Michael Wood is a freelance jou
Newcastle. As a journalist he
throughout Sheffield, gaining
procedure. He also reviews bo
dedicated to crime fiction.

       𝕏 x.com/MichaelHWood
       f facebook.com/MichaelWoodBooks
       ⊙ instagram.com/MichaelWoodBooks
       BB bookbub.com/authors/MichaelWood

Also by Michael Wood

Dr Olivia Winter series

The Mind of a Murderer

DCI Matilda Darke series

For Reasons Unknown

Outside Looking In

A Room Full of Killers

The Hangman's Hold

The Murder House

Stolen Children

Time Is Running Out

Survivor's Guilt

The Lost Children

Silent Victim

Below Ground

Last One Left Alive

Standalone

The Seventh Victim

Vengeance is Mine

Short Stories

The Fallen

Victim of Innocence

Making of a Murderer

THE DEVIL'S CODE
A Dr Olivia Winter Thriller

MICHAEL WOOD

*To Martin and Shannon
I'm glad you're enjoying my books
Michael Wood*

One More Chapter
a division of HarperCollins*Publishers*
1 London Bridge Street
London SE1 9GF
www.harpercollins.co.uk
HarperCollins*Publishers*
Macken House, 39/40 Mayor Street Upper,
Dublin 1, D01 C9W8, Ireland

This paperback edition 2025

1

First published in Great Britain in ebook format
by HarperCollins*Publishers* 2025

Copyright © Michael Wood 2025
Michael Wood asserts the moral right to
be identified as the author of this work

A catalogue record of this book
is available from the British Library

ISBN: 978-0-00-861888-9

This novel is entirely a work of fiction.
The names, characters and incidents portrayed in it are
the work of the author's imagination. Any resemblance to
actual persons, living or dead, events or localities is
entirely coincidental.

Printed and bound in the UK using 100% Renewable Electricity
by CPI Group (UK) Ltd

All rights reserved. No part of this publication may be
reproduced, stored in a retrieval system, or transmitted,
in any form or by any means, electronic, mechanical,
photocopying, recording or otherwise, without the prior
permission of the publishers.

To Chris Schofield (again, I suppose).

Extract from a notebook allegedly written by Isaac McFadden

Hello, how are you?
I'm fine thanks, you?
I'm good.
That's all a complete lie. They're just words we say to each other out of politeness, and, together with the painted-on smiles, we accept those baseless words as being the truth. If we're being honest with each other, the conversation would go much differently.
Hello, how are you?
I'm in agony. I hate my job, my kids are driving me mad, I'm pretty sure my husband is cheating on me and I'm two months behind with the mortgage. You?
The same. I don't think I've ever felt so lonely since my wife died. I cry every night, I rarely eat, I'm drinking far too much, and last week I found a lump that I'm scared to get checked out.
That's the truth. That's what we hide from the world.
When I'm looking for a victim, I watch them, I follow them, I observe them before I go and talk to them. And when I do strike up a conversation, I don't listen to a single word they say.

My opening line is always "Hello, how are you?" or "Are you all right?" They always try to assuage me, a complete stranger, that they're fine. I know they're not. They know they're not. They know that I know they're not fine. To get to the truth, you need to look into their eyes.

Eyes never lie.

Ignore the fake smiles. Don't listen to a single word that passes their lips. Watch their eyes. They're not fine.

They're in pain.

They're tortured and tormented.

They're lost.

They're perfect.

They're already dead.

Chapter One

EARSDON, TYNE AND WEAR

Friday 1st March 2024

The silver Citroen Picasso was driving at a steady speed along the desolate, waterlogged A1. Rain was pouring down in sheets, visibility was poor. A weather warning was in place from the Met Office telling people to only travel if their journey was essential. This was the essence of an essential journey.

Isaac McFadden was concentrating on the road ahead. Both hands on the steering wheel, gripping hard, Roy Orbison blasting out of the speakers singing 'You Got It', drowning out the sound of the rain lashing against the windscreen and battering the roof. Isaac was a huge fan of The Big O. It was his go-to music whenever he'd had a hard day or felt like taking a trip down memory lane to happier times. On his honeymoon, he'd serenaded his wife with his rendition of 'Pretty Woman'. He'd even surprised himself by how good a singer he was, though he could never replicate Roy's purr.

'You Got It' ended in dramatic style to be replaced by 'I Drove All Night'. Isaac smiled to himself. He felt like he'd been driving all night already.

He had left the village of Earsdon behind him. Hopefully it

wouldn't be long before he saw a sign for Eshott Airfield, not that he could see much through the rain.

In the rearview mirror, a flash caught his eye. He eased off the accelerator and turned his attention to the mirror. There it was again. In the blur of the rain-splattered back window, a blue light was dancing. It was growing bigger as it came closer. He turned off the music and through the hammering of rain on the roof, he heard a blast of a siren. There was a police car behind him.

'Shit,' he muttered to himself.

He must have been speeding. When he was lost in a mind trip listening to his favourite artist, everything around him was forgotten, including how fast he happened to be driving. He already had six points on his licence. He blamed Meatloaf for those last three. He began to slow down.

The police were bound to ask him what he was doing out at this time of night in these treacherous conditions. What if they breathalysed him? He tried to remember when he last had a drink. He'd had a bottle of lager about four hours ago. Actually, no, it was two bottles. Would that take him over the legal limit? Was it still on his breath? It probably was.

'Shit!' he said again, much louder.

Another blast from the siren behind. They wanted him to pull over. He had no choice.

Isaac took several deep breaths and gave himself a quick pep talk.

This is fine. This is going to be okay. Yes, the weather is bad, but you're on an essential journey. Your dad is ill. He's got cancer. No, he's got Alzheimer's and you're going to check on him to make sure he's okay. It'll be fine.

'What if they offer to accompany me on the rest of my journey?' he asked himself.

No. They wouldn't do that. Surely. The police are far too busy for that kind of thing. Aren't they?

He pulled over to the side of the road, put the gear into neutral, and turned off the engine. He watched in the rearview mirror as the police car came to a stop behind him. The blue lights continued to flash. A uniformed officer climbed out from the driver's side. A beat later, another uniformed officer got out from the front passenger side.

Does it take two to ask me where I'm going?

A tap on his side window made him press the button and lower the window a touch. A blast of cold wind and rain hit him in the face. He squinted.

'Good evening. Nasty night, isn't it? I wasn't speeding, was I?'

'Good evening,' the police officer said, shouting to be heard above the elements. He'd only come a few feet from his car, but he was already drenched. 'No, you weren't speeding, Sir. Can I ask where you're going to on a night like this?'

'Yes. I'm going to see my father. He's got Alzheimer's. He called me and he's a bit scared with the weather. I thought it best to go over there.'

'I see. I'm sorry to hear that. Where does your father live, sir?'

Shit. Shit. Fucking shit.

'Where does he live?'

He had no idea what lay ahead beyond Eshott Airfield. Although, there was a sign. What did it say? Thirston. He was sure it said something Thirston. But was it West Thirston or East Thirston? Did it matter? If there was a West Thirston, there was bound to be an East Thirston.

'West Thirston,' he said.

'You're going the long way round, aren't you?'

'Am I? I mean, yes, I am,' he said with a nervous smile. 'I thought it best to stick to the main roads in this weather. I don't want to get stuck if any of the smaller roads are impassable.'

'Very sensible.'

Isaac looked back in his rearview mirror. He couldn't see where the second officer was.

'Do you realise one of your back lights is out, sir?'

'Oh. Is it?'

'Yes.'

'Is that why you pulled me over?'

'It is, yes.'

'Oh. Right. I see. Well, no, I didn't realise that. I'm sorry. I'll have it checked first thing in the morning.'

'It doesn't necessarily have to be a fault. I can take a look. It could just be a loose connection.'

'Could it?'

'If you'd like to open the boot, we'll take a quick look.'

'Ah. That's... that's very kind of you, but I really need to go and see my dad.'

'It won't take long.'

'But... I mean, you're soaked. I can deal with it tomorrow.'

'I'm not going to get any wetter than I already am,' he said with a grin. 'Just pop the lid, sir, won't take two minutes.'

'I'd rather wait until...'

'It is actually an offence to be driving with a rear light out, sir.'

'Is it? Ah. Right.'

He made no attempt to move.

'The boot?' The police officer asked.

Isaac turned to face the road. 'I'm sorry. I'd really rather wait until I can take the car to a garage.'

'Is there something in the boot you don't want us to see?'

'I need to get to my father,' he said, his voice barely audible.

'Sir, I'm going to ask you to step outside of the vehicle, please,' the officer said, opening the car door and allowing a torrent of wind and rain to enter.

Isaac remained where he was.

'What's going on, Alan?' the second officer asked, coming to the front.

'He doesn't want us to see what's in the boot.'

'Why?'

'No idea. Sir, please, step out of the car.'

Isaac didn't move.

'Have you been drinking at all today, sir?'

'I really need to go and visit my father,' he said, calmly, quietly.

'I'll go and get a breathalyser,' the second officer said.

The first officer reached into the car for the catch to open the boot. Isaac grabbed him by the wrist.

'You really don't want to do that.'

'Alan!' the officer called out.

Alan came running back. He took out his taser and held it at arm's length.

'Sir, let go of my colleague.'

They were at a stalemate. Isaac, eyes fixed firmly on the road ahead, refused to let go of the wrist of the police officer. The second officer aimed the taser directly at Isaac. The rain was lashing down, getting harder with every minute.

Eventually, Isaac released his grip, and the officer pulled his arm away.

'Very slowly, take off your seatbelt, and get out of the car,' he said.

He had no choice. He unclipped his seatbelt, swung his legs around and stood up, ignoring the rain thrashing down on him. He stood taller than both officers, but his height didn't intimidate them.

'Step away from the vehicle.'

He released a breath and took two steps away from his car, standing in the middle of the A1. His hair was plastered to his head. His shirt was sticking to him. He shouldn't have gone out tonight. He knew it had been a mistake.

The second officer still had his taser aimed at him while the first went around to the rear of the car. He opened the lid and looked inside. In the darkness, he couldn't see a thing. He detached a torch from his utility belt and shone it inside. He opened his mouth to say something, but turned and vomited before the words could come out.

Chapter Two

BLYTH, NORTHUMBERLAND

Saturday 14th December 2024

Eleanor McFadden had been dreading this day. She knew the evidence against her father was overwhelming. She knew he was facing a life sentence, but at the back of her mind was the tiniest glimmer of hope that he would be found not guilty, that he would be returning to the home she grew up in. Unfortunately, that wasn't to be. The foreman of the jury had stood up tall and straight-backed and cleared his throat in readiness.

'Do you find the defendant, Isaac McFadden, guilty or not guilty of the murder of Sean Bridger?'

Dramatic pause.

'Guilty.'

Eleanor had closed her eyes and put her head down. She felt a hand on her back, rubbing her, soothing her. Everything around her became a blur as the judge spoke and sentenced her father there and then to a minimum jail term of twenty years. She hadn't looked at her father as he'd been led away, but she was sure she could feel his gaze burning into her.

Eleanor decided to strike while the iron was hot. She needed to take control of the nightmare she was in. This horror film she found herself in needed to end sooner rather than later and it would only do so when she confined everything that had happened before now to the history books. The day after sentencing, she woke early, not that she'd slept much, and drove over to her father's house. She had no idea what she would do with it. She doubted anyone would want to live in a house where a man had calmly cut a body into twelve pieces, but the sooner it was off her hands, the better.

The house hadn't been lived in since Isaac was arrested and charged. Eleanor had only been here twice since, both times to collect a few items of clothing for her father to wear while he was kept on remand. Lesley Quinn next door had been keeping an eye on the place, picking up the mail, making sure the house was secure and contacting Eleanor when the odd window had been broken by vandals. She'd then got onto her dad's friend Hal, across the street, who'd taken care of any repairs, and he'd kindly cut the grass and trimmed the bushes. She'd delegated tasks to other people, but this one she had to take control of herself.

Eleanor entered the cold living room. She was wearing black. She thought it was fitting for the occasion. She threw her bag down on the armchair and sat on the sofa. Last week had been her twenty-eighth birthday and she'd celebrated it by sitting in a courtroom listening to a pathologist helping the prosecutor explain in painstaking detail how it was possible to cut up a body into transportable pieces. She had to keep reminding herself it was her father they were talking about, and she wasn't living in some Netflix docudrama about a deranged psychopath.

Lesley followed her in. She was dressed as if ready to tackle a massive spring-cleaning project. Her hair was tied up, and she wore oversized combat trousers and a jumper that had seen better days. In one hand she held a bottle of milk, in the other, a roll of black refuse sacks.

'Do you want me to make us a cup of tea before we start?' Lesley asked. 'I think I'll go and flick the immersion on, actually. It's perishing in here, isn't it? I've kept the heating on a constant low. It shouldn't take too long to warm up.'

Eleanor hadn't heard what she said. Her eyes were fixed on the mantelpiece and the framed photographs showing happier times for the McFadden family. She wanted to cry when she looked at her mother's smiling face staring out at her, but she didn't think she had any tears left. For the first time, Eleanor was glad her mother was dead, so she wouldn't have to suffer through all this.

'There we go,' Lesley said, coming back into the living room. 'Give it half an hour and it should be toasty warm. I've put the kettle on. Do you want a tea? Eleanor?'

'Sorry?' Eleanor asked, looking up.

'Tea. Would you like a cup?'

'No.'

'There's some whisky in the cupboard.'

'I think it's a bit early for hard liquor.'

Lesley sat next to her on the sofa and grabbed her hand, enveloping it in hers and rubbing it hard to warm her up. 'You've had a shock. We all have, but you more than most. If you want something to numb the pain, then bugger what time of day it is.'

Eleanor shook her head.

'It'll be all right, you know,' Lesley said.

Eleanor turned to look at her, took in her features, the lined face, the makeup, the sickly placating smile that she'd been wearing since her father was arrested. Surely it was hurting her by now.

'Will it?' Eleanor asked, a stern tone to her voice. 'How? How will it be all right, Lesley? Can you explain that to me?'

It was a while before she answered. 'People soon forget. They move on.'

'They might. I won't.'

'It's going to take time, Eleanor. You can't expect something like this not to have an impact on you. You just have to take one day at a time. I know it sounds like a cliché, but with each day that passes, you'll feel stronger.'

Eleanor was tired of hearing platitudes. She took her hand back, stood up and went over to the fireplace, where she picked up a framed photograph of her mother and father on their wedding day.

'I'm just glad Mum isn't here to see what's happened. It would have killed her.'

'He might not have...' Lesley began, then stopped herself.

Eleanor quickly turned around. 'What? He might not have turned into a murderer if Mum had still been here? Do you really believe that?'

'I... I'm... I don't know, Eleanor.'

'No. Neither do I.' She walked over to the bay window and looked out at the street. Life was continuing as normal. She recognised an elderly woman with a shopping trolley – Mrs Cathcart. She didn't know her Christian name. She remembered her from her youth, always smiling, always bringing her sweets and allowing her to play in her garden during the school summer holidays because it was the end house and therefore bigger than theirs. Mrs Cathcart had purposely crossed the street that last time Eleanor saw her. She was being shunned. Guilt by association.

'Lesley.' Eleanor turned back. 'Do you think it was true, what the prosecution said, about Dad being stopped before he could commit more murders? Do you think he was a potential serial killer?'

'I don't know about that, Eleanor. I'm no expert in these things. I don't think we should dwell on it, though, do you? Maybe we should just be thankful that there was only one victim.'

'I suppose. Will you... you know, visit him in prison?'

'I'm not sure. I've been asking myself that question for months. I suppose it depends on what prison he's sent to. Do you want to see him?'

Eleanor wiped the tears from her eyes. 'He's my dad,' she choked.

Lesley jumped up and went over to her. She held her bony shoulders and pulled her close in a tight hug. Lesley had been like a surrogate mother to Eleanor since her real mother had died when she was only five years old. When Eleanor was a child, Lesley's hugs had been warm and nurturing, and that's exactly how it felt now. Eleanor's father had never been one for hugging, but right now it was what she needed. She was eternally grateful to Lesley for sticking by her through all this. Since Isaac's crime had been made public, she was being shunned right, left and centre. Eleanor had been seeing someone casually, though it had ended as soon as Isaac's name was printed in the newspaper. She had been glad she wasn't from a large family, but the few distant aunts and uncles she did have, dotted around the country, had ignored her calls, and she had noticed friends on social media were unfollowing her by the dozen. Colleagues had stopped inviting her on nights out, neighbours stopped taking in parcels, and Eleanor's windowsill had been bereft of birthday cards last week.

'What am I going to do?' she asked, looking at her only friend with tear-filled eyes.

'You're going to survive,' Lesley said with a catch in her throat. 'You're going to face this with your head high because you have done nothing wrong. And I'll be with you as much as you want me to.'

Eleanor tried to smile but it wouldn't come through the tears.

'Thank you.'

'You've nothing to thank me for. Now, I'm going to make us both a mug of coffee and, screw what time it is, I'm dropping in a dash of whisky. Then we'll go upstairs and sort through your dad's clothes. We'll see what you think he might want and the rest we'll either sling or I'll take them to a charity shop. Is that okay with you?'

Eleanor wiped her eyes with the backs of her hands. 'Yes. Thank you, Lesley.'

The house felt different.

As Eleanor stood in her father's bedroom, doors to the fitted wardrobe wide open, it felt alien. She felt like an intruder. She tore off a black bin bag from a roll and started to fill it. All of this could be sorted out properly later, when she was back in her own home. Right now, she just wanted to bag everything up and leave.

The Devil's Code

Cardigans, shirts, trousers, jumpers, T-shirts, they were all bundled into a bag. Tied up when full, then on to the next one. Eleanor hadn't realised her dad had so many clothes, and she was pretty sure there were boxes in the loft containing jackets and coats.

She sat on the edge of the double bed and rolled her sleeves up. She was getting hot and sweaty, and the disturbance of dust was causing her to itch and sneeze.

'How are you getting on?' Lesley asked, coming into the bedroom. 'I've boxed up all the kitchen things. I don't know if you want to take a look at them, see if there's anything you want.'

'No, I don't think so.'

'I didn't realise your dad had so much stuff. I'm going to have to...' She stopped as her eye caught something through the window. 'He's a nosey so-and-so, that Hal Garfield,' she said. 'I've seen his blinds twitching on and off all morning. I bet he's itching to come over here. I saw him in the Co-op last week. He only asked me what you were doing with your dad's golf clubs. Cheeky sod.'

Eleanor stifled a smile. 'He's welcome to them.'

'Then he can pop down to the charity shop and buy them. Skinflint.'

'I should go over and see him. He's been good to me since Dad was arrested.'

'Just be careful what you say to him. He's like an old washerwoman. Anyway, I'm going to make a start on the back bedroom if you want me,' Lesley said, giving Eleanor a big smile and leaving the room.

Eleanor remained still, both hands on the bed beside her. She remembered running in here as a child on a Sunday morning, seeing her mum and dad having a lie-in, and jumping up and down on the mattress to wake them up. Looking back on her childhood, she remembered it with fondness. Her mother was always smiling and laughing. Her dad was slightly firmer in Eleanor's upbringing, but he told great stories and always took her to the beach for trips and adventures at the weekends when the weather was fair. Eleanor wasn't looking at her life through rose-tinted glasses. There was photographic evidence of her idyllic childhood. But now it really was tainted by what her father had turned into. The man who sat on her bed every evening and invented a new story about giants and ogres to send her off to sleep with an adventure in her head to live on in her dreams: she couldn't see him as a man found guilty of murdering and dismembering a twenty-year-old man. It wasn't the same man. It couldn't be.

Eleanor opened the top drawer of the bedside cabinet. The usual detritus of people with a nighttime routine lay in a disorganised state. She found a silver watch belonging to her mother that she hadn't seen for years. She picked up the delicate object and looked at it with a smile. Then she remembered the rest of her mother's personal items. The police had searched through the house when her father was arrested. Had they looked through everything?

She went over to the fitted wardrobe and threw open the door. She dropped to her knees and pulled up the carpet. Beneath, the end floorboard was loose. She took it up and reached inside where her mother's jewellery box was. Inside, there was more than just an antique necklace and diamond earrings, there was a lock of Eleanor's hair from when she was a baby, the ID tag that had been placed around her wrist after she was born, and a small velvet bag containing a few of her baby teeth. She closed the lid of the box and held it tight against her chest. Treasured memories.

Eleanor was about to replace the floorboard when something else caught her eye. She leaned down and reached inside. There was an oak keepsake box Eleanor had never seen before. She pulled it out, wiped off the layer of dust with the sleeve of her jumper, and rested it on her lap. Inside was a small leather-bound notebook. It was A5 in size and very slim. There couldn't have been more than twenty pages to the whole book. It looked handmade. She opened it and saw her father's neat scrawl on the first page. A hint of her father's writing that she'd seen on Christmas and birthday cards her whole life. It made her smile.

What was written made no sense to her. It was a chart of some kind, but it was all random words.

She returned to the box. At first glance, it seemed like it was filled with trinkets, memorable items from her father's past, maybe things he and her mother had collected along their life journey together. The more she looked, the more she realised she was seeing these items for the first time. None of them belonged to her father. He wasn't the type of man to wear a sovereign ring. It was too small for his fingers, anyway. He'd never wear a St Christopher necklace and why would he own a single stud earring? She rifled through the box and found a passport at the bottom.

Lesley came into the room holding up her mobile phone. 'Eleanor, I've just had a text from Hal. Listen to this... What's wrong?'

Eleanor looked up at her. 'I found this box under Dad's wardrobe. What do you make of this?' She handed her the notebook.

She sat on the bed and opened it. She stared at the pages, the writing. A frown developed on her forehead.

'I... I have no idea,' she said, genuinely perplexed.

'What do you think all these are?' Eleanor asked, showing her the contents of the box. Her voice was shaking with fear. Her mind had raced to a dark conclusion. She was hoping Lesley could offer a sensible explanation.

Lesley rifled through the box. She picked up the ring, a pair of glasses, a cheap Casio wristwatch.

'They're not Dad's, are they?' Eleanor asked.

'I'm not sure. I've never seen him wear a watch like this. He had that one his father gave him, didn't he?'

'Then there's this.' She handed her the passport.

She didn't take it from her at first. They made eye contact. Both knew they were thinking the same thing.

'It's a Polish passport,' Eleanor said.

'Why would your dad have a Polish passport? Isn't your family Irish?'

'It's not his.'

'Whose...?' She couldn't finish her question. She took it from Lesley and opened it. The photograph was of a young man with blond hair. He was handsome, giving a hint of a smile to the camera. The date of birth told them he was twenty-one.

'These aren't Dad's,' Eleanor said. 'Nothing here belongs to Mum, either. I don't think they're keepsakes. I think they're trophies.'

Lesley shook her head. 'Trophies? What do you mean?'

'There are twelve items in this box. And look here, in the notebook, at that table at the back, there are twelve entries. What if Dad has killed more than one person? What if these belong to his victims?'

Lesley had the notebook gripped firmly in both hands. She looked down intently at the pages, a blank expression on her face. 'Victims?' she asked. 'What are you... what?'

'This chart or table or whatever it is, it makes no sense. It's like it's written in code or something.' Eleanor climbed to her feet. 'I need to call that detective.'

'What? Why?'

'Maybe the prosecution was wrong. Maybe Dad wasn't a future serial killer. Maybe he was an actual serial killer and he's kept a log of his victims written in some kind of secret code.'

'Secret code? Eleanor, listen to yourself. People don't write secret codes.'

'They do when they have something to hide. I'm going to call DI Sutton. He needs to see this. I'm sure there's a department within the police force that's good at cracking codes.'

She left the room, leaving Lesley sitting on the bed. She looked back down at the cream pages and took in Isaac's neat handwriting.

'Jesus Christ, Isaac, what have you done?'

Chapter Three

MIDDLESEX UNIVERSITY, LONDON

Wednesday 15th January 2025

'When we hear the term "serial killer", we think of a white male having dysfunctional relationships, engaging in animal torture and arson and wetting the bed well into their teens, of someone who was physically and or sexually abused as a child, a loner of low intelligence in a meaningless job, if they can hold down a job at all. This is no longer the case. The modern serial killer has evolved and has the ability to maintain a double life: both a seemingly happy family man with a good career, a loving wife and children and a wide social group, and an evil monster, a butcher of innocent victims, a destroyer of lives, and not just those of the people he has killed. He will leave a trail of devastation in his wake.

'As I've said, my work isn't an exact science. There isn't a form to fill in where you tick boxes and get a result back saying if a person is or isn't a future serial killer. However, there are red flags that we can look for that should give us an indication that this person requires treatment before they reach the point of no return.

'Extreme antisocial behaviour is a possible indicator. Antisocial personality disorder is defined as someone who shows no remorse or guilt. Searching for these signs has become increasingly difficult in recent years with the rise of social media, and negative aspects of comparing our lives with others having a detrimental effect on our mental health, causing us to withdraw from a reality of social interaction to protect ourselves further. We shouldn't judge a person who fears a crowded place as having homicidal tendencies.

'One factor we have seen increasingly among the young is a propensity towards voyeurism. Again, this is also linked to social media. There are some who live by Instagram and TikTok, who post their entire lives online. It doesn't take much for a developing brain, an impressionable person, to become fixated on someone they've only seen through the screen of their mobile phone. It will get to a point where merely watching them online isn't enough.

'And then there's the entertainment factor to be considered. The rise of streaming platforms and the number of true crime documentaries and dramatisations in recent years have popularised the serial killer, elevating them to almost celebrity status. Is this fuelling the minds of the young to give them a level of fame to grasp for? I'm going to talk about this more in our next lecture. However, does anybody have any questions about what we've discussed today – or in readiness for next time?'

Dr Olivia Winter stepped back from the lectern, stood away from the microphone and let out a heavy sigh. She usually enjoyed giving lectures. She enjoyed watching a captive audience listening to what she had to say, to her imparting her knowledge and wisdom – except on a Monday morning, when the majority of her students were nursing hangovers and Olivia used creative licence to gain their attention.

Over the last few months, Olivia's attitude to her lectures had changed. She could feel the eyes of every single person in the lecture hall burning deep inside her. They weren't so much listening as analysing what she was saying, waiting for her to say something that they could jump on and question her about, something that would pick holes in her approach to forensic psychology, or her understanding of it. She often noticed students frantically scribbling down notes at a time when she wasn't saying anything they would need in a potential future career as a psychologist or criminologist. What were they writing? And was it about her?

She took a deep breath and looked out at the packed auditorium. Several hands went up.

'Gavin,' she said, choosing a thin young man on the front row wearing a baggy red jumper and blue jeans. He seemed to be trying to grow facial hair, but his face appeared reluctant to comply, as the hair was patchy.

'You've mentioned social media quite a lot in your lecture today, and you've said a few times that people should be careful what they post online, but isn't that stamping on people's freedom of expression and victim-blaming?'

'No. Not at all. Obviously, you don't know who is monitoring your social media pages, but it's basic common sense to be careful what you post. It's not only potential serial murderers who could be watching you but people looking to commit fraud as well. If your bank account is emptied simply because you posted an innocuous photograph of a new wallet someone bought you for your birthday without realising your card details were within shot, shouldn't some of the blame fall on you for being so naïve? I would never dictate what people should and shouldn't reveal about themselves. We do, after all, live in a democratic society. However, we should be aware of the dangers that are out there. Not everyone is as good as you or I. If you, Gavin, have over a thousand followers on Instagram, can you be sure they're all interested in your insightful wit and social commentary?'

'He should be so lucky,' Timothy, the young man to his left, commented to a ripple of laughter from those close by.

'Lucy.' Olivia pointed to a young woman who was always in the front row.

'You just said that a serial killer could maintain a loving family life and have a wide social circle, then you said what typifies a serial killer is someone with extreme antisocial behaviour. Isn't that contradictory?'

'Yes, it is. Which is why I said it's difficult to spot a serial killer. If someone wants to kill, and continue to kill, and have a high body count, they need to be savvy about what people like me are looking for. These are the ones who kill without compulsion, the ones who kill for the sheer pleasure of it, and not because of some personality disorder. It's all about manipulation.'

Lucy frowned. 'But surely, for someone who can do that – manipulate those around them – that suggests a personality disorder.'

'No. It suggests a dark and devious mind. Don't confuse someone with a lack of empathy as having a fault in their genetic or personality makeup. Mary.' Olivia pointed to a woman three rows back from Lucy who had a mass of curly brown hair whipped up into an untidy beehive.

'When it comes to the glamorising of true crime with all these documentaries and podcasts, do you think there's a study that should be done on the psychological impact on the survivors of those crimes and the relatives of the perpetrators? Surely the conveyor belt of Jeffrey Dahmer and Ted Bundy and all the others will affect those directly involved and their survivor's guilt or PTSD.'

Olivia could feel the temperature in the room drop. Everyone knew what Mary was alluding to. It was less than a year since Olivia's true identity, daughter of the infamous Riverside Killer, was revealed to the world by the tactless and reviled British press.

'You're right. Producers of such shows should take into consideration those left behind. You often hear them say that a particular programme has been made with the consent of all the survivors or the families of the killer. I'd like to think sensitivity is high on the producers' emotive radar, but I think money, advertising and ratings come first.'

'Were you contacted by the production company who are making the drama about your father?'

Olivia was pretty sure she heard a collective intake of breath at the direct question regarding her personal life.

She looked around at the sea of expectant faces. How many of them were taking this course to get a real insight into the mind of a murderer and how many were simply ghouls who wanted, one day, to write about being close to the daughter of a serial killer? After all, publishers and programme makers grasped any tenuous link to a celebrated killer. How long would it be before Netflix produced a six-part series from the point of view of Jeffrey Dahmer's dry cleaner?

'Yes. They did,' she simply answered. 'And I told them I wanted no part in the making of the drama. The source material of the script was the book written about my father. They didn't need to ask me as the rights to the book were purchased from the author. They contacted me out of courtesy.'

'Will someone be appearing in the drama playing you?' Mary asked.

'Playing a younger version of me, I assume so. I won't be watching to find out. Though, fingers crossed, they've made me a six-foot leggy blonde,' she said with a faux smile.

A ripple of nervous laughter ran around the room.

'Now, I believe that's all we have time for today. Next lecture is the open discussion, so if we can have some insightful psychological questions to tax us all, that would be something to look forward to. Enjoy the rest of your week.'

Olivia turned off the microphone and began getting her papers together as the room quickly emptied. Every lecture always ended with a personal question. Usually she skirted around them, or point-blank avoided them, but occasionally she felt she needed to answer them. Was there someone among her students who was noting down all the answers and building up a profile of her? By the end of the course, would they know more about her than she knew about herself? Maybe she should rethink lecturing.

Leaving the university, Olivia made her way to where she'd parked her scooter. Driving a car in London wasn't for the faint-hearted and Olivia didn't have time to sit in traffic. A cold wind blew around her and she pulled up her collar. She turned the corner and stopped dead in her tracks. She looked up at the large billboard across the road. In the centre, a man was glaring at her, his steely gaze staring deep into her soul. She didn't know him. She knew his name and that he was a relatively famous actor, not that he had appeared in anything Olivia had seen. It wasn't who he was that made her stop and brought a lump to her throat; it was who he represented. It was to be his biggest starring role to date: playing Olivia's father, Richard Button, in a new drama starting next month on ITV.

Loving husband. Devoted father. Vicious serial killer.

The tagline screamed out in red at the top of the poster. For viewers, this was going to be a gripping drama that would give them something to talk about with their colleagues the following morning. How many would think about the real people behind the actors' performances? This wasn't entertainment. This was real life, Olivia's life, and it was about to be turned into glossy fiction.

Chapter Four

Olivia parked her black Honda PCX125 outside the office on George Street in Westminster.

It was a nondescript building. A stranger to the area would think it was a delightful townhouse. Those who knew London would think they were the consulting rooms of a private doctor, a psychiatrist or maybe even a private dentist charging exorbitant fees. Nobody would know that behind the black door lay the headquarters of the Behavioural Science Administration. It was a grand name and 'headquarters' was a slight exaggeration. Two leading doctors in forensic psychology and a secretary hardly matched anything the FBI in America could offer.

Funded by the Home Office and several universities, Olivia and Dr Sebastian Lister's remit was to lecture around London on an ad hoc basis as well as travel the world talking to incarcerated serial killers in the hope of discovering what turned a person into a killer in the first place. Information and research were shared with similar organisations around the world, and while some people might be embarrassed to welcome a delegate from Quantico to this end-of-terrace house that was the heart of England's psychological fight against serial murder, Olivia and Sebastian weren't. The main draw for visitors was Olivia herself. The daughter of a serial killer, the survivor of a serial killer, Olivia had first-hand knowledge of what it was like to look evil in the eyes and win. That was something a suited, desk-bound agent of the FBI might give their right arm for.

Olivia took off her helmet and ran her gloved fingers through her short hair. She walked up the black and white chequered tiled steps and pushed open the front door. Daisy Leatherwood, receptionist, secretary, personal assistant, office manager, baker of cakes and queen of everything, was sitting behind her desk wearing headphones and a perplexed expression. Olivia guessed she was trying to keep up with Sebastian's speedy dictation. When she saw Olivia enter, she switched off the recorder and looked up at her with a friendly smile.

'I really wish Sebastian would slow down when he's dictating his reports. There was actual smoke coming from my keyboard earlier. I type. I'm not changing a wheel in the pitstops at Silverstone.'

'I heard that,' Dr Sebastian Lister said, coming down the stairs holding Stanley, Olivia's miniature Dachshund, in his arms.

Olivia took the dog from him.

'Could you please just slow down? Just a tad,' Daisy pleaded.

'I shall try.'

'That's all I ask.'

'How was the lecture?' Sebastian asked Olivia.

'Fine. I spoke. Students pretended to listen. Repeat every day for the rest of my life,' she said.

'Only another thirty-something years until retirement.'

'By the way, you've got a visitor,' Daisy said, nodding towards the meeting room.

'Who?' Olivia frowned. She wasn't keen on unsolicited visitors. They never brought good news with them.

'A detective inspector from Newcastle.'

Olivia looked to Sebastian, worry written on her face. 'The police? Why would someone from Newcastle come all the way down here?'

'He wouldn't say,' Sebastian said. 'Don't worry. It's nothing to do with your father. I already checked.'

Olivia breathed a sigh of relief. She had spent her career interviewing serial killers. Occasionally, one of them took a shine to her and bombarded her with emails, letters, cards, deranged ramblings of what they'd like to do to her. She would get a call if one had escaped or, God forbid, been given parole. She quickly thought and couldn't recall ever having dealings with a killer from Newcastle.

'Do you want me to take Stanley?' Sebastian asked.

'Please,' she said, slightly distracted.

'I'll stay down here. Give me a shout if you need me.' He was always looking out for Olivia, and she smiled warmly. Turning to the closed doors of the meeting room, she took a deep breath, painted on a confident smile and went through.

The man waiting for her was sitting at the table. He hadn't heard her come in. His head was down and judging by the expression on his face, he was deep in thought, lost in whatever was occupying his mind. He wore a heavy frown, and his eyes were glassy. He was in a world of his own.

Olivia cleared her throat.

He looked up at her and the look of sadness quickly disappeared to be replaced by a strained smile. He jumped to his feet. He was wearing a knee-length grey reefer coat, tight black trousers and large boots. His hair was a huge mass of glossy black. Olivia would kill for that kind of shiny, wavy hair. The smile lit up his face and she found herself melting straightaway, despite the cold air in the room. He was handsome, with beautifully straight teeth, smooth skin and sharp cheekbones. His fragrance was sweet and understated.

'Hello,' she said. 'I believe you're waiting to see me.'

He held out a hand. 'That's right. Detective Inspector Linus Sutton. Northumbria CID.'

She shook his hand and didn't want to let go. His grip was firm yet his skin so soft.

'I don't believe I have a connection to Northumbria,' she said, pulling out a chair and sitting down. 'Sorry, can I get you a coffee or something?'

'I'm fine. Your receptionist has already made me two.'

'So, what can I do for you? It must be something important for you to come all the way down from Newcastle.' She looked past DI Sutton and out into the street. That bloody red Vauxhall was there again.

Sutton cleared his throat. 'Have you heard of Isaac McFadden?'

Olivia ignored the car outside and searched her memory. It didn't take her long to find what she was looking for. She took a keen interest in all murder investigations, serials or one-offs. 'Convicted of murdering twenty-year-old homeless man Sean Bridger, I believe.'

'That's him.'

'He was sentenced to life with a minimum term of twenty years. The case is closed, isn't it?'

'The case is, yes. However, while his daughter was clearing out his house, she found a box in Isaac's bedroom. Inside there were some items that she couldn't identify and a notebook in which he… well, to be honest, we don't know what it is he wrote. We think it might be a list of his victims, and we think the items found might be trophies.'

'Victims? Plural? None of this came out at the trial, though, did it?' she asked, a heavy frown on her face as she thought back to all the stories she had read online throughout the court proceedings.

'No, it didn't. Isaac was… he didn't give much away when it came to telling his version of events.'

'He didn't take the stand, either, did he?' Olivia asked.

'No. He even refused to enter a plea.'

'Unusual for a serial killer to remain silent once caught.'

'This book that his daughter found contains a chart or a table, written in code, possibly, that we believe could identify more victims.'

'Is it genuine?'

'Eleanor, that's his daughter, says it's her father's handwriting.'

'I'm assuming you've interviewed Isaac about it.'

The Devil's Code

'I have. I've been to see him several times in prison. He refuses to talk about it.'

'Why have you come all the way down to London to see me?'

'To get your insight. I've been reading up on the remit of the Behavioural Science Administration. This is the kind of thing you'd be interested in, isn't it?'

'It is,' Olivia said, trying not to let the look of excitement appear on her face. Anything that could open up the inner workings of the mind of a serial murderer was always welcome. 'How many entries are there in this table?'

'Twelve. And there are twelve items that we believe represent one for each victim.'

'Twelve? Surely you'd know if you had twelve unidentified bodies on your patch.'

'I'd like to think so. However, I don't believe they are all from within our boundary. One item amongst the collection is a Polish passport. Also, the victim Isaac was arrested for, Sean Bridger, was homeless, and originally from Yorkshire. It was a sheer fluke that we managed to identify him.'

'Have you looked for the person the Polish passport belongs to?'

'Yes. Piotr Czajkowski. He left Poland in early December 2023 to go travelling. Nobody has heard from him since.'

'Was he listed as a missing person?'

'No. Nobody knew he was missing. They just thought he was travelling across Europe.'

'When was he last in touch with friends or family?'

'He wasn't.'

'Didn't anyone think it strange that they didn't receive a postcard?'

Sutton shrugged. 'Obviously not. He had very little family. His last surviving relative, his grandmother, died a month before he went away. According to local police, he didn't have many friends, and none he'd likely send a postcard to.'

Olivia listened intently to Linus Sutton. He had a soft, smooth voice, with just a hint of a Geordie accent, which grew stronger the more impassioned he became.

She stood up. 'I'm sorry, I'm going to need a coffee. Are you sure I can't get you another?'

'I'll have a tea, please. If I drink any more coffee, I won't sleep for a week.'

She went into the attached kitchenette and flicked on the kettle.

'Isaac McFadden,' she said. 'Does he have a criminal record?'

'No.'

'Really? Nothing at all before the murder?'

'Nope. The only slight against his name was six points on his driver's licence. He was squeaky clean.'

Olivia paused. A cold feeling swept over her. People didn't simply become serial killers. They didn't wake up one morning and decide to kill and have the level of competence that allowed them to get away with killing twelve people. Isaac had to have committed a crime in the past, something that led to an escalation into becoming a serial murderer.

'Tell me more about Isaac,' Olivia said as she began to prepare the drinks.

Sutton reached beneath the table for his rucksack and took out a folder. He placed it in front of him but didn't open it.

'From the off he answered, "No comment" to every question we put to him. He told us nothing about the body in the boot of his car, how it came to be there, whether he'd killed him, how he picked him up, nothing. Even when we asked him to confirm his name and address, he answered, "No comment." He refused a solicitor and had so much self-control he sat for hours while we bombarded him with questions. He sat staring blankly at us. He didn't once ask for a drink, something to eat, or to go to the toilet. He was like an automaton.'

Olivia chewed her bottom lip as she thought, pouring boiling water into the mugs. 'Very cool. Very calm. Very in control of his emotions. I'm assuming you tried every tactic in the book to get him to open up. Did you mention his daughter to him?'

'Many times. We said he should consider her and how she would feel having to watch her father on trial for murder. Nothing. We might as well have been talking to the wall.'

'Either he completely shut himself off from reality in his guise as a murderer or he really didn't care about his daughter. What does she say of her father?'

She brought the mugs in on a tray along with a jug of milk and a bowl of sugar.

'She thought he was the perfect dad. His wife, her mother, died many years ago from cancer. He's always been there for her. She had an idyllic childhood. She didn't have a bad word to say against him.'

'A loving family,' Olivia offered. Her own childhood had been similarly idyllic. Were murderers so good at manipulation that they managed to fool their loved ones, or did they go above and beyond to avoid the telltale signs of their darker half? If that was the case, then Olivia's childhood, like that of Isaac's daughter, had been a complete lie. She threw that thought away. Happiness with her mother and sister was the only pure memory she could cling to.

'Quite. What she said about him doesn't tally with the man we interviewed,' Sutton said.

'No,' Olivia mused. 'When he was first arrested, Isaac's clothes will have been tested by forensics. Did he have anything on them connected to the victims?'

'No. They were clean. No traces of blood or skin samples. Nothing under his fingernails either. Yes, he could have changed his clothes and showered, but we also tore through his home, and we didn't find a single trace of Sean Bridger anywhere. Well, not then, anyway.'

'But you have since?'

'When Eleanor brought us the box with the notebook and the trophies, we went back to the house. Fortunately, she hadn't done anything with it. We had a forensic team literally take the place apart. We found minute traces of blood in the garage. Three different strands of DNA were extracted, one of which belongs to

Sean Bridger. Unfortunately, we can't match the other two to anyone on the National DNA Database.'

'And you tested those other two against Isaac's daughter?'

'Yes,' Sutton stated firmly, almost annoyed at having his approach to his job called into question.

'I'm sorry,' Olivia said, picking up on the tone of his voice. 'I didn't mean to suggest you'd been sloppy or anything. I just wanted to check all bases were covered.'

'Trust me, I wouldn't be here if they hadn't been. We've exhausted all forensic avenues and questioned those we can question multiple times.'

Olivia nodded. 'This notebook...' she began, leaving the question hanging in the air.

Sutton opened his folder. He pulled out a stack of stapled A4 pages. He didn't hand it over straightaway.

'This is a photocopy of every page in the notebook Eleanor McFadden found. There's also a list here of the items found along with it. There are no dates attached to any of the entries and several different pens and coloured inks have been used. What we need to know is if this is genuine, and if there really are more victims out there. If so, who, and where?'

Olivia couldn't take her eyes from the printout. She was itching to go through it all, sit down in her darkened office, doors shut, curtains closed, all distractions from the outside world obliterated, and scrutinise every single line, sentence, word, syllable, and get deep inside the mind of, potentially, a prolific serial killer.

'I'm not good with cryptic crosswords, but I'll see what I can do,' she said, hoping her flippancy would stop her salivating to get her hands on the paperwork.

He handed it to her across the table. She took it from him in both hands and felt its heft. Psychologically, it weighed a tonne.

'Have you shown anyone else this?' She looked down at the cover page. It was blank. She could see the print from the text on the page beneath, tantalising her. She wanted nothing more than to open it and read the horror within.

Sutton snorted a laugh.

'What is it?' She looked up.

'I showed it to Professor Hatch at Newcastle University. He...' Sutton stopped. He didn't seem to know how to finish his sentence.

'Didn't want to get involved,' Olivia volunteered.

'Something like that. You know him?'

'I know of him. I think he's running down the clock until retirement.'

'I got that impression. He told me to contact you, actually.'

'Really?' Olivia noticed Sutton's cheeks redden slightly. He looked away. 'What were Professor Hatch's exact words?'

'Are you sure you want to hear them?'

Olivia stifled a smile. 'It would be helpful to know, when our office sends out Christmas cards, whether we should bother sending one to Newcastle.'

Sutton took a breath. 'Professor Hatch said that if we wanted the insight into a twisted psychopath, we should ask the infamous Olivia Winter. His words were, "They don't come more twisted than her." I'm sorry.'

'Oh, he's definitely off the Christmas card list.'

Sutton let out a guttural laugh which seemed to light up his face. Olivia found herself laughing, too.

She looked back down at the printout and began to flick through the pages. She didn't want to seem too eager. She didn't want to add to her reputation of being 'twisted'.

'Can I keep this?'

'Of course. I'd prefer it if you didn't show it to anyone, though.'

'I won't,' she lied. As analytical as her brain was, she relied heavily on her partner Sebastian Lister to help her. 'Did you work on the McFadden investigation or are you just getting involved now?'

'I worked on it from the beginning.'

'At any time did you think he might be responsible for more deaths?'

Sutton sighed. 'I couldn't read him at all. He was a closed book. He was too calm during the interviews.'

Olivia went back to the printout. She flicked through more pages, taking in the wording and the layout of the text.

'Do you want me to leave it with you?' he asked.

She looked up. 'Sorry,' she smiled. 'I was getting submerged there. Erm, how long are you down for?'

'Just overnight. I'm back on the train mid-morning tomorrow.'

'Okay. Well, how about I look over this tonight and you come back tomorrow, and we can go from there?'

'That works for me,' he said with an appreciative smile.

'Shall we say nine o'clock?'

'Fine. Well, I'd better be going,' Sutton said, standing up. 'I can count on one hand how many times I've been to London, and I always get lost. It'll be a miracle if I get back to my hotel.'

'Would you like me to give you directions?'

'No. I'll be fine. Thank goodness for Google. I'll see you tomorrow.'

Olivia watched as Linus Sutton picked up his bag and left the room, flashing her a smile over his shoulder, though it didn't quite reach his eyes, as he closed the door behind him.

Olivia returned to the journal. She opened the front cover and read the first page.

> Now I lay me down to sleep,
> I pray the Lord my soul to keep,
> In the morn should I awake,
> Point me to a life that I should take.

'Bloody hell!' Olivia uttered.

Chapter Five

There was a knock on the meeting-room door. It opened without Olivia calling out. Stanley trotted in first followed by Sebastian.

'Oh, you are awake then?'

'Sorry?' She looked past him and out into the street. It was dark. How long had she been in here on her own? She looked at her watch. More than an hour had gone by since DI Sutton had left. It didn't even seem like five minutes.

Sebastian was forty-four, ten years older than Olivia. He was average height and carrying a little extra weight around his middle which was a never-ending struggle for him to try and lose. He lived in Finsbury Park with his four children and had been a widower for two years, having lost his beloved wife to breast cancer. As much as he tried to hide it, he felt her loss greatly, and many a time his face belied his constant reassurances that he was fine.

Sebastian and Olivia met years ago when Sebastian was writing a book about her father, the infamous serial killer Richard Button. He had wanted to interview her as the sole survivor. She immediately said no, but something drew the two of them together and they remained firm friends. It was a long time into their friendship before Olivia told Sebastian the full story of what it was like living with a man she thought of as the perfect father, the man who murdered her mother and younger sister and who tried to kill her. Sebastian knew everything about Olivia, and never betrayed her confidence. She trusted him completely.

Sebastian pulled out a chair next to her and sat down. 'Something's keeping you engrossed.'

'Isaac McFadden,' Olivia began. 'Does the name ring a bell?'

'No,' he answered immediately.

'You don't keep an eye on the news, do you?'

'Definitely not. If I want to spend my evenings being depressed, I'll look at my energy bills.'

There was a light knock on the door, followed by an even lighter yap from Stanley. Daisy came in carrying a tray.

'I thought you'd both like a hot chocolate. I brought my Velvetiser in from home. Nobody uses it. This should warm you both up.'

Olivia took a mug from the tray. 'I can't remember the last time I had a hot chocolate.'

And then she could. Her mind immediately took her back to her last Christmas with her mum and her sister. They were in their happy home in Kingston-upon-Thames decorating the Christmas tree, tinsel draped over every item of furniture, baubles rolling everywhere, as her mother, Geraldine, struggled with a knotted string of lights and Olivia and her sister, Claire, planned with military precision where each ornament was going to go. Claire sipped at her hot chocolate and gave herself a chocolate moustache. She refused to wipe her upper lip, saying she wanted to be able to smell the chocolate as she drifted off to sleep.

'Olivia,' Sebastian called out, bringing her back to the present.

'Sorry?'

'You drifted.'

Olivia looked around her. Daisy had gone.

'Mental flashback.'

'You all right?'

'Fine.' She gave one of her stock smiles, took a sip of the

smooth hot chocolate and placed the mug down on the desk, away from Stanley. 'Anyway, as I was saying, Isaac McFadden. He was arrested last year somewhere in Newcastle when police pulled him over during a storm and found a body in the boot of his car.'

'I remember now. Wasn't it cut up into pieces?'

'It was. He gave "no comment" answers to everything, refused to enter a plea and spent his entire trial looking bored to tears. No surprise that he was found guilty and sentenced to life. Fast forward to a few weeks ago and his daughter was cleaning out his house and she came across a notebook. In it, there's a code she couldn't decipher. She took it to the police and they couldn't understand it either. However, they think it might be a table of Isaac McFadden's victims. They think there could be another twelve of them out there.'

'Surely they'd know if they had a serial killer on their hands,' he said.

'That's what I said. But the man Isaac was arrested for killing was homeless and estranged from his family. It could be possible his other victims had dropped off the radar, too.'

'I'm guessing that's the book that's been keeping you so engrossed.'

'Only a photocopy. How are you with cryptic crosswords?'

'I prefer a Wordle,' Sebastian said, coming round to her side of the table so they could read it together.

Sebastian sat back in his chair and took a deep breath. 'Well, I'd be lying if I said I understood all that. In fact, I'd be lying if I said I understood any of that.'

Olivia remained silent as she continued to gaze at the code she had already looked at several times. Then she said, 'Me neither. But it's an insightful journal. That section where he wrote about choosing his victims, not listening to what they said but looking into their eyes to see if they're for him or not.'

'We all do it. How many times do I ask you how you are, and you simply say you're fine even though we both know you're not.'

'For the most part I am fine. And when I'm not fine I don't want to talk about it, so it's easier to say I'm fine.'

'Count yourself lucky you were never asked by Isaac McFadden,' Sebastian said, almost flippantly.

Olivia didn't respond. She had returned to the code.

'What do you think?' Sebastian asked.

'I can't make up my mind,' she said.

'What are you pondering?'

'Firstly, why would someone keep a record of the people they'd killed?'

'To look back over it and marvel at their handiwork.'

'Why write it in code?'

'So that should it fall into the wrong hands, they won't know what it means.'

'But if you hide it somewhere private, somewhere only you know the location of, there's no need for a code, is there?'

'No. Where was the notebook found?' Sebastian asked.

'Beneath the floorboards of a fitted wardrobe. It was in a box with items the police believe are trophies from his victims.'

'Who knew about the hiding place?'

'Well, his daughter for one. She found it, after all. I think he was hoping it would be found one day. DI Sutton said that in his police interviews he was very stoic. He replied, "No comment" to every question, and nothing rattled him. He refused to enter a plea or take the stand at his trial. He sentenced himself before he even set foot in the courtroom. He remained silent because he knew this code would be found and the police would go begging to him for answers.'

'He was manipulating the investigation from the moment he was arrested.'

'He was.'

Olivia took her laptop out of her bag. She turned it on and entered Isaac's name into Google. She looked down a few articles until she found what she was looking for.

'Here we are. Isaac was pulled over by police during a storm. One of his rear lights was out,' she began, reading from the screen. 'The police officer offered to take a look inside the boot, but Isaac's behaviour made them think he was hiding something...'

'Which he was,' Sebastian interrupted.

'At the point where Isaac was pulled over, he must have known that this was the end, that he'd finally been caught. However, he's hidden all his victims in locations that haven't yet been found so during any police interview they'd only question him about the one body in the car. He could have answered their questions and been charged and sentenced for the one crime. That's it. Game over. But he didn't. He remained silent and allowed a shroud of mystery to envelop him. When this code turns up, police immediately believe it to be genuine because of his strange behaviour.'

'So, is it genuine or is it the workings of a disturbed individual with massive delusions?'

Olivia thought for a moment. 'I... I'm not entirely sure at present,' she said, slowly.

Sebastian studied her. He seemed always to be able to read what she was thinking simply by looking at her. 'You want to go up to Newcastle and visit Isaac McFadden?'

'If I speak to him, I'll be able to work out if he's written these words and if they're from his mind or from experience.'

Sebastian nodded. 'I can see that. Look at those interviews we've been doing this past year with killers around the world. I'm guessing you've noticed the ones we've always gone back to are the ones we've conducted ourselves rather than ones other people have done.'

'I wondered if you'd noticed that,' she said with a wry smile.

'What about your work here? You've got lectures planned for the next month and we've got the guy from California coming a week on Monday. Or is that why you're suddenly charging up to the other end of the country?'

'Professor Monroe is only coming to promote his own book. We said we'd meet him if we could fit him in. We'll just say we can't. Besides, do you really want to spend leisure time with someone who is completely bald on top but has a straggly ponytail down his back? I bloody don't.'

'Not really. Did you see his Instagram photos of his holiday in Mexico?'

'I'm trying to block those from my mind. Moving swiftly on from a sixty-year-old with a paunch in budgie smugglers, can you cover my lectures?'

'You know I can. Though, Olivia, is there another reason why you're so keen to get out of London?'

Olivia frowned at him.

'I've seen the billboards going up for the drama about your dad. Are you sure you're not just running away?'

'They do have billboards up in Newcastle, you know,' she said, playfully.

'Don't be pedantic. You know what I mean. Unfortunately, journalists know where you live and where you work now. Once this drama hits the screens, they're going to be coming to you for a comment, or at least hoping to snatch a photo of you in tears on your doorstep. Are you trying to avoid the scrum?'

'Of course I am.'

'I knew this would happen. Olivia, when I was approached to sell the rights of my book I asked you on thirteen different occasions – I kept a record – if you minded. You said no every single time. You obviously do mind.'

Olivia stood up and went over to the window. She pushed open the slats of the Venetian blind and looked out into the darkening afternoon. The red Vauxhall had gone.

'Selling those rights has paid for Tilly to go to America to study. It's paid for Alistair to go on that school trip to Iceland, decorated the twins' bedroom, and covers your bills for several months.'

'But at what cost to you?'

She turned back to him. 'Obviously, I would have preferred if they'd turned it into a musical.'

'Now you're being silly.'

'I just want to get out of London for a while. I'm feeling… stifled. The billboards seem to be all over the place. Whenever I go into a shop, I see your book with its new TV tie-in jacket glaring at me. I know I'm not, but I feel like I'm being watched. I've lost my anonymity. All my neighbours now know who my father is, and I feel their gaze lingering on me. At least in Newcastle, nobody will know I'm there.'

'I worry about you.'

'I know you do. You don't need to, though.'

'Would you like me to look after Stanley?'

'Yes, please.'

'Shall we see if we can crack this secret code?'

Olivia's face lit up. 'Go on, then. Though if A equals one, I'm going to be seriously pissed off at Isaac McFadden.'

Chapter Six

BYKER, NEWCASTLE

It hadn't been much of a funeral service for Rona Landy. It lasted barely twenty minutes and the congregation of only six people were soon herded out of the chapel. As they stood in the entrance, none of them knowing what to do next or what to say, the next funeral was getting ready to begin. Rona had been just thirty-eight when she died. Less than a week after discovering a lump in her breast last summer, she was diagnosed with stage five cancer. Her decline was rapid, and doctors warned her she might not see Christmas. She managed to cling on to spend a final festive season with her son, see in the new year and wish him happy birthday on the fifth of January, and then she succumbed to death a week later.

Thomas Landy had grown up a great deal over the past six months. Seventeen years old, he should have been enjoying his teenage years at college, learning to drive, having nights out with friends, discovering freedom and what life had to offer. Instead, he deferred his A-Levels and put his life on hold as he nursed his mother through her final months. She was all he had. He wasn't prepared to lose her yet.

His eighteenth birthday should have been one of drunken decadence. He should have been scouring the clubs of Newcastle, getting drunk, waking up in the middle of the afternoon the next day and not remembering a single minute of the night before. Instead, he sat on his mother's bed and unwrapped the Hugo Boss watch she'd asked one of the carers to order online for her. She didn't even have the strength in her body to hand him the gift. The carer, Lucy, had had to do that for her.

He loved it. He put it on, kissed his mother and promised he would wear it every day for the rest of his life. He spent the rest of the day by her side, watching comedy films from the 80s on the TV in her bedroom. It was a day filled with sadness and tears. Both of them knew they didn't have much longer to spend with each other. They tried to smile at Goldie Hawn and Kurt Russell's unconventional romance in *Overboard* and Whoopi Goldberg's attempt to gain access to the British Consulate in *Jumpin' Jack Flash*, but their laughs were false. Death was already in the room and biding his time before he took Rona by the hand and led her away.

It was another week before Rona breathed her last. Two hours before she died, Thomas sat on the edge of the bed next to her and held her hand. They didn't need to speak. Everything had been said. They were content to be with each other.

'Tom,' she began. Rona had never shortened her son's name before, but she no longer had the energy for multisyllabic words. A short sentence could take several minutes for her to get through. 'Do me. A. Favour.' Her words were barely audible. She didn't sound like his mum. Her voice was slow and slurred. Thomas didn't rush her. He remained by her side and listened intently. She would get her words out eventually. 'Live. Your life.' She took a few slow breaths. 'Enjoy. Your. Self.'

'I will,' he said. He wanted to cry. He knew he was losing his mum, and he wasn't ready. But he didn't want her to see him already beginning to struggle without her.

'Do,' she continued. 'Do. Everything. At least. Once.'

He turned to look at her. She had a soft smile on her dry lips. She winked at him. She made him smile.

'I intend to,' he said, finding the bravado from somewhere.

'Love. You.'

They were her last words to her son.

Rona's carers couldn't make it back to the house. The woman next door, Janet Wray, had put on a bit of a spread to toast Rona's life and had spent the morning cleaning up the living room and kitchen for the guests.

Thomas unlocked the front door. He picked up the few letters and cards that had been delivered while he'd been at his mother's funeral and led Janet and three of the nosier neighbours into the house.

In the kitchen, Thomas stood in silence. He looked around him. A year ago, this house was full of life. His mother couldn't cook a meal without having Kim Wilde or Bananarama blasting at full volume and dancing around the kitchen. Many a time he would come home from college, and he'd hear an 80s classic from up the road. Rona would be singing away as she peeled vegetables or prepared the pork chops. Thomas wanted to remember his mother as she lived, always with a smile on her face, happy, having fun, but whenever he thought of her, she was in bed, her face distorted in pain, tears running down her cheeks.

From the living room, he could hear Janet and the other women from Cheviot Mount talking about the poor turnout at the funeral and reminiscing about Rona, all with their mouths full of hastily made sandwiches and shop-bought sponge cake. Thomas was certain they'd only come for the free food. It would save them having to cook a meal this evening.

When had he become so cynical? His mother wouldn't have come out with a comment like that. A cruel, untimely death of a loved one did that to a person.

He sat at the table and looked at the post. A few stiff white envelopes obviously contained sympathy cards from people he wouldn't know. They could be opened another time. There was a brown envelope, which meant it was something important, serious and grown-up. This kind of missive fell to Thomas now.

He was eighteen. He was the only adult here. He ran his finger under the flap and took out the letter. It was from Newcastle City Council.

He read the letter. It didn't make any sense to him, so he read it again.

'Thomas, are you coming through?' Janet asked. She stood in the doorway to the kitchen and looked down at Thomas. He had tears running down his face. 'What is it? What's the matter?'

'The council say I can't live here anymore,' he said. He swallowed his emotions. 'Mum was the tenant, not me, and as a single person, I don't qualify for a three-bedroom house.' He looked up at Janet. 'They're throwing me out.'

Extract from a notebook allegedly written by Isaac McFadden

1	A1	SCORN HEIGHT YELLING (NAVY)	DOG RISEN (ANGERS) GARDEN	BLACK GREEN GREEN BLACK 3/6/4/21	*
2	O1	BAIT ANGEL COG (KITE)	DREADING ORIGIN GANDER (GRINCH)	BROWN GREY BLACK BLACK 0/?/?	&
3	F1	SCREAMED TOUCH (ALLEN) GATE	NOISY (ONION) UNWELL NUN	BROWN GREEN GREEN BROWN 8/6/2/24	*
4	J5	HOUSE (ANCIENT) GRASS GARAGE	(SLEEVE) NAMETAG INDIA DARK	BROWN WHITE BLACK BLACK 12/6/1/21	(
5	N2	MEWS ANSWER STATION (TEA)	(SCARF) MINIMUM ENERGY GRAM	BLACK BLACK BLACK BLACK 0/6/?	%
6	J6	RELY OCTAGON (COLD) KEY	(CHICKEN) ZOOMING OLD GHOST	YELLOW YELLOW WHITE BLACK 10/6/?	%
7	M4	JUICE ELECTRICITY LEAVES (SOUTH)	MISERY INCEPTION NINE (KING)	BROWN BLACK BLACK BLUE 6/6/1/20	&
8	M5	NATURAL (JOANNA) ATTITUDE VEIL	CHRISTMAS HOUSE ELDERS (BORDER)	BLACK GREY BLUE BLACK 0/5/7/20	(

The Devil's Code

9	A6	DIVE ENVELOPE NIGHT (SAUSAGE)	(SILK) AGED GLOVE ALIVE	BROWN WHITE BLACK BLACK 15/6/3/23	*
10	O3	POSTAL ACTION (CAT) TRANSPORT	(SHARP) ISLAND NEVER NEWS	YELLOW BLUE BLUE BLUE 9/6/19	&
11	J9	CONDUCT ORANGE (RUN) NEWT	POLITICAL (WALK) GRAPHIC EDITION	YELLOW WHITE BLACK BLACK/WHITE 8/6/21	(
12	M6	DATE EATEN EDGE (POPPY)	HELPFUL INDEED CRESCENT (HEAT)	BROWN BLUE BLUE BLACK 12/5/10/20	£

Chapter Seven

There were twelve entries in total in Isaac McFadden's cryptic chart and none of it made any sense, at least not to Olivia and Sebastian. It didn't seem to matter how many times they read it, nothing became clearer.

'I can only work out the first column and that's only because it's in numerical order.' Sebastian said, sitting back in his chair and folding his arms.

Olivia remained silent. She was bent over the printout, her eyes glued to the text.

'Should we take the columns individually or go across the rows?' Sebastian asked.

'I'm not sure,' Olivia mused, finally looking up. 'Each column must refer to something, obviously, but then each row is about each individual victim, I assume. Okay,' she said, standing up. She ran her fingers through her hair. 'Let's take this one row at a time. We can guess that the first column refers to the number of the victim. So, one. Now, what does A1 refer to?'

'I don't know. Maybe it's the road he picked his victim up from.'

'But in the next row it's O1. There's no road called O1, is there?'

'No.'

The Devil's Code

'So, it's not a road then. What else can A1 refer to?'

'Paper size?'

'Again, there's no paper size called O1.'

'Maybe it's a grid reference to an A–Z road map,' Sebastian said. 'You look up something in the index, it tells you what page it's on, then which square. Numbers along the top, letters down the side. We just need to work out which A–Z and which page these refer to.'

Olivia nodded. 'That makes more sense. It could be either where he picked his victims up or where he buried them.'

'Or where he took them to kill them.'

'I wonder if there were any A–Z maps found in Isaac's house,' Olivia mused. 'I'll make a note to ask DI Sutton tomorrow.' She reached into her bag and took out a hardback notebook and pen. She scribbled inside.

'So, we definitely think this is a grid reference thing then?'

'It can't really be anything else, can it?'

'I wouldn't have thought so. A1, O1, F1, J5. Unless they're the beginning of a postcode.'

'I hadn't thought of that,' Olivia said. 'Where is A1?'

Sebastian went over to the corner of the room where his battered briefcase was. He took a tablet out and turned it on.

'There isn't an A,' he said. 'There's AB which is Aberdeen and AL which is St Albans.'

'No others beginning with A?'

'No.'

'Maybe he knows what the A refers to and doesn't want to narrow it down to either Aberdeen or St Albans and just uses the first letter. So, it could be AB1 or AL1.'

'Aberdeen is a big place. I'm guessing AB1 would cover a large area. It doesn't really narrow it down, does it?'

'No. I think a map grid reference is more likely than a postcode,' Olivia said.

'I hope so. Look at entry number five. That's N2. N is North London. That's a massive area.'

'Okay. So, the second column could be a map grid reference.

We just need to find which map Isaac was working from. Columns three and four are very similar. A list of four words in each, one of which is bracketed in each entry.'

'Scorn. Height. Yelling. Navy. Dog. Risen. Angers. Garden,' Sebastian read. 'It's like a round from *Only Connect*,' he said.

'What's *Only Connect*?' Olivia asked.

'It's a gameshow.'

'I don't watch gameshows.'

'Oh. Well, there's a round in *Only Connect* where there are sixteen words, seemingly random, but they can be put into four categories of four connecting items. Maybe each of these four words have a single common meaning. They could refer to the victim or where he's buried them.'

'Scorn. Height. Yelling. Navy. What could that refer to?' Olivia asked.

It was a while before Sebastian replied. 'I… I don't know. I mean, if it refers to a place and Isaac stayed local to the North East then we need someone who is an expert in that area. I think I've only ever passed through on the train.'

'Say he is copying this *Only Connect* programme. Are there words in this round that appear in brackets?' Olivia asked.

'No.'

'Then what's the point of them?'

Sebastian screwed his face up while he tried to think of a solution. 'Maybe he needs one word to stand out somehow. So, navy, in this case, could mean…' He left the sentence hanging in the air as he thought. 'Is there a Naval yard in Newcastle?'

'I don't know.'

'Navy blue the colour? Could Isaac have been wearing navy blue when he killed him and wants that reminder?' Sebastian shrugged. 'Are you getting a headache? I am.'

Olivia went back to the code. 'Scorn. Height. Yelling. I suppose, if you're being scornful to someone, you could be yelling. And maybe you're yelling from a height.'

'The Angel of the North is very high. It looks over Newcastle.'

'It's a bit of a tenuous link, isn't it?'

'Very tenuous.'

'Let's leave the gameshow round and move on to the fifth column. "Black, green, green, black." That could mean anything. What's black and green?'

Sebastian sat back in his chair and looked up to the ceiling as he thought. 'Isn't there a make of chocolate called Green and Black's?'

'There is, but what does that have to do with anything?'

'I don't know. It was the first thing that came to mind. Every fifth column is just a list of four colours.'

'Number five is "black, black, black, black". What the hell can that refer to?'

'Black seems to be in every entry. Could that refer to it being dark? Maybe he killed all his victims at night.'

'Why would he need to remind himself of that?' Olivia asked.

'Say black does refer to it being dark, what could green represent?' He thought for a moment. 'Grass is green.'

'Yes, and so are sprouts, cabbages, avocados, caterpillars, cactus and bloody go signs at a traffic light,' Olivia said, getting riled up. 'Green could mean anything. Black could mean anything. I'm no good at cryptic crosswords or sodding anagrams. I mean, he obviously expected this to be found or he wouldn't have written it in this way, which means he's like all the other serial killers we've met over the years. They want to keep taunting the investigators even after they've been caught. Isaac McFadden is in prison. He's lost his freedom, and this is all he has left to hold onto, and if there are a dozen more victims out there, then he can spend the rest of his life drip-feeding little nuggets of information to torment the police with.'

'If that's the case, do you really want to go and have a face-to-face meeting with him?' Sebastian asked.

'What do you mean?'

'He'll know who you are. Dr Olivia Winter. Serial killer survivor and famous forensic psychologist—'

'I'm not famous,' she interrupted.

'You are. Whether you like it or not, you're known throughout the world as a serial killer obsessive. You study them. You visit them in prison and question them at length. You're even related to one. I know you don't care what the media say about you, but me and Daisy do. We read the stories. We look on social media. By not reading them, you can pretend they don't exist, but the fact of the matter remains, people know who you are. Isaac McFadden will know who you are. Whatever he tells you will need to be taken with a large pinch of salt. He'll delight in besting the great Olivia Winter.'

Olivia sighed and slumped down on the seat in the bay window. Stanley jumped down from the table and jumped up at her legs. She lifted him up and snuggled him on her lap.

'So, what do I do? Do I go and see him or try and work this out on my own?'

'By all means, go and see him. But you need to remember that things have changed for you now. In the past, you've visited prisons and talked to killers, and they've just known you for being a psychologist who's written a few books on serial killers. Now, they know you as Richard Button's daughter, as someone who fought her father and survived, as the person who single-handedly tracked down Jamie Farr and killed him before he could kill you. People on social media are already referring to you as a real-life final girl.'

'I don't know what that means.'

'Jamie Lee Curtis in *Halloween*. Neve Campbell in *Scream*. They're both final girls. The killer comes after them God knows how many times, kills their friends, but they're always left standing by the time the credits roll.'

'I'm not a fictional character.'

'No. But the lines between fiction and reality for a lot of people are very blurred. Can I give you some advice on this one, Olivia?'

'You know you can.'

'Stay under the radar. If you go and see Isaac make sure it doesn't get out to the public. If people see you as a real-life Laurie Strode, they might try and hunt you down to test their theory.'

'Am I allowed to ask who Laurie Strode is?'

'Bloody hell, Olivia, stop watching things with subtitles and give popular culture a try from time to time.'

She laughed. 'Sorry.'

'All I'm saying is that if you allow yourself to be caught up in a high-profile media storm, you'll attract a high number of undesirable people – horror film fans who can't quite grasp what they see on screen isn't real, psychos who want to try and take down the woman who has managed to survive two serial killer attacks.'

'I'd hardly say I've survived,' she said, wiping a tear away before it managed to fall.

'Survived physically.'

Olivia snuggled Stanley a little tighter. 'Should I help DI Sutton or not?'

'Only you can answer that question.'

'No, you can answer it, too. I trust you explicitly.'

'Help him. That's what we're here for, after all. If it turns out Isaac McFadden has killed a dozen people and it gets out that the Behavioural Science Administration turned down the police, we'd be in some serious shit with the Home Office. Besides, Isaac's in prison. It's not as if he's an active serial killer who can hunt you down to try and stop you.'

'That's comforting.'

'As a rule, we don't work on active investigations. Last year was a one-off, and only because you were close to one of the victims. Once this TV drama is off the screens, the interest in you will quickly fade as soon as the next series of *Bake Off* begins, and you can return to a life of anonymity. In the meantime, stay low.'

Olivia placed Stanley back on the table and went round behind Sebastian. She wrapped her arms around him and kissed him on the cheek.

'Thank you for your kind words. Thank you for being there for me.'

Stanley yapped.

'For us,' Olivia corrected herself.

Chapter Eight

Olivia rode home through the dark streets of London on her scooter wearing a specially adapted rucksack-cum-papoose she found online to hold Stanley in. It wasn't ideal, and she was pretty sure it might be illegal, but she could think of no other way of getting to and from work with a Dachshund without driving a car.

Olivia lived in Modbury Gardens in Camden, a four-storey townhouse in an exclusive cul-de-sac. It was far too big for a single woman and a tiny dog, but it was her home and she felt comfortable here. Just about.

She pulled up outside her house and looked up at it. To anyone else it would look as if it was occupied. Lights had been timed to turn on and off at irregular intervals once darkness had fallen. She'd timed the radio and television to come on in different rooms at certain times to give the illusion people were enjoying an evening at home, should anyone want to invade her personal space. If she thought about it, Olivia would call herself paranoid, though she preferred to think of it as being cautious. Twenty-first-century London was not a safe place. Olivia had been born and raised in the capital. She lived here. She worked here. Her father killed her here. She might not have physically died when he murdered her mother and sister and stabbed her multiple times at the age of nine, but she had been mentally and emotionally dead ever since. To her, London meant death, crime, fear, murder, danger and horror. Yet she had no intention of leaving it.

She put Stanley on a lead and took him for a walk around the block for him to stretch his little legs and do his business. They didn't stay out long. He had a large, and secure, back garden to be free in.

As she approached her house, a couple came down the steps from the property next door. It had been empty for months since the Abbots had moved to Germany on business. She hadn't known them. Olivia wasn't the neighbourly sort. She said hello, smiled and nodded if she saw any of her neighbours in the street and she'd received a few Christmas cards, though she had no idea why anyone would send a card to someone they didn't know. 'To No9, Merry Christmas from the Coker family at No12.' She could see the motive behind it, the friendliness, but it was a faux greeting. Why wait until Christmas to approach someone you wanted to say hello to?

'Good evening,' the woman said.

'Good evening,' Olivia replied. She didn't stop, trotted up her front steps and took her keys out of her pocket to make a swift getaway into her own home.

'Excuse me,' the woman called out. 'Do you live here?'

Olivia turned. 'Yes.'

'We've just been looking around next door. It's a beautiful property.'

Olivia didn't say anything. It wasn't that she was tongue-tied and couldn't think of anything to say, it was simply that she was uncomfortable and found small talk pointless and a waste of time.

'What's it like around here? The neighbourhood?' the woman asked.

Olivia looked around her. All the houses had their curtains closed and lights on behind them. Behind those closed doors, people were living their lives. Whether they were happy, sad, rowing, making love, ignoring each other or simply sitting down to an evening meal in silence was of no consequence to Olivia.

'It's a pleasant neighbourhood,' Olivia said. 'People tend to keep to themselves.'

'That's good. That's just what we're looking for, isn't it, Ben?' she said, looking back to the man Olivia guessed was her husband.

'Absolutely. I work from home so peace and quiet would be ideal.'

Olivia would never describe London as being peaceful and quiet. In the distance, the sound of two sirens competing with each other could be heard. She turned away and back to her house.

'We'll definitely be putting in an offer,' the woman quickly called out. 'We could be neighbours.'

Olivia glanced back over her shoulder and smiled.

'I'm Natalie. I'm a registrar at the Royal Free. This is my husband, Ben. He's a forensic psychologist.'

This caused Olivia to stop in her tracks. She turned back to face the couple. She took out her mobile phone, accessed the security app and turned on the overhead lights above her front door, lighting up the whole of the exterior, and bringing the couple more into focus. They squinted in the brightness of the light.

She studied the couple. The penny dropped. She almost sniggered. It was clever. Seven out of ten for ingenuity.

'I'd have thought you'd have used different names,' she said.

'I'm sorry?' Natalie asked.

'I don't know you, but I thought I recognised your so-called husband from somewhere. Ben Latimer. Crime Correspondent for the *Daily Mail*. I've replied to three of your emails politely refusing an interview, yet you still persisted with your requests. I make a point of knowing the people who pester me. And you couldn't have been looking around next door as I had an email from the Abbots a week ago saying they've taken the house off the market as they've decided to come back to live in England. For journalists, your research skills are terrible.'

Olivia entered her house and closed the door behind her. She would have liked to slam it, but she didn't want to give them the satisfaction of knowing they'd riled her.

'Fucking journalists,' she said as she unclipped Stanley's lead and allowed him to run into the kitchen for a drink.

On the back of the front door, Olivia had installed a cage to collect any mail posted through the letterbox. She had done this when she found Stanley shredding a letter from her GP inviting her for a smear test. Three letters had been delivered today. One stood out more than the others as it was in a pale yellow envelope. She didn't need to open it to know who it was from. She took the letters from the cage and followed Stanley into the kitchen. She tossed the two circulars on the island and the yellow envelope went into a drawer with the others. Unopened.

Stanley had eaten and was now running around the back garden, which was lit up with motion sensor lighting like an alien invasion. Olivia stood in the back doorway, freezing cold, heavy cardigan pulled tightly around her as Stanley yapped at decaying leaves being swept around by the light winter breeze.

She looked up at the house next door, in continuous darkness for the past few months. The house beyond had its curtains drawn, lights on in almost every room, the shadows cast displaying the normality of family life within.

Stanley yapped, making her jump. She looked down to see he'd brought her a soggy tennis ball for her to throw.

'Not at this time of night, young man,' she said.

Olivia had inherited the dog from a friend of hers, Jessica Sheffield, a detective with the Metropolitan Police who had been murdered last year by a serial killer. Olivia blamed herself. Jessica had come to her for help, but Olivia always stated she didn't work active investigations. She changed her mind, but it took Jessica's murder for her to do so. Had she been more flexible in her thinking, Jessica might still be alive.

Stanley trotted back up the steps and into the house. She

closed the door and locked it securely. He jumped into his little bed in the kitchen and made himself comfortable. Olivia pulled out a stool at the large island and sat down. She needed to eat as she'd only had a sandwich at lunchtime, but she had more important things to think about. This code written by Isaac McFadden was gnawing away at her mind. She needed to try and break it, to understand it. If there were twelve victims out there, they needed finding so their families could say goodbye to them.

Olivia poured herself a large glass of white wine, took a notebook from her bag and the printout given to her by DI Sutton, and read through the code once more. Still it made no sense to her at all. It was random, but there had to be a key to it somewhere, even if it only existed in Isaac's head.

She drained her glass and looked down at Stanley, snoozing in his bed. She felt light-headed. She needed something to eat. She could be healthy. There was salad in the fridge. She had grains, pulses, lentils and quinoa she could use to beef up the lettuce and beetroot, but what Olivia really wanted right now was comfort food. Twenty minutes later, she was sitting in the living room on the Chesterfield sofa tucking into a fish finger sandwich made with thick slices of white bread. Stanley was by her side, eyes wide open, waiting for leftovers. He would have a long wait.

Olivia's house was on four floors, but she never went down into the basement. Many people in the cul-de-sac had adapted their lower-ground levels to let out as self-contained flats. Olivia's remained empty. She didn't even use it for storage. It was a forgotten place.

The ground floor was where Olivia mostly lived. There was a large kitchen, a cosy living room and a bedroom with en suite. It was tastefully decorated and looked more like a suite in a five-star hotel. It was all Olivia needed to be content, and it saved Stanley tiring himself out trying to run up and down stairs every time Olivia went to bed.

The first floor was one large room that most people in the street used as a spacious living room. Olivia used it as an office for the days she worked from home. Bookcases spanned the walls from floor to ceiling, filled with texts on psychology and criminology. She had a desk in the corner where she typed up her notes and lectures and a large refectory table in the middle of the room where she liked to spread out to do her thinking. That was where she was heading now with the printout of Isaac McFadden's journal in one hand and a bottle of wine and glass in the other. Naturally, Stanley followed.

The top floor of the house was where Olivia rarely went. It was decked out with everything concerning her father and the crimes he committed, the women he killed. When she was feeling at her lowest, when she wanted to try and understand what had caused a seemingly happy family man to turn into a serial killer, she went to the top floor and punished herself further.

Olivia began to read through the code again, though she had no idea why. She leaned back in her seat and drained her wine glass. She really shouldn't drink so much, especially on a weeknight, especially when she had a meeting with the detective at nine o'clock in the morning. She looked at her watch. It was almost midnight. Maybe sleeping on it would help, though she knew for certain she would be awake long before first light. She always was.

Tucked up, with Stanley snoozing at the foot of her bed, Olivia lay with her eyes wide open. Sleep refused to come. The confrontation with the sneaky journalists earlier was one of the many things preying on her mind. What other tactics would they resort to in order to get a few words out of her in the run-up to the dramatisation of her father's killings? Now they knew her address, would it be better if she moved? Why should she? She loved this house.

She sat up and switched on the bedside lamp. On the bedside

table sat a framed photograph of her mother and sister, taken in happy times, before evil entered their lives. She thought about them both every single day and missed them so much it physically hurt. One question she had always wanted answered was: why had her father turned to murder? Why had he killed so many people? Why had he killed her mum and sister and tried to kill her? Last year, she finally got the answer when she built up the courage to visit him while he was recovering from a heart attack in hospital. He'd told her, simply, that he killed because he could, that he'd enjoyed it. She refused to believe that as a motive. She refused to believe her father, a man she loved as a child, took pleasure from killing other people.

She climbed out of bed, slid her feet into slippers, grabbed her dressing gown and headed for the kitchen. She needed tea, and she needed chocolate. Stanley didn't even flinch.

As she made a mug of tea and searched the cupboard for something chocolate-coated, she had a thought. There might not be twelve more victims out there somewhere. There might only be eleven. Isaac was caught with a victim in the back of his car, but maybe Sean Bridger was victim number twelve rather than thirteen. Maybe Isaac had already written his entry into his code before he left the house to dispose of the body.

12	M6	DATE EATEN EDGE (POPPY)	HELPFUL INDEED CRESCENT (HEAT)	BROWN BLUE BLUE BLACK 12/5/10/20	£

'Huh,' she said to herself.

She read the twelfth entry several times. It meant nothing to her. It might as well have been written in a foreign language. Her eyes kept going back to the row of numbers in the fifth column. 12/5/10/20. What did that refer to? Was it another map grid reference? Could '20' refer to the year? Was it 2020? '10' could mean the month, which was October, '5' could be the date, but what did '12' mean? Was it the time? Was it twelve o'clock on the fifth of October 2020? If so, he couldn't have been the most recent victim as Sean Bridger was killed in March 2024.

'Maybe it has nothing to do with date and time at all,' she said out loud. 'The only way I'm going to know if this refers to the last victim is by finding out everything there is to know about Sean Bridger.'

Extract from a notebook allegedly written by Isaac McFadden

Thanks to programmes like Silent Witness, the plethora of shite from the CSI franchise and the many documentaries on true crime detection and forensics, everyone in the world knows what police and scene of crime officers look for when they enter a crime scene. We know that every contact leaves a trace, that no matter how much you scrub and scrub and scrub at a tiled floor, you're not going to remove every speck of blood. A killer can be caught with one strand of hair, and DNA can be taken from everything.

There was a case in the news not long back about a victim who had been killed and dumped, their body dragged by the ankles into woodland. The CSIs swabbed the ankles of the victim and found sweat deposits from the killer's fingers. Who would have thought of that?

It's not possible to remove every piece of trace evidence, but it's possible to minimise what is left. I take my victims apart. For one thing, it allows for ease of transportation when taking them to the dumping site. But the implement used needs careful consideration. A chain saw is going to be noisy, the neighbours might hear, and the blood spatter is going to be messy. An axe, again, it will be loud, and fragments of bone and tissue could fly off at random. A hand saw will also produce splinters of bone and will not make for a clean cut. Pathologists will easily be able to detect what kind of instrument was used. And there are some parts of the body that are thicker than others. The femur is the longest, heaviest and strongest bone in the human body. That's going to take some hacking into.

Blades need to be precise; they need to be easy to handle and easy to come by, and above all, they need to be razor sharp. The dismemberment of a body is a laborious process but with the correct tools, it's relatively easy, and, surprisingly, it can be quite therapeutic once you get started.

Chapter Nine

Thursday 16th January 2025

Olivia was the first to arrive at George Street. It was still dark, and a layer of frost made the chequered tiles difficult to walk on as she climbed the steps to the front door. She didn't put Stanley down until they were inside. He immediately ran into the meeting room, where he had a bed in front of the radiator.

Olivia followed, went into the kitchenette and flicked on the kettle. She needed a strong coffee to wake her up. She was shattered. More than usual. Isaac McFadden had haunted her dreams, causing her a restless night. She woke several times and by six o'clock, two pillows were on the floor, the duvet was half hanging off the bed and Stanley had moved to his own bed in the corner of the room, probably for some peace and quiet, bless him. Olivia was struggling to understand why Isaac had written a code in the first place, and what lay behind his laissez-faire attitude to his court case.

By the time DI Linus Sutton arrived, a little after nine o'clock, Olivia had devoured a bacon sandwich brought in by Daisy and downed three strong black coffees. She was feeling more presentable and alert. Sebastian had been late; his twins, Robert and Catherine, playing up on their way to school. He had only just sat down in the meeting room and arranged his notes when there was a knock on the door.

'Sorry for my appearance,' Linus said as he stood in the doorway. He was wearing a shirt and tie, waist-length reefer coat, boots and tight tracksuit bottoms. 'I only brought one pair of smart trousers down with me and let's just say the hotel make their eggs a little runnier than I'm used to.'

Olivia smiled and beckoned him in.

'I rarely stay in hotels,' Linus said. 'Usually when...' He stopped himself and his face dropped. 'I was surrounded by businesspeople in designer suits and smelling of expensive fragrances. I felt like a complete outsider.' He tried to laugh to make up for his discomfort, but there was something troubling him, something weighing him down emotionally, and Olivia surmised it ran deeper than the headache Isaac McFadden was giving him. However, Olivia was pleased to find she wasn't the only one who was socially awkward in strange places.

'Can I get you a coffee or anything?'

'I'd love a coffee, thank you. I'm not sure what that was at the hotel, but I think it had been made the night before.'

Olivia went into the kitchen. 'I hope you don't mind, but I showed Isaac's code to a colleague of mine, Dr Sebastian Lister.'

Linus looked to Sebastian. 'You're the bloke who wrote the book about...' He tailed off.

'That's me,' he said with what looked like a painful smile. They shook hands.

Olivia quickly continued, 'I know you asked me not to show it to anyone, but he's incredibly discreet, and I value his opinion more than anyone else I've ever worked with.'

Linus looked impressed. 'High praise indeed. Have you both been able to come up with anything?'

Olivia carried a tray into the room. She placed it in front of Sutton. He ignored the milk jug and sugar bowl and inhaled the strong coffee. A satisfied smile appeared on his face. He took a sip.

'Now that's proper coffee,' he said.

'We haven't come up with anything conclusive, I'm afraid.

However, I do have more questions. I know you've been to see Isaac McFadden many times and he hasn't opened up to you. Do you think he'll see me?' Olivia asked.

'I can ask him.'

'Thank you. Regarding the code, I wondered if the last entry refers to his final victim, Sean Bridger.' Olivia sat in a chair close to Linus. She tucked her short hair behind her ears. 'I've read this code countless times and it's meaningless to me. Obviously, it will mean something to Isaac. But what? However, if the final entry refers to Sean Bridger, then it might be possible to crack the code. So, what can you tell me about Sean?'

Linus placed his mug of coffee down on the table and made himself comfortable as he sat back and crossed his legs. 'Sean was a troubled lad. According to his parents he was a good boy until he went to secondary school and got in with the wrong crowd. By fourteen he was shoplifting, skipping school, smoking and drinking. He was taking drugs by sixteen and a dealer by seventeen. They tried everything to get him back on the straight and narrow, but nothing worked. When he was eighteen, he stole his father's car and sold it for two hundred pounds to a bloke in a pub. That's when they finally gave in and called in the police.

'Sean was arrested and served six months in a Young Offenders Institution. On his release, he went straight back to his old ways. However, he didn't go back home to his family in Harrogate. He came up north to Newcastle. His parents didn't see him again after the day he was released. His mother wanted to view the body. I had to tell her he'd been dismembered.'

'Good grief. That can't have been easy,' Olivia said.

'It wasn't. She literally collapsed in front of me and had to be sedated.'

Olivia had the printout open in front of her. She looked down at the page, at the final entry of the code.

| 12 | M6 | DATE EATEN EDGE (POPPY) | HELPFUL INDEED CRESCENT (HEAT) | BROWN BLUE BLUE BLACK 12/5/10/20 | £ |

'We were wondering if M6 could refer to a map reference, like you get in the back of an old-style street A–Z. Were any found in Isaac's house?'

Linus squinted at the ceiling as he searched his memory. 'I'm not sure. I'll have to check.'

'The list of trophies. Do any of the items belong to Sean?'

Linus sighed. 'I went through them all with Sean's mother. That was a long hour. She had so many questions about each item. Eventually she said she was around ninety per cent certain the necklace with the St Christopher medal belonged to Sean.'

Olivia made a note in a pad beside her. 'The four words in the third and fourth column, do they refer to Sean Bridger in any way? His personality, his appearance, where he lived or where he was found?'

'No. Trust me, I've looked at this code until I can barely focus and it's meaningless,' Linus said. 'They just seem like random words.'

'They have to mean something,' Sebastian said. 'To Isaac, they refer to something specific about his victim in order to trigger a memory.'

'We have the names of two victims, Sean Bridger and Piotr Czajkowski from Poland. I've put together as much as I can about both victims, and I cannot find an entry that matches either of them. Obviously, it would make sense for the last one to refer to Sean Bridger, but I can't work out the key. I'm sorry.' Linus looked genuinely troubled not to be able to move the investigation even slightly forward.

'What was Sean like when he arrived in Newcastle? Did you speak to his friends up there?' Sebastian asked.

'He knew very few people in Newcastle. The few we managed to track down told us what they knew.' Linus paused and took a breath. 'Sean was selling his body for drug money. He looked younger than he was, and men took advantage of that. By all accounts, he was raped several times.'

'Jesus,' Sebastian uttered. 'Was there any sign of sexual assault during the post mortem?'

'No. According to the pathologist, there was no evidence of recent sexual activity.'

'How did Isaac come to find him? Did you show his photo to Sean's friends?'

'We did. They'd never seen him before.'

'Had Isaac picked him up as a rent boy?' Olivia asked. 'I know he has a daughter, but is Isaac gay, bisexual?'

'Eleanor says not. We can't find any connection between Isaac McFadden and Sean Bridger.'

'Could Isaac have been Sean's dealer?' Sebastian asked. 'Didn't I read somewhere that Isaac worked as a sales rep for a medical company?'

'He was but he didn't sell medication. He sold things like hospital beds, surgical hoists, commodes.'

Olivia leaned back in her seat and sighed. They were getting nowhere.

'I'm struggling to understand the colours mentioned in each entry, too,' she said. 'At first, I wondered if it was skin colour. Black and brown are mentioned in all entries but one, the tenth one.'

'I thought that, too. Sean Bridger was white. He was very pale.'

'Did Isaac beat him to death?'

'No. He was strangled. Were you thinking of being beaten black and blue?'

'Yes, I was,' Olivia said. 'But that doesn't tell us what the brown refers to. I know he was dismembered, but did you ever find the clothes he was wearing?'

'Yes. They were in a bag in the boot of Isaac's car, along with the body parts. Sean was wearing blue jeans, a hooded jumper and black trainers.'

'What colour was the jumper?'

'Hang on.' Linus leaned down to his rucksack and took out a tablet. He switched it on and began scrolling through various folders. 'I couldn't have your Wi-Fi password, could I?'

'Sure. Can I get you another coffee?'

'I'd love one, thanks.'

Olivia handed Linus a card that gave him the Wi-Fi information then headed into the kitchen. She could do with another coffee herself after hearing about Sean Bridger's tortured life. Yes, a lot of it was of his own making. Nobody forced him into a life of drink and drugs, but if he'd accepted help, he might still be alive today. He'd landed on a path of self-destruction and couldn't find a way to get off. She found that incredibly sad, especially for someone so young.

'Can I ask about Isaac's internet history?' Sebastian asked. 'I'm guessing your team went through his computer, tablet or whatever he had.'

'He had a desktop computer at home and a tablet, a personal smart phone and a work one. We also took his work tablet. Those he used for work were clean, as was his mobile. The only questionable searches on his computer were pornography. Nothing illegal. A mixture of straight and gay porn, though.'

'Was Isaac seeing anyone?'

'Eleanor didn't know him to be romantically linked to anyone following the death of her mother.'

'When did she die?'

Linus checked his notes. 'September the first, 2002.'

'She wouldn't have been very old.'

'No. As Eleanor saw it, he dedicated himself to raising her on his own.'

'The perfect father,' Sebastian mused to himself.

Olivia came back in with the coffees.

'Sean Bridger was wearing a navy-blue hooded jumper,' Linus said. He handed her his tablet, which showed the clothes found in the back of Isaac's car lined up neatly on a table in the mortuary suite.

'Blue jumper, blue jeans, black trainers. Blue, blue, black,' she said, pointing to the code.

'What's brown?' Sebastian asked.

'If not his skin colour, perhaps his hair?' Olivia guessed.

'It was a dark blond if memory serves. I do have a photo of his head, but it's from the mortuary, it's... well, it's not attached to his body.'

Olivia swallowed hard. She'd seen all kinds of disturbing photographs over the years in her research of serial killers, but it didn't get any easier. 'Let me look,' she said, coolly.

Once again, he turned the tablet to her.

Olivia took a breath as she looked at the severed head of the young man on a stainless-steel gurney.

'I'd say that was more light brown than dark blond, but that's just my view.' She handed it to Sebastian, who agreed with her.

'So, it could refer to hair colour. Hair colour, then clothes,' Linus said. 'And if we apply that theory to the entry above – yellow, white, black, black slash white – we get blond hair, white top, black trousers and black and white shoes.' He looked relieved at a possible breakthrough.

'It's a working theory,' Olivia agreed. 'If you can find out when this Piotr was last seen and what he was wearing, you might be able to identify a second victim.'

'Apart from a stamp in the passport, there's no sign of him in England at all,' Linus said. 'There's something I need to tell you both. It might help you get a better insight into the type of man Isaac McFadden is.' He cleared his throat, selected another file on his tablet, placed it on the table and pushed it towards them.

The photo showed Sean Bridger laid out in the autopsy suite. His limbs and body had been put back together, though it was clear where he had been cut up. Linus leaned over the tablet and pinched the screen, zooming in on an area on his left leg.

'If you look at where the body was cut,' Linus began, 'you can see there is bruising all over the limbs. The next photo –' Linus flicked the page over to reveal pictures of Sean's internal organs '– shows the heart and lungs, which appear paler than we'd usually expect them to be. The pathologist is one hundred per cent certain that Sean Bridger was still alive when Isaac began cutting him up.'

'Bloody hell!' Sebastian exclaimed, a hand reaching up to his mouth.

Olivia turned away.

'That's not all,' Linus said. He paused as if to compose himself. 'I'm not going to ask you to study these photos to spot it, but Sean Bridger wasn't hacked to pieces, he wasn't cut up, he was taken apart.'

'What?' Olivia asked. She leaned forward to get a better look at the photo on the tablet.

'No bones were cut,' Linus said. 'Sean was found in a dozen pieces, but he was taken apart at the tendons and muscles that were holding the bones together.'

'Oh my God,' Sebastian said. 'How do you do something like that?'

'You'd need to speak to the pathologist. He did tell me, but a lot of it went over my head.'

Olivia pinched the touch screen and zoomed in. 'He took him apart while he was still alive,' she said, more to herself, to process what she was seeing. 'Can I speak to the pathologist?' she asked Linus.

'Sure. I'll get you his details. I mean, have you ever come across anything like this before?'

Sebastian shook his head.

'No,' Olivia said. 'When I was reading the section in Isaac's notebook last night about cutting up his victims, something didn't make sense. Now I know. He never mentioned cutting. He talked about taking them apart. This is a level of disturbing behaviour I've never come across before. I can't understand how Isaac has managed to evade the law for so long, not appear on the police radar, yet commit a crime of this atrocity.'

Linus cleared his throat and continued.

'What about the row of numbers in the fifth column? 12, 5, 10, 20. Can you work out what that might mean?'

Olivia sniffled. 'Erm, well, at first I thought they might be a map grid reference, then I thought maybe a date: fifth of October, 2020 and maybe the 12 referred to a time, twelve o'clock, but Sean was killed in 2024, so it can't. Was his birthday on the fifth of October?'

Linus consulted his tablet. 'No. April seventh.'

'But he was twenty years old, wasn't he?'

'Yes.'

Olivia chewed her bottom lip as she thought. She quickly snatched up the printout and looked at the final entry, then the others in the code.

'How tall was Sean Bridger?'

'Oh, erm . . .' Sutton went back to his tablet. 'A hundred and seventy-eight centimetres. Five foot ten.'

'That's it,' she said. 'Well, it might be it. 12, 5, 10, 20. He was twenty years old and five foot ten.'

'And the twelve?'

'Shoe size?'

'He was an eight.'

'Weight? Could he have been twelve stone?'

'He was much lighter than that.'

'But if the five and ten refer to him being five foot ten and the twenty refers to his age, the twelve has to be something personal to…' Olivia stopped and put a hand to her mouth.

'What is it?' Sutton asked.

Olivia closed her eyes. She felt sick.

'What's wrong?'

She opened her eyes and took a deep breath. 'Can you show me that photo of Sean fully laid out again?'

'Really?'

'Please.'

Linus handed over his tablet.

Olivia looked down. There he was, twenty-year-old Sean Bridger, his body parts assembled in order to make him whole again. She counted the different pieces. She struggled to speak. She was on the cusp of crying.

'Twelve pieces,' she said, quietly. 'Twelve pieces. Five foot ten. Aged twenty. 12, 5, 10, 20.'

'Fuck!' Linus exclaimed.

They remained silent as they absorbed the horror that this code, this chart, represented.

'So,' Linus began. 'The entry above contains the numbers 8, 6, 21. That could be eight pieces, six foot, and twenty-one years old.'

'Possibly.'

'Jesus Christ! What kind of a sick monster was he?'

'How can nobody know anything about this?' Sebastian asked, incredulously. 'What did his neighbours say about him?'

'Oh, they all thought he was the perfect neighbour. How could he keep all this to himself?' Linus asked.

Olivia shook her head. She was speechless. She looked down at the photograph of Sean Bridger, dissected and put back together again on a mortuary slab like a macabre jigsaw puzzle. This took horror to a whole other level. Very little scared Olivia, but right now, she was petrified.

Chapter Ten

Not long after Linus Sutton had left, backpack on, heading to the train station for his journey back to Newcastle, Sebastian asked Daisy if she would take Stanley out for a long walk around the block. Dog walking had been added to her list of talents.

Olivia and Sebastian were now alone in the office at George Street. He went into the meeting room and closed the door behind him. He opened his mouth to say something, but Olivia got in first.

'What do we know about people who dismember corpses?' she asked, looking up from her notebook.

Sebastian pulled out a chair opposite her and sat down. 'Well, we know that there are usually five…'

'No,' she interrupted. 'What do we, you and I, know about people who dismember corpses?'

'Nothing. I've never interviewed a killer who cut up his victims.'

'Me neither. This is the perfect opportunity to expand our knowledge and he's right here in the UK. No long-distance flights to the US or Japan for a change.'

'You don't have to convince me that this would be vital

information, but why do I get the impression that you're waiting for my approval?'

Olivia reached across the table. Her reach didn't quite get halfway. 'I love you to... Oh. I was going to say, "I love you to pieces," but perhaps I shouldn't say that. But I do. I love you, Sebastian, and I respect you. I wouldn't feel comfortable going up to Newcastle if I didn't have your support.'

'You always have my support. I just... Whenever you go away, I always wonder if you're not running away from something.'

She sat back and folded her arms. 'I think this time I am. There were two reporters outside my house when I got home last night. And there's been a car parked out front the last few days.'

'Red Vauxhall?'

'You've noticed it, too?'

'I called Foley and gave him the registration number. It belongs to someone who works on the *Mirror*. He's having a word with him.'

Olivia shook her head and looked down.

'I should never have sold those rights,' Sebastian added.

'We talked about this. Thirteen times, remember? You've already had a massive increase in sales of the book and it's getting translated into more languages. You need this money for your kids.'

'But at what cost?' he asked, reaching across to her.

She took his hand in hers. 'What's a little more mental torture to someone who is already screwed up beyond all help?' She smiled.

'You're not as screwed up as you make out. A lot of it is an act so people don't get too close. You use your trauma as a defence mechanism.'

'Don't tell anyone.' She winked.

'Promise me three things,' Sebastian began. 'You'll keep in touch. You'll share what you find out. And you won't allow Isaac McFadden to get under your skin.'

'Poor choice of words,' Olivia said with a hint of a smirk.

The penny dropped. 'Shit. You know what I mean. Stop splitting hairs.'

'I promise,' she said, crossing her heart.

'Good. Now, do you want to know my theories about body dismemberment?'

'I'd love to.'

'Okay. First of all, it's rare. Fewer than five per cent of murders involve dismemberment. However, some psychologists believe there are five different kinds of homicidal mutilation. The most common is defensive. It helps in hiding or moving the body to a burial location or for getting rid of evidence or to make identification more difficult.'

'Isaac mentioned in his notebook about the ease of transportation,' Olivia interrupted.

'True, but I think he's got a little bit more enjoyment out of it than merely making a body easy to dispose of. The second is aggressive, where the acts of killing and dismemberment are one and the same, usually as a means of torturing the victim. The third is offensive, where the dismemberment is the real purpose of the murder all along and is mostly associated with lust and necro-sadistic murders. Usually, in this case, death is by strangulation.'

'The PM report said Sean Bridger was strangled,' Olivia said.

'If Sean Bridger was sexually abused either before or after death, if his genitals were removed or mutilated, then this would be your kind of killer. We're talking sadomasochistic. Isaac would have used the victim's body to perform sex acts with after death.'

'The PM report stated there was no evidence of recent sexual activity.'

'So, we can rule that out.'

'What are the other two forms of dismemberment murder?' Olivia asked.

'The next one is psychotic, where the killer has completely lost touch with reality. He may say he's hearing voices or suffer from some kind of delusion. The fifth kind of killing is one we associate with the world of organised crime, whereby dismemberment is a way of sending a message to others.'

'Like a Mafia hit?'

'Yes.'

'Which category does Isaac fit in?' Olivia pondered.

'I'd say psychotic. I'm not saying he's heard voices telling him to dismember his victims, but it takes a person with a complete lack of empathy and an inability to experience emotions to sit and calmly cut a person into twelve pieces. Don't forget, throughout his police interview, Isaac answered, "No comment" to every question. Throughout his trial, he remained in his seat, not reacting at all to what was going on around him. He showed no remorse whatsoever for killing and mutilating Sean Bridger. He's separated himself from the Isaac McFadden his daughter and colleagues knew, to become a violent, composed and controlled killer.'

'If I go and talk to him, he's not going to help me in any way, is he?'

'No. He doesn't care about his victims. He has no interest in whether their bodies are ever found or in giving the victims' relatives closure. I think that's why he's written this code, so that he can read back and remember what he's done, because at the time of murdering and dismembering he was on a whole other plane.'

'I'm not going to be able to get inside his head, am I?'

'No. And you shouldn't want to, either. However, there is something you can do to try and get him to open up to you.'

'What's that?'

'You can feed his ego. Yes, he has the upper hand because he knows the key to the code, he knows where the bodies are buried, but he doesn't have anyone marvelling at what he's done. If you, the renowned Dr Olivia Winter, tell him that he's something new, something you've never come across before, something you want to study and understand, he'll tell you. He won't be able to resist.'

'So, I have to go in there as his number-one fan?'

'I'm afraid so. Just don't turn into Kathy Bates.'

Olivia laughed. 'I know who that is.'

Sebastian's face hardened. 'Olivia, I'm serious. Don't let him try to manipulate you. You're there to understand him, not support him. If he gets inside your head, you're fucked.'

Chapter Eleven

CIVIC CENTRE, NEWCASTLE CITY CENTRE

Wednesday 22nd January 2025

Thomas Landy had had no success trying to find a solution to his living problems over the phone. He eventually made an appointment with a housing officer at the Civic Centre and hoped that someone would be able to help him.

He was kept waiting for twenty minutes after his appointment time before a woman, Rosa Glass, who barely looked older than him, called his name. She led him into a tiny office, closed the door behind them, but deliberately opened the blinds so people could see in.

'Now, Mr Landy, I've been reading your emails and looking over your circumstances,' she said in a sickly voice.

Thomas noticed how she didn't apologise for keeping him waiting.

She opened a slim cardboard folder and took out a few sheets of paper.

'Let me just confirm: your mother was a council tenant and you lived with her. She died recently and you don't qualify to live on your own in a three-bedroom property. That's right, isn't it?'

'Yes,' he said, already exasperated. He had repeated this same line over and over again every time he called and struggled to be understood.

'And there's no other family for you to live with?'

'No. My mother was an only child. As was my father. My father died when I was two years old. Both sets of grandparents are dead. There's literally just me,' he said, a catch in his voice.

Rosa Glass looked up at him. She gave him a faux sympathetic smile. 'I'm sorry to hear that,' she said, without a single hint of emotion behind the words. 'Now, are you working at present?'

'No. I was at college, but I deferred my course when my mum fell ill. I was hoping to go back now, though.'

'Okay. Will you be going back or are you just thinking about it?'

'I will be going back.'

'Good. You will qualify for a one-bedroom flat or a studio apartment and we can help you with hardship funds and the various benefits open to you as a student. Obviously, you'll get a discount on your council tax. In the wake of the cost-of-living crisis we can help you with gas and electricity, too.'

Thomas suddenly felt overwhelmed. The bills at home all came out of his mum's bank account via direct debit. He'd had everything switched over to his account when he went to the bank and closed his mum's accounts, transferring what little money she had left into his. Gas, electricity, TV licence, council tax, he had no idea about any of this. He was eighteen, for crying out loud. He should be at college finishing his A-Levels, going out every night with Dean and Rick and Hakan and getting pissed, not sitting in a council office that reeked of desperation and sweat, on the verge of homelessness.

'Unfortunately, at present, we don't have any one-bedroom flats or studio apartments available. We can put you in touch with a housing association and the same benefits to help with rent and council tax will still apply. However, we are pushed for time as you're due to be out of your mum's house within the next ten working days.'

'I'm aware of that.'

'We do have emergency accommodation available. They're usually hostels and B&Bs.' She pulled a face. 'They're not very nice, but it's a roof over your head, that's the important thing. And it is only temporary.'

'Temporary? For how long?'

'Unfortunately, it could be a while before a property becomes vacant. Are you sure you don't have anyone you can stay with? A friend?'

'No,' he said, flatly. 'Look, what do I do with all my stuff? I'm living in a three-bedroom house. I've got all my mum's furniture – sofas, wardrobes, fridge, cooker. If I'm going to be staying in a B&B, what do I do with all that?'

Rosa looked at him blankly. She shrugged.

'I'm actually asking you for advice here,' he said, raising his voice slightly.

Rosa glanced out of the window towards the open-plan waiting area.

Thomas suddenly realised why she opened the blinds. It was so somebody would notice if she was attacked by her visitor. Thomas wasn't like that. He would never hurt anyone. But he'd fallen on hard times. He was asking the council for help. They obviously tarred all desperate people with the same brush.

'You could sell them, I suppose,' she said.

'They're my things. They're my mum's things,' he said, choking back his tears.

'I don't know what to say to you, Mr…' she looked down at her file. 'Landry.'

'Landy,' he corrected her, struggling to hold back his rage.

'Would you like me to fill you out an application for emergency accommodation?'

Thomas looked around him. His eyes were caught by posters on the walls offering help for asylum seekers and women suffering domestic abuse, or children being groomed online, or the elderly who couldn't afford their heating. Where was the poster for a teenager whose mother had just died and who was homeless? Where was the targeted help for him? He didn't want to live in a shitty B&B on his own. He didn't want to have to sell the sofa his mother loved, or the dressing table she'd inherited from her mother, or the cooker she worked hard to save up for. They were her things. They were *his* things. He wanted them. He *needed* them. He wanted his mum now more than ever.

Outside the council offices, Thomas allowed the sleet and icy wind to cut into his face. He leaned against the building and looked up at the sky. He was crying. He felt like he was falling down a hole and there was no bottom. He wiped his eyes with the damp sleeves of his coat. Across the road, a man layered up against the elements was selling copies of *The Big Issue*. He felt the urge to cry again. How many people were on the verge of losing everything? Before his mum became ill, she often struggled from month to month with the rising costs of bills and food. She often joked about running on empty in the days leading up to payday. Once she fell ill, the money from the government and charities came pouring in. Where was it when she really needed it? How much longer would it be before he was standing on a street corner selling *The Big Issue*? He was supposed to be going back to college in September. Thomas wanted to be a vet. He loved animals. He always had done. It was all he'd wanted to do since he was a small child. He had the grades and the aptitude. He just needed a break. One small break.

Chapter Twelve

DI Sutton emailed Olivia everything he had on Isaac McFadden. Interview transcripts, video files, statements from his daughter, colleagues, neighbours and friends. Before she headed off to Newcastle, Olivia wanted to know everything she could about Isaac, about his life before, during and after the killings and about the investigation as a whole. If Isaac was as prolific a serial killer as the evidence suggested, the last thing Olivia wanted was to go into the interview room with him unprepared. He would be able to tell straightaway that she hadn't done her homework. Right now, he had the upper hand, and he would continue to do so until Olivia cracked his code and the bodies were found. However, Olivia had to show him that she was more than a match for his intellect.

Sebastian had agreed to take one of Olivia's lectures while she spent the day at home studying the interviews and statements. After showering and taking Stanley on an amble around the block, she went up to her home office. Stanley had a bed in there and made himself comfortable while Olivia sat at her desk, turned on her computer and opened the video file of the first interview with Isaac McFadden. She had already read the transcript so knew what questions were coming and his responses, but she wanted to see his reactions, his movements, the subconscious telltale signs of lies.

The camera in the interview room was high up and angled to focus on Isaac. He was sitting alone, having refused a solicitor. From this point of view, Olivia could only see the backs of the heads of his two interviewers, DI Linus Sutton on the left and DS Shona Lees on the right. Isaac had had his clothing removed upon arrest and was wearing a white Tyvek forensic suit. His hair was neatly swept back. Before pressing play, Olivia leaned in and took in his body language. His shoulders were relaxed, his face wasn't tense or frowning in panic or worry. He seemed the embodiment of calm.

'Mr McFadden, can you tell us about what was found in the boot of your car when you were pulled over earlier this evening?' Linus asked.

Isaac remained still, his fingers interlocked in front of him on the table. It was a while before he spoke.

'No comment.' His voice was steady and perfectly pitched.

'For the benefit of the recording, in your car, police officers found three industrial waste sacks containing body parts and clothing. How did they get there?'

'No comment.'

'Who is the person in the bags?'

'No comment.'

'Did you kill them?'

'No comment?'

'Where were you taking the body parts?'

'No comment.'

Isaac's tone didn't waver once. He seemed to be remarkably in control of his emotions for a man who had been found with a dead body in his car.

'Mr McFadden, you've refused a solicitor. However, as this interview isn't progressing, I would like to ask you again if you would like to see a solicitor?'

'No comment.'

'You're not even going to answer a simple yes or no question?'

'No comment.'

'Mr McFadden, answering "No comment" to every question is not going to look good when this goes to court, and believe me, it will be going to court. You've been found with a dead, mutilated body in the back of your car. Now, for your own sake, please, tell me who the body belongs to.'

'No comment.'

The interview was paused.

Olivia sat back in her seat and watched the still image on screen of Isaac McFadden. She could perfectly understand why Linus Sutton hadn't been able to read him. She couldn't either. If he had killed twelve people, why wasn't he being smug? Why wasn't he lording it over the police that they'd caught a prolific killer, that he'd been able to murder a dozen people without once appearing on their radar?

The second interview with Isaac McFadden was conducted the following day. The victim, Sean Bridger, had been identified through his DNA, which was stored on the National DNA Database following a previous arrest in Newcastle for supplying drugs.

Before pressing play, Olivia looked closely at Isaac again. His hair wasn't as smooth, and he hadn't been allowed to shave. He hadn't been provided with a change of clothes and he was looking uncomfortable in the paper suit he had been wearing for almost twenty-four hours. Was this a tactic by DI Sutton and his team, to make Isaac ask for something, in the hope of moving this investigation further forward? Very probably.

'Mr McFadden, we've identified the body in the back of your car as belonging to Sean Bridger.'

Isaac didn't say anything.

'Do you know this person?'

'No comment.'

'We've spoken to your daughter…'

Olivia paused the video. It was the first time Eleanor had been mentioned. She took the footage back a few seconds and played it again. There wasn't a flicker of emotion on his face at all.

'… she doesn't know the name Sean Bridger. Who is he to you?'

'No comment.'

'Someone you work with?'

'No comment.'

'A friend?'

'No comment.'

'A lover?'

'No comment.'

Olivia watched that last question being asked again. She wanted to see if there was any flicker in his eyes at the mention of a possible same-sex lover. There wasn't.

'The postmortem examination was carried out earlier this morning. We believe Sean Bridger was strangled. Did you strangle him?'

'No comment.'

'Did you use your hands or a ligature?'

'No comment.'

'A hair was found between two fingers of Sean's left hand. The DNA in that hair matches yours. Can you explain how it got there?'

'No comment.'

'Mr McFadden, the evidence shows that you killed Sean Bridger, you cut him up and you were prepared to dump his body somewhere. Can you confirm that?'

'No comment.'

Linus released an audible sigh. 'I'm going to charge you with Sean Bridger's murder. Is there anything you would like to say before I do so?'

'No comment.'

'Very well. Isaac McFadden, I am charging you with the murder of Sean Bridger. You do not have to say anything, but it may harm your defence if you do not mention, when questioned, something which you later rely on in court. Anything you do say may be given in evidence.'

The fact Isaac hadn't said anything since he was brought into the police station made the caution a moot point. He remained still and fixed his gaze on DI Sutton as he read the police caution. The interview was terminated.

Olivia couldn't understand what game Isaac was playing. She needed to think. She needed to clear her head. She decided to take Stanley for a walk.

Olivia could walk for miles when she had some thinking to do. When she was on her own, that was fine. Unfortunately, with a miniature Dachshund for company, a long walk was out of the question. She looked down and saw his little legs going like the clappers to keep up with her. She apologised to him and slowed down.

'Why does someone remain silent when they're being interrogated?' she asked Stanley as he cocked his leg.

He looked up at her with his big brown eyes and tilted his head to one side as if genuinely listening to her.

They walked on.

In the war, captured soldiers remained silent and only gave their name, rank and serial number. They didn't speak because they were protecting their comrades and their country from capture and invasion. They had something worth keeping silent for. So, what was Isaac McFadden keeping silent for?

According to DI Sutton, the only person Isaac had in his life was his daughter Eleanor. Was he keeping quiet in order to protect her? But from what? She already knew he was a killer. She was also the one to find the code book and the box with the trophies. Surely, he must have realised she would eventually need to clear out his house and would come across his stash. Did he honestly believe she wouldn't be curious and look further into it? Would he rather have her think he had only murdered one person, not twelve? Would it make any difference to how she felt?

Olivia stopped dead in her tracks. Stanley kept walking and was pulled back by his lead. He gave a little yelp. She bent down and picked him up.

'Oh, I'm so sorry, Stanley,' she said, kissing him on the nose. 'It's just… I think I might have worked out why Isaac replied "No comment" throughout his interview.'

A gust of wind caused her to shiver in the cold January afternoon.

'Let's go home,' she said, turning and heading back to Modbury Gardens. 'And while you're tucked up in your comfortable bed, chewing on a Schmacko, I'll try and find evidence of Isaac having a partner in crime.'

Chapter Thirteen

NORTHUMBRIA POLICE, FORTH BANKS POLICE STATION

A knock on DI Sutton's door caused him to look up from a report he was struggling to make sense of. DCI Diane Wise stood in the doorway.

'How was your trip to London?'

'Oh, fantastic,' he said. 'Had dinner at the Ivy, took in a show.'

'And the infamous Dr Winter?'

'She's much smaller than I expected.'

Diane pulled out a chair and sat down. 'Is she going to help us?'

'She said she would. I emailed her everything I've got this morning.'

'You are keeping this to yourself, aren't you?' she asked, looking over her shoulder and out into the CID suite. 'I don't want the press hearing about us consulting with a forensic psychologist. Nor do I want to hear the words' – she lowered her voice to barely above a whisper – '"serial killer" mentioned anywhere until we have definite proof.'

'I haven't told anyone.'

'Good. Now, Linus, on a personal note, how are things?'

'Fine.'

'That's a lie. I'll ask you again. How are things?'

He swallowed hard. 'They're fine. I promise.'

'You haven't booked the second of February off.'

'I've no intention of booking the second of February off.'

'It's the first anniversary…'

'I'm aware,' he interrupted. 'If it's all right with you, I'd rather just carry on as normal.'

'Are you still seeing the therapist?'

'No.'

'Why not?'

His phone began to ring. He looked down at the display and saw that it was Eleanor McFadden calling.

'Do you mind if I get that?'

She stood up and headed for the door. 'If I was a suspicious person, I'd say you orchestrated your phone ringing at that time.' She smiled and winked as she left the room, closing the door behind her.

Linus picked up his mobile, took a deep breath and swiped to answer the phone.

'Eleanor, what can I do for you?'

'Hello. I… I… well, I was just ringing to see if you'd made any progress on the… you know, the notebook and the items,' she said, his voice oozing with nerves.

Linus had told Eleanor that she was welcome to contact him at any time if she had any questions regarding the investigation. Eleanor had taken him up on that and called a couple of times a week for an update.

'I'll be honest with you, Eleanor, I'm afraid we haven't, not yet. However, I've been speaking to an expert in psychology who is looking into the code for us. Hopefully she'll be able to come up with something we haven't thought of.'

'She. Who?'

'I'm afraid I can't reveal her name, Eleanor.'

'Oh. Right. I see. No, of course, not. I'm sorry. I'm… I'm…'

'Is there something you wanted to tell me, Eleanor?'

'I don't know,' she said. 'I can't make sense of anything right now. I've been looking back over my life, my time with Dad, the times we went on holiday when I was a child, the school plays he came to see me in and when he cheered me on at sports days. Were they genuine times? Was he being my dad then or was he looking around and choosing his next victim?'

Linus didn't know how to answer that question. He wished Olivia Winter was in the room with him. He could hear the agony in Eleanor's voice, the pain and sadness radiating down the phone line.

'Eleanor, the forensic psychologist I mentioned is coming up to Newcastle at some point. Would you like to speak to her? She'll have more of an understanding of what you're going through than I have. She might be able to help you.'

'Will she be able to tell me why my dad became a killer?'

Linus was hoping Olivia would answer that question for him. 'I don't know. Possibly.'

'It's frightening, isn't it? You never really know what people are like. Even those closest to you, those you love and respect. You don't know what's going on behind their eyes, in their heads.'

'Eleanor…'

'I'm sorry for interrupting you, DI Sutton.'

The call ended.

Eleanor McFadden was sitting on an armchair in her living room. The curtains were drawn, the television was on with the sound muted. The room was lit by a single standard lamp in a corner. Darkness was falling. Another day over. Another day that had passed by in a blur. Eleanor had no recollection of what she had done today. She'd slept late, having eventually fallen asleep during the small hours from exhaustion. Around lunchtime, she became hungry but couldn't be bothered to cook anything. She fancied a big bowl of cereal but was low on milk. She hid her unwashed hair beneath a beanie hat, put on a pair of jeans over her pyjama bottoms, buttoned up her coat to the neck so people wouldn't see her pyjama top beneath and headed for the shops.

She hadn't given her neighbours any thought during her

father's trial. She woke early, drove to the court and by the time she stumbled over her front doorstep it was late and pitch-dark. She hadn't seen anyone to talk to properly for months.

The automatic doors of the Co-op yawned open, and she stepped inside, squinting beneath the brightness of the strip lighting. She headed for the cereal aisle and picked up a couple of boxes of Crunchy Nut Cornflakes. She went to the fridge and grabbed two four-pint bottles of milk. She turned and headed for the self-service counter, then stopped in her tracks. Right in front of her, glaring, gawping at her, was her next-door neighbour, Alice Dee. Her face was unreadable. Her eyes were wide and her mouth agape. She was clearly shocked to see Eleanor, but why? She hadn't done anything. She was simply out buying milk and cereal. Why the stare?

'Hello, Alice,' Eleanor said, quietly. She suddenly caught a taste of her own breath. It was stale. She couldn't remember the last time she'd brushed her teeth.

'Eleanor. It's...' She looked her up and down. 'It's lovely to see you. How... how are you?'

'I'm fine,' she said, trying to smile. She wasn't sure it came off as a smile. It felt more like a grimace. 'How are you?'

'Oh, you know, the usual. This winter seems to be dragging on, doesn't it?'

'I can't say I've noticed.'

'No. Well, you wouldn't have.' Her face dropped and began to redden in embarrassment. 'What I meant was that, I mean, well, you've had a lot on your plate recently, haven't you?'

'You could say that.'

'Listen, Eleanor,' Alice began, stepping closer and placing a comforting hand on Eleanor's arm. 'If you ever want to talk about anything, you know where I am.'

'Thank you. That's kind of you to say,' Eleanor said, and suddenly felt a warmth within. Maybe she could face the real world again after all.

She smiled, said goodbye and headed for the till. As she

turned left at the bottom of the aisle, she could hear the chatter in the background.

'Is that who I think it is?'

'Isaac's daughter? Yes. I wouldn't have the nerve to show my face in public, would you?' Alice said.

Eleanor couldn't pay for her shopping fast enough and rushed home just as the tears began to fall.

Now, sitting cross-legged on the armchair, second bowl of cereal of the day on her lap, she flicked through the channels before settling on *The One Show* on BBC One. It was comforting viewing, though it depended which guests they had on. She recognised the actor sitting on the sofa but couldn't recall his name. She might as well watch it. She had nothing else to do.

'So, this is the first time you're playing a real person. You've always played fictional characters in the past, and now you're playing a serial killer, the infamous Richard Button. What's it like to play someone real?' the interviewer asked.

'I relied heavily on the script,' the actor said. 'And I read the book by Sebastian Lister, which was very detailed.'

'According to the press you even went along to the prison where Richard Button is being held and spoke to him, is that right?'

'Yes. He actually got in touch with me, asking if I wanted to ask him anything.'

'How does he feel about you playing him?' she asked with a smile.

'He said he was pleased, but we'll see after he watches it.'

'Will he watch it?'

'He said he would.'

'So, what did you talk about?'

'That has to remain between us, I'm afraid,' he replied, teasingly.

'Did you speak to anyone else in preparation with the role? Richard's daughter, Olivia Winter, she's a prominent forensic psychologist. She knows a great deal about the mind of a murderer.'

Eleanor didn't hear the answer. She tuned them out. She put the bowl of cereal on the floor beside her chair and stood up. She looked all round her untidy living room for her laptop, eventually finding it on the floor beneath the coffee table. She plugged it in and switched it on. Googling Olivia Winter, she first went to Wikipedia and gave her entry a quick read, taking in the highlights. Daughter of serial killer Richard Button. Mother and sister stabbed to death when Olivia was nine years old. She was also stabbed, four times, and survived. She went to live with her grandparents and changed her name, later becoming an eminent forensic psychologist yet keeping her true identity a secret. It was only revealed last year when she survived an attack by serial killer Jamie Farr in London.

An idea struck Eleanor. If anyone knew how to survive the actions of a serial killer, it would be Olivia Winter. Eleanor could learn so much from her.

Chapter Fourteen

At the exact time agreed upon, Olivia's laptop rang out the tune of an incoming Zoom call. She accepted and smiled at Dr Boyd Hailstones. Olivia hadn't known what to expect from a man with such an unusual name. She tried not to trivialise, but certain names conjured up certain images and nothing came to mind with Hailstones, apart from the obvious.

Boyd Hailstones was somewhere in his fifties with a shock of thick wavy hair that was more salt than pepper. He was clean-shaven, slim and had a humorous twinkle in his eye. When he introduced himself, his deep Scottish burr was so quiet, Olivia had to turn up the volume.

'Thank you for agreeing to talk to me,' Olivia said.

'You're welcome. I've heard of you, of course. It's delightful to finally see you in person.'

Olivia was struggling to get used to complete strangers knowing who she was. It made her uncomfortable.

'I want to talk to you about Sean Bridger's post mortem,' she said, getting straight down to business. 'I've spoken to DI Sutton, and he told me you believe Sean was still alive when Isaac McFadden began cutting him up. Is that correct?'

'It is. A most disturbing case. It's definitely one of the more unusual post mortems I've ever carried out. I'm not afraid to admit it's given me many sleepless nights.'

Olivia knew exactly how he felt.

'I'm sorry to put you through it again, but can you explain how Isaac could go about dissecting the body while Sean was still alive?'

'The toxicology results showed a high dosage of a local anaesthetic agent, specifically bupivacaine hydrochloride. It's a major nerve block. It would have been injected into the space around the nerve Isaac was planning to cut in order for it to sort of bathe the nerve, rendering the cut painless to the victim.'

'There would have been a great deal of blood loss, though, wouldn't there?'

'Absolutely. However, that can be limited, providing Mr McFadden was knowledgeable in tying off blood vessels to stem the flow.'

'He would need expert knowledge of medical procedure?'

'He would need expert knowledge of *surgical* procedure.'

'At the trial you mentioned in questioning that Isaac needed to have surgical knowledge, yet the defence stated Isaac had no medical training whatsoever. The prosecution really dug into his background to try to find if he had ever obtained such knowledge, and couldn't find anything.'

'That's right. I believe all they could find was an attendance of a first-aid course and moving and handling training to go with his job.'

'Is there any way you can think of where Isaac could have discovered this kind of information on how to administer a nerve block and to tie off blood vessels?'

'He certainly wouldn't have got it by watching *Casualty*,' Boyd said with a wry smile. 'As I said in my testimony at the trial, Isaac either found a way to enrol on such a medical course under a different name – though the length of time it would take to learn all this would have left a huge, questionable, gap in his life and CV – or he had somebody with him who already had that knowledge.'

The Devil's Code

A tick in the box for a possible second killer.

Olivia cleared her throat. She looked down at the notes she'd been making. 'Where would Isaac have been able to get bupivacaine hydrochloride?'

'I shudder to think. However, we both know how anything and everything can be bought from the dark recesses of the internet these days. I'm sure a five-minute Google search would have sent him in the right direction,' he said, almost depressingly.

'How long would it have been before Sean died?' Olivia asked, dreading the answer.

Boyd paused before answering. 'I can't answer that one. I only hope it was very early on.' There was genuine emotion in his voice. 'If Isaac McFadden is as proficient in surgical procedure as he appears to be, then he would have been able to draw out the death of this poor young man. Sean would have gone into trauma. He may have passed out with the shock of seeing someone removing a part of his body. It's possible Isaac McFadden could have waited, possibly even brought him round, before continuing with his dissection.'

Olivia felt a shiver. She pulled her cardigan tighter around her. She felt sick. The silence between them grew while Olivia took in the enormity of Boyd's claims.

'I'm aware that you've conversed with all manner of killers around the world,' Dr Hailstones continued. 'Have you ever come across anything like this before?'

Olivia swallowed the bile rising in her throat. 'No. I haven't.'

'It is possible to take a body apart without sawing through bones. They're held together with muscles and tendons that can easily be cut with the correct tools. All you'd need is a scalpel and a very sharp blade. As I mentioned before, a search on Google will inform you where the veins and tendons are on the body. I'm no expert, but I would also say it would take a complete psychopath to put another human being through the torment Sean Bridger was put through.'

'I couldn't agree with you more, Dr Hailstones.'

'Is there anything else you would like to ask me?'

'Not at the moment.'

'Well, you have my email address. Please feel free to contact me at any time if you require further information.'

'Thank you.'

'Good luck to you, Dr Winter.'

The call ended.

Olivia sighed. The atmosphere in her office was suddenly incredibly heavy. She was going to need all the luck in the world to try to understand Isaac McFadden.

Chapter Fifteen

Thursday 23rd January 2025

Olivia had found a replacement for her lecture. Sebastian had cancelled his and they'd both instructed Daisy to move any Zoom calls to another day. Any phone calls that came in, she was to take messages, and once the door to the meeting room was closed, they were not to be disturbed under any circumstances. Unless Stanley needed to pop out to pee.

They were sitting at opposite sides of the large table, laptops open, both with a copy of Isaac's code in front of them, pads and pens at the ready, and the coffee machine was on standby.

'I couldn't sleep last night so I did some research into Isaac McFadden,' Sebastian began.

'Why couldn't you sleep?' Olivia asked, picking at a croissant.

'Well, I'm guessing I could have slept perfectly well if it hadn't been for Robert's toothache. Of course, that kept Catherine awake. I was watching sodding *Barbie* at five o'clock. As I dropped them off at school, she told me she'd enjoyed getting up early and could we do it again tonight?'

'Tell her yes but she'll have to watch *Oppenheimer* this time.'

'Anyway, between what Linus Sutton sent you and what I've

been able to find online, I think I can paint a pretty interesting picture of Isaac McFadden. Are you sitting comfortably?'

Olivia sat back in her seat and held her coffee mug in both hands. 'Ready when you are.'

'Isaac made the news before he even opened his eyes. At seventeen seconds past midnight on Thursday, the first of January 1970, the midwife cut the umbilical cord and Isaac McFadden was brought into the world – the first child born in England in the 1970s. His proud parents, Peter and Susan, were featured on the inside pages of their local newspaper holding their beautiful child.' Sebastian passed Olivia a photograph he'd printed off the internet.

'He's got his father's nose,' she said.

Sebastian continued. 'Born and raised in Jarrow in South Tyneside. His mother was a housewife and his father worked at the local coal mine, a five-minute walk from their terraced two-up, two-down house. Isaac wasn't an academic child and required additional help from teachers to understand basic maths and English. He was a slow learner and was the last in his class to be able to tell the time and tie his shoelaces. He often seemed to be distracted by other things going on around him and found it difficult to focus on his lessons. He left school at the age of sixteen in 1986 with no qualifications.'

'Where did you get all that from?'

'That was from the prosecution in the lead-up to the trial. As a child, Isaac was close to his father, Peter, and always wanted to work alongside him down the coal mine when he was old enough. By the time Isaac left school, the majority of the coal mines were closing down in the North of England and Peter had been out of work for eighteen months following the closure of the local pit. Isaac took a job on the production line of Carter, Weddle and Thropp, a local shoemaker. His job was to cut the leather and line up the templates for the holes to be pressed for the laces to thread through. He was known to be quiet yet conscientious. He had to concentrate hard to be able to perform his tasks. He didn't mix with any of his colleagues, preferring to go straight home after his shifts.'

'Wow. The prosecution really did their homework, didn't they?' Olivia asked.

'All that came from a statement given by Joyce Simmonite.'

'Who's she?'

'She was secretary to Mr Weddle of Carter, Weddle and Thropp. Now, while Isaac was at Carter, Weddle… you know, I'm just going to call them CWT. It's easier. Isaac was made redundant from CWT in 1992 at the age of twenty-two. Now, tucked away on page five of her statement, Joyce Simmonite mentioned that she knew Isaac's parents, particularly his mother. She says that while they were a close family, Susan McFadden was very strict and ruled her house with an iron fist. When Isaac was made redundant, the first thing he said was, how was he going to break the news to his mother?'

'Was he scared of his mother?' Olivia asked.

'Joyce didn't say. She did go on to say that it wasn't just Isaac she ruled over but her husband, too. Joyce's husband worked in the mine with Peter, and he'd told her that Peter hated being at home during the day. He'd do anything to be out of the house.'

'Did he say why?'

'I've no idea. Haven't you read any of what Sutton has sent you?'

'I've glanced,' she said, hesitatingly. 'I was distracted after speaking to Dr Hailstones.'

'Yes, and thank you for your graphic email at half-past midnight,' Sebastian said, shooting Olivia a daggered look. 'Anyway, following this, Isaac had a string of jobs, mostly cash-in-hand, as a labourer on building sites, painter and decorator, and lastly as a delivery driver. All his former colleagues and bosses said he was a diligent worker who never had a sick day and was a true grafter. In later years, following his marriage to Louise Phipps in 1995, he worked as a sales rep for MediSupplies UK, a medical company that sold equipment to hospices, hospitals and nursing homes. Meeting Louise seemed to have been a turning point in his life as he went to evening classes to gain the qualifications he missed out on at school and learn essential computer skills. At MediSupplies UK, his territory covered the entire North of England from the border with Scotland down to Harrogate in North Yorkshire. Once again, he was described as being an exceptional worker who never had a sick day. The only blot on his employment record was in 2002 when he took an extended period of leave following the death of his wife from cervical cancer. He was off for six months while he worked out a future for himself and Eleanor, who was only five years old.'

'So, at the age of thirty-two, Isaac found himself widowed and left to bring up a daughter on his own,' Olivia said. 'That can't have been easy.'

'Tell me about it,' Sebastian said, who had also found himself widowed, with four children to support. Fortunately, Tilly was nineteen and very independent, leaving Sebastian with twelve-year-old Alistair and seven-year-old twins to contend with on his own.

'I've read the statements from Eleanor,' Olivia said. 'There is no mention of Isaac having any other relationship.'

'Well, bringing up a child on your own and holding down a full-time job tends to take up quite a large chunk of your day,' Sebastian said, speaking from experience.

'Yes, but even as she grew older, there's no mention of Isaac having any kind of a personal life. Eleanor becomes a teenager, and off she goes with friends, then she goes to university. All it says about Isaac is that he worked. I doubt Eleanor would have minded if he'd married again.'

'There's a statement somewhere from Isaac's neighbour,' Sebastian said, scrolling through his laptop.

'Lesley Quinn. Yes, I've read it. She helped Isaac out a lot when Eleanor was small and calls him a doting family man.'

'Maybe Isaac wanted to keep a low profile so he could kill without attracting attention.'

Olivia mused on that statement. 'It's possible, I suppose.' She held up her empty coffee mug. 'Fancy a refill? Then I'll dazzle you with my research.'

They took a break while Olivia refreshed their coffees and Sebastian woke Stanley up to take him for a quick trot around the block so he could get up close and personal with a few lampposts. Back in the meeting room, work resumed.

'Question: why would Isaac reply "No comment" to every question put to him during police interviews?' Olivia asked.

'Because he's hiding something,' Sebastian answered without having to think.

'What's he hiding?'

'More bodies.'

'What else?'

Now Sebastian was stumped. He thought for a moment. 'Well, maybe he's not hiding something as such, maybe he's trying to protect Eleanor from the truth coming out.'

'But the truth is going to come out because he's left his trophies in his wardrobe along with a headache-inducing code book.'

'True. Maybe he has some other secret he doesn't want to be exposed.'

'Go on,' Olivia prompted.

Sebastian looked at her. 'You already know, don't you?'

'I have no proof. It's just a theory.'

'Are you going to share it?'

'Before I do, you seem to know a great deal about Isaac's life. Is there any reference to him having studied medicine or medical procedures?'

'Of course not. He had trouble tying his shoes when he was younger. I doubt he knows anything about medicine.'

'Agreed. So, what if the reason Isaac remained quiet was because to speak would be to reveal he has a partner in crime?'

'You think he's killing with somebody else?'

'Somebody who knows how to obtain –' she looked down at her notes '– bupivacaine hydrochloride and knows how to administer it. Also, they know how to tie off blood vessels to stop

Sean Bridger from bleeding to death, and physically be able to take a body apart without vomiting all over it.'

'He works for a medical company,' Sebastian said.

'He's a salesman. He doesn't need to know how to inject someone with a nerve blocker.'

'But one of his customers might.'

'Also, look at our two victims. We've got Sean Bridger. Now, he's addicted to drugs and he's selling his body. Isaac could have found him and lured him that way. I've no idea how he managed to find Piotr unless he, too, was either selling himself or was gay and Isaac took advantage of that.'

'But we don't know if all the victims are male, let alone gay,' Sebastian interrupted.

'Precisely. If Isaac was using one single way to lure his victims, procuring rent boys, or finding victims on the gay scene or via gay sex apps, then DI Sutton would already know about it. Someone will have made the connection that there are twelve victims from the gay community disappearing. The fact they haven't makes me think all these victims are completely different and I don't think one man alone could lure them all in.'

'A double act.'

'Look at Isaac McFadden for a moment,' she said, swinging her laptop around to face Sebastian. The screen featured a still of Isaac in the interview room at Forth Banks Police Station. 'He doesn't stand out in any way, does he? He's not overly good looking. He's of average height and average build. He goes to work every day and he comes home in the evenings. What else does he do? Nothing. He's keeping well below the radar. Why? Because he's a killer and he doesn't want to get caught. However, when he finally is caught, why isn't this mild-mannered man crumbling and confessing chapter and verse? Because his partner is still out there, and he's protecting them.'

'Who is his partner? Eleanor?'

'I don't know, and I won't know until I talk to her. Do we know of any families who kill together?'

Sebastian inhaled as he sat back and thought. 'There's the

infamous Kelly family in America in the 1880s. Mother, father, son and daughter. I think they killed about eleven people between them. Then there were those two sisters, Christine and Léa Papin, in France in the 1930s.'

'It may not be Eleanor, though. Don't forget, she brought the trophies and the code book to the police.'

'But she wasn't alone when she found it. She was with the neighbour, Lesley Quinn, who was helping her clear out the house. Eleanor could have known it was there all along and knew she wouldn't be able to get it past Lesley without her noticing, so pretended she didn't know of its existence.'

'True.'

'On the other hand, we could have ourselves a *folie à deux*.'

Olivia's eyes widened.

'If we have, which one is Isaac McFadden, the primary or the secondary?' she asked.

'The fact he's remained quiet and is literally giving nothing away suggests he's the secondary. The primary, the more dominant one, is still out there, and he's protecting them.'

'If that's the case, then we have to ask ourselves if the primary will continue killing on their own, or begin the search for a replacement secondary.'

Chapter Sixteen

'Lesley!'

As soon as she heard her name being called, she rolled her eyes. She'd been shopping, bought too much and was struggling with lifting the heavy bags from the boot of her car. She stood up straight and saw her neighbour Hal Garfield trotting towards her from the house next door. She frowned at him. He lived directly opposite. There was no reason for him to be next door.

'What are you doing at Isaac's house?' she asked.

'I thought I heard something,' he said, slightly out of breath. 'I was putting my bins out and I heard glass breaking. I thought I'd better check it out. The last thing Eleanor wants is those kids back causing trouble. In the right light you can still see the graffiti on the garage door.'

Leslie gave him a weak smile and returned to her shopping. She didn't like Hal. He was nosey, always prying into people's affairs.

'Did you find anything?' she asked.

'Sorry?'

'At Isaac's house. Did you find a broken window or anything?'

'Oh. No. It must have come from somewhere else. You know how sound travels when it's quiet. Anyway, I'm glad I've caught you,' he said. Hal was somewhere in his forties and worked in computers. He had told Lesley about it once, years ago, but he spoke for fifteen minutes non-stop, and she still wasn't any the wiser as to what he did. He was single and Lesley had never seen him with anyone. Why he needed a three-bedroom house was beyond her. 'I called round the other day, but you weren't in.'

'Oh,' she said. She was in. She had heard him knocking but remained upstairs and silent in the hope he'd go away.

'Have you seen Eleanor lately?' he asked, lowering his voice when he said her name as if there was a curse attached to it.

'I saw her last weekend,' she said.

'How is she doing?'

'As expected, I suppose. It's not easy having your father sent to prison for life for murder.'

'No. I guess not. Did she… I mean, has Eleanor said what she's going to be doing with the house?'

Lesley glanced at the house next to her where Isaac had lived. To see it locked up and unlived in was sad.

'I think it's a little early for conversations like that, Hal. She's still taking in everything that's happened.'

'Right. Understood,' he said with a smile. He backed away a couple of steps, then stepped back towards her. 'It's just… listen, if she does mention selling it, do you think you could let me know?'

'You want to buy it?'

'Well, it's bigger than my house. Bigger garden, too. I could grow vegetables.'

'Hal, I'm not going to bring the subject up when I see her. It's not exactly tactful, is it?'

'No. I understand. But, if it comes up, if you could point her in my direction. Thanks, Les. Anyway, must be getting back. I've got an Osso Buco on the go. I don't want it spoiling. Look after yourself,' he said, retreating down the drive and waving at her over his shoulder.

Lesley watched him go. She hated that he'd shortened her name without asking permission. It gave the impression they were friends, when the only reason they spoke was simply because they lived opposite each other. She slammed the boot of her car closed and looked up at Isaac's house. She gave a sad smile and shivered in the cold. As she went back to her house, she turned on the front doorstep and saw Hal across the road standing at his door. He held up a hand to wave to her, a ridiculous grin on his face that she could see even from right over here. Out of politeness, she waved back.

Chapter Seventeen

BYKER, NEWCASTLE

Sunday 26th January 2025

Thomas Landy was sitting in the living room of his home, his former home. It was no longer his home, despite the fact he had another week before he was forced to vacate the premises. He'd asked among his friends to see if they could let him have a spare room or even a sofa for a week or two until he sorted himself out, but they'd moved on. He'd dedicated the last year to looking after his mother. He'd forfeited his college education, holidays, birthday nights out, weekends away, and they'd all formed other friendship groups. Diana Peacock was going out with Craig Sheldon. A year ago, she hated Craig Sheldon. Aria Mukherjee had left Newcastle and was backpacking solo around Europe. His best friend all through secondary school, Darren Claypool, had dropped out of college and was working at HMV in the Metro Centre. There was a time he would have called and told him all about that. Thomas's mother had taken priority. Now she was gone, he had nobody left.

There was a knock on the door. It made him jump, even though he was waiting for it. He took a breath and looked around the room one last time in its usual state. His mum had spent days decorating it. She spent weeks choosing the right sofa. They were her things, and he was having to let them go.

He opened the door to a rough-looking man and woman. He tried to act tough, like this was his house, but he had never felt so alone before in his life.

'Hi,' he said.

They didn't say anything.

'You've come for the sofa?'

'Well, we haven't come for tea,' the man said. He walked in without being invited. The woman followed, her eyes stuck on Thomas. She didn't bother putting out her cigarette and continued to smoke as she came in. His mother hated the smell of smoke. She would never have allowed her into the house.

Thomas ran after them into the living room.

'I don't know,' the man said, studying the sofa. He gave it a kick. 'It looks more knackered than your photos suggested. What do you think, Shell?'

'I doubt this is from John Lewis. Who are you trying to kid?' she scoffed at Tom.

'It is from John Lewis. It was bought in the January sales four years ago. It's been well looked after. Honest.'

'Yes, and this is real Prada,' Shell said, flashing her jacket.

'Look, we've come all this way. We may as well take it off your hands, but we're not giving you hundred quid for it,' the man said. 'We'll give you thirty.'

'Thirty? No. It was over a thousand brand-new. It's fine. There's nothing wrong with it. Nothing's ever been spilled on it. They're the original cushions and everything.'

'You'll never get a hundred quid for it. It's faded from the sun. You can tell. You can always tell,' he said, trying to sound like he knew what he was talking about.

Thomas knew they were trying to get a fast one over on him. There was no way he was giving it to them.

'Look, I'm sorry you've had a wasted journey, but I think I'll wait for other offers.'

'You what?' the man said, he pushed passed Shell and loomed over Thomas.

Thomas looked up at him, at the moth tattoo on his neck. He tried not to wince at the smell of stale tobacco on his breath.

'You taking the piss?'

'What? No.'

'You've had us come all the way out here in the cold, now you don't want to sell it to us?'

Tom swallowed hard. 'I will sell it to you. For a hundred pounds, as we agreed.'

'But it's not worth hundred quid. I already told you. Now, if you don't want to sell it to us, fine, we'll go, but you're giving me petrol money. I want thirty quid off you.'

'What? No. I'm not giving you any money.'

'You either give me the sofa and I give you thirty notes, or you give me thirty notes for a wasted journey. What's it to be, lad?' he asked, slapping Tom softly on the cheek.

Thomas was sitting on the bathroom floor. He'd vomited everything he'd eaten today down the toilet, yet he was still retching. Tears were streaming down his face. This wasn't fair. He had done nothing wrong, yet he felt as if he was being punished by everyone he came into contact with. The council was treating him like scum, people were taking advantage of him because they could, his friends had deserted him, and his mother had left him when he needed her the most. Why was this happening to him?

Eventually, he stood up. He wiped his mouth with the sleeve of his jumper and walked down the stairs into the empty living room. As soon as he saw the space where his mother's beloved sofa used to be, the tears returned.

'I'm so sorry,' he choked. 'I'm sorry, Mum. There was nothing I could do.'

He dropped to his knees.

'Where the fuck do I go from here?'

Chapter Eighteen

KING'S CROSS STATION, LONDON

Tuesday 28th January 2025

Olivia had spent the best part of a week living and breathing everything there was to know about Isaac McFadden, his daughter, his work, his dead wife and his childhood. She had spoken to DI Sutton in Newcastle on several occasions, sharing her theories, though she was still no closer to cracking the code. She hoped, by talking to Eleanor and others who had played a part in Isaac's life, as well as visiting the man himself in prison, she would be able to work something out. Linus told her he had spoken to Eleanor, and although she was still struggling to understand how her father could have murdered twelve people without her knowing about it, she was happy to sit down and talk to Olivia.

It was another bitterly cold day. Olivia had checked the weather forecast in Newcastle and it was four degrees colder up north than it was in the capital. She had packed her suitcase with heavy jumpers, thick socks and boots. She hated leaving Stanley but knew he would be in good hands with Sebastian and his children, though she made the kids promise her they wouldn't overfeed him. Stanley knew how to twist them around his little paw when it came to handing out Bonios.

She looked up at the announcement board in King's Cross Station. Her train to Newcastle hadn't yet been assigned a platform. She was surrounded by a wall of noise: commuters chatting amongst themselves or calling out to their fellow travellers to keep up, parents chastising slacking children, teenagers talking on their mobiles with the speaker on so their entire conversation could be overheard. Add to this the constant updates from station announcements and it was a cacophony. Olivia couldn't wait until she was on the train in the first-class carriage, relaxed in the quiet space with her thoughts and her research.

She had plenty of time before her train was called so headed for WHSmith to buy some snacks for the journey. A man not looking where he was going, too distracted by whatever he was glaring at on his phone, bumped into her wheeled suitcase. He apologised and Olivia waved him off, but his eyes widened as he looked at her as if he knew her. She quickly turned away.

Olivia grabbed a packet of mint humbugs and a large bar of Galaxy. She looked up for where to pay and was hit with a row of paperback books, all featuring the actor playing her father. His picture took up the entire cover, a sinister grin on his face. He looked nothing like her father, but it was what the picture represented that struck Olivia. She froze, transfixed, looking at the man the whole world would soon associate with her dad, the man who had tried to kill her.

A hand reached out beside her and picked up a copy.

'Wonderful actor, isn't he?' she said to Olivia.

She didn't reply. The woman hurried off to pay for her book. Did she think she was reading fiction, a cheap crime thriller to occupy her for a few hours on her journey, only for her to cast the rest of it aside unread once she reached her destination? This was real. This was true life. This was *her* life.

The announcement boomed out around the station. Her train was ready to board.

Sitting comfortably in a single seat facing forwards, Olivia took out the printout of Isaac McFadden's code and her tablet. She had read through the information Sutton had sent her, and her own notes, many times, but she always liked to be prepared when interviewing a serial killer. Killers were, by design, manipulative, and if Isaac really had killed twelve people, with the aid of a partner, without anyone close to him discovering it, he was obviously a grand master of manipulation. If Olivia showed one sign of weakness or unpreparedness, Isaac would see right through her, and she could kiss goodbye to any hope of getting anything from him.

'Can I get you a hot drink?' the steward asked her.

'Can I have a very strong black coffee, please?'

'Of course,' she smiled. 'Would you like anything from the menu?'

'Not right now, thank you.'

Within a couple of minutes, the steward was back with the coffee. 'It's as strong as I can get it. I can keep topping it up if you want. Just give me a shout.'

'Thank you,' Olivia smiled. She took a sip. It was weak. She would need several of these if she was going to read about the dark crimes of a serial killer. She didn't want to have too many, though. She would hate to have to break her rule of ever attempting to use the toilet on a moving vehicle.

Olivia had been sent a list of Isaac's customers by MediSupplies UK. She had found their locations on a map and saw that he covered a large area of northern England in the course of his work. Although based in Newcastle, he had very few customers there. He went as far west as Whitehaven and Barrow-in-Furness, as far south as Harrogate, and occasionally headed into Scotland as far as Lockerbie and Dumfries. In between, there were large areas of open countryside including the North Pennines, the Lake District National Park, the Yorkshire Dales National Park and the Forest of Bowland. And that was just to start with. Add the countless rivers, canals and reservoirs, forests, woods and parks, and Isaac could have dumped his victims anywhere. If his code didn't reveal a location, it would be nigh on impossible to locate them.

Three of Isaac's customers stood out as being particularly close to him. They had appeared in his diary most often, and he had taken them out for dinner on several occasions, according to his expense accounts. Melanie Knox in Carlisle, Vanessa Charlton in Cockermouth and Chris Cohen in Middlesbrough. Olivia didn't know much about them at present, but Sutton and his team were working on it. Hopefully, she would know more within a day or two.

Olivia leaned back in her seat and had another sip of her bland coffee. She was struggling to understand who Isaac could be in league with. According to the list of his customers, there were no doctors, surgeons, nurses, dentists or anyone who would have acquired medical knowledge through their work. He dealt with managers. Besides, would he really involve someone he worked alongside? How would it come about that they had a shared interest in killing people? Why was Isaac's life such a blank? Even Olivia, in her almost monastic lifestyle, had someone she was close to in Sebastian Lister.

Olivia closed her notebook. She had no choice. She needed to use the toilet. She held her breath throughout the ordeal, hovering over the seat, and washed her hands several times, using the sanitiser she always kept in her bag. She decided against having any more coffee and returned to her tablet.

Isaac wasn't a prolific user of social media and only had a Facebook page where he posted photographs of when he was out with Eleanor for a meal or a walk along the beach at Whitley Bay or Sandhaven. It would seem that Isaac enjoyed the countryside, hiking in particular, as he posted sprawling views of the stark landscape with comments attached, saying how many miles he had walked. Did he go alone or with a friend? Other than the ones with Eleanor, nobody else was ever tagged into the posts and there were no selfies either. Isaac listed his hobbies as walking, hiking, spending time with his daughter, local history and preservation. Did he partake in these hobbies on his own or did Eleanor join him? Or someone else?

Another question Olivia was struggling to answer, based on what she had learned about the affable, gentle, hard-working and decent Isaac McFadden, was what had turned him into a killer in the first place. And not just a killer, a butcher of people. Had he finally snapped? Had he looked back on his life, his tame, safe existence, and realised there was more than being a sales rep and father? If that was the case, why didn't he do something worthwhile? Why not walk the length of the country to raise money for charity, or volunteer at a homeless shelter or offer a spare bedroom to a refugee? Why go over to the dark side? At what point in his life did he wake up one morning and decide to kill someone?

Olivia looked around her at the other people in the first-class carriage. Most seemed to be businesspeople hammering away on laptops, occasionally looking at their phones and having intermittent conversations, many of which ended with the classic line, 'You're breaking up, I'll have to call you back.' There were two elderly women sitting at a table opposite her. They were sharing a bottle of wine and chatting quietly, laughing as they flicked through a glossy magazine. They were both well dressed, understated make-up, sensible shoes, a hint of a sharp perfume. Olivia guessed them to be in their late seventies. She doubted they'd ever had any murderous intentions.

In front of them was a man Olivia estimated to be in his forties. He was vastly overweight, his gut pushing hard to turn his shirt buttons into missiles and fire them across the train carriage. His brown hair was receding, his goatee was unkempt, and his leather shoes were scuffed. He studied the screen of his laptop as if it was the most important thing in the world to him. It probably was. He had two mobile phones and a tablet lined up on the table. He looked the very definition of a workaholic; a heart attack waiting to happen. Olivia didn't think he was the type to snap and run havoc with a gun or machete. If he snapped, he'd keel over and die at his desk. She almost felt an ounce of sympathy for him. He really should take a look at his lifestyle and make some serious changes if he wanted to reach his fiftieth birthday.

A woman on a single seat, further up the carriage, put down her mobile phone, reached into her bag and picked out a paperback book. Olivia caught a glimpse of the cover. It was the TV tie-in edition of *The Riverside Killer* by Sebastian Lister. She was more than halfway through. Olivia wondered what she would think if she knew the only survivor of Richard Button's reign of terror was sitting less than five feet away from her. Would she be tuning into the adaptation next month? Very probably. Olivia turned away.

She angled her head and leaned out into the aisle so she could see the young man sitting close to the back of the carriage. He was in his late twenties, she surmised. He was wearing a fitted suit. The trousers had ridden up and revealed plain black socks. He had neat blond hair, perfectly coiffed, a firm jawline and a smooth complexion. He wasn't reading, he wasn't working, he wasn't scrolling through his phone, he was sitting perfectly still, gazing out of the window as the train turned everything into a blur as it whizzed through England. What was he thinking? Olivia wondered. He had an intense stare. His gaze seemed to be fixed on something far in the distance. It couldn't be anything beyond the window as the train was going too fast. He was obviously lost within his own thoughts. What were they?

He turned and looked at Olivia. He must have sensed he was being stared at as his eyes latched onto hers. He didn't smile. He didn't acknowledge her. He held her gaze. Olivia blinked and looked away, down at her tablet. She waited a few seconds and risked a sneaky look back up. He was still locked on her. There was something troubling about this young man. The smart suit, the perfect hair, the smooth skin, the handsome face: it was a veneer. What was he covering up with his professional appearance?

'Would you like to order from the menu now?' the steward

asked Olivia, making her jump. 'I'm sorry. I didn't mean to startle you.'

'No. It's fine. I was… I was just thinking. Erm, there's actually nothing I fancy. I think I'll wait, thank you.'

'No problem.'

The steward went on her way, asking Olivia's fellow first-class passengers if they required any more drinks. When she arrived by the side of the young man in the perfect suit, he waved her away without even looking at her. For such a young man, he had an air of confidence usually associated with a man of experience.

Olivia shook her head. He could simply be a very confident man. There didn't have to be a dark side to him. Maybe he had achieved everything he had set out to do so far in his personal and professional life. Maybe he was truly happy and exactly where he wanted to be in the world. Did he have to be a potential serial killer? Did he have to be sitting in first-class on LNER plotting his next kill?

Olivia looked down at her notes. The last thing she had written was: *at what point had Isaac decided to kill?*

She looked back up at the young man. She had the urge to ask him the same question.

Chapter Nineteen

Olivia didn't tell DI Sutton the time of her arrival in Newcastle. She had the feeling he would be waiting for her at the train station to take her straight to the police station to get stuck into discovering how prolific a killer Isaac McFadden was. What Olivia really wanted, after a three-hour journey, was to shower, change her clothes, have a drink and something to eat, and prepare herself for what was to come.

Like any other train station, Newcastle's was busy with passengers gawping at the boards or racing for the platforms. Olivia looked for an exit sign and quickly made her way towards it.

Daisy had booked her a standard king room in the Crowne Plaza, a four-star hotel in the Stephenson Quarter of the city. It was close to the train station, only an eight-minute walk away. She had no idea where it was, having never been to Newcastle before, but didn't want to look foolish by getting a taxi and arriving before she had even managed to secure her seatbelt.

She followed the blue dot on her phone, dragging her heavy wheeled suitcase behind her. It was cold in Newcastle and Olivia was glad she had checked the weather forecast and dressed in layers. There was a biting breeze blowing in off the Tyne. She checked in and made her way up to her room. She was pleasantly surprised by how spacious, warm and comforting it seemed. She had no idea how long she would be staying in Newcastle. However, if she was sticking around for the foreseeable future, she would be very happy in this room.

She went over to the large picture window, peeled back the sheer curtains and looked out at the view, expecting to see a buzzing metropolis with designer buildings and flashing lights. The first thing her eyes landed on was the logo for Northumbria Police. The main station was right across the road from her hotel.

'Thank you, Daisy,' she said to herself. She had asked her secretary to make sure she was close to the station, but she hadn't expected to be on its doorstep.

She relaxed on the bed. She didn't realise how tired she was until she lay back and felt herself sink into the deep memory-foam mattress. She decided to close her eyes for a few minutes, recharge her batteries, then get something to eat and read her notes for tomorrow.

Four hours later, Olivia opened her eyes. She quickly sat up and looked around at the strange, dark room. It was a few, long, seconds before she realised she was in a hotel room in a strange city and not the comfort of home. She must have been more tired than she thought. She let out a heavy sigh. She stood up, closed the curtains and turned on the lights. Her large suitcase was in the middle of the room. She decided she might as well make the room feel as close to home as possible while she was here, and began to unpack. The first thing she removed from her bag was the framed photo she kept by her bed at home. It showed her mother and sister in the sunlit back garden of their home in Kingston-upon-Thames. They were smiling to the camera, the picture of happiness. It was Olivia's favourite photograph and as much as it tugged at her heartstrings, it made her smile when she looked at it. She placed it on the bedside table so it would be the first thing she saw in the morning when she woke.

Next she removed her laptop and notebooks and assembled them on the fitted desk. One of the notebooks dropped onto the floor. As she picked it up, a photograph fell out. Turning it over, she saw it was a snapshot of her with Ethan Miller, her... it was difficult for Olivia to describe her relationship with Ethan. They were casual acquaintances, though he wanted to take things further. Before he left for the Amazon rainforest on the second of January, he had told Olivia he loved her. She hadn't reciprocated. She didn't know how. She had no idea what her feelings were towards Ethan. She was fond of him. She had a great deal of respect for him. He made her laugh. The sex was off-the-planet amazing. But love? Olivia didn't know what that felt like. That wasn't technically true, as she loved Stanley. Dogs were different. Dogs were loyal.

The photograph was a selfie of her on the back of Ethan's motorbike. They were both smiling broadly into the camera. Olivia had her arms wrapped around him, holding him tight, her head resting on his leather-clad shoulder. Ethan's eyes lit up with the flash. His designer stubble had felt so good against her smooth cheek. She felt herself smiling. Ethan could be good for her. But she knew she couldn't open herself up to him. She refused to allow herself to be vulnerable with a man and risk being hurt. When Ethan returned from the Amazon next month, she would tell him they could never work.

She placed the photo on the desk and looked around at her room, her home for the foreseeable future. It was devoid of character and personality. It was as empty as she was. It was perfect.

After a luxurious shower, she put on her bathrobe and sat down on the bed. She was hungry but wasn't in the mood to get dressed and go down to the hotel restaurant. Daisy had given her a potted history of Newcastle and told her about the nightlife and the plethora of eateries the city had to offer. There was plenty of time for Olivia to explore. Right now, she didn't want to go out, so she called down for room service. While she waited for it to arrive, she opened her laptop and looked at the typed-out version of Isaac's code and her own notes alongside it.

12	M6	DATE EATEN EDGE (POPPY)	HELPFUL INDEED CRESCENT (HEAT)	BROWN BLUE BLUE BLACK 12/5/10/20	£
12th Victim	?	Could poppy refer to drugs?	?	Description of Sean Bridger? Brown eyes. Blue top. Blue jeans. Black shoes. Cut into 12 pieces. 5ft 10. Aged 20.	?

If 'poppy' did refer to drugs and the police knew Sean Bridger was a drug addict, what did the other three words refer to and why was 'poppy' in brackets? Did the first letter of each word mean something? Together, they spelled 'deep'. Had Isaac been planning to bury Sean deep underground before he was pulled over by police? Together, 'date', 'eaten', 'edge', 'poppy' meant nothing. Not to Olivia. What did they mean to Isaac? She had so many questions she wanted to ask him but doubted he would answer. Killers like Isaac enjoyed being in control.

A knock on her hotel-room door told her room service had arrived. She opened the door to a young man holding a heavy-laden tray. She let him in, told him to put it down on the desk and rummaged around in her pocket for a tip. She found a single two-pound coin. It would have to do. He thanked her and left.

The smell of perfectly cooked beef, roasted vegetables and gravy made to the ideal consistency made Olivia's stomach growl. She hadn't eaten anything substantial since breakfast. She sat down and tucked in. She couldn't eat fast enough.

Meal over, she logged on to the hotel's Wi-Fi and checked her emails. There was the usual spam from organisations she subscribed to, the majority of which she deleted unread. Sebastian had forwarded her something for her to cast her eye over. Daisy had sent her an article entitled 'Fifteen amazing things to do in Newcastle', which she bookmarked.

Logging onto the BBC News website, she skimmed the main headlines. She tried to avoid the news as much as possible. It was all bad, about conflicts and suffering around the world. She couldn't take on more horrors. She went to the world news page to see if there was an active serial killer gaining momentum or if an unwitting one had been captured by police. There was nothing to pique her interest. She was about to log off when something caught her eye. At the bottom of the page, she saw her name within a headline: WHY THE FASCINATION WITH OLIVIA WINTER?

She didn't want to read the article. The launch of the drama of her father's killings was rapidly approaching and media outlets were milking the story for all it was worth. Richard was a hot topic. As was his sole survivor. She didn't want to click on it but knew it would keep her awake if she didn't have a peek. She gave in to her urge for self-flagellation and clicked on the story.

WHY THE FASCINATION WITH OLIVIA WINTER?

A year ago, Dr Olivia Winter, forensic psychologist, was hailed a hero as she tackled a violent serial killer and ended his reign of terror that had been gripping London for months. Footage of her being wheeled into the back of an ambulance, suffering four stab wounds, giving the thumbs-up sign to a nearby detective, went viral and the search was on for the world to find out more about this incredibly brave academic.

It wasn't long before her true identity was revealed. Olivia Winter was born Olivia Button, daughter of infamous serial killer Richard Button, whose life is about to be turned into a four-part drama beginning on ITV1 next month. On the 21st of December 1999, Richard, being pursued by police, went home and murdered his wife and six-year-old daughter. He was caught in woodland at the back of the suburban home in Kingston-upon-Thames, stabbing the nine-year-old Olivia, who managed to survive her injuries.

Why did Olivia grow up and choose a career where she would surround herself with serial killers? She works for the Behavioural Science Administration based in Westminster and travels the world to interview incarcerated serial murderers in the hope of discovering what makes a person kill. But is Olivia really trying to understand her father's actions? Is she searching for closure? Is she really the right person to interview a serial killer when she could so easily be blindsided by her father's crimes?

Professor Andrew Tanner at the University of California, Berkeley, said: 'The trauma Dr Winter faced as a child is something nobody can comprehend. Even if she has been seeking help with a therapist over the years to talk through her issues, there are going to be occasions when something will trigger her memories and send her back in time to that night when her father was unmasked as a serial murderer. Sitting across a table from a serial killer will no longer be a one-sided affair for her. The killer will know who she is, what she went through, and they will use that against her. Dr Winter is going to face closer scrutiny by her peers in her future publications as they will want to know just how clouded her judgement really is.'

Ms Winter is single and lives alone in north London. She has written extensively on the mind of a murderer. Her first book, The Secrets of a Serial Killer, won the non-fiction Crime Writers' Association award. Her second, depicting the life of Joseph Lansbury, known as the Seattle Slasher, was a New York Times bestseller, and her most recent book, The Psychopathy of a Serial Killer, published in 2021, was seen by many as a seminal manual in understanding the make-up of a murderer.

Can someone who has survived a serial killer, not once but twice, really have an open mind when she's sitting across the table from a murderer who is revealing the Technicolor details of their crimes? Is Olivia just a little too close to be able to understand what lurks within the mind of a murderer?

Olivia sat back in her seat and shook her head. She had heard of Professor Andrew Tanner, but never met him. She hoped, now, that she never would. She had heard via Sebastian and Daisy that some people within her circle were questioning her research and interviewing methods in the aftermath of her true identity being released. There was nothing the great British public enjoyed more than the downfall of someone who had worked hard to achieve their position.

With the bravado brought on by the alcohol she'd consumed from the minibar she did something she had never done before. She googled her own name. She clicked on news and read the headlines written about her: 'WHO REALLY IS OLIVIA WINTER?' – 'THE TRUTH BEHIND RICHARD BUTTON'S FINAL VICTIM AND THE REASON HE KEPT HER ALIVE' – 'WHAT DOES DR WINTER'S RESEARCH TELL US ABOUT DR WINTER HERSELF?' – 'SURVIVING A MURDEROUS ATTACK: WHAT IS GOING ON IN OLIVIA WINTER'S HEAD?'

'So, that's what people are saying about me,' she said to herself.

If her identity had been revealed when she was first attacked by her father at the age of nine, she would have received an outpouring of sympathy from the public. But as an adult, as a doctor, as a forensic psychologist, her work is called into question. There is no sympathy for an esteemed figure in society. If she went on *BBC Breakfast* and burst into tears as she relayed the horror of what she went through as a child, the viewing public would be on her side. She would probably be inundated with requests for more media appearances, then the inevitable offer to appear on *Strictly Come Dancing* or *I'm a Celebrity*, to have her open her heart further while chewing on a kangaroo's testicle. That was not the life she wanted. She wanted to live in the shadows and be ignored, let her work speak for itself. But now that was being called into question simply because she refused to be dissected in the media.

Olivia slammed the laptop closed, pushed back the chair and went over to the minibar. She hoped there was a decent supermarket nearby with a good selection of wine. She grabbed a handful of miniatures and slumped onto the bed. Screw the hangover and the befuddled brain tomorrow, tonight she needed oblivion.

Olivia woke with a start. She often did. She rarely remembered her dreams but they always seemed to jolt her awake.

She sat up and wiped her eyes with the backs of her hands. She hadn't fallen asleep, merely nodded off on the bed in a drunken stupor. She looked at the time on her phone. It was a little after three o'clock.

Olivia couldn't get back to sleep. She flicked on the kettle, put the complimentary dressing gown around her shoulders and opened up her laptop. The hours of darkness, when not used for sleeping, may as well be put to good use. She didn't have Stanley to talk to, so work was the next best thing to occupy her mind.

She read more about Isaac, about his life, his childhood with a meek father and a domineering mother, his return to college in his mid-twenties to get the qualifications he'd missed out on at school, the making of a true family man. It seemed strange to Olivia that he had it all – good career, wonderful child – and it wasn't enough. Would he have become a killer had his wife not died? That was an unanswerable question.

Looking back on her notes, Olivia saw that Isaac's wife Louise died on the first of September 2002. He wasn't captured until 2024. How long was he killing for, and did his code give her any hints? She looked back at the printout. Nothing stood out, but then an idea came to her. She fumbled through the pages until she found what she was looking for. Isaac and Louise had married on Friday the first of August 1997. Isaac was born on the first day of 1970. The first day of the month seemed to follow him around. His wife even died on the first of September. When he was born, he would have been told he was something special, having got into the newspapers as the first child born in England in 1970. Who chose the day for their wedding? Did he kill his victims on the first day of every month?

Olivia went back to the code, to the second column in particular.

A1
O1
F1
J5
N2
J6
M4
M5
A5
O3
J9
M6

If she was writing a code to list all of her victims in, she would have a column of dates so she would remember when they were killed. Is that what this was? She ignored the numbers and looked at the letters: A O F J N J M M A O J M. They were all initials of the months of the year: April or August, October, February, J could either be January, June or July. It fitted. The second column could be when the victims were killed. The first three in the table were

A1, O1, F1, that could be April or August 1st, October 1st, February 1st. But then why had he switched to J5, which could be the fifth of January, June or July? She doubted those were the dates of the deaths at all. They had to mean something else, but she had finally cracked the second column, she was sure of it. Surely that could help in tracking down missing people if they all disappeared on or around the first day of the month.

Extract from a notebook allegedly written by Isaac McFadden

The first dead body I saw was my father's. Mum told me not to see him. She said it would upset me, but I wanted to say goodbye. I hadn't been able to do that while he was alive. I knew he was ill. It was obvious. The amount of coughing and wheezing, the vomiting, the blood-stained tissues in the bin. It would have taken a complete idiot not to see that he didn't have long left. But I couldn't face it. I loved my dad. He was my whole world. I couldn't say goodbye to him.

He died while I was at work. I was called into Mr Weddle's office, and he sat me down, told me Mum had called and that I needed to go straight home. He didn't tell me why. He didn't need to. I knew. Dad had already been taken away.

A week later, it was the funeral and Dad was brought back into the house in an open coffin for people to say goodbye. I begged and pleaded with Mum to let me see him. In the end, she gave in. I walked slowly to the coffin and looked inside. I had no idea who that man was. He was clean with neat hair. He was wearing a smart suit and a navy tie. I'd never seen him in a suit before. He looked nothing like my dad. I even asked Mum if she was sure it was him.

I watched as the lid was put in place and screwed down. It was lifted and carefully taken out of the house, put into the back of the hearse, and driven away.

It wasn't far to the church, and it was a fine day, so we walked. Mum was struggling to hold back the tears, so was everyone else who attended. But I wasn't. I didn't feel anything. Who was that man in the coffin? It wasn't my dad. He looked nothing like my dad.

Chapter Twenty

Wednesday 29th January 2025

'Welcome to Newcastle,' DI Linus Sutton said. He had a smile slapped on his face, but it looked as if it was causing him great pain. Olivia was an expert in masking her true feelings and she could spot a faker a mile away. What was Linus hiding?

Olivia stood up from the chair where she'd been kept waiting in the spacious and bright atrium of the Northumbria Police Headquarters.

There was something strange going on with Linus that Olivia couldn't quite put her finger on. Admittedly this was only their third meeting, but he hardly made eye contact with her, and he was radiating a sadness that manifested itself in his lolloping gait and his slumped shoulders. She felt like she was looking at a male version of herself.

'Thank you,' she said.
'How was your journey?'
'Long.'
'Hotel okay?'
'Yes. Very cosy.'
'Excellent. We're upstairs,' he said, hesitantly leading the way.

'Erm, there's something I should probably tell you before we begin.' He stopped at the bottom of the stairs, blocking Olivia's path. He turned to her.

'What is it? Has something happened?' she asked, taking in his drawn expression.

'No. Nothing like that. It's just… well, we're not running a full investigation into Isaac McFadden right now. My boss doesn't seem to think we have enough evidence to throw the resources of a full team at it.'

Olivia mused on this. 'I can see that,' she said.

'So, for the moment, it's just you, me and a very junior DC.'

'Oh. Well, I'm sure between the three of us we can locate twelve bodies hidden somewhere in an area the size of a small country,' she said, flippantly.

Linus smiled at her remark, but it didn't reach his eyes. He must be the only person in the country whose smiles looked like he was going to burst into tears.

Olivia looked around at the open-plan space as they made their way along the top floor towards a room at the back of the building. She felt the cold stares of the inquisitive fall upon her as she passed police officers and civilian staff. News of her arrival had spread quicker than Covid throughout the entire building, it would seem. She imagined her name had risen in the Google search engine rankings and they'd know so much more about her than she would ever know about them. Suddenly, Newcastle didn't seem far enough away from London to act as an escape.

'I've typed up an updated version of the code,' Sutton began. 'I've included our theories regarding the colour of clothing, age, height and… how many pieces we believe each body was cut into. If we could find where one was located, at least, it would be a help.'

'I may have cracked the second column. I think they're the months of when each victim was killed. However, it's the list of the four words in two of the columns I can't get my head around,' Olivia said. 'They don't seem to mean anything. I'm wondering if Isaac's daughter might know. Did you go through the code with her to see if it made any sense?'

'When she brought it in, she said she couldn't understand it. It meant nothing to her. Personally, I think she was glad to hand it over. We're just through here, on the left.' Sutton directed her along a corridor with threadbare floor tiles. 'I've explained to Eleanor who you are, the fact you're a forensic psychologist and helping with the code. She… sorry, she said she already knows who you are.'

'I should think the whole country knows who I am right now,' she said as she saw two women standing in a doorway, glaring at her. She couldn't hear what they were saying to each other.

Linus opened a door to a small room that contained a single table with six chairs around it. That was the only furniture. There was an underlying fusty smell as if there was something dead behind one of the radiators. There were a couple of tasteless, generic prints on the walls, a whiteboard and half-opened Venetian blinds at the window.

'We're in here. It can't be easy for you at the moment, with the drama seemingly everywhere. It was advertised twice during *Emmerdale* last night.'

She looked at him as she placed her case on the table. She smiled. 'You're a soap opera fan?'

'I… no. It… it was just something to have on in the background.'

Olivia could tell she had hit a raw nerve. She looked down at his left hand. He wasn't wearing a wedding ring but there was a white band on his finger where it used to be.

'I used to do that; have the TV on in the background for some noise. Now I just talk to my dog. Do you live on your own?'

Linus didn't answer. Something out in the corridor caught his eye and he immediately jumped upon it, opening the door and beckoning a young man inside.

'Olivia, this is DC Ryan Sweetland. He'll be helping us.'

Olivia tried not to judge upon appearances, but Ryan Sweetland looked as if he was on work experience from secondary school. He was of medium height, around five foot eight, very slightly built and wearing a fitted checked shirt and black trousers. Olivia wondered if he'd bought them from Next's children's department. She looked down at his feet. His matte black boots couldn't be more than a size six. She turned to Linus, then back to Ryan. So, this was the crack team that was going to unmask a serial killer. A DI who was clearly going through some kind of personal torment and a DC who would probably need to be put down for a nap in an hour's time. If Olivia was meant to be the sane and in-control one, then may God have mercy on them all.

'Nice to meet you,' Ryan said, holding out his hand.

Olivia smiled. She took his hand in hers. It barely gripped her. 'And you.'

'I know he looks about twelve, but he does have a very sharp mind,' Linus said, as if reading Olivia's thoughts.

Twelve? Olivia would have guessed younger.

'Now, I've had the case files brought in.' Linus indicated the boxes stacked in the corner of the room. 'I thought we could run through everything so we know we're all on the same page. How does that sound?'

'Fine.'

'Before we begin, would you like a coffee?'

'I'd love one, thank you.'

'That's my cue to do a Costa run. I'll be ten minutes,' Ryan said, leaving the room after taking Olivia's order of a strong black Americano.

'He's a child,' Olivia said to Linus.

'He has an IQ of 165 and graduated from university two years early. He has a degree in mathematics and in clinical psychology and is studying criminology in his spare time.'

'What the hell is he doing in the police then?'

'I ask him that every day. He says he wants to understand the human condition. I thought he'd be perfect working on this.'

Olivia immediately changed her mind about DC Sweetland. In this case, appearances clearly were deceptive.

Twenty minutes later, Ryan returned with three Costa takeaway cups and a square of millionaire's shortbread for each of them. When they were all settled and ready to begin, Linus took out a printed copy of Isaac's original code and the new one he'd made from the information he and Olivia assumed to be correct. Olivia filled them both in on what she and Sebastian had been talking about regarding the psychology of a killer who cuts up their victims. Linus was listening intently while Ryan frantically made notes on his tablet.

'If Isaac is this great organised killer who's planned everything, every victim, every kill and dismemberment, then from his point of view, he's got away with his crimes, apart from Sean Bridger,' Linus said. 'He's languishing in prison with the knowledge that there are eleven other victims out there we know nothing about. He's not going to tell us anything, is he?'

'No,' Olivia stated. 'However, we need to look at another angle here. Isaac was caught by accident. He obviously planned to continue killing. Yet throughout his interviews and trial, he gave nothing away as to motive or where he buried his victims. All you have is one man with one body in his car.'

'What are you saying?'

'It is very possible that Isaac wasn't working alone and that he's remained quiet to keep his accomplice safe.'

Linus's eyes widened. He sat back in his seat and blew out his cheeks. 'You mean, there's a second killer out there?'

'It's a possibility,' Olivia said calmly. 'This level of organisation, where you have twelve victims yet only have knowledge of one of them, is almost unheard of. One man, keeping all this to himself, I find incredible. I don't believe someone wakes up one morning and decides to kill, let alone become a serial killer. When you identify a killer and look back at their lives, at their past crimes, you see an evolutionary process that led them to become a prolific killer. Isaac doesn't have that kind of past. He doesn't have a criminal record. However, if there were two of them, and they sat down and decided to kill, they could have come up with this structure of the type of victim to go for, how to kill them, how to dispose of the body, who could alibi them if they were ever questioned. I don't believe Isaac McFadden could do all this on his own, not from what I've read about him.'

'But surely Isaac fits the description of a psychopath,' Ryan said. 'Someone like that could very well kill twelve people, cut them up, hide their bodies and keep it to themselves.'

'I agree,' Olivia said. 'If Isaac is working alone, he clearly has the mentality to separate the killer version of himself from the supposed normal version of himself where he's able to hold down a job and interact with his daughter.'

'Split personality,' Linus said.

'Dissociative Identity Disorder,' Ryan corrected him.

Olivia smiled to herself. She was very impressed with Ryan.

'In the interviews between DI Sutton and Isaac I've watched, Isaac has remained stoic throughout. Nothing fazes him. You could threaten him with the hangman's noose, and he wouldn't bat an eyelid. Even at the first mention of his daughter, Eleanor, the person he is supposedly the closest to in the whole world, he doesn't flinch. There is nothing there. There is no reason for him to remain quiet. Yet he does so.'

'What does that tell you?' Linus asked.

'It tells me that there is someone out there who Linus holds in higher regard than his daughter, someone he is protecting.'

'But we've been through his entire life,' Linus said, frustration rising slightly.

'You have. But you need to look closer. There are three of Isaac's regular customers who stand out as people Isaac has paid particular attention to. Whether he was simply schmoozing them for their business or it goes deeper, I don't know, but you need to look at Melanie Knox, Vanessa Charlton and Chris Cohen.'

'Isaac has been doing this job since the turn of the century. Do you think this goes as far back as that?' Linus asked.

'I really don't know,' she said. 'When I first looked at the code I thought it was a fairly recent thing. Now, I'm not so sure. I'll admit, I'm struggling to understand Isaac here. I'll know more once I've spoken to Eleanor, and to Isaac himself.'

Linus took a final bite of shortbread and a lengthy sip of coffee. His brow furrowed as he thought. 'So, let me get this straight. Have we got a serial killer couple on our hands and there's still one out there?'

Olivia took a breath. 'It's one theory. I'm guessing you both know what a *folie à deux* is.'

'The subtitle of the *Joker* sequel,' Linus said.

Ryan smiled. 'It's a delusion or mental illness shared by two people who are incredibly close to each other.'

'That's right.'

'Myra Hindley and Ian Brady. Fred and Rose West. Nathan Leopold and Richard Loeb,' Ryan said.

'I've never heard of those last two,' Linus said.

'Basically, *folie à deux* is two people who both have some kind of psychological disorder, though one will have it more prominently than the other,' Olivia said. 'When they meet and their disorders are shared, it is incredibly dangerous. Now, on their own they might not kill, but together, well, we can see what happens simply by looking at the Wests and Hindley and Brady. There is always one who is more powerful than the other. An instigator who pushes them further than merely having murderous delusions.'

'So, are we looking for a Myra or a Rosemary to Isaac's Ian and Fred?' Linus asked.

'Not necessary,' Olivia replied. 'His partner in crime could easily be male.'

'Leopold and Loeb,' Ryan added.

'I'm going to have to look those two blokes up. But how has Isaac been able to lead a perfectly normal life, marrying, having a child, a good job, if he's been killing all this time?' Linus asked.

'If this does go as far back as the early 2000s, maybe even earlier, then Isaac McFadden is one of the most in-control and dangerous psychopathic killers I've ever come across. However, if it's more recent, then it's possible that Isaac's disorder has lain dormant for most of his life and only came to the front when he met his partner in crime.'

'Isaac is the submissive one?' Ryan asked.

'I think he is. If he was the dominant one, once caught, he wouldn't care about his submissive partner being still out there and free. He'd give chapter and verse to his crimes, revelling in them. The fact he's remained silent tells me he's the secondary and the primary is still walking the streets.'

'So, again, how do we find this second person? We've literally been through Isaac's life,' Linus said.

'Yes, you have. And I believe you've already interviewed them.' Olivia pointed to the box files behind her. 'Are all the interview statements in those boxes?'

'Yes.'

'Then there's your killer.'

'Bloody hell,' Linus said.

The trio took another break and Linus popped to the toilet, leaving Olivia and Ryan alone in the small room. Ryan was unloading the boxes while Olivia was scrolling through her notes on her tablet.

'Have you checked missing persons lists for any people who have a likeness to Sean Bridger?' she asked.

'Yes. And we're getting updates all the time. The problem is, Sean Bridger wasn't listed as a missing person. We don't know if any of the other victims are even being missed by family or friends.' Ryan sat down. 'That makes me feel incredibly sad. I mean, surely someone is missing these people.'

'You'd hope so, wouldn't you? But people fall off the radar for all kinds of reasons. I think we should keep an eye on missing persons but maybe we need to talk to the homeless charities, too, especially those within the North East for now. They'll know the regulars and they'll notice when they go missing. If that doesn't give us anything, we need to widen the net, especially to areas where Isaac had his regular customers.'

'That might not be possible at the moment,' Ryan said, pulling a face.

'Why not?'

'Well, like DI Sutton said, it's just us working on this at the moment. That kind of search requires manpower, and we just don't have it allocated to us. CID is stretched to the limit as it is. I could get pulled off this at any moment if a major incident develops, and DI Sutton is also heading an inquiry into a drugs bust.'

There was a light knock on the door. It opened and a man in an ill-fitting suit stepped in holding an envelope. He looked at Olivia, his gaze lingering a tad too long for her liking. He turned to Ryan.

'Sheldon, I'm still waiting for your money for Jack's get-well present.'

'Sorry,' he said. He bent down to pick up his rucksack from beneath the table, took out his wallet and rummaged around inside.

'You're Olivia Winter,' the man said.

'It would appear so.'

'Here you go?' Ryan handed over a five-pound note.

'A fiver? Don't go mad.' He snatched the note from him and left the room, clocking Olivia once more.

'Who's that?' Olivia asked.

'DC Lowel,' Ryan said, as if it left a nasty taste in his mouth.

'He called you Sheldon.'

'From *The Big Bang Theory*. He's intelligent, socially awkward, finished university ahead of his peers,' Ryan said, looking down at his notes, his face reddening.

'Do they all call you that?'

'Most of them. The older ones call me Doogie. I had to look that one up.'

The other detectives might consider the nicknames to be good-natured ribbing, but Olivia could see from Ryan's face that they hurt. This went further than office banter.

'Ryan—'

'Oh,' he said, interrupting her. 'Would you like to see Isaac's original notebook?'

Ryan pulled out a leatherbound A5 book from the evidence box and handed it to her. The leather was deep red, the book well made. Olivia would have bought it herself if she'd seen it on sale somewhere. This definitely wasn't from a chain store. She opened the front cover; nothing was written on the title page. As she leafed through it, she took in the neat, tiny handwriting. There were no spelling errors, no crossing out of words, no pages torn, no mistakes at all. An alarm bell rang in Olivia's head.

'It's strange. I don't know why I didn't pick up on this while reading the photocopy.'

'What is it?' Ryan asked.

'It's too neat. It's too perfect. Obviously, we don't know when he wrote this. Had he just killed, was he planning a kill, was he thinking about a former kill? Either way, his mind would have been all over the place, yet this is all perfectly structured and neat. There are no misspellings or crossings out. This isn't written by someone with a murderous mind.'

Ryan looked at Olivia with rapt attention.

She continued, 'Either he wrote his ramblings elsewhere and transferred them to this book when he was calmer, or…' She paused while, in her head, she sorted the words she wanted to say. 'Or…'

'Or?' Ryan asked.

'It could be a few things. Isaac could be so cool and calm that killing a person has no effect on him whatsoever, which, frankly, scares the living daylights out of me. Or it was written purposely with the intent to throw the police off the scent. Or somebody else wrote this book.'

'But it's Isaac's handwriting. We've checked,' Ryan said.

'He could have copied it. The more I'm finding out about Isaac

McFadden, the more I'm starting to think he's not working on his own here. Now, I never go to see a killer until I've done my homework, and if Isaac has covered his tracks so well that we don't even have a second suspect on the horizon, I'm going to have to be shit hot when I go and see him or he'll eat me alive.'

'How dangerous can he be? He's in prison,' Ryan said.

'And that's the worst place he can be,' Olivia said. 'He's got absolutely nothing left to lose.'

Chapter Twenty-One

BYKER, NEWCASTLE

Thomas Landy took one last look around the empty living room. He didn't feel sad about leaving. After everything the council had done to him over the past few weeks, they could have their house back and shove it up their arse. All he thought about when he looked in the empty rooms was his mother. She loved this house, despite it not being hers to own, and she looked after it as if it was. It was always neat, clean, tidy and tastefully decorated, and even though she hated gardening, she made sure the lawn was always trimmed and the weeds eradicated. This was her home, their home, and now it was a shell.

Following the council's strict instructions, Tom had had to get rid of everything in the property, including the carpets. He had spent the week ripping them all up, rolling them down the stairs and leaving them in a pile outside for the council to collect for the rubbish skip next week. Due to his circumstances, they were waiving their rubbish collection fee. If he'd had the money, he would have told them what they could do with their so-called generosity.

On Wednesday, Janet Wray from next door had taken Thomas in her car to donate the last of his mother's possessions to charity shops around Newcastle. She had offered him her sofa for a couple of nights until he could go to the B&B on Friday, but he turned her down, saying he was staying with a friend. He didn't tell her he was kipping on the empty living-room floor in a sleeping bag.

At the front door, Thomas took one last look over his shoulder. He wanted to cry, but he had no more tears left, and he didn't know who he would be crying for anyway. He lifted his heavy rucksack onto his shoulders, picked up the bulging holdall, his entire life's possessions in two bags, and left the house. He slammed the door behind him, locked it and posted the key back through the letterbox.

Thomas made his way by bus to Benwell. It was a tired-looking area of Newcastle, seemingly forgotten by the council. Houses were in disrepair, gardens overgrown, roads filled with potholes. Nobody seemed to care about where they were living.

He struggled with his bags, which seemed to be getting heavier with every step of his journey. He pushed the door to the Egremont open and stepped inside. Straightaway, he wanted to turn around and leave. There was a thick stench of grease and fried food. The thin carpet was brown and stained. An elderly man sat behind a desk in the corner of the hallway. His grey hair was thin and swept across his scabby scalp in a comb-over. He wore a beige cardigan that looked a couple of sizes too big for him. He was bent over a newspaper. He looked up at Tom, his sunken eyes boring into him.

'Yes?' he asked, his voice heavy with phlegm.

'I believe there's a room booked for me by the council.'

'Oh, you believe there is, do you?' he mocked. He moved the newspaper to one side to reveal an old and stained keyboard. 'Name?'

'Thomas. Thomas Landy.'

He typed slowly and with one finger. 'Well, Thomas Thomas Landy, you're in luck. The council have indeed booked you one of our more gracious rooms.' He pulled open a drawer, grabbed a key and tossed it to him. 'The front door is locked at eleven o'clock every night. No visitors staying overnight, no toasters, microwaves or air fryers in your room. Breakfast is served between seven and nine every morning and clean the bathroom after you've used it. The amount of complaints I get about hairs in the drain is unbelievable.'

'Aren't the bedrooms en suite?' Thomas asked, looking towards the stairs.

'Sorry, your Lordship, the penthouse suite is taken. I'll have the key back if you're going to kick up a stink.'

'No. It's fine. I just… it's fine. Honest.'

'Right. Here, before you go up, put your scribble on this form here.'

'What's it for?'

'It's to say you've arrived and so the council will release the funds to allow you to live in such splendour.'

Thomas stepped forward. With a shaking hand, he picked up a sticky biro and began to fill in the form, putting his full name and telephone number in block capitals.

'So, just got out of prison, have you?' the man asked.

Thomas looked up. 'No,' he said, firmly.

'No. I didn't think so. You haven't got the hardened look about you. What's happened to you then?'

'My mum died. We lived in a council house. They wouldn't let me stay in it on my own.'

'Oh.' The man's face softened. 'I'm sorry. Council are a bunch of bastards. This place only stays open because they pay for immigrants and ex-cons to stay here. Look, a word to the wise, son, don't leave anything valuable lying around in your room. Take everything with you when you go out, and…' He stopped and looked over his shoulder to make sure there was nobody listening in. 'Do everything in your power to make sure your stay here is as short as possible.'

Thomas swallowed hard. He wanted to thank the man for his advice but was worried that if he said anything, it would release a torrent of tears. Instead, he nodded, picked up his bag and headed for the stairs.

The label on the key told Thomas he was on the third floor in room sixteen. He walked up the stairs. In the background, he could hear the sounds of the B&B. Loud music he'd never heard before was coming from somewhere, the sound of a baby crying from somewhere else. He passed one room with the door ajar. He glanced inside and saw a woman sitting on a bed wearing only a bra and pants.

'You my twelve o'clock?' she asked in heavily accented broken English.

'No,' he said.

'Well, piss off then.'

Thomas hurried along the corridor, up the next flight of stairs and found room sixteen. He unlocked it, scurried inside and locked it behind him.

He could perfectly understand why the council was keeping this place open. Nobody in their right mind would voluntarily spend a night here. The walls were tobacco yellow and stained with damp patches. The same brown carpet as everywhere else in the building was frayed and the floorboards beneath were visible in places. The curtains stank of stale air and as he sat on the bed, he heard several springs groan under his weight. He felt like he needed a shower just by being in this room.

A door slammed in the corridor, making Thomas jump. Heavy footsteps descended the stairs.

'You're a tight bastard, Barry. Don't bother coming back until you bring me what I'm owed,' someone yelled.

Thomas closed his eyes tight.

'I wondered how long it would be. Can't we go a day without you screaming, Dawn?'

'And you can fuck off as well, you old bastard!'

Thomas wrapped his arms around himself. He started rocking back and forth. How the hell had it come to this?

Chapter Twenty-Two

Linus had arranged for him and Olivia to go out to Heaton, where Eleanor McFadden lived, and interview her together. Ideally, Olivia would have liked to interview her alone, but Linus stated that if Isaac did have a partner in crime, at present the likeliest suspect was the only person they knew about whom he was genuinely close to, and that was his daughter. He couldn't allow Olivia to go into her house, alone, and question her about her father's crimes. Reluctantly, Olivia agreed.

Linus booked out a pool car and Olivia watched out of the window as Newcastle passed her by. She marvelled at the buildings, some of them very old, with ornate cornicing.

During the drive, Olivia kept stealing glances at Linus as he concentrated on the road. A sadness emanated from him. He had the faraway look of a man on the verge of bursting into tears. When he had work to concentrate on, he gave it his full attention, but now, as he was driving, his mind was clear and whatever was troubling him jumped to the surface. His eyes were glassy with tears, and he kept sniffling to rein in his emotion.

'Are you originally from Newcastle?' Olivia asked, for something to say to fill the silence.

'Hexham. Not far.'

'Ah.' She had no idea where that was. She was hoping he would elaborate, but he didn't.

'Is everything all right?' she asked.

'Yes. Fine. I hope you've packed some thick jumpers; it's going to get colder. There's snow forecast for the weekend,' he said, clearly wanting the topic of the conversation to move away from him.

'I'll be fine. Are you sure you're all right? Something's changed since you came to London.'

They pulled up at a red light. Linus opened and closed his mouth a couple of times as if to say something but changed his mind.

'It's just the January blues. I get like this at this time of year.'

Olivia wasn't convinced. 'No, you don't.'

He turned to look at her. He quickly turned back to gazing through the windscreen at the still traffic ahead.

Olivia could see Linus was in great emotional pain. 'Talking is the hardest thing in the world,' she said. 'It's also the most important. It can save lives. You can talk to me, you know. I'm a complete stranger, and sometimes that's better than talking to someone you know. I won't judge. I won't tell anyone. I'll help you if I can.'

'Why do you want to help me?' he asked, gaze fixed firmly ahead.

'Because you're a good guy. I can see that.'

Olivia was brilliant at giving people advice. She was terrible at accepting it and even though she knew what she had to do in order to achieve some form of equilibrium, she refused to do it. Olivia was, and always would be, a complete fuck-up. Around her, she saw good people like Sebastian Lister and Ethan Miller, and she needed them to stay good. She needed to know there were good people in the world, otherwise what was the point in any of this?

'You know all about me, don't you?' she began. 'You know who my father is, you know what happened to me as a child.'

'Yes.'

'I've never confronted that. I should have done, but I haven't. I've locked it all away, thinking that if I ignore it, it'll all go away. Last year, my father had a heart attack. I was encouraged to go and see him and make my peace, just in case he died and I'd later regret it. I didn't want to go but I went along, and I saw him. He survived and it wasn't long before I saw the evil in him come to the surface. Nothing had changed. I actually hate myself more for going to see him in hospital, and it's one extra thing I'm beating myself up about. I'm doing everything wrong. Linus,' she said so he'd turn to face her. 'Please, do not turn into me.'

His bottom lip began to wobble. He bit down on it hard. He opened his mouth to speak but the car behind beeped its horn. The lights had changed to green. Olivia waited for him to say something more. She could see him wrestling with indecision. She was in for a long wait.

Eleanor's house on Mundella Terrace in Heaton wasn't easy to find, and the satnav took Linus down a small alleyway beside Heaton Baptist Church that he probably shouldn't have driven down. There was no designated parking space but fortunately it was the middle of the day and most people were at work, so they found somewhere to park with ease.

The weather was deceptive. As they'd driven here, Olivia had had to pull down the visor to protect her eyes from the dazzling sun in the brilliant blue sky, but as she opened the door, a blast of cold air hit her.

She looked around her. It seemed like a quiet, unassuming neighbourhood. Tree-lined pavements, Victorian-style terraced houses, some with attics and large bay front windows. The front gardens were no bigger than a postage stamp, but people seemed to keep them neat and tidy. It appeared to be a pleasant place to live.

Linus knocked on the black door with a gloved fist and stood back. It wasn't long before it was opened, and Olivia was almost taken aback by what she saw. Admittedly, she had only seen Eleanor in photographs, but she was always well turned out, hair neatly tucked behind her ears or tied up in a bun, designer clothing that fitted her perfectly. Even in the paparazzi snaps of her on her way to court she looked elegant and poised. The woman Olivia saw before her looked as if she'd endured a five-day bender and been dragged out of bed. She was wearing grey tracksuit bottoms and an oversized hoodie with a suspicious food stain on the left breast. Her hair was all over the place, knotted, lifeless, her dark roots showing.

'Eleanor, we're not early, are we?' Linus asked, looking at his watch.

'No,' she said, stepping to one side to allow them to enter.

'Eleanor, this is Dr Olivia Winter I was telling you about.'

Eleanor closed the door behind them. She briefly looked Olivia up and down. She gave her a sad smile. 'Nice to meet you.'

'And you,' Olivia replied.

The hallway was bright with a high ceiling. There was a musty smell about the place. Windows hadn't been opened for a while and Eleanor had done little cleaning. She led the way into a spacious living room with bare floorboards, a leather sofa and expensive artwork on the walls. There was a matching armchair in the crook of the bay window.

'It's strange,' Eleanor began. 'I've just seen the actor playing your father on *Loose Women*.'

Olivia had been about to sit down but stopped. She looked over to the muted television to see a row of women behind a desk chatting animatedly. Eleanor picked up the remote and turned it off.

'He was on *The One Show* the other night, too,' Eleanor continued. 'There's a lot of buzz around that drama at the moment, and here you are in my living room.'

'The producers will want the millions they've spent on it to be matched in viewing figures, I suppose,' Olivia said agreeably, with an over-the-top smile. She sat down on the sofa, Linus next to her.

'He gave a good interview. You don't realise how much

research goes into playing a character, do you? You think they just read the script and say the lines. He actually visited your dad in prison a couple of times. Oh my God, I'm so sorry,' Eleanor gasped. She slapped a hand to her mouth. 'That was so insensitive of me, wasn't it? I bet you think I'm a right bitch.'

'No. It's fine.' She waved her off.

'I'm talking about it like it's not real, but it is, isn't it? For you, it's your life on screen. That must be… I don't know… horrible to see it dissected like that.'

'I've no intention of watching it. I've lived through it. I don't need to be reminded.'

'No. Of course not. No. Sorry.' Eleanor sat on the armchair, perched on the edge. 'I suppose, if everything turns out to be true about my dad, they'll be clambering all over each other to want to make a drama about it, too. True crime dramas are pretty hot at the moment, aren't they?'

'I'm afraid so.'

'I hope I can be as strong as you are about it, should it happen.'

Olivia felt anything but strong.

'Can I get you a drink?' Eleanor asked them both.

'I'm fine,' Linus said.

'I'd love a coffee,' Olivia said.

'Okay. Sure.'

'I'll have one too, seeing as you're making one,' Linus added.

Eleanor stood up, gave them both a brief nod and a smile and left the room.

'Here's a tip,' Olivia said, leaning close to Linus and lowering her voice. 'Always accept the offer of a cup of tea, even if you don't want one. They leave the room, and you can have a good look round. You can learn a lot about a person by how they've decorated their home.'

'I've never thought of that. So, what does Eleanor's living room tell you about her?'

Eleanor's home was simple in its style. There were very few possessions or unnecessary ornaments on display. What there were were clearly expensive. Eleanor had good taste. The rugs scattered on the floor were thick and plush, the television on the wall was huge and not a cheap brand. All wires were hidden. Not a single device in sight. No Blu-ray player, no Sky box, no games consoles. Shelves either side of the fireplace were neatly packed with paperbacks. There were a few well-thumbed Penguin Classics by Austen, Gaskell and Hardy, a complete set of Harry Potter novels in the covers designed to attract the adult reader, and books by Sally Rooney, Dawn O'Porter, Donna Tartt and Dolly Alderton. A wide variety of fiction.

'Well, it's not easy to tell at the moment. It could do with a good clean. I'm guessing since she found all that stuff in her dad's bedroom, she's been moping about the place feeling sorry for herself. However, it's minimalist in its decoration, bare floors, expensive furniture. Eleanor is a very unfussy kind of woman, no nonsense, she knows her own mind and what she wants out of life. She's probably got a plan of where she wants to be in five, ten, twenty years' time. Although everything is on hold at the moment.'

'Wow, you're good,' Linus said, impressed.

'She also has a tortoiseshell cat named Teddy, she had spaghetti Bolognese for her evening meal last night, and she's having an affair with the man directly opposite who works as a dental hygienist.'

Linus's mouth fell open. 'Where did you pick all that up from?'

'I didn't. I'm joking,' she said, nudging him. He smiled. It was a genuine smile. The first genuine one she had seen. It lit up his face.

Eleanor came back into the room carrying a tray with matching mugs and a full cafetière. She set it down on the coffee table and poured out the drinks, releasing a strong aroma of coffee. She told Olivia and Linus to help themselves to cream and sugar.

'You'll want to ask me all about my dad, won't you?' Eleanor asked. She sat back on the armchair and tried to relax, but her body language was giving her away. She was tense and awkward, uncomfortable in her own home.

'Whatever you want to tell me.'

'I honestly don't know where to begin. It still doesn't feel real. This time last year, I was sitting where you are now looking at holidays for the spring with my boyfriend. We were thinking of Corfu. Less than six months later, I don't have a boyfriend, my dad's being held on remand for murder, and I've had to leave work.'

'How long had you been seeing your boyfriend?'

'About four months. Not long. We weren't serious. I knew he wasn't the man I was going to marry, but we had fun together.'

'How soon was it, after your father was arrested for murder, that you split up?'

'Less than a week,' she said, an iciness in her voice. 'He gave me some shite about us not working out for a while and maybe we should have a break. I remember calling him, telling him he'd left some of his things here. He just told me to bin them. Bastard.'

'What did you do for work?'

'I was a team leader at Webber Addams. They're a digital marketing company. They didn't actually ask me to leave but suggested I take some time away to re-evaluate things. It doesn't look good for a company to have a team leader who keeps crying.'

'Will you go back?'

'Would you?'

'No. I don't think I would.'

'They were really good about me leaving, actually. They treated it like a redundancy, so I got a good payoff.'

'What are you doing at present?'

Eleanor seemed reluctant to answer. 'Very little,' she eventually said. 'Not good, I'm aware. I shouldn't be spending my days alone watching daytime TV, but I don't know, I just can't face the world at the moment. I go to the shops across the road, and I feel like everyone is looking at me, talking about me behind my back. Do you get that?'

'I used to.'

'Throughout the whole trial I kept expecting someone to say there had been a massive error and that they'd got the wrong man. Even after his sentencing I was waiting for the phone to ring and it would be the police saying they'd arrested the real killer and could I go and pick my dad up. Silly, isn't it?'

'It's not silly at all,' Olivia said. 'Our parents tell us how to know right from wrong. They teach us how to behave in the world. We're here because of them. When they do something wrong, it's a huge blow and you start to question everything.'

'He cut a body up into twelve pieces,' she said, struggling to maintain a grip on her emotions. 'How? Why? I don't understand. Can you explain it to me? Because I'm clueless.'

'I really wish I could,' Olivia answered, truthfully. 'Eleanor, the book you found.'

'It's real, isn't it? And those things, they were all trophies of his victims.'

'That's what I'm helping the police look into.'

'You wouldn't be here though if you didn't think it was genuine, if you didn't think my father had killed twelve people. Oh God,' she said, putting her head in her hands. 'It sounds so... I don't know. It's like I'm talking about someone else. My father has killed twelve people. I can't get my head around it. I can't even begin to...'

Olivia didn't say anything. She was waiting for her to fill the silence. People in Eleanor's position wanted answers and they would look to people like DI Sutton and herself to give them. They'd want to ask as many questions as they could, and in doing so they'd reveal so much about their own thought processes.

'Eleanor,' Linus began. Olivia inwardly sighed. She would have preferred the silence to grow, for Eleanor to become awkward and start talking again. 'Are you seeking help? Are you talking to anyone?'

'I had a couple of sessions with a therapist,' Eleanor said. 'I... I couldn't settle. I became paranoid wondering if... I just... I couldn't open up like that to a complete stranger.'

'It's not easy. Therapy isn't for everyone,' Linus said.

Olivia looked across to him. She could see in his eyes that he was speaking from experience.

Eleanor grabbed a tissue from the box on the coffee table and wiped her eyes. 'The problem is my mind won't settle. I keep thinking that my entire life has been a lie. Everything I thought was real and true has been a complete lie.'

'No. Not everything,' Olivia said. 'You had a mother who loved you. You have thirty years of memories of holidays and birthdays and Christmases. Happy times.'

'They're tainted.'

'No, they're not. You just think they are. At the moment, everything is still incredibly raw, and it will be for a while. You think back to a time that you thought was happy and you wonder if your father was plotting to kill while you were unwrapping a birthday present, or if he was eyeing up his next victim while teaching you to ride a bike. We can't know what other people are thinking at any time, but you can look back on those times with a smile, at a time when you were at your happiest.'

She blew her nose and gave Olivia a pained smile.

Olivia reached down for her mug of coffee and took a sip. 'Lovely,' she said. She'd tasted better, but it made her smile grow. She needed Eleanor to be compliant, and any compliment would do right now.

'I'd like to ask you some questions. DI Sutton and his team may already have asked you them, and they're not going to be easy questions, but the answers will help.'

Eleanor took a deep breath to prepare herself. 'That's fine. Go ahead.'

'The young man who was found in the boot of his car, Sean Bridger, did your father know him?'

'I've no idea.'

'Had he mentioned the name before?'

'No.'

'Did *you* know him?'

'No.'

'How do you think your father met him?'

'I'd rather not think about that.'

'Why not?'

'DI Sutton has told me all about Sean Bridger. He was

estranged from his family. He was a drug addict. He stole things to sell so he could buy drugs. I suppose it's not beyond the realms of fantasy to guess he might have sold himself at one point or another. I'm just worried he sold himself to my father and he bought him.'

'Are you worried your father is a homosexual?'

Eleanor winced. 'No. It wouldn't have bothered me at all. What would have bothered me is him paying for sex with twenty-year-olds.'

'Were you close?'

'We were when I was younger. Work took up a lot of my time.'

'After your mother died, was there anyone else in his life? A girlfriend?'

'No.'

'Not at all?'

'No. I remember when I was about ten years old asking if he was going to marry Lesley Quinn next door,' she said with a warm smile. 'I wanted Lesley to be my new mum.'

'What did your dad say to that?'

'He said nobody could replace Mum and he wouldn't even try.'

'What about as you got older, became more independent and went out with your own friends, wasn't there anyone for your dad then?'

She shook her head. 'He just worked.'

'Would he have told you if he was seeing anyone?'

Eleanor paused for a moment while she thought. 'I like to think so. We talked about... well, we talked about most things. When I was a teenager, I got up to all kinds of shit. I really experimented with my youth. Dad was a great support. I think if he'd met someone else, he would have told me. Dad loved Mum. He still loved her. He was fine on his own. Perfectly fine.'

Olivia thought Eleanor was defending her father too much. The man was a serial killer and the whole country would very soon know about it. But if there was any scrap of dignity she could hold onto regarding her father, she would grab it tightly with both hands.

'Looking back, is there anything that stands out about your father? Anything that suggests a red flag?'

Eleanor shook her head.

'Tell me about your dad's friends,' Olivia asked.

'He didn't have many. There was Lesley next door. Hal across the road. His social life seemed to involve people he worked with. If he wanted a meal out or anything he'd take one of his clients to dinner.'

'What about holidays?'

'He went hiking and camping occasionally.'

'Who with?'

'Himself, mostly.'

'Did you ever go with him?'

'God, no. I like a firm mattress. I could never get comfortable in a tent.'

Olivia wasn't getting anywhere with Eleanor's answers. If anyone should know anything about Isaac, it should be his daughter. She was either holding back or genuinely didn't know.

'Eleanor, about this notebook you found. Did you read it?'

'Some. I couldn't... I...'

'Is your dad the type of person to create such an elaborate, cryptic code?'

'I don't know.' She shrugged. 'A year ago, he was just my dad. He worked hard, he went hiking, he watched Formula One and drank craft beers. Now, he's a fucking serial killer. I feel...' She stopped herself.

'Go on,' Olivia prompted.

'I don't know. When Mum died, Dad took on the role of both parents. He always put me first. He was always there for me when I needed him. I'm not looking at my past through rose-tinted glasses, he really was the best dad I could ask for. Was that all fake? Was he faking it so I wouldn't find out who he really was? How long was his killing spree going on for? I... I'm really struggling to understand everything, and it hurts. In here,' she said, slamming a fist against her chest. 'I'm knotted up inside and I can't... I can't...' She gave in to her tears and bent double, rocking back and forth.

Olivia and Linus watched, impotent. There was nothing either of them could say or do that would make Eleanor feel any better about the situation she found herself in. Only a handful of people could sympathise, and although Olivia was one of them, no words of comfort came to mind.

As Eleanor sat in the armchair, head in hands, crying her heart out, Olivia saw herself as she was, aged nine, discovering that her father was a serial killer and had murdered her mother and sister. When she'd regained consciousness in hospital, her gran and grandad were by her bed, tears streaming down their faces as they told her everything. She wanted to scream. She wanted to shout. She wanted to run away from everything.

That was how Eleanor was feeling now and any soothing words Olivia could say would sound bitter and hollow. There would come a time when Eleanor would be able to function in the world, but it wouldn't be for a while.

'Eleanor, tell me something good about your dad,' Olivia said, eventually.

Eleanor looked up at her with tear-filled eyes. 'Like what?'

'I don't know. Just share a good memory.'

She thought for a moment, her face a map of frightening emotions. Soon, it began to soften and, very slowly, the darkness seemed to fall from her face and a small smile appeared.

'When I was eight, I wanted to be Mary in the school nativity play. I wanted that part so much. But I didn't get it. I was devastated. I cried all the way home, all through tea, and even walking upstairs to bed I was in floods. I can still picture it. I ended up having to play a wise man at the last minute when one of the boys vomited during the dress rehearsal. The next morning was Saturday. I woke up, and Dad was sitting on the edge of my bed. He'd brought me my breakfast and told me to stay in bed until he came to fetch me. When he did, he told me to put my dressing gown on and come downstairs. He'd turned the whole living room into a stable. I've no idea where he got the straw from,' she said with a huge smile on her face. 'He got Lesley to play the innkeeper. Gran was still alive then. She played the angel. I still laugh now when I think about her sitting on the dining table with a fag hanging out of her mouth. Dad was Joseph, and I was Mary. We put on a little play together. Just the four of us. It was so much fun.'

All three were grinning by the time Eleanor finished her story. She looked away from them, saw her living room, and reality dawned. The smile quickly faded.

'How can one man be two different people?' she asked.

'Killers, particularly serial killers, tend to disassociate themselves from their real lives when they're killing. It's as if they're two people. You could have been sitting together on this sofa watching the news about one of his victims and it would be as if he was hearing about it for the first time. It would never enter his head that he killed him.'

'So, he could have gone out, killed someone, then come round here and had a few drinks while watching a film with me?'

'Yes.'

'And, from his point of view, it would have been as if it was a normal day?'

'Yes.'

'How can he do that?'

Olivia only knew the scientific answer, not the personal one. She thought it prudent not to say anything.

Olivia and Linus didn't stay much longer. As they were leaving, Olivia gave Eleanor her card. She told her to contact her at any time should she have any questions or think of anything that might help. She seemed to soften then, knowing there was someone out there who might be able to help her come to terms with what she was going through.

'Well, what do you think?' Linus asked as they made their way back to the car.

'She's all over the place. It's understandable, obviously, but that makes her incredibly difficult to read.'

'You don't think she's Isaac's partner in crime?'

'I never cross anyone off the list until I have absolute proof, but I can't see it.'

'So, that leaves us with no suspects then.'

'Only X.'

'Formerly known as Twitter. You think Elon Musk is involved?' Linus said with a smile in his voice.

Olivia turned to him and took in his grin. It was good to see him show a lighter side, even if it was only briefly.

'X is a person we've yet to identify. X is someone incredibly important in Isaac's life who hasn't appeared on the radar yet, or who has but is keeping their murderous persona deeply hidden.'

Back in the house, Eleanor was standing in the middle of the living room, looking out through the slats of the blinds at Olivia and Linus chatting as they walked back to the car. She would have loved to hear what they were saying.

She liked Olivia. She seemed to know what she was talking about, and she came across as strong and professional. After reading about her online, she had expected someone with more emotion attached to them. She was also shorter than she imagined. She watched the car drive away and returned to the armchair. She sat back and closed her eyes.

Eleanor lost time. She had no idea how long she sat in that chair, struggling to compose herself. Her mind had wandered. It had shut down in order for her to relax, get her breathing under control and stop the agonising horrors tormenting her. She was battling hard to cope with everything that was happening around her. This darkness was new to her, and she didn't like it.

She went into the kitchen and made herself a peppermint tea.

The book *The Riverside Killer*, by Sebastian Lister, was on the kitchen table. She picked it up and took it back into the living room with her. She was three-quarters of the way through and had left Post-it note arrows on various pages she wanted to revisit and research when she was finished.

As Eleanor settled and read about the day after Richard Button had murdered his wife and youngest daughter, and almost killed Olivia, a thought struck her. There was only one way to get through this horror and that was to claim it. The press was going to be on her doorstep again once the news of her father's code and his many victims was released. She needed to take control and own her victimhood.

Chapter Twenty-Three

Transcript of Zoom conversation between DC Ryan Sweetland, Northumbria Police, and Vanessa Charlton, manager of Meridian Homes North West.

> RS: Thank you for agreeing to talk with me. Can you tell me about your relationship with Isaac McFadden?
>
> VC: It was purely a professional relationship. As you know, he worked for MediSupplies UK and we bought everything we needed from them.
>
> RS: We've looked through Isaac's diaries and we've highlighted the customers he's spent the most time with and we've found three people who he saw more than any others. You're one of them. He took you out to dinner several times, didn't he? What did you talk about?
>
> VC: They were business meals. Meridian Homes owns five nursing homes and they're adding to their portfolio all the time. When they bought a new property, I contacted Isaac, and he came over to discuss what we need. Discussing it over dinner was a more relaxed environment.

RS: Did you ever talk about anything personal?
VC: Well, obviously, we didn't talk about business all the time. We're not robots.
RS: Can you elaborate?
VC: We talked about our families, hobbies, the usual things.
RS: I hope you don't mind me being blunt, but did Isaac ever seem interested in taking things further? Did he ask you out in a romantic sense?
VC: No.
RS: Never?
VC: I… no. Never.
RS: Mrs Charlton, I'm getting a sense that…
VC: All right, if you must know… Shit. Look, I had a little too much to drink one evening while we were out. I shouldn't have done, and I regretted it the next morning. I mean, I'm married, for crying out loud.
RS: Something happened between the two of you.
VC: No. I made a pass at Isaac, and he brushed me off. He was very polite about it, and he didn't mention it again when we met the time after. He was a gentleman.

Transcript of Zoom conversation between DC Ryan Sweetland, Northumbria Police, and Christopher Cohen, owner of Cohen Distributions Ltd, Middlesbrough.

RS: Mr Cohen, thank you for agreeing to talk to me. According to his records, you were one of Isaac McFadden's longest serving customers. You've known him for more than ten years. Can you tell me what he was like?
CC: He was a good bloke. He knew his business. He was confident. Funny. Personable.

RS: He took you out to dinner on several occasions, too.
CC: Yes. Well, you've got to have some perks in sales. His company was paying so we had a few meals in some top restaurants.
RS: What did you talk about during your meetings?
CC: Work, mostly. But it can't be all work, can it? Know what I mean?
RS: So, the conversation did turn personal?
CC: Oh yes.
RS: Can you elaborate?
CC: You're a bloke. What do you think two single blokes talk about once the wine has started flowing?
RS: I need you to tell me, Mr Cohen.
CC: Well, like I said, we were two single blokes. He travelled around a lot with work, he told me a few stories about the women he met, how a few went back to his hotel room if he was staying over.
RS: He slept with his customers?
CC: I very much doubt there was much sleeping going on.
RS: Did he give you any names?
CC: No names. Just details.
RS: Did you ever know Isaac to be in a relationship with anyone?
CC: No. He never said. Everything was just casual for him. His job suited him perfectly. He wasn't one for settling down.
RS: Did you ever go out with Isaac when it wasn't business-related?
CC: I did, yes. Only once. He came over for a meeting and I'd turned fifty that week. I asked if he fancied joining me for a few drinks and we hit the bars around Middlesbrough.

RS: Did you see him with any women?
CC: I lost bloody count, mate. We ended up getting separated, though. I met an ex of mine who I hadn't seen for about fifteen years, and things were rekindled. No idea what Isaac got up to. I called him the next day and he said he'd taken someone back to his hotel. Oh, I've just remembered, he did tell me he was seeing one of his neighbours casually. Julie somebody.

Ryan ended the call with Chris and sat back in his seat, a heavy frown appearing on his face. Two conversations with two people Isaac spent a great deal of time with, and they gave conflicting statements about the type of person Isaac was. Vanessa Charlton said he was the perfect gentleman and didn't take advantage of her when she made a pass at him, and Chris Cohen made Isaac out to be a complete ladies' man.

'Would the real Isaac McFadden please stand up?' Ryan said to himself.

Chapter Twenty-Four

Isaac McFadden's former home was a corner house overlooking Ridley Park and very close to the River Blyth. It was a strange-looking house with the upper floor windows in the roof, two tall chimney stacks and an attached garage that seemed to have been plonked on the end. There was a driveway and a wraparound garden with a high privet hedge to hide the house from the street. The journey from Eleanor's house had taken almost forty minutes due to traffic on the A19.

'What do you think about the relationship between Isaac and Eleanor?' Linus asked as he turned the engine off. Olivia remained still. She hadn't even removed her seatbelt.

'From the outside it looks like Isaac sacrificed any kind of a personal life to raise his daughter on his own following the death of his wife, which was incredibly laudable. However, they don't seem very close, do they?'

'I thought that. Eleanor didn't mention them doing things together. Obviously, I don't expect them to go on holiday together, but there was no talk of going out for a meal or to the cinema.'

'No. But then Eleanor did say she got up to all kinds of shit when she was a teenager. Did whatever it was drive some kind of wedge between the two?'

'It could have done. My dad didn't speak to me for months when I was fourteen and he caught me drinking at a party.'

'Naughty boy,' Olivia playfully chastised him. She removed her seatbelt and made to get out of the car.

'He totally over-reacted. I was grounded for a month for having two cans of Stella. I did vomit in his car on the way home, so maybe that's why he was so pissed.'

'You think? Are you close to your father?'

'We speak every weekend. He lives in Brighton with his second wife. My mum died when I was twenty.'

'I'm sorry.'

Linus nodded. 'She suffered with her nerves a lot. She was a fragile woman.' He cleared his throat. 'Shall we go inside then?'

'Absolutely,' Olivia said. She had found another layer of sadness to Linus. But that wasn't the only thing that was causing him such torment, something closer to the present was giving him a shroud of sorrow.

There was something about setting foot inside the house of a serial killer that filled Olivia with a sense of dread – but also one of excitement. Killing another person was the most extreme thing a person could do. Seeing how they lived, how they filled their home, would give her an insight into their mind.

They walked up to the front door. While Linus was unlocking it, Olivia glanced around her. It was an innocuous-looking street. Other houses also had high fences or high shrubbery to act as a barrier from their neighbours. She wondered, briefly, what had happened to the supposed friendliness of the north.

'Did your team speak to the neighbours?' Olivia asked.

'Yes.'

'And?'

'You've seen their statements.'

'Yes, but, what impression did you get? I thought people up north were supposed to be friendly and polite and always chatting over the garden fence. You'd need to be eight feet tall to talk to the people next door.'

'People are only friendly to those they know. Everybody is busy with their own lives these days. The time of chatting over the fence while you're hanging out your washing is long gone.'

He entered the house and left Olivia on the doorstep. She looked around once more. There was an upstairs curtain twitching at a house across the road. People might no longer be friendly, but it didn't stop them being nosey.

Inside, the house was just as cold as outside. There was no heating on and a fusty smell in the air. As she entered the living room, Olivia took a camera out of her bag, a Nikon D7500, and took a few snaps. The house was devoid of life. The furniture was still in place, picture frames still adorned the walls, yet there was no atmosphere. It had the cold feeling of an unlived-in house, even though there were all the signs of a family still being present. It was the *Mary Celeste* of homes.

'Why are you taking photos?' Sutton asked from the doorway.

'It gives me a sense of who Isaac was in his private life,' she said, taking a photo of a framed family picture on the wall: mother, father, daughter, all happy and smiling. The picture of happiness. 'I can't feel anything in here. Isaac hasn't lived here for so long that there's nothing to cling onto, but I can take away an image of what he surrounded himself with, what was important to him.'

'What was important to him?'

'Family, obviously.' She indicated the many photo frames. 'He genuinely loved his wife and daughter, there's no denying that.'

'Yet he was willing to ruin everything,' Linus said as he picked up a photo frame and studied it.

'He won't have seen it like that. You don't kill someone thinking you're going to get caught. You do everything you can to make sure you *don't* get caught. Up until he was pulled over in the storm, Isaac had mastered that. He really was untouchable.'

'So why did he do something so ridiculous as try to get rid of Sean's body during a storm?'

'He either got complacent and thought he really was uncatchable, or he'd had enough and wanted to be caught. Although I never believe that reason. If you want to stop killing, then just stop. You don't need to risk spending the rest of your life being locked up.'

Linus went through to the kitchen, leaving Olivia in the living room. She lowered her camera as she walked over to a sideboard. A framed picture had caught her eye. It showed Isaac in the middle of a field, a tent in the background. He looked windswept, with hair all over the place and ruddy cheeks, yet he had a broad grin on his face. He was enjoying nature. Eleanor said he went away mostly by himself. The question Olivia had was: who was taking the photograph?

'There's a jar of coffee but no milk,' Linus called out from the kitchen. 'Fancy a cup?'

'Go on then. It might help to thaw me out,' she said, heading into the kitchen. 'What does Eleanor plan on doing with the house, do you know?'

Linus was spooning instant coffee into two mugs in the clean yet out-of-date kitchen.

'I've no idea. You wouldn't want to move in here, would you?'

'No. I'm guessing she'll make a loss. Someone will snap up a bargain.'

'If you want to live in a house where a man chopped up twelve people.'

'Can the garage be accessed from inside the house?' Olivia asked.

'Yes. It was a recent addition. I asked Eleanor about it after Isaac's arrest. It was installed in 2010 and there's a door in the hallway that'll take you through.'

Linus led the way while the kettle was boiling and unlocked the internal door. The garage was freezing. The wind had picked up outside and was causing the steel door to rattle. He turned on an overhead light. There were two strip lights, but only one worked, the one closer to the up-and-over garage door. Olivia stepped onto the concrete floor.

'Everything's been taken away,' Linus said, his voice echoing around the empty space.

All that remained was metal shelving on the far wall and a few paint tins.

'What was in here?' she asked, taking several photographs from different angles.

'There was a chest freezer.'

Olivia quickly turned to look at him and raised a questioning eyebrow.

'Only food inside it. Forensics went over every single inch of it. They found nothing to suggest a body, or body parts, had been inside. If there had been, they'd been securely wrapped up beforehand. There were plastic crates that contained medical equipment for his work, things he needed to deliver. Again, they were all tested. A couple did contain minute traces of blood. We can't get anything from them, unfortunately. Apart from that, all the usual car stuff you expect to find in a garage.'

Olivia stamped hard on the floor. 'You haven't taken this up?'

'It hasn't been tampered with in any way. The concrete laid by the company is exactly as it was in 2010. There was no need for us to dig it up.'

'What car did Isaac drive?'

'A Citroen Picasso. Bought brand-new in 2021.'

'That's a decent-sized car, isn't it?'

'Yes.'

Olivia stood in the middle of the garage and looked around her.

'A chest freezer and storage boxes. Would you have said this garage was cluttered?'

'Not overly, no. Why do you ask?'

'With those shelves, it would be a very tight squeeze to get a Citroen Picasso in this space. He didn't use this garage to park his car. I mean, without a big chest freezer and if he put those shelves on the back wall, he probably could have done, but not how it was.'

A gust of wind rattled the steel door. Olivia jumped at the echoing sound.

'It's not sound-proofed.'

'No.'

'Did the neighbours hear anything coming from in here? Any cries or screams or anything that stood out?'

'They say not.'

Olivia looked around her. 'Did anyone else have access to this garage?'

'As far as we know, just Eleanor.'

'Did the neighbours notice any strange visitors, anyone coming late at night, or when Isaac wasn't here?'

'They didn't say. What are you thinking?' he asked, leaning against the door frame and narrowing his eyes.

'At the moment, I'm still trying to work something out in my head. I'd rather keep my thoughts to myself if that's all right.'

'You're the expert. I'm not going to laugh if you say you've evidence Isaac wasn't of this world.'

Olivia laughed. It echoed.

The kettle clicked off in the kitchen.

'Have you seen enough?'

Olivia nodded. 'Can I get a copy of the photos your team took when everything was in here?'

'Sure. I'll send them over when we get back.'

'Thanks.'

They went back into the house and Linus poured boiling water into the mugs. He handed a mug to her bearing the KitKat logo.

'Thanks.' She took a sip. It was bland.

'I'm reading a couple of your books at night. I'm trying to understand more about what you do. I'm guessing you'd call Isaac an organised killer.'

'I would, yes.'

'That kind of killer is someone with a great deal of brain power, someone who can manipulate the crime scene and other people, so the attention isn't drawn to them. If all that's true, how do you know what you can and can't trust when you look around this house or talk to McFadden in prison?'

'You have to trust physical evidence. Several spots of blood were found in this garage belonging to different people. You have to accept that the garage was used to cut up the victims. That's a fact. So, you base the rest of your research and planning from this point. You put yourself in Isaac's shoes and you work out his journey to the disposal of the bodies. He's living in a built-up area, so it's natural he would wait until nightfall so fewer people might spot him. Look at maps and find where the likely disposal points would be. He's not going to want to travel far with a body in his car, so he needs to get rid of it quickly.'

'But what we would see as a potential disposal site might not be one for a psychopathic killer like Isaac.'

'Which is why we try and find out as much about Isaac as we can so we can think like he does.'

Linus pulled a face. 'Really? That's what you do? You try to think like a serial killer? Jesus, Olivia, how are you able to function, having all that inside your head? I'd be a complete basket case by now.'

Olivia gave one of her knowing smiles. To Linus, it would show she was in control, and nothing fazed her. To Olivia, it was a defence mechanism. The truth was, she was a complete basket case. She should not be doing this job if she wanted to survive to a ripe old age.

Olivia stood in Isaac's bedroom and looked out of the window. It was at the front of the house and overlooked the park opposite. She could see warehouses in the distance.

'What's at the other side of the park?' she asked, taking a photograph.

'Blyth Harbour,' Linus said. 'There's an historic lightship not far from here and a yacht club.'

'Beyond that would be the North Sea.'

'Yep. Not far at all.'

'If he dumped body parts out to sea, we may never find them.'

'We checked with the harbour offices and Isaac never rented a boat or approached anyone with a boat moored there. According to Eleanor, Isaac didn't know anyone with a boat.'

Olivia turned back to the room. A king-size bed took up most of the space. Fitted wardrobes were still filled with Isaac's clothes.

'When Eleanor found the notebook and came to us, she was in the process of clearing out the house. We asked her to leave it as it was for the time being in case we needed to do further testing.'

'Is she in a hurry to sell?'

'I'm not sure. You wouldn't want to hang onto it, though, really, would you?'

'No,' she said, thinking of how long it took her grandparents to sell her family home, and the loss they made on it. 'I'm finding it hard to believe that if Isaac killed twelve people, he somehow had to bring them to the house, maybe unconscious but still alive, before killing them and dismembering them in his garage, then leaving to dispose of the parts. How can no one in this street have realised something strange was going on here?'

'People tend to keep themselves to themselves.'

'But they're going to notice Isaac coming and going at different times of the day and night. The fact he's an organised killer means that he's going to try to outfox potential witnesses. That means he won't bring a victim back here at the same time every day. He'll change the time. Sometimes it'll be midday, sometimes the middle of the afternoon, sometimes the early hours of the morning. How can nobody have noticed the erratic times he was keeping?'

'Reading the witness statements, they all say that basically Isaac was the kind of person you didn't really think about until you saw him. He blended into the background.'

'None of the witness statements mentioned seeing someone come to the house regularly, did they? Apart from Eleanor, he had no friends, no partner, come to visit.'

'No.'

'Not once. Not one person worth mentioning in twenty-odd years. Don't you find that strange?' Olivia asked.

'A little. But if it's purely innocent, you're not going to remember, are you?'

'But finding out your neighbour is a murderer will make you question everything, and that includes the people who come to the house.'

'Going back to Isaac having a partner, you said there's always a dominant and a submissive one. Does that always have to be the case?' Linus asked, crossing his arms as he leaned against the wall.

'There are usually three categories for couples who kill. The first is a dominant who coerces a submissive to murder. The second is a dominant who gets together with someone who appears to be good, but will harbour demons of their own, to go on to murder. The third can actually be the worst. You get two bad people, both of whom are too cowardly to act alone, but they join forces, and their dysfunctional relationship leads them into acts of evil.'

'I can't see Isaac being a cowardly sort of person.'

'Me neither. The fact there are traces of blood from different people in the garage, and the fact the neighbours didn't see anyone unusual come to the house, makes me think Isaac is the cool, calm, dominant one. *However*, he remained silent throughout his interviews and the court case. He's not speaking to the police when you question him about the code. He's covering up for someone. A dominant wouldn't protect a submissive like that.'

'So, if Isaac is the submissive one of the partnership and the dominant one is still out there, what will they be doing now? Will they continue killing on their own?'

'Maybe. Or maybe they've got another submissive waiting in the wings.'

Extract from a notebook allegedly written by Isaac McFadden

I sit back, knackered, mentally, and physically exhausted, and look at the scene in front of me. It genuinely looks like a scene from a horror film or an abattoir. The floor is awash with blood. There are body parts scattered everywhere; legs, arms, torso, organs, head. I can't see for red.

I have to take a break here. I need to settle myself down, compose myself. I also need to revel in what I've got in front of me. This used to be a person. A few days ago, this was a young man walking around going about his business, unaware of the horror about to come his way. Now, he's in pieces on the floor.

I don't usually give him a pronoun. He doesn't physically exist anymore. What is in front of me is meat, flesh, bone. This isn't a person. It's raw materials.

I like to sit back, have a cup of tea, and look at what I've done. Am I sorry? No. Is it worth all the effort and risk taking? Yes. Fuck, yes.

Chapter Twenty-Five

Olivia left Isaac's house, leaving Linus to lock up and make sure it was secure. She headed for the car, buttoning up her coat and putting on her gloves.

'Are you a journalist?'

Olivia looked around her to see where the voice was coming from. Her gaze eventually fell on a woman in the doorway of the house next door. She was conservatively dressed in muted colours. She had her arms folded across her chest and a severe look on her face.

'I'd have thought you'd bled that family dry. Can't you just leave them alone? Can't you leave us all alone, for crying out loud?'

'I'm not a journalist,' Olivia said.

'Documentary film maker. Investigative reporter. Whatever you call yourselves, you're sick.'

Linus, upon hearing the exchange, ran over to the dividing fence.

'I don't know if you remember me. DI Sutton. Northumbria Police. It's Mrs Quinn, isn't it?'

'That's right.'

'She's with me. This is Dr Winter. She's a forensic psychologist.'

'Is she indeed?'

Olivia opened her mouth to speak but Linus got in first.

'Have you been receiving unwanted attention from the media, Mrs Quinn?'

'We did once the trial was over. It's died down since. I thought it was starting up again. I'm sorry,' she said, turning to Olivia. 'No offence meant.'

By the look on her face, Olivia assumed Mrs Quinn wasn't used to making apologies and found they had an unpleasant taste.

'Mrs Quinn, have you lived here long?' Olivia asked.

'Coming up to thirty years.'

'Would it be possible for me to talk to you?'

'What about? I've said everything I know about the family. Can't you just let poor Eleanor try and come to terms with what's happened?'

'Mrs Quinn,' Linus began, 'I can't go into details, I'm afraid, but Dr Winter is working with us to try to understand more about Mr McFadden. It would be useful if she could talk to you.'

Mrs Quinn seemed to think for a long moment. She looked Olivia up and down, as if judging her on appearance alone. Eventually, she acquiesced by releasing a heavy sigh.

'I suppose you'd better come in then.'

She turned and went back into the house, leaving the front door ajar for Olivia to follow.

'I don't recall reading her witness statement,' Olivia said. 'Did she say much?'

'Very little. She was very protective of Eleanor. She didn't want to tell tales.'

'Which means she knows tales to tell.'

'You think?'

'Only one way to find out,' she said, making her way over the border to next door.

'Do you want me to come in with you?'

She thought for a moment. 'Erm, no. I think I might do this on my own. I'll play the girls banding together card. I think Mrs Quinn might appreciate that.'

'How will you get back?'

'Well, in London we have these remarkable things called taxis,' she said with a smirk.

Linus smiled. 'We're a bit backward up in the north. You'll need to call for a pony and trap.'

Olivia watched as Linus made his way back to the car. The slow gait and slumped shoulders revealed more about him than he would realise. When left on his own and with nothing to occupy his mind, his thoughts went quickly over to the dark side.

Lesley Quinn was somewhere in her mid-fifties, though the dyed shoulder-length hair and the make-up made her look younger. Once Olivia was close enough and took in the lines around the eyes and the softening of the jawline, she managed to arrive at a rough estimate of her age. The iciness of the woman on the doorstep had thawed and she welcomed Olivia into her home.

'I'm afraid I can't offer you a cup of tea or anything,' Lesley said. 'I thought I'd be terribly modern and have one of those boiling hot water taps installed. Unfortunately, it's stopped working on me. Someone's supposed to be coming out to look at it. I'd been putting off updating the kitchen for years, but I finally got around to it last summer. I wish I'd never bothered, with all the problems I've had,' she said. 'First it was the waste disposal, now it's the hot water tap,' she said with a smile.

'That's fine,' Olivia said. She sat down on the chintz sofa and looked around her at the neat, spartan room.

'So, you want to know about Isaac, don't you?'

Olivia nodded. She took a notebook from her bag and flicked to a fresh page to take notes. 'Did you know Isaac well?'

'I thought I did,' she said. 'I've been here since 1995. Isaac and his family moved in a few years after me. That house had been empty for ages. It needed a lot doing to it. But they made it into a family home, him and his wife. They only had a couple of happy years before she died. That was tragic.'

'Isaac took it badly?'

'He did seem to fall apart. I helped with Eleanor for a while. I took her to school, picked her up. Isaac just needed a bit of time on his own to grieve, to get used to Louise not being around anymore.'

'What was it that brought him out of his grief?'

'Eleanor had an accident at school. She fell over in the playground, hit her head hard, and the school rushed her to hospital. Personally, I think they over-reacted, but it had the desired effect on Isaac. He realised he'd been neglecting her. After that, he was a changed man. He put Eleanor first before anything.'

'He must have been very grateful to you for stepping in to help with his daughter.'

'Oh, he was,' she smiled. 'I still helped if he was going to be late home from work or if he had to travel far and needed someone to take Eleanor to school. I work from home, you see, always have done.'

'What do you do?'

'I'm an accountant. I've got my own business. I have an office upstairs.'

'When Isaac was arrested…' Olivia began.

Lesley's face soured. 'Don't remind me. It was like something from a TV drama. All those police cars and vans pulling up outside with their lights flashing. They went through that house like nobody's business. Frightened the life out of me. Then they came knocking on here. Late at night it was, too. I had two plain-clothed detectives in my living room questioning me in my nightie. I didn't get much sleep that night, I can tell you.'

'Did they tell you what had happened?'

'They didn't go into details. They said Isaac had been arrested and could I tell them what he was like as a person.'

'What did you say?'

'Well, I just told them the truth. He was a family man. He still doted on Eleanor, despite her growing up and moving away. He was hard-working, quiet, friendly, everything you want from a neighbour, really. I called Eleanor up after they'd gone. She was at the police station at the time and said she'd pop round in the morning, which she did.'

'And she told you why Isaac had been arrested for murder?'

Lesley paled. 'I'm afraid to say she did. I've known Eleanor since she was a bairn. She used to call me Auntie Lesley growing up. Eleanor told me everything, though I wished she hadn't done.'

'What did you think?'

'I didn't believe it at first. I couldn't. I'd been in Isaac's house. I'd been in there alone with him. What if…' She swallowed hard. 'It doesn't bear thinking about, does it? I mean, why? Why did he do it?' She looked at Olivia as if expecting her to answer.

Olivia didn't respond. She found it was best, in these situations, to say as little as possible, and allow the other person to do the talking.

'I suppose it could have been a moment of madness. I've known Isaac for… well, a long time. I never would have thought…'

'In your statement to the police you told them that you didn't want to tell tales. That usually suggests there are tales to tell.'

Lesley froze. She didn't even blink. Olivia knew this meant one of two things. Either she was searching her memory for what she could reveal, or she was trying to conjure up a lie to cover what she really knew.

'There are no tales to tell. Isaac… well, he was just a regular family man.'

'Was there anyone else after his wife died?'

'No,' she answered quickly.

'Nobody casual?'

'No.'

'Did you ever see visitors come to the house?'

She shook her head.

'Did Isaac ever ask you to babysit while he was going out with someone, a date, or a friend?'

'No.'

'Do you know if he asked anyone else to babysit Eleanor?'

'No. He always asked me if he needed me. It was usually for

work purposes. You know he was a salesman? Sometimes he had to go over to the Lake District or there was one time he had to go up into Scotland. He said he didn't know if he was going to be late back with traffic and everything so would I mind Eleanor when she came home from school. That was generally all, really.'

'Right,' Olivia said. She looked down at her notes. She hadn't written anything that would help her. 'Did you attend the trial?'

'I did. Not every day. I couldn't stomach some of the things they were talking about. I went for the sentencing to support Eleanor.'

'Have you been to see Isaac in prison?'

'No. Well, you don't, do you?' she said, almost embarrassed at turning her back on him.

'I suppose not. Lesley, is there anything you can tell me about Isaac, anything that stands out as odd or strange over the past thirty years he's been living next door, anything that stands out to you?'

'Like what?'

'I don't know. Anything that could help us understand Isaac better.'

Lesley frowned. 'Why are you asking now? Is this to do with those things Eleanor found in her dad's bedroom?'

Olivia nodded.

'Oh my goodness, then she was right,' she said, more to herself. 'They were trophies, weren't they? Is Isaac a serial killer?'

'The police are wondering whether Isaac might be responsible for more crimes. They've brought me in to help them understand the psychology behind a killer,' Olivia said noncommittally.

'How many…' She paused, swallowed hard, and composed herself. 'How many do you think he…?' she asked, her hand rising to her chest and fiddling with a cross on a chain around her neck.

'We don't know that either.'

'Good grief. It goes from bad to worse. I don't know what to believe about anyone anymore.' Lesley stood up and went over to the window, looking out into her back garden. 'The press is going to be all over this again, aren't they? They're going to be knocking on my door night and day. Poor Eleanor.'

Lesley turned her back on the window. A tear escaped her right eye and ran down her face.

'You liked Isaac, didn't you?' Olivia asked.

She nodded. 'He was a good man. He'd do anything for anyone. He was so… good-natured.' She shook her head. 'I can't believe any of this.'

'Are you married?'

'What? No,' she answered quickly.

'Did anything happen between you and Isaac?'

'No,' she said, almost wistfully.

'But you wanted it to.'

Lesley snapped out of whatever thought was at the front of her mind and turned to Olivia. 'Of course not. Isaac was a neighbour and a friend. That's all. If there… No. He loved his wife. The memory of her, you know?' She was clearly floundering. Her cheeks had blushed. She did have feelings for Isaac – perhaps not now, but she had done in the past. 'Look, I have work to do. You've taken up enough of my time.'

'Of course,' Olivia said. She closed her notebook and placed it back in her bag. 'If you think of anything…'

'I have DI Sutton's number,' she interrupted.

As she left the house, Olivia couldn't help thinking that Lesley Quinn had been holding a candle for Isaac over the years. She'd helped with his daughter when his wife died and been a close friend ever since. Had she been hoping for a romance to develop? Olivia thought so. However, it hadn't happened. Why not? Maybe Isaac kept her at arm's length, so his murderous ways weren't discovered. Yet, if Lesley loved Isaac, was she keeping tabs on him from afar? Was she watching his house, wondering if he was bringing a girlfriend back with him one night? If so, what had she seen that she hadn't told the police, or Olivia, about?

Chapter Twenty-Six

Olivia stood on the pavement at the bottom of Isaac's driveway. She was scrolling through Google, looking for a local taxi firm to pick her up.

'Want to know about the murder house?'

She looked up to see where the voice was coming from. At the house directly opposite Isaac's, a slim man stood on the front doorstep. He beckoned her over.

Olivia looked down as she crossed the road, trying to hide her smile. She loved a nosey neighbour, though not when they lived in the same street as her.

Hal Garfield stood back and allowed Olivia to enter his home. He greeted her with a broad smile, introduced himself and closed the door firmly behind her. The hallway was spacious and bright, neat, tidy, and there was a strong aroma of an air freshener that caught at the back of Olivia's throat. He showed her into the living room.

'Can I get you a cup of tea?' Hal asked from the doorway.

'That would be lovely, thank you.'

'Bag or leaves?'

'Oh. Whichever's easier for you.'

'Right. Won't be a mo.'

Olivia glanced around the room. It was an assault on the

senses. Nothing matched. The carpet contained many random patterns and colours. The curtains were in a dark green velour fabric, and it was difficult to tell what colour the walls were as every available space was filled with framed prints and bookshelves. She placed her bag on the sofa and went over to the shelves to look at the spines of the well-thumbed paperbacks. They were mostly true crime books and crime fiction novels. There was even a copy of *The Riverside Killer* by Sebastian Lister, and there were a couple of her own, too.

Hal interrupted her thoughts by entering the room carrying a tray with two cups and saucers and a matching teapot. He placed it down gently on the coffee table and began to pour. While he did so, Olivia opened her bag and turned on the digital recorder she always kept in there. Hal seemed eager to speak to her. Maybe he had juicy information to impart.

'I know who you are,' Hal said with a sly grin.

'Do you?'

'You're Dr Olivia Winter, aren't you?'

'I am.'

'I thought I recognised you. I've got a couple of your books,' he said, nodding to the shelves.

'So I see.'

'You've got an amazing analytical mind.'

'Thank you.'

'How are you doing now? You were stabbed last year, weren't you?'

'I was. I'm doing very well, now, thank you,' she said, taking the cup and saucer from him.

'Help yourself to milk and sugar,' Hal said, taking his own cup and sitting down on the armchair opposite her. His eyes lingered on her as if he was studying her. 'They've been advertising that drama about your dad a lot on telly recently. I'm in two minds whether to watch it myself,' he said. 'I love a true crime but I'm not sure about a dramatisation. You never know how much creative licence they've taken. Have you been shown an advanced screening?'

'Erm, no. I haven't.'

'I just wondered how true to life it really was.'

'Mr Garfield,' Olivia began.

'Hal, please. Mr Garfield always reminds me of that cartoon cat,' he laughed.

'Hal. Did you know Isaac well?'

'I like to think so. He was a good bloke. He worked hard. He'd do anything for anyone if you asked him. We were on the same pub quiz team. Some of the answers he seemed to just pull out of nowhere, you wouldn't believe it. Sport was his specialist subject.' He took a lingering sip of his tea. 'You see, I'm not mechanically minded, and I've got a clapped-out Punto that I'm reluctant to trade in. Whenever I had problems, Isaac would come over and take a look at it for me. In return, I'd pop over to his whenever he needed anything doing with his computer.'

'You work in computers?'

'I do. I work for a local company who provide IT support to small and medium-sized businesses throughout the North East. I've been there since they began twenty-one years ago and love it as much now as I did on my first day.'

'That's very rare.'

'I just love anything when it comes to computers. I could probably strip one with my eyes closed,' he laughed.

'And you enjoy true crime, too,' Olivia said, eyeing up the shelves.

'Oh. I do. I mean, I know enjoy isn't the right word. It's more of a fascination really. I can never get my head around how and why someone would do some of the things they do, but I can't stop reading about it. I watch all those true crime documentaries on Netflix. I listen to all the podcasts, too. Me and a friend started one about true crime, but we didn't get many listeners, so we packed it in.'

Olivia suddenly felt uncomfortable and began to wish Linus was with her. There was a fine line between someone with a healthy interest in something and an obsessive fanatic. Hal was hovering very close to crossing that line.

'How did you feel when you heard about what Isaac had done?'

'Initially I was shocked, obviously. You don't expect to find a killer living bang opposite you, do you? The more I thought about it, though, the more I could understand it. Isaac, bless him, he was married, lost his wife, struggled bringing Eleanor up on his own, was doing a job he didn't exactly love. He's a prime example of someone snapping and railing against the norm, isn't he?'

Olivia bent forward to pick up her mug to hide rolling her eyes. She wasn't a fan of armchair psychologists.

'The police are looking into whether Isaac may have committed more than one murder.'

'Of course he did.'

Olivia raised an eyebrow.

Hal leaned forward on his chair and lowered his voice, as if he was afraid of being overheard. 'I spoke to Eleanor. She told me what he'd done to that young man in the back of his car. He'd chopped him up into twelve pieces. Well, that's not a first murder, is it? You don't wake up one morning, decide to become a killer, and be an expert in dismembering a body. I didn't say anything to Eleanor, I could see she was struggling, but I said it to Lesley opposite. I said, there'll be more victims out there. I'd put my house on it.'

'You said Isaac was on your pub quiz team. Did you see him a lot socially?' Olivia asked, wanting to get Hal away from whatever he'd picked up on *Unsolved Mysteries*.

'On and off,' Hal said, thinking as he spoke. 'I went camping with him once. Not my cup of tea. Half an hour to warm up a tin of beans. And I couldn't get comfortable in a sleeping bag.'

'You went camping with him?'

'Just the once.'

'Did you take his photograph?' she asked, remembering the framed picture on display in Isaac's living room.

'No. Why would I do that?'

'Just wondering.'

'The house,' Hal began. 'Is that where he killed his victim, or victims, I suppose?'

'The police believe so, yes.'

Hal stood up and went over to the bay window. He peered through the slats in the wooden venetian blind. 'It's a shame. It's a lovely house.'

'Did you go in there much?'

'Like I said, I popped round whenever he needed help with his computer. I sometimes stayed for a cup of tea and we'd have a chat.'

'What did you chat about?'

'Anything and everything really.'

'I've been speaking to his neighbour, Lesley Quinn. She said Isaac had never had a partner during the thirty years he's been living there. Did he ever confide in you about seeing someone?'

Hal went back to his armchair and sat down. 'He was seeing someone.'

'Really?'

'Someone from work. A woman in the office. It was only casual. He said he'd been on his own too long to settle down again.'

'Did he tell you her name?'

He thought for a moment. 'No. I don't think he did. If he did, I can't remember it.'

'Lesley, across the road, didn't mention this.'

'No. You see, Lesley was a bit keen on him. I think she was hoping they'd end up together.'

'Did she tell you this?'

'She didn't have to. It was written all over her face every time she saw him.'

'Was Isaac aware of Lesley's feelings?'

'He guessed as much. She'd drop everything for him if he wanted her, especially when Eleanor was young. He just saw her as a neighbour and a friend.'

'How did you first find out about Isaac being a killer?'

'When the police came screaming up in their cars the night he was arrested. I went over and spoke to Lesley. Neither of us could believe it. I mean, I know everyone says things like that when someone is arrested for something huge, but Isaac a killer? Definitely not.'

'Have you changed your mind now that's he's been found guilty?'

Hal let out a heavy sigh. 'I've had to change my mind. The jury found him guilty. What else can I think?'

'Have you been to see him in prison?'

'I haven't. Not yet. I will do, though. I thought I'd leave it for a while, let him settle in. Have you spoken to Eleanor?'

'Yes.'

'Did she mention what she was planning on doing with the house?'

'No.'

'Oh. That's a shame. As I've said, it's a lovely house,' he said, going back over to the window and looking at it again through the slats of the blind.

'Hal, is there anything you could tell me that might help the police with their investigations?'

'Not off the top of my head,' he said without thinking. 'Ooh, while you're here, you wouldn't sign your books for me, would you? I promise not to put them on eBay.'

'Of course,' Olivia said with a painted-on smile.

Hal took the battered paperbacks from the shelf and handed them to her. She took a pen from her bag and scribbled on the inside page.

'I suppose it would be inappropriate to ask you to sign *The Riverside Killer*, wouldn't it?'

'It would. Yes,' she said, firmly.

'Just thought I'd ask. Could we have a selfie?'

Olivia decided it was time for her to leave.

Chapter Twenty-Seven

DC Ryan Sweetland was composing an email when his mobile rang. He looked at the screen, didn't recognise the number, but swiped to answer anyway.

'DC Sweetland,' he said.

'Hello. It's Melanie Knox. I'm so so sorry,' she began.

Sweetland had tried, and failed, on four occasions to begin a Zoom call with Melanie, one of Isaac's more regular customers, over in Carlisle.

'We've had some strong winds out here over the past couple of days and it's thrown my internet right out. I cannot apologise enough,' she said in a loud voice with a hint of an Irish accent.

'That's fine. It can't be helped.'

'Do you want to conduct the interview over the phone?'

'Sure.'

'And you wanted to talk to me about Isaac McFadden, that's right, isn't it?'

'Yes, it is. I'm afraid I can't go into too many details but we're looking into Mr McFadden's background as new evidence has come to light that makes us believe he may have committed further crimes.'

'Further crimes? I'm guessing you're talking about more murders.'

'That's what we're currently trying to ascertain.'

'I see. Wow. You think you know someone.'

'We've been looking through Isaac's diaries and he had many appointments with you over the past couple of years.'

'Yes. I run a couple of private care homes out here. They're not huge. We only take in around a dozen residents at each one, but we're able to give them the attention and support they require.'

'And you used MediSupplies UK?'

'Yes. I can't say we're one of their biggest customers, but I'd highly recommend them.'

'Was it Mr McFadden you always dealt with?'

'Yes. The first time I called up, he came out to see me and I told him what I required, and he made sure we received everything on time. He seemed to know his products, and his selling skills were top-notch. I found myself buying more than I wanted,' she said, giving a hint of a laugh.

'You got on well?'

'We did. I think in a sales position you need to be personable, and Isaac certainly was that.'

Ryan could tell she was smiling as she spoke. 'I'm not sure how to put this without sounding too indiscreet,' he began. 'I've looked at your sales record with MediSupplies UK and it seems Mr McFadden took a rather keen interest in you as a customer. He took you out for a meal more than any of his other customers.'

Melanie snorted a laugh. 'There was a... connection between us. As I said, we got on well from the start. We had similar interests out of work.'

'The relationship turned personal.'

'That's the polite way of putting it, yes.'

'You liked him?'

'I did.'

'Did he ever give you cause for concern?'

'In what way?'

'Well, given that he was arrested for murder, were there any times you thought you might be in danger?'

'None whatsoever,' she said, firmly. 'He was kind, considerate, caring. He was a gentleman. I must admit, I was more than shocked when I saw the news about his arrest. Now you say you think there are more victims. He certainly hid that side of him very well. I always thought I was a good judge of character. Obviously not.'

Ryan cleared his throat. 'I hope you don't mind me asking, but, when you saw him outside work, what did you do? I mean, sorry, I don't mean…' he floundered.

Melanie laughed again. 'Let me save you the embarrassment. I won't go into details, but he did stay at my flat a few times rather than a hotel. We used to go walking and hiking together. I even joined him camping a couple of times.'

'Really?'

'Yes. I'm a big fan of the great outdoors.'

'Did Isaac ever talk about his daughter?'

'Eleanor? Yes. He spoke about her often. He was incredibly proud of her.'

Ryan sighed. He had been hoping for a juicy revelation. 'It seems as if Isaac might have been leading a whole other life. Is there anything you can tell me that you think could help us work out how and why Isaac became a killer?'

She thought for a moment. 'I'm afraid not. I know when I saw it on the news about him being arrested, and then his picture was shown, I was shocked. He was the last man I'd ever have expected to have murdered someone.'

'Right. Well, thank you very much for your time,' he said, dejected.

'You're welcome. Good luck with the investigation.'

Ryan ended the call and slumped in his chair. He had been reading up on the psychology of leading a double life and had discovered that around seventy per cent of men and fifty per cent of women have extramarital affairs – essentially, leading a different life to the one their partner and close family and friends believe they have. However, in Isaac's case, it's not an affair he was concealing, but murder, and on a grand scale.

The problem with leading a double life is that eventually it will spiral out of control and the person will take further and further risks so that the two different lives remain separate. The question troubling Ryan was: how far had Isaac gone in preventing his daughter and his work life from intruding on his crimes? Did he have a second home somewhere in a different name? Did he have other bank accounts?

There was a tap on the glass door that made him jump. He looked up to see DC Lowel standing in the doorway.

'Sheldon, afternoon briefing, you're wanted. If you can tear yourself away from thinking you're in an episode of *Mindhunter* and fancy doing some real police work,' he said, heading for the briefing room.

Ryan rolled his eyes. He turned off his tablet and dragged himself up out of his seat. As much as he enjoyed his job, the research and the understanding of the criminal mind, he was liking being a detective less and less each day.

As he left the room, he glanced back and saw Isaac's face in the centre of the murder board. He could see how alluring the thought of a double life was when you weren't enjoying your current one.

Chapter Twenty-Eight

As Olivia made her way back to her hotel in a taxi she thought long and hard about how her first full day of working in Newcastle had gone. She couldn't give herself an answer. She'd received conflicting statements from the people she'd spoken to. Eleanor had said her father wasn't interested in a relationship, yet Lesley, next door, clearly had feelings for him. Had she made them known to Isaac? If so, how had he reacted? Then, nosey neighbour Hal said that Isaac had confided in him that he'd been seeing someone. Why had Isaac felt the need to change character depending on who he was talking to? The only way she was going to find out was by visiting Isaac McFadden and speaking to him face to face. Only then would she know just what kind of a man she was dealing with. Right now, she needed a drink.

Olivia went to the hotel bar and ordered a vodka. Neat. No ice.

It was dark outside, yet it was still only early evening. There was nobody else in the bar apart from the staff. She lifted herself onto one of the stools and drank the vodka back in one mouthful.

'Heavy day?' the barman asked her.

'You could say that.'

'Another?'

'Please.'

'Are you eating in the hotel tonight?'
'I am, yes.'
'Do you want me to set up a tab?'
'Put everything on room 407.'

He poured her another drink, a large one this time, and walked away, leaving her to her dark thoughts.

All of Olivia's thoughts were dark. She spent her days trying to understand serial killers. And when she wasn't at work, she was at home with her own darkness deep within her, waiting for a quiet moment when it would snatch at her attention.

'*Run.*'

That voice. Such a short word, but there was so much power behind it.

Olivia had come home from visiting a friend on Tuesday the 21st of December 1999. The house was quiet. She wondered where everyone was. She looked in the living room and the kitchen. There was nobody there. She walked up the stairs, slowly, quietly, wondering if her mum or her sister were planning an early Christmas surprise for her. She looked in her own room. Empty. She looked in her sister Claire's room. Empty. She pushed open the door of her mum and dad's bedroom and froze. What she saw defied belief. It wasn't real. It couldn't be.

On the bed, her mother lay, half propped up by the headboard. Her sister was in her lap. Red. There was red everywhere. Claire was dead. Her mother was struggling to stay alive. Her breathing was short and erratic. Out of the corner of her eye, Olivia detected movement in the en suite.

'Run,' her mother said. '*Olivia! Run!*'

She said it again now inside her head. Olivia had run that night. She'd run for her life, but her father still caught up with her. He should have killed her. He had plenty of time before the police arrived. Why hadn't he killed her?

'Run.'

That voice wasn't inside Olivia's head.

She blinked hard.

'Olivia. Run!'

She looked around her. There was nobody there.

'I love you, Livvy.'

Only one person called her Livvy. Where the hell was that voice coming from?

She turned back, looked up at the television above the bar. It was the trailer for the drama about her father, about her life. The actor playing her father was following a woman down a lonely, darkened street. She looked back over her shoulder, fear etched on her face. Her father grabbed her from behind, put his hand over her mouth and dragged her into nearby woodland. A piercing scream rang out and Olivia's blood ran cold.

'The true story of one of Britain's most chilling serial killers, Richard Button,' the voiceover said in a harsh, tense voice, *'The Riverside Killer*, begins Monday at nine on ITV and ITVX.'

Olivia staggered off the stool. It toppled to the floor. She could barely stand up.

'Someone can't handle their drink,' she heard the barman say to a colleague as she trundled out of the bar towards the lifts.

Olivia had had panic attacks before, many times, but she had always managed to hide them, or she'd been in her own home alone, or with Sebastian, who had been able to cover for her. Right now, she was alone, in a strange city, in a hotel she didn't know the layout of, and she felt like she was dying. She fell into an oversized potted palm, picked herself up and slammed herself against the lift doors. She fumbled along the wall and stabbed at where she thought the buttons were.

Olivia had no idea how she'd managed to get into her hotel room. One minute everything was a blur as she stumbled into the lift, the next she was lying back on her bed, staring up at the ceiling tiles and concentrating on her breathing. She was cold. She felt sick. She wanted to cry, but the tears wouldn't come this time. She climbed off the bed, stumbled to the window and pulled back the curtains. She opened the window and leaned out, taking in huge lungfuls of freezing cold air. She took in the sounds and smells of a strange city. Traffic, conversations, a train pulling into the nearby station, laughter, the rancid odour of fumes mixed with whatever was emanating from the Tyne. Olivia shivered and fell back into her room, pulling the window closed.

Sitting at the desk, she blew out a heavy sigh and looked down at her mess of paperwork. The forensic psychologist within was eager to find out everything she could about Isaac McFadden, but right now, she had no interest in him whatsoever. She just wanted to get the first train back to London and to the relative safety of her home in Modbury Gardens.

Her eyes fell on the photograph of her and Ethan, and she felt a warmth inside her. He was a good man. After Sebastian, he was the best man she knew. He was kind and honest and gentle and… he was far too good for her. When he came back from the Amazon, she knew he'd come straight to see her, tell her he loved her again, and would expect a response. How could she tell him how she felt? She had no idea of her feelings. Like Eleanor had said earlier, she was numb. She couldn't love Ethan. She wasn't capable. Yet, right now, she wanted Ethan more than ever. If they were both in London she could have called him, asked him to come over on his bike, dressed head to foot in leather, asked him to fuck her hard and rough, to hurt her, to bite her, to pound her into oblivion. How could a relationship grow based on that? She tucked Ethan's photo beneath a notebook. Out of sight, out of mind.

Chapter Twenty-Nine

Thursday 30th January 2025

Olivia sat at the window of her hotel room, curtains wide open, gazing out at a pitch-black Newcastle. It was the early hours of Thursday morning and freezing cold. She had endured a fitful sleep of only a couple of hours, and woken, trapped in a cocoon of duvet wrapped around her. She'd wrestled herself free and went over to the window, duvet over her shoulders, and looked out at the sprawling city. It was calming to watch over a metropolis in slumber. In the hours of daylight, it was a cacophony of noise. In the early hours of the morning, it was practically a ghost town.

There were very few people about at this time – taxi drivers, shift workers, emergency service crew members, insomniac dog walkers, and those with more nefarious motives. Olivia blinked hard. She couldn't even enjoy the hours of darkness, when everything was stripped back to the basics of empty roads and pavements. Everyone had to have an unwholesome reason for being out at this time. Why couldn't the man across the road in the oversized coat and beanie hat simply be heading for the train station to go to work? Why did Olivia look at him and assume he was a rapist looking for his next victim stumbling, drunkenly, out of a nightclub? A young man stepped up to a cash machine, looked around him and inserted his card. Why did Olivia think it wasn't his card, that he'd stolen it, forced his victim to reveal their PIN before stabbing them, and was now planning to empty their account?

That was how her mind worked. It was always switched on and seeking out alternative motives for people's actions. She always thought the worst of people, never the best. It took a long time before she trusted anyone new. It had taken years for her to feel comfortable in Sebastian's company, to share her innermost thoughts and feelings knowing he wouldn't try to get them published somewhere. Everyone else she kept at arm's length. If they didn't have the bullets to fire, they couldn't shoot her.

Following a long and scaldingly hot shower, Olivia dressed and headed for the police station, stopping off at a Costa en route to get drinks and snacks for Linus and Ryan.

She entered the small room to find Ryan on his own. He was wearing earbuds and looking seriously at his laptop. Olivia hesitated in the doorway.

'It's okay, you can come in. I've just had a Zoom call. It's ended now,' he said, closing the laptop.

'I've brought drinks. Linus not in yet?'

'Yes. He's in with DCI Wise and she can be a bit of a talker so he might be a while,' he said with a smile. 'I need to talk to you about what I discovered yesterday about Isaac,' he said, taking the coffee proffered by Olivia and inhaling the aroma. 'I spoke to three of his customers and they all said conflicting things about him. I've printed off the transcripts of the conversations.' He handed her the sheets.

Olivia removed her coat and sat down.

'I've had the same response chatting to Eleanor and his neighbours. Now, Lesley was clearly attracted to Isaac. According to Hal, he knew about her feelings yet did nothing. Maybe he didn't find her attractive, but Eleanor said he wasn't interested in a relationship with anyone, yet Hal said he was seeing someone at his office.'

'I'll give the office a call, ask if they knew who it was,' Ryan said, making a note.

'Who's this Julie?' Olivia asked, reading Ryan's interview transcripts.

'The only one I've been able to find is Julie Packard. She lives at number 8. A few doors down from Isaac. I've made a note to give her a call later. Why would someone be completely different around all these people? Surely, even the most accomplished liar would trip themselves up at some point.'

'Some people lie if they have low self-esteem. They want to impress people in order to be accepted. I don't think Isaac needed to worry about that. Lying gives a person control over a situation as they're manipulating it. On one level, it's a defence mechanism to stop someone from getting close and seeing their true self and vulnerability. In Isaac's case, he's creating a different character of himself so that the real Isaac McFadden isn't revealed.'

'But these people talk to each other. Surely Lesley and Hal and Julie chat about their neighbours. It's what you do.'

'He hasn't said anything to them that's all that different. It's his customers who he's told dissimilar stories to, and they're unlikely to ever meet up.'

'He really did manipulate everyone around him, didn't he?'

'It would appear so.'

'I feel sorry for his daughter,' Ryan said. 'Oh, I nearly forgot, I thought you might like to see these.' He brought up a box from beneath the table. 'It's the trophies found hidden in Isaac's house.'

Olivia took the cardboard box from him, pulled back the flaps and lifted out the dark oak box first. 'Is this the box found in Isaac's wardrobe?'

'Yes.'

'You don't happen to know where, or when, he bought it, do you?'

'No,' Ryan said. 'Eleanor said she'd never seen it before.'

All the items had been tested for prints and DNA. Only Eleanor and Lesley's prints were discovered on a few items, and they admitted to handling them when going through the box. There was a partial thumbprint belonging to Isaac found on a lens of the pair of glasses.

Olivia picked up the small, creased photograph of the young boy and girl. She studied it. 'They look like they could be brother and sister.'

'We think they might be twins,' Ryan said. 'We've had that photograph in every national newspaper, on the local news, and it's on our website. Nobody has come forward to say they recognise it.'

'They may not be English,' she said as she brought the photograph closer and squinted at it. 'When would you say this was taken – late 90s, early 2000s?'

'I'm not sure,' Ryan said.

'The furniture in the background looks dated but the clothing of the kids isn't. They're either in the house of an elderly relative or… I don't know, maybe Eastern European, Russian, perhaps.'

'It might belong to the guy whose passport is in there,' Ryan said. 'I can't pronounce his surname.'

'No,' Olivia said, firmly. 'I think each item refers to a different victim. The passport and the photograph are separate.' She placed the picture, carefully, back in the box, and lifted out the chain with the St Christopher medal. 'The patron saint of travellers,' she said to herself. 'The young lad from Poland, tell me about him.'

'We don't know much about him. He lived with his grandmother in a village just outside Gdansk. He wanted to travel so he saved up, bought a plane ticket and said he was off to England,' Ryan said. 'He told a friend that he'd work his way back home via Portugal then up through Spain, France, Belgium, Netherlands and Germany. He had it all planned out.'

'And the stamp on the passport tells us he arrived in England on December the sixteenth 2023,' Olivia said, looking at the passport. She flicked to the back and studied the photograph of a young Piotr. He was a handsome young man with floppy blond hair and the vaguest hint of a smile on his thin lips. 'So, where has he gone?'

Ryan didn't say anything.

'Is this jewellery worth anything?' Olivia asked, picking up the black Zirconia ceramic ring.

'No. It's all costume stuff. The diamond stud isn't real either, in case you were wondering,' Ryan said.

'I hate to say this, but I think we're going to struggle to identify these victims at all.'

'What makes you say that?'

'Sean Bridger was estranged from his family. Piotr Czajkowski left home to go travelling. Nobody has come forward to claim the photograph of the two kids. I think these are all people who have lost their way. Whether they've run away to escape their lives or been abandoned, or their families have turfed them out, they're all lost. Isaac found them. He saw something in them that he could take advantage of. That's why you don't know that there are twelve victims out there – because nobody is looking for them.' Olivia's voice had taken on a dark, sad, tone.

'There must be something we can do,' Ryan said.

'Find their bodies.'

'How? Where do we even look?'

'Everywhere.'

There was a bang on the glass, making them both jump. They turned and saw DC Lowel walking past.

'Bazinga!' he called out before putting his fingers to his head in the shape of an L. L for loser.

Ryan looked down as if concentrating on his work.

'Ryan, do you enjoy being a detective?' Olivia asked. She'd noticed the way his face had dropped.

He looked up at her. 'I'm guessing you can tell whether a person is lying or not.'

'Most of the time,' she said, a smile in her eyes.

'So, if I tell you that I love being a detective, what will you say?'

'I'll say that the smoke alarm will go off soon because your pants are on fire.'

He gave her a brief smile and returned to his laptop.

Olivia took out her phone and composed a text message to Sebastian: 'Do you think we have enough work on to take on another member of staff, particularly one with an IQ of 165?'

Chapter Thirty

By lunchtime, Olivia was developing a headache. She and Ryan had been going through missing persons reports as well as studying the trophies and trying to crack Isaac's code. Linus had come in and asked her to accompany him to DCI Wise's office so she could be introduced to his superior and fill her in on what they were working on. The ten-minute chat was succinct, and Diane Wise had offered Olivia anything and everything to help with the investigation, quickly followed by telling her there was no extra money available to assign more officers to the case. It was a conversation of contradictions.

Olivia decided not to take Linus's offer of a bite to eat in town. She wanted to be alone with her thoughts for a while, try to make sense of what she had learned yesterday from Eleanor, Lesley and Hal, and put her own anxieties in a locked box in the deep recesses of her mind. It was true that serial murderers were great manipulators. Isaac had been able to manipulate his own daughter into thinking her father was the best. He'd blindsided Lesley next door, as well as neighbour Hal and all of his work colleagues, into believing he was a hard-working family man. The best person out of all of these to talk to again was Eleanor. She was the closest to Isaac. He would have had to work hard in order to convince his daughter he was who he wanted her to believe he was. Just what was hiding in Eleanor's subconscious about her father that even she didn't know about?

Olivia ran her fingers through her hair, gripping it hard and pulling at it, causing her pain. She needed to try and crack this code. Maybe, hopefully, it would reveal the whereabouts of the victims, which, in turn, could reveal more about the killer, and the second possible killer.

She walked to the Quayside with her satchel across her shoulder and decided to explore Newcastle on foot. If she was going to call this city home for the foreseeable future, she might as well know more about where she was living.

She had heard a great deal about the famous Baltic Centre for Contemporary Art, which she planned to visit, and she would like to see the Angel of the North close up. There was a gorgeous building on the opposite side of the river which Olivia had to look up. It was the Glasshouse International Centre for Music, also known as the Sage. She'd have a look on their website back at the hotel, find out what attractions they had in the coming days and weeks and see if anything took her fancy.

As she strolled along the Quayside, she felt her body relaxing as she took in the calming river views and the bars and pubs, comfortably lit and oozing with welcoming atmosphere. As much as Olivia wanted to go into one or two of them and drown her sorrows in alcohol, she knew it was a slippery slope. She'd treat herself to a gin and tonic back at the hotel.

The further she walked, the fewer people she saw. She walked under a beautifully designed iron bridge, crossed over the road and continued to follow the river. She had no idea where she was going, but with a smartphone you were never really lost anymore. She could always turn back when she wanted to.

A cold wind was blowing. Olivia raised the collar of her coat and looked at her watch. She'd been walking for well over an hour and had missed lunch. Her stomach grumbled, reminding her she needed fuel if she was going to concentrate on her task of cracking Isaac's code. She looked around her and had no idea where she was. She turned back and headed for her car. She had passed a few pubs and restaurants on her walk; she'd pop in, have a sandwich and a glass of wine, something to lubricate the brain cells.

Olivia found a bistro that looked homely and not too busy. While waiting for her chicken risotto to be prepared, she sipped a delicious Sauvignon and took out her laptop. She looked over at the next table where an elderly couple were dining and smiled at the woman. Olivia had no idea why people found it strange to eat out alone. She did it all the time. She would never taste great food if she didn't. She had chosen to live a life alone and keep people at arm's length. Occasionally she went for a meal with Sebastian, and she and Ethan had gone out a couple of times, though it was always a prelude to amazing sex.

She shook her head. She had lost concentration. Another reason to kick the Ethan issue into touch. She needed to focus, and a man would hinder that.

Opening up a file, making sure she didn't have any postmortem photos on show in case the people behind glanced over her shoulder while they were tucking into their prosciutto, she selected the code she was adding her own notes to and hoped reading it for the three thousandth time would cause something to click into place.

12	M6	DATE EATEN EDGE (POPPY)	HELPFUL INDEED CRESCENT (HEAT)	BROWN BLUE BLUE BLACK 12/5/10/20	£
12th Victim	March or May	Poppy = drugs?	?	Description of Sean Bridger? Brown eyes. Blue top. Blue jeans. Black shoes. Cut into 12 pieces. 5ft 10. Aged 20.	?

It didn't. It was still as confusing as ever. She looked at the final column. Why a pound sign? What did it mean? Had Isaac paid Sean Bridger? Sean had sold himself to men for sex in order to buy drugs; is that what it referred to? The symbol in the entry above was an open parenthesis; what could that possibly refer to?

She looked at the code as a whole again. Every time she read it, she seemed to have more questions about it. Yes, it was Isaac's handwriting, Eleanor had confirmed that, but why write it in the first place? Why did he need to keep a chart of his victims? It was narcissistic to keep a record so he could read it and marvel at his accomplishments, but from what she had heard about Isaac, he was anything but narcissistic. Nothing about the psychology of this killer fitted with what Olivia was discovering about Isaac.

She sighed and looked down at her laptop keyboard. The letter 'S' had faded. The letter 'A' had disappeared completely. She wondered what the most common letter in the English alphabet was. She wondered how long she had had this laptop for and if it was time for an upgrade. It did seem to be running slower lately and the number '3' button stuck when she pressed it.

Her eyes widened in realisation. 'Oh my God,' she said to herself. She looked back at the code on the screen, down at the keyboard, back to the code. 'The sick bastard.' The couple opposite looked up at her. She apologised and scrambled around in her bag for her mobile. She searched for Linus's number and hit call.

'Olivia, what can I do for you? Have you got lost?' he asked, breezily.

'Are you anywhere near a computer?'

'I'm always near a computer. What do you need?'

'Look at the code…' The waiter arrived at her table with her chicken risotto. 'Oh, sorry, erm, let me just move this,' she said, holding the phone in the crook of her neck and trying to find somewhere for her laptop. 'Thank you. Sorry, again. Are you still there?' she asked Linus.

'Yes. Where are you?' he asked.

'I'm in a restaurant.'

'Do you ever just take a break for food? Do you always have to be working?'

'Yes, I do. Have you got the code in front of you?'

'Yes.'

'Right. The final column. The one with the symbols.'

'Go on.'

'It's been staring at us all this time. The symbols are all on the top row of numbers on a standard computer keyboard.'

'Oh yes. So they are.'

'Don't you see what this means? He's marking his victims out of ten.'

'He's… you think?'

'Sean Bridger. The last victim. He put a pound sign in the last column. The pound sign is the number three on a keyboard. He's marked him three out of ten. The entry above that has an open parenthesis sign, that's the number nine. Nine out of ten.'

*	8
&	7
*	8
(	9
%	5
%	5
&	7
(	9
*	8
&	7
(	9
£	3

'Jesus Christ. That's beyond sick.'

'Tell me about it. Why would you give that a rating? I mean, what are you basing it on? If the victims resisted or how loudly they screamed?' Olivia caught the eye of the elderly couple at the next table again. She mouthed an apology and lowered her voice. 'Sean Bridger scored the lowest. Only three. Why? Did he mean nothing to him or was it what Sean represented, the fact he was homeless and selling himself for drug money? Why would Sean only score a three?'

'If you're expecting an answer you'll have a long wait.'

'You need to get me an appointment to see Isaac McFadden as soon as possible.'

'I've been on to the prison. Will Saturday morning do you?'

'Perfect.'

She ended the call, apologised once again to the couple opposite and began to tuck into her cooling risotto. It tasted good, but her appetite had gone. She could only manage a couple of forkfuls before she realised she didn't have time for eating. Now she had cracked another column in the code, she needed to give it more attention. She raised her arm and asked for the bill.

She quickly left, leaving a hefty tip for the waiter. She headed for the hotel. It was going to be a very long night.

Chapter Thirty-One

What kind of a man would mark his killings out of ten? On what scale was he judging Sean Bridger to be a three and the victim before him a nine? Talking to Eleanor, Olivia had assumed Isaac McFadden to be a perfect father, a hard worker who wanted to look after his child following the tragic early death of his wife and her mother. If Olivia hadn't seen Isaac's police interviews with her own eyes and read the transcripts, she would have thought the killer and the father were two completely different people. A man who can withstand police interrogations and answer 'No comment' to every question for hours on end has to be cool, calm and collected. Isaac wasn't just cool, he was ice-cold, and this rating system proved that. Add into the mix the contrasting information gleamed from Lesley Quinn and Hal Garfield and it would seem that Isaac McFadden wore many hats depending on who he was with.

Olivia locked the door to her hotel room behind her and closed the curtains. She wanted to try and understand more of this code, and she couldn't allow any distractions. Olivia didn't care if she was awake all night; she was seeing Isaac face to face in two days. She needed to have the upper hand in their conversation as The Iceman would give her nothing.

She took a bottle of water from the minibar, opened it and took a lengthy swig. It was cold and refreshing and she hoped it would wake up her brain, focus her mind on the task at hand. She brought up the code on her laptop and concentrated on the second column. She was ninety-nine per cent sure the letters referred to the months of the year but had no idea what the numbers meant.

A1	April, August
O1	October
F1	February
J5	January, June, July
N2	November
J6	January, June, July
M4	March, May
M5	March, May
A5	April, August
O3	October
J9	January, June, July
M6	March

M6 could refer to May, but as Sean was found in the back of Isaac's car on the first of March, Olivia guessed M stood for March. But why six? It wasn't the sixth month; it was the third. Sean wasn't killed on the sixth, it was the first. He wasn't the sixth victim either, he was the twelfth. If Sean Bridger's entry referred to March, then the M5 could refer to May, but that didn't make sense on a chronological basis as May comes after March in the calendar. Unless Sean's March was the following March.

'Oh my God, I've got it!' Olivia exclaimed. She remained silent for a long moment while she arranged her thoughts. The more she thought about it, the more sense it made.

'M6 refers to March. M5 is the M month before, making it May, and the M4 refers to the previous March before Sean's death in his March. The numbers refer to how many months of the same letter have passed since the first killing. I've got you, you sneaky bastard.'

A1	First A month	April 2021
O1	First O month	October 2021
F1	First F month	February 2022
J5	Fifth J month	July 2022
N2	Second N month	November 2022
J6	Sixth J month	January 2023
M4	Fourth M month	March 2023
M5	Fifth M month	May 2023
A6	Sixth A month	August 2023
O3	Third O month	October 2023
J9	Ninth J month	January 2024
M6	Sixth M month	March 2024

That had to be it. Olivia was sure. And she knew how much the first of each month meant to Isaac. He was born on the first of the month. He was married on the first of the month. His wife died on the first of the month. Sean Bridger was killed on the first of the month. It was just possible that all of these victims were killed on the first of the month in their corresponding years. If that was the case, it drastically narrowed down the field of missing persons and could lead to them discovering more about the code and potentially tracking down their bodies.

She rang Linus. It took him a while to answer.

'Am I interrupting anything?' she asked as he sounded groggy.

'Yes. My sleep. Do you have any idea what time it is?'

She didn't have a clue. She looked at her phone. How could it be almost one o'clock in the morning already?

'Ah. I'm sorry, Linus. I didn't realise. Do you want me to call back in the morning?'

'I'm awake now. What have you got?' he asked, stifling a yawn.

Olivia filled him in on cracking another column and talked him through the process.

'That should make it easier to track down any victims listed as missing persons,' he said. 'I'll get Ryan on to it first thing in the morning.'

'Excellent. Again, I'm sorry for waking you.'

'That's quite all right. Now, turn your laptop off and get some sleep.'

'Will do. Goodnight, Linus.'

'Yeah. Night,' he said, his voice already sleepy.

Olivia was still buoyed. She had cracked two more of the columns in the space of a few hours. That just left columns three and four where both had four seemingly random words, one of which was bracketed. The more she studied them, the more she didn't have a clue what they could possibly mean. If she didn't mention them to Isaac on Saturday, he would realise she hadn't been able to decipher the full code and would enjoy her failure. However, if she admitted she was in the dark, he would delight in having bested her. Was it better to not mention the code at all, or maybe mention it as if it was meaningless and not giving her sleepless nights?

From the minibar she took a can of gin and tonic and drank it in two long swigs. Alcohol helped her to relax, and if she was to be any use to Linus and Ryan tomorrow, she needed to get a decent night's sleep.

While waiting for the alcohol to kick in, she went into the bathroom, changed and brushed her teeth. Then she climbed into bed, sank into the memory-foam mattress, wrapped the duvet around her and closed her eyes. She tried not to think about what dreams would haunt her tonight. Usually, the amount of alcohol she drank caused her to forget her dreams. She doubted she would forget on only one gin and tonic.

Olivia opened her eyes to the darkness. Something had woken her. As much as she was enjoying her time away from London, staying in hotels was never fun. It was like being in hospital, there was always something happening in the building that could wake her up. There was a beeping noise coming from somewhere. It wasn't from the corridor. It sounded like it was coming from inside her room.

She sat up in bed, reached across to the bedside lamp and flicked it on. She picked up her phone and looked at it. There was an alert on the alarm system she had on her house.

Given the job she did, and the people she had met around the world over the years, it was no surprise that Olivia suffered from paranoia occasionally. There was only one place she felt safe and secure: that was her home, and she intended to keep it that way. She had sensor lights at the front and back, cameras over all entrances and alarms on all windows and doors. She had an app on her phone whereby she could control everything and see live feeds from the cameras wherever she was in the world. Right now, there was a fault with the alarm on the back door.

Fully awake now, Olivia logged on to the security app and opened the camera above the back door. It was still pitch-dark so she couldn't see anything. She turned on the sensor light and the garden lit up like an alien invasion. She zoomed in on various points, but nothing seemed to be out of place and the back door didn't seem to have been tampered with in any way.

She hit reset and waited a few seconds for the app to reconfigure, but the alert still flashed up.

'Shit,' she said to herself. She looked at the time. It was just before seven o'clock. There was no way she would be able to get back to sleep now, and she knew there was one other person who would be awake at this time. She selected Sebastian's number and gave him a call.

'Good morning, Olivia,' he said, breezily. 'You're up early. How's the North East?'

'Bloody freezing. Sebastian, before you head into work this morning, can you stop by my house? I've had a security alert on the back door. I've looked on the camera, but I can't see anything out of place. Any chance you can investigate for me?'

'Sure. No problem.'

'Thanks. It's not been the same since that storm before Christmas when the power went out. I've had the company out twice and they say it's working fine.'

'I'm sure it's nothing. It's probably a fox or something come too close to the house. You know how sensitive these things can be. I'll go after I've dropped the twins off at school, that okay?'

'Yes. Fine. Thank you, Sebastian.'

'So, how's everything going? Have you cracked more of that code yet?'

'I think I may have. I'll drop you an email later.'

'Who is this new member of staff you've got lined up?'

'He's a DC here in Newcastle. He's wasted as a copper, Sebastian, and he's incredibly intelligent. He'd be invaluable when it comes to researching.'

'Let me crunch some numbers before you talk to him about it.'

'Thank you.'

'When are you paying a visit to Isaac?'

'Tomorrow.'

'Whose idea was that?'

Olivia frowned. 'Erm, what do you mean?'

'Tomorrow is the first of February. You know the first of the month is an important date to him. Hang on a minute…

Catherine, I don't know where your shoes are, sweetheart. If you put them away like I told you to whenever you took them off, we wouldn't have this conversation every morning. Sorry,' he said, coming back to the conversation. 'Where was I? Oh yes. Isaac was born on the first. It made the newspapers, so he's gone through life thinking he was special in some way.'

'I think he might have killed all his victims on the first of the month,' Olivia said.

'It would certainly seem likely.'

'Surely, he can't have manufactured his wife dying on the first. Unless he finished her off.'

'I'm guessing his daughter is too young to remember anything about it.'

'The woman who lives next door to Isaac has been there longer than he was. She helped with Eleanor after his wife died.'

'Would he have confessed to her that he killed her? He didn't kill her like he did his other victims – maybe she was in pain, so he killed her to end her suffering. Is there any way of finding out?'

'I'm not sure. I'll look into it. The thing is, there is nobody Isaac is close to who he would confide anything like that to.'

'What about this neighbour?'

'I'm not sure. I'll pay her another visit.'

'One other thing, Olivia, when you go to see Isaac tomorrow. Remember, it's a special day for him. He'll want it to be a memorable day.'

'He's in prison. Every day is like any other.'

'Yes, but tomorrow something different is happening. He's got you visiting him. Right now, you're hot property. The drama about your life is starting on Monday night. He's going to want to remember your visit for years to come. Be very careful.'

Olivia ended the call to Sebastian claiming she needed to run to the toilet. Suddenly, she was very nervous about meeting Isaac on Saturday.

Chapter Thirty-Two

Olivia didn't usually bother with breakfast. A strong coffee or two and a slice of toast or maybe a piece of fruit was what she settled for at home. However, the hotel did an excellent breakfast, and she was thoroughly enjoying her Belgian waffle with a selection of fruits and maple syrup to accompany her customary strong black filter coffee. It really set her up for the day, and by the time she entered the office at Forth Banks she was full of energy. She decided that when she returned home she would seriously rethink her morning routine.

'We think we might have identified another victim,' DC Ryan Sweetland said as Olivia entered. His face was lit up with a huge smile of achievement.

'How long have you been here?' she asked, looking at her watch.

'I'm always in early. I don't need much sleep,' he said.

Linus was at the whiteboard filling in more of Isaac's code. 'That'll catch up with you when you get older. I could have a full eight hours and still be knackered.'

'It takes me about three nights to get eight hours,' Olivia said, taking off her coat and sitting down.

'Are you a member of Insomniacs Anonymous, too?' Linus asked her.

'Who do you think came up with the name of the club?' She winked.

Ryan cleared his throat. Looking at him, head down over his tablet, it was obvious he struggled with small talk and was more confident when the conversation pertained to work matters.

'Sorry, Ryan. Go on,' Olivia prompted.

'Thanks. Now, from what we know about the code so far, I've worked out each of the months backwards going from Sean Bridger being killed in March 2024. I also wondered if, as Isaac seems to have a thing about the first day of the month, he killed his victims on the first of each month.'

Olivia decided not to interrupt and tell him she and Sebastian had already come up with that.

He continued, 'If that's the case, entry six on the code has J6 in the second column. I've worked this out to be January 2023. The first of January is also New Year's Day. I thought any missing person report, or someone being murdered on that day would have more prominence in the news.'

'Hang on,' Olivia said, as she opened her laptop and brought up the code on screen.

6	J6	RELY OCTAGON (COLD) KEY	(CHICKEN) ZOOMING OLD GHOST	YELLOW YELLOW WHITE BLACK 10/6/?	%

'If you look at the fourth column, 'yellow, yellow, white, black' gives us someone with blond hair, a yellow top, white trousers and black shoes. Using the rest of the theory we can guess he was six foot, age unknown and –' Ryan swallowed hard '– he was cut into ten pieces. So, I put "missing person on New Year's Day 2023" into Google and this is what we've got.' He handed Olivia a printout.

She took it from him and looked down. She saw the smiling face of a young man who looked no older than a teenager. He had blond hair, dazzling blue eyes and such an infectious smile she found she was smiling back at him.

'Shane Waterhouse from Thornhill in Sunderland. He was reported missing by his mother on New Year's Day 2023,' Ryan said. 'He'd come to Newcastle the day before to stay with a cousin. They were going out to Powerhouse in Newcastle to celebrate New Year.'

'And what happened?' Olivia asked.

'They went out at ten o'clock. The place was packed. Shane and his cousin saw the New Year in together and they got separated in the crowd. He didn't see him after that.'

'So, what happened with this cousin? Did he just go home when he'd had enough?'

'He met someone and went back to their flat,' Ryan said, uncomfortably.

From a file, Linus took out a photograph. 'This was taken at around ten o'clock on December the thirty-first 2022.' He handed it to Olivia. It showed two young men grinning for the camera. 'Shane Waterhouse, as you can see, was wearing a yellow long-sleeved polo shirt, white jeans and black boots. If you look closely, you can see he also has a Casio watch on his right wrist. He was six foot and twenty years old. He matches the description perfectly.'

'Okay,' Olivia said.

'You don't look too pleased,' Linus remarked.

'I had all the victims in my head as being people who'd fallen off the radar and were estranged from their families for some reason. This one, he's missing and people are missing him.'

'We would have come across him eventually,' Ryan said. 'I've got a huge list here of missing people in and around the North East. I've since checked, and Shane Waterhouse is on the list.'

'Now we know the dates of when the others either went missing or were killed, possibly, we can focus more on the missing persons list. If more of Isaac's victims are missed by family and loved ones, we should find them,' Linus said. His tone was buoyant at hopefully making some progress with identifying the victims.

'It's good news. It is,' Olivia said. 'It's just not what I was expecting.' She looked back down at the photograph of the smiling Shane Waterhouse. She took a breath and slowly blew it out. 'So, what about the rest of the code? "Cold" and "chicken" are in brackets. What could they mean?'

'"Cold" could mean that it was cold. It was New Year, after all,' Ryan said.

'It's a bit obvious,' Linus suggested.

'Maybe it will get obvious once we have more information,' Olivia added. 'What about "chicken"? Is there a chicken farm or a chicken factory nearby? Maybe he was dumped near a KFC. Or are there any place names including "chicken"?'

'I'll dig out the map,' Ryan said.

Olivia's frown deepened. 'I'm really struggling with columns three and four. I can't see them just being random words, they have to mean something. But what? Does column three relate to where the victims were picked up and the fourth to where they're buried?'

'Shane Waterhouse was last seen at Powerhouse,' Ryan said. 'It's possible he could have been picked up from there. I can't see how "rely", "octagon", "cold" in brackets, and "key" relate to a nightclub.'

'Some columns make sense, like the months, the markings out of ten and the numbers referring to age and height, but columns three and four with the different words make no sense,' Linus said. 'What if they're nothing to do with pickup and burial points? What if they're just random words that will remind Isaac of the victim?'

'They're not random words,' Olivia stated. 'Nothing about this code is random. They mean something. They have to.'

'But what?' Linus asked.

'I don't know. But I'll find out. I promise you.'

'So, where do we go from here?' Ryan asked.

'I've been on to the sergeant who is handling the Shane Waterhouse case,' said Linus. 'I'm going to ask him to take the Casio watch to his mother and see if she recognises it. If we can get him officially recognised as a victim, that will make three with Sean Bridger and Piotr Czajkowski. I'll then try and get an investigation opened and we can get more people on this.'

'In the meantime, I think trawling missing persons reports to try and locate more victims will help. Shane was from Sunderland, you said. I'm guessing that's not in your remit.'

'No, it's not,' Linus said. 'Like I said, we need to cast our net wide.'

'I think, if you remain in the perimeters of where Isaac went for his work, you should find your other victims there. Speaking of Isaac's work, any more news from his other colleagues or customers?' Olivia asked.

'Yes, actually,' Ryan said. He frantically scrolled through his tablet, which seemed to be permanently by his side, and found what he was looking for. 'I spoke to the office manager at MediSupplies UK, Doreen Bliss. She's been there for years and she told me all the sales reps are male and of the seven female office-based staff, none have had a relationship with Isaac McFadden. She put me on speakerphone so I could ask them all. Also, since Covid, none of the sales reps have been in the building. All meetings are done via Zoom.'

'So he lied to Hal about seeing someone from work,' Olivia said.

'I also called the neighbour, Julie Packard. She gave me a right earful,' Ryan said. 'She said she liked Isaac as a neighbour and sent him a Christmas card every year, but that was as far as their relationship went. When I told her he'd told someone he'd been seeing a neighbour called Julie, she flew off the handle. She's been married to her husband for more than twenty-five years and never once looked at another man, blah, blah, blah.'

'More lies from Isaac,' Olivia said.

'Is there anything he says that we can take as being true?' Ryan asked.

'I have no idea, which is going to make my meeting with him tomorrow very interesting.'

Chapter Thirty-Three

MODBURY GARDENS, LONDON

By the time Sebastian Lister turned into Modbury Gardens, most of the residents had left for work, so finding a parking space was not a problem. Olivia generally parked her scooter on the pavement at the bottom of her steps. She didn't have to worry about designated spaces. He looked up at the house as he ascended the stone steps. From this angle, everything seemed to be fine and in order.

He unlocked the door, opened it, and stepped inside. He waved his fob in front of the alarm and the warning beeping stopped. He closed the door and turned to look in the cage at the back of the door that contained the post. There were a couple of white and brown envelopes, but what stood out most was the number of yellow envelopes sitting in the cage.

He took them out and began to look through them as he walked into the kitchen. All of the yellow envelopes had been handwritten, and they had all been hand delivered, as there was no stamp in the top right-hand corner. Surely, if someone knew Olivia well enough to hand deliver a letter on a regular basis, they knew her well enough to know she was out of the city at present.

He slapped the letters down on the island and went to examine the back door. He unlocked it, opened the door and found what was once a pigeon, its innards and feathers splattered all over the step.

He pulled a face. 'Bloody cats,' he said to himself. He went back into the house and set about looking for a bin bag and a bottle of bleach.

Sebastian's phone began to ring. It made him jump. He took it out of his coat pocket, saw it was Olivia calling and swiped to answer.

'I had a notification that my alarm had been turned off. I guessed it was you,' she said. 'How is everything?'

'Fine. Apart from what appears to be a crime scene on your back step. There are pigeon guts all over it.'

'It's probably that ginger cat from two doors down. It's an evil little thing.'

'I'll get rid of it for you.'

'The cat or the pigeon?' Olivia asked, playfully.

'The pigeon. I'm not in the hitman game just yet.'

'Thanks, Sebastian.'

'By the way, you've had some post delivered. There are a lot of yellow envelopes in your cage.'

'Just throw them on the counter. I'll deal with them when I get back.'

'Did you know they were hand delivered?'

'What?' Olivia asked.

Sebastian sensed an edge to her voice.

'I... I didn't give it any notice. I wonder if the others are,' she said, almost to herself.

'Others?'

Olivia didn't say anything.

'Olivia, what others? How many of these have you had?'

'I don't know. It doesn't matter. I know exactly what they are.'

'What are they?'

'They're from Richard. He knows yellow was my mum's favourite colour.'

'But you haven't been gone long enough to have received this many. These are being posted through your letterbox more than once a day. This isn't him writing to you. This is bordering on harassment.'

'Which is why I don't open them.'

'Have you reported him?'

Again, Olivia didn't say anything, which told Sebastian more than any words could.

'Olivia, you need to report him to the authorities.'

'What good will that do? He's in prison on a whole life tariff. What punishment can they possibly give him that's any worse than that?'

'Olivia...'

'Look, Sebastian, I'm going to have to go. I'm needed. You'll find everything you need under the sink in the utility room. Give Stanley a kiss from me. Bye.'

She quickly ended the call before Sebastian could say anything. He released a frustrated sigh and looked down at the yellow envelopes. They all seemed to be of the same thickness. He guessed they contained one sheet of paper, two at the most. What could her father possibly find to say that would warrant all these letters?

Sebastian decided to open one. He knew it would be against Olivia's wishes, but he hadn't told her how many had been delivered so she wouldn't miss one, he hoped.

He tore open the envelope and pulled out the paper inside. He unfolded it and read the single sentence written in the middle of the page:

You <u>need</u> to come and see me.

Dad.
xxx

Sebastian chewed his bottom lip while he thought of what to do next.

'Screw it,' he said to himself as he picked up another envelope and ran his thumb under the flap. Once again, another single sheet of paper with the same sentence written. Did they all contain the same thing? It would seem so. Why was Richard Button suddenly so anxious to see his daughter? The last time they met was the previous year, when Richard was in hospital following his heart attack. Why now? Was it because of the drama starting on Monday night? There was only one way he could find out.

Chapter Thirty-Four

BENWELL, NEWCASTLE

Thomas Landy made his way back to the Egremont B&B in Benwell. It had been a long and tiring day. He'd been into every shop, café, restaurant and pub he could find, asking if they had any jobs available, and all had turned him down. It was the wrong time of year to be job hunting. Businesses had put on temporary staff to see them through the festive period but now that was over, they didn't need extra staff during the leaner months when shoppers tightened their purse-strings while waiting for their first credit card bill and bank statement of the year.

Tom had also been calling on his friends, the few he had left, to see if they could either lend him a bed for a couple of weeks or help him find alternative accommodation. He hated living at the Egremont. He couldn't relax so he couldn't sleep. His bedsheets had a nasty smell to them. His mattress was thin and painful. The noises from the other rooms were sounds he'd never heard before and they were frightening. Several times his door handle had been rattled or someone had knocked in error, frightening him further. He didn't trust the lock and had taken to pushing the chest of drawers in front of the door before he went to bed, though it was so flimsy, he felt a few hard kicks would soon have it toppling over.

It was pitch-dark. Thomas had been walking the streets since first light. He was cold, shattered and hungry. He needed a shower, and he needed a bloody good cry. He'd spent the entire day being rejected and it had affected his mood. He was so tense and taut he was worried what he might do if he were to snap.

He turned the corner, his backpack heavy on his shoulders, and stood stock still at the sight in front of him. The Egremont was surrounded by haphazardly parked police cars with blue flashing lights. A uniformed officer was stretching crime scene tape around the entrance and a few people were struggling into white paper forensic suits like he'd seen on *Silent Witness*.

He walked slowly to the front door, looking around him, taking in what he assumed to be an active crime scene. Something had happened, but what?

'Sorry, you can't go in there,' someone said in a deep voice, blocking his way.

'But... I...' He was almost embarrassed to say this was his home. 'I live there.'

'Not tonight you don't,' he said, before walking off.

Thomas turned around to study the scene, mouth agape.

'Thomas!' The man on reception – Raymond, Thomas had found out his name was – beckoned him to the side of the road.

Raymond pulled his thin cardigan around his thin frame. He looked freezing cold.

'What's happened?' Thomas asked.

'A couple of hours ago, a man came to see her in number nine. There's a load of shouting. Next thing, bang, bang, bang, three shots rang out. Bloke comes out, calmly walks past me to the door, with a smoking gun in his hand. I tell you, Thomas, I've seen some things in my time working here, but that's the first time I've seen a bloody gun.'

'Oh my God. Is she dead?'

'Dead? Of course she's bloody dead. Her brains are all over the fucking ceiling. You know in films where someone gets shot and you just see a dot on their forehead where the bullet's gone in? All lies. There was nothing left of her.'

'Jesus!' Thomas said, turning back to look at the building. 'So, why can't we go in?'

'It's a crime scene.'

'But... what are we going to do?'

'I'm waiting for my Malcolm to come and pick me up. Not ideal, as me and his wife don't get on, but Malcolm won't see me out on the streets. I know about him and Sally,' he said with a smirk.

'What about me? I've got nowhere to go.'

'Isn't there anyone?'

Thomas shook his head. His bit his lip to stave off the tears.

'It'll probably only be for tonight, maybe tomorrow night at the most. Surely someone can give you their sofa.'

He shook his head again.

'Fucking hell, Thomas, you've been left in the shit good and proper, haven't you? Look, it's not ideal, I know, but pop along to one of the hospitals and sit in a waiting room. If anyone asks, tell them you've got a relative in surgery or A&E or something. If they quibble, move to another waiting room. It's warm and it's dry. Hopefully they'll let us back in tomorrow.'

'All my stuff's in there.'

'I'll keep an eye on your things.'

Thomas nodded his thanks to Raymond, turned on his heel and headed back the way he came.

'Thomas!'

He turned around at Raymond calling his name.

'Here, take this,' Raymond said, holding out a ten-pound note. 'It's all I've got on me. My wallet's in the reception drawer. Buy yourself a burger or something.'

A tear rolled down Thomas's cheek. He didn't want charity, but he literally had nothing left in the world right now. He reluctantly took it from him.

'I'll pay you back,' he choked.

'I'll see you tomorrow.'

Thomas turned and walked away, his head down, dragging his feet. He was cold. He was tired. He had no energy left at all. He felt a fine rain start to fall and looked up at the cloudless sky with an infinite number of stars stretching out across the galaxy.

'Where do I go from here, Mum?' he asked.

He waited for an answer, but one didn't come.

Chapter Thirty-Five

Eleanor hadn't moved from the dining room table for hours. She had been meticulously reading *The Riverside Killer* by Sebastian Lister, underlining sentences she felt were important and making notes on a pad about things Olivia Winter had gone through that were relevant to her own situation. She was engrossed and hadn't noticed the day had ended and darkness had fallen.

She sat back, aching from being hunched over the book. She stretched her muscles and yawned. She was shattered.

Olivia was a survivor. Everybody said so. She had endured the horror of seeing her mother and sister dying in a pool of blood in front of her. Her father had chased her with a carving knife in his hand. She had slipped into unconsciousness watching the police wrestle him to the ground and arrest him. The story had gripped the nation, and it was headline news for weeks as, at first, the public thought Richard Button had simply run amok and killed his family. When it was discovered he was a serial killer with four more victims, the media had a field day. Serial murderers were rare in Britain so they were going to milk this for everything they could get.

What had happened to nine-year-old Olivia when she had woken up in hospital and been told by her grandparents that her mother and sister were dead, that she would have to go and live with them, that her entire life had been turned upside-down? Sebastian's book didn't go into any of that. Richard's victims were given the respect they deserved, but once Olivia had gone into hiding, she was only fleetingly mentioned. The missing years of the only survivor were what the readers wanted to know about. An innocent nine-year-old was all alone in the world. Did she see a child psychologist? Did she have nightmares? Was she withdrawn? Did she start wetting the bed again? When she became a teenager, did she go off the rails, experiment with sex, drink and drugs? Nothing was known about Olivia until she started gaining recognition as a forensic psychologist, and then, last year, she exploded into the limelight when her true identity was revealed.

Eleanor was a survivor. Her father had killed twelve people, it would seem. She was the survivor of a serial killer, just like Olivia. Would Sebastian Lister write a book about her father, or would Olivia? She was here, after all. She was talking to the police, to Olivia, and visiting her father in prison. Would her life be turned into a TV drama?

She opened her laptop and scoured the internet for someone she could talk to, someone who would be interested in hearing all about her. Once she found the contact details, she grabbed her phone and dialled. It was a while before she reached the person she was looking for, because she was passed round various departments.

'Hello, is this Damien Littlejohn?' she asked.

'Speaking.'

'My name is Eleanor McFadden. My father is Isaac McFadden. He was sentenced earlier this month for…'

'Murdering Sean Bridger, yes, I was in court for the sentencing. How can I help you, Miss McFadden?' He sounded harassed, as if it had been a long day and he was desperate to leave and go home.

'The police have been to see me. They're looking into whether my father may have killed more people.'

'Really?' he asked, his interest piqued.

'While I was clearing out his house, I found something I'd never seen before. I took it to the police, and they think they might be trophies of his victims. They think he could have killed twelve people in total.'

'Twelve?' he almost squeaked in delight. 'Twelve victims? That's... wow. I mean, how come the police didn't know about this before?'

'I don't know. They've brought in a forensic psychologist to help them. Dr Olivia Winter.'

'Dr Winter!' he exclaimed.

Eleanor could hear him almost salivating.

'If they've brought in Dr Winter then they must really think your father is a serial killer. Have you spoken to her?'

'Yes. She came to my house to interview me.'

'What's she like?'

Eleanor was thrown. Why wasn't he interested in her? 'Erm, she's smaller than I expected. She knows her stuff, though.'

'Will you be seeing her again?'

'I'm not sure. I might be. Mr Littlejohn, the reason I called you was because I was wondering if you'd like to interview me about my father, about his crimes.'

'Yes. Yes. I'd be very interested,' he said, perking up.

'How much would you pay for an exclusive?' she asked, a smile appearing on her face.

Chapter Thirty-Six

BENWELL, NEWCASTLE

Thomas Landy hadn't looked for anywhere to sleep. He'd left the Egremont behind him and dragged his feet to a destination unknown. He was tired. His legs ached after spending the day looking for work. He'd hardly eaten. The Egremont might be a shithole, but, for now, unfortunately, it was his home, and he had been looking forward to throwing himself onto the bed and falling asleep from exhaustion. Now, he had nothing. He was homeless.

He wanted to cry, but he didn't even have the energy for that. He came to a stop at the entrance to St John's Cemetery and propped himself up against a stone pillar. He was numb. He was shattered. He needed to sit down before he fell down. Looking into the graveyard, he decided to make this his home for the night.

It wasn't ideal. It was freezing cold, a harsh frost twinkling under the sodium of the streetlights, but it would have to do. Thomas Landy was out of options.

He entered the cemetery and staggered amongst the gravestones. He found a bench and sat down. It was cold. He lay on his side, using his rucksack as a pillow. He lifted up his hood to protect his head from the cold and closed his eyes. Right now, he didn't care if he died in the night from hypothermia. At least all his problems would be over.

'Excuse me.'

He opened his eyes. Had he really heard a voice or was it in his head?

'Hello. Are you all right?'

He sat up and looked around him. Someone was approaching him out of the darkness.

'Hello. I saw you come into the cemetery. Are you planning on sleeping here tonight?'

Thomas swallowed hard. There was a painful lump in his throat. He nodded and fought hard to hold back his tears.

'It's just for tonight. I'm staying in a bed and breakfast but there's been a… something's happened and I can't stay there tonight. I promise, I'm not going to do any damage. I just need to sleep for a couple of hours.'

'Don't you have anywhere you can go?'

He shook his head. He could feel the emotion rising inside him.

'I'm sorry, but you can't sleep in here.'

It was a while before Thomas said anything. Tears rolled down his freezing cold cheeks. His bottom lip wobbled. He couldn't hold back his torment any longer.

'My mum's dead,' he choked. 'I've literally nothing left in the world. I'm on my own. I just need to sleep for a little while.'

The person flicked on a torch and aimed it at Thomas's face. He squinted, blinded by the light.

'You're just a child.'

'I'm eighteen,' he protested.

'You're shaking.'

'That's because it's bloody cold. Look, I know I shouldn't be here. I'm sorry. But it's just for tonight. It's just for one night,' he pleaded.

'I'm sorry. I can't allow you to sleep here.'

Thomas was frustrated, angry, sad, in mental torment, but he was too drained to do anything about it. He was defeated. He lifted himself up off the bench and struggled to put his backpack on his shoulders.

'I can offer you my sofa if it's just for one night.'

Thomas looked up. 'Really?'

'Yes. But, like I said, it can only be for one night.'

'That's all I need. Thank you. Thank you so much,' Thomas said, more tears rolling down his cheeks. 'You don't know how much this means to me. I'm so grateful.'

His good Samaritan smiled back. 'Follow me.'

Chapter Thirty-Seven

HM PRISON FRANKLAND, COUNTY DURHAM

Saturday 1st February 2025

Frankland Prison had been extended many times since it was first opened in 1983 with just four wings and 108 cells in each wing. Now, there were almost one thousand category-A male prisoners, each in a single occupancy cell, and a specialist DSPD (Dangerous and Severe Personality Disorder) wing had opened in 2004. Frankland was only one of five Dispersal prisons throughout the UK and had been dubbed Monster Mansion due to the many convicted murderers, high-risk sex offenders and those convicted of terrorism-related offences. Former inmates included Charles Bronson, Colin Pitchfork and Harold Shipman. Current inmates included serial killer Levi Bellfield, Islamist terrorist Michael Adebolajo and London nail-bomber David Copeland.

Olivia had been in many prisons around the world. Some seemed luxurious and plush, others degrading and filthy. The people she had spoken to were hardened criminals who had committed the worst acts imaginable against other people. Olivia had been held hostage, spat at, attacked, physically and sexually assaulted, had all manner of filthy language thrown at her, yet she still continued to go back to these places for more. She needed to understand that darkness in the minds of these people. It was an obsession.

As she approached the main entrance to Frankland Prison, she didn't give the building a second glance. Even a Victorian monolith didn't scare her. Buildings were harmless. It was the people inside who needed to be approached with caution.

The routine in attending prisons is roughly the same the world over. No mobile phones are allowed, and visitors are told not to hand anything to the prisoners under any circumstances. Therefore, Olivia arrived with the minimum about her person. She left her mobile and bag safely locked in her hire car. She didn't wear any jewellery or a belt or shoes with laces. She didn't have any ties or slides in her hair and there were no zips on her clothing. However, she still had to go through the expected rigmarole of being searched and stepping through an X-ray scanner.

Olivia didn't make notes when she was meeting with a serial killer. Pausing the conversation while she made extensive notes acted as a barrier and disrupted the flow of whatever they were talking about. She didn't record her interviews either, unlike Sebastian. She wanted the conversation to appear as natural as it could be. A digital recorder, a pad and pen, they all acted as tools to show Olivia had a professional interest in who she was talking to and she wanted the person on the other side of the table to see her as a confidante, someone they could open up to. Anything important said, she remembered, and once she was away from the interview room, she made detailed notes. What needed to happen between Olivia and whoever she was interviewing was for them to simply converse. No distractions. Nothing to alert the killer that he, or she, had said something meaningful to Olivia. This way, the killer's manipulations would not be shown to affect her in any way, and they would have no idea if their deception and scheming were working.

The meeting with Isaac McFadden was by special arrangement. This wasn't a normal visit to a prisoner by a friend or family member. Olivia was helping the police with a serial murder investigation. A room had been set aside for her to meet Isaac in, and as the door was unlocked and opened, Isaac was already waiting for her.

Dressed in blue tracksuit bottoms and a blue jumper, he was sitting at a table in the middle of the room. His hands were cuffed to the table. Behind him was a door with a large Plexiglas window on either side where two prison guards stood watch. Should anything happen, they were on hand to charge in to subdue the prisoner.

The door behind Olivia closed. She was alone with Isaac McFadden.

'Good morning, Mr McFadden. Thank you for seeing me,' she said in a polite, friendly voice. She pulled out the chair opposite and sat down.

First impressions counted, more so when meeting a psychopathic killer. She could not show any fear or nerves. She had to be confident and treat Isaac the same way she would treat Sebastian and Daisy or Linus and Ryan.

'You're welcome,' he said with a smile. His voice was soft and quiet, quite different from when he was interviewed by DI Sutton at Forth Banks Police Station. He had been in prison for less than two months but already he was a changed man. Gone was the conviction in which he replied 'No comment' to every question Linus threw at him. His shoulders had sunk, and he'd clearly lost weight as he adapted to prison routine and food.

Olivia returned his smile as she quickly studied him. His hair was cut short, dark brown, greying at the temples. His face was lined in all the usual places, but he didn't look old. Prison pallor hadn't set in yet. His eyes were blue and dull. The sparkle she'd seen in photos had long gone. His jawline, once firm, was now softening with age. He was clean-shaven and smelled clean. Olivia looked down at his cuffed hands and took in the long, slender fingers with neatly trimmed nails. Those fingers had strangled the life out of Sean Bridger. They'd held all manner of instruments used to cut up his body into twelve pieces. How many more had those smooth hands killed?

'How are you?' she asked.

'I'm fine.'

'Settling in?'

'You make it sound like I've started a new job.'

'You're going to be spending the rest of your life here. It's important to be comfortable.'

'I'm in a single cell smaller than my bathroom at home. I'm locked in at eight o'clock every evening. I have to shower with twenty other men and my meals aren't exactly prepared by a Michelin-starred chef. Comfort isn't high on the list of priorities here.'

'You're an intelligent man, Mr McFadden. Did you never think of the consequences of what you were doing? Surely you must have known you'd end up in prison at some point.'

He looked Olivia deep in the eyes and leaned forward.

'No comment.' There was a ghost of a smile on his lips.

'We're not in a police interview room now. This conversation isn't being recorded and I have no authority over you. I'm assuming you know what my job is. Why did you agree to see me if you weren't prepared to answer any of my questions?'

'I wanted to meet a survivor.'

The mind games had begun. Isaac knew who she was: not just Dr Olivia Winter, forensic psychologist, but Olivia Button, daughter of Richard Button, infamous serial killer. Sebastian was obviously correct; everybody did know her.

She had no idea what her expression was when he called her a survivor. Did she flinch? Did she roll her eyes? She sincerely hoped not. If he noticed a change in her, he would know which buttons to press in order to elicit a reaction.

'We're all survivors of something, Isaac. May I call you Isaac?'

He nodded. 'May I call you Olivia?'

'Of course.'

'Olivia. Olivia,' he said, sounding out the name. 'Olivia Button.'

She sniggered. 'Yes, very good, you know who I am. It's not exactly a secret. Can we turn the conversation back to you?'

'I'd much prefer to talk about you,' he said, leaning even closer.

'That's not why I'm here.'

He sat back in his seat and sighed. 'DI Sutton couldn't get anywhere with the notebook found in my wardrobe, so he ran to an expert.'

'It makes for fascinating reading.'

'You can understand it?'

'Yes. Sean Bridger. Twenty years old, five feet ten inches tall, with brown hair and wearing a blue jumper, blue jeans, and black shoes, cut into twelve pieces on the first day of March 2024.'

He looked at her, waiting for her to continue. When she didn't, he gave a knowing smile. He knew she hadn't cracked the whole code.

'Are you going to go through all twelve?'

'Not yet.'

'No. You can't, can you?'

'All victims have yet to be identified.'

'Or found.'

'I've been speaking to your daughter,' she said, changing the subject. She watched closely for a reaction at the mention of his child. He swallowed hard. 'She speaks very highly of you. It can't have been easy raising a young child on your own after your wife died. But you did a wonderful job. Eleanor is a lovely young woman.'

'Yes. She is.'

'I'm afraid Eleanor is struggling at present. She's finding it hard to understand what you've done, why you've done it. It's not easy to discover the person you love and respect most in the whole world has been hiding a completely other life from you. Trust me, I know. It makes you question everything. Eleanor is wondering if she ever knew you at all.'

'My daughter knows who I am. She knows who I am to her.'

'That's not the same. Turn the tables. How would you have

reacted if the police came to your door and told you Eleanor had killed twelve people?'

He didn't answer that. He couldn't.

'I love my daughter,' he eventually said.

Olivia believed him. There was real emotion in his statement.

'Then why did you destroy everything?'

Isaac didn't reply. He looked down at his hands.

'What was so important to you that you would risk losing everything you loved and had worked so hard at?'

Olivia waited to an answer. She didn't get one.

'Shall I tell you what Eleanor is doing now? She's lost her job.' Isaac quickly looked up at her in horror. His eyes were filled with tears waiting to fall. 'She kept bursting into tears at work. Her company made her redundant, so she'd get a financial package to keep her afloat for a while. She rarely leaves the house. She's numb. She's in shock. She's scared for her own future, especially when news of how many people you really killed has hit the press. You've single-handedly destroyed her life.'

'I love her,' he said, barely audibly.

'You have a funny way of showing it. What happened, Isaac?'

He looked back down at his hands again.

'What happened in your life that made you want to kill someone?'

He shook his head.

'I'm here to help you,' she said, reaching forward and placing a hand on top of his. He flinched. He looked at her. There was confusion on his face.

'I'm not just here to help the police,' Olivia said. 'That's not what I do. I want to understand you. I want to help you understand yourself. I've met Eleanor, and I like her. I'd like to help her, too.'

Reluctantly, he nodded.

Olivia removed her hand and sat back. 'Will you help me to understand you?'

'You want to know about my childhood?'

'Whatever you want to tell me.'

'You want to know if I was abused as a child, if my parents hit me, if I wet the bed until I was a teenager, if I went around pulling the wings off flies and legs off spiders, is that it?'

'Not at all.' Olivia was prepared for this. The modern killer was savvy about what made a killer: the bed-wetting, the fire-setting, the harm to animals. The internet made Olivia's job harder, but not impossible. 'I know you had a happy childhood. You loved your father and mother. You weren't born into a rich family, but you lived well. Although not naturally academic, you were settled in school. There were no reports of you bullying anyone or being bullied. I've no idea what age you stopped wetting the bed, and to be perfectly honest, I don't want to know.'

'So, you're not one of those people who believe a bed-wetter is a future serial killer?'

'Bedwetting is incredibly common. It affects one in fifteen seven-year-olds and can affect one in seventy-five teenagers. Causes can be a urinary infection, frequency of urination in the daytime and something as simple as not going for a pee before bed.'

'Oh. Fair enough,' Isaac said.

Olivia smiled. 'Would you like to tell me about your childhood, your earliest memory?'

He frowned as he thought. It was a while before he answered. 'I'm not sure I can recall my earliest memory. We went to the coast a lot. Dad was never one for spending a day in the house. Whenever he could, he liked to be out and about. We went to the park, to the beach, to the countryside.'

'Would that be all three of you, including your mum?'

'Yes. We'd be kicking a ball or throwing a frisbee or skimming stones. Then we'd have fish and chips in the car and come back home. It was fun.'

'Would you have liked a brother or sister?'

'I never thought about it.' He shrugged. 'I was happy with it just being the three of us. Besides, we didn't have much money.

I'm not sure my parents would have coped with another mouth to feed.'

'But they could cope with one child?'

'Yes. We weren't rich, but we always had food on the table. Mum always cooked a roast on Sunday,' he said with a smile.

'Did you have a favourite parent?'

He looked away and his brow wrinkled. He'd clearly never given this much thought before. 'I… I'm not sure. I don't think so.'

'You're of the generation where there was usually one breadwinner in the household. The man went out to work while the woman stayed at home to look after the house and raise the family. Is that how it was for you?'

'Yes,' he said, a winsome smile appearing on his lips.

'Your father was the master of the house.'

The smile fell. 'I wouldn't say that.'

'Your mother ruled the roost?'

'She had… she had her own ideas of how a family should behave.'

'And what were they?'

'She liked a clean home, a faithful husband and a well-behaved child.'

'Did she get those?'

It was a while before Isaac answered. 'Yes,' he said.

Olivia studied him. There was a deep, pained look in his eye. He was thinking back to his childhood. His father returning home from working down the mine. He'd be filthy and reek of sweat. How did his mother react to that? And what about Isaac when he was a small boy, out playing with friends during the summer holidays, running in the woods, getting into scrapes and coming home with grazed knees and clothes covered in grass stains. She decided to leave that for now. It was obviously a sensitive subject for Isaac. He loved his parents and he was looking at his childhood through rose-tinted glasses.

'Your parents weren't old when they died, were they?'

'No. Dad was only fifty-four. He worked down the coal mines his whole life. Black lung, they call it, or coal workers' pneumoconiosis if you want the full title. Mum died later. She was sixty-seven. She had a massive heart attack in her sleep. She never really got over Dad dying. They were a happy couple. They genuinely loved each other.'

'It can't have been easy for you.'

'No. At the time it wasn't, but, well, it's the circle of life, isn't it? Your parents die. You replace them. Then you die and your children live on. There isn't room for all of us to live for ever.'

Olivia nodded. She immediately thought of her own mother, and her sister Claire. People can't live for ever, but it would be nice if they stuck around for a while. She banished the thoughts. She needed to remain on topic. She couldn't let Isaac get into her head.

'You wanted to follow your father into mining, didn't you?'

'I did. I mean, it's a horrible job, and it eventually killed him, but he really did love it,' Isaac said, wistfully. 'Then Margaret Thatcher got her hands on it and killed the whole industry.'

'How did your dad take it?'

'He was a changed man after that. He got a job on a building site, but he hated it. It wasn't long afterwards that he fell ill. The doctors signed him off. He never worked again.'

'So, what happened? Did your mum have to go out to work?'

He nodded. 'She had two jobs. One in the local Co-op on the tills and at a bakery in the evenings.'

The dynamic in the family home had shifted. Peter McFadden was home all day while Susan worked two jobs and was the breadwinner. Did Peter feel emasculated? Did Susan's domineering behaviour escalate? How did a young Isaac fit into this new world order?

'Your first job was at the shoemakers Carter, Weddle and Thropp,' Olivia said, deciding to move on. 'Did you enjoy it?'

'God no. The work was tedious. The people were great, though.'

'Did you enjoy working for MediSupplies UK?'

His eyes lit up. 'Oh yes. I loved it. I felt like my own boss, travelling around, nobody looking over my shoulders.'

'Freedom.'

'Yes.'

'Which now you don't have.'

'No,' he said, his face taking on a resigned look.

'I've been chatting to the people who know you, or, rather, those who thought they knew you. I'm receiving conflicting reports,' Olivia said. 'Eleanor said you were content with being on your own. Lesley Quinn was obviously holding a torch for you,' Olivia noticed his eyes twinkle at the mention of Lesley's name. 'Hal Garfield told me you were seeing one of your customers and Chris Cohen told police you were seeing your neighbour Julie, who vehemently denies this.'

A smile spread across Isaac's face. He looked down at his hands. When he looked back up, the smile had been replaced by a smirk.

'Would the real Isaac McFadden please stand up?' Olivia said.

He let out a throaty laugh.

'You've manipulated so many people over the years. How long has this been going on? Does anyone know the real Isaac McFadden? Do you?'

Isaac didn't say anything.

'You've painted a picture of yourself as the perfect family man who looked after his daughter, brought her up single-handedly, worked hard to provide for her and sacrificed his own happiness for her, but it's not true at all, is it? You've used your own child as an alibi to deflect who you really are, a disturbed and violent man.'

'Is that what you think I am?'

'Having a body cut into twelve pieces in the back of your car seems to point to that. Unless you didn't put it there.'

He raised an eyebrow, asked an unsaid question.

'For a man to have committed twelve murders and not appear on the police's radar, you will have needed help to cover it up. You haven't been working alone all these years, have you? You have a partner out there.'

'Is that what you think?'

'It's what I know,' she replied, confidently.

'Dazzle me,' he said, sitting back in his chair, a gloating expression on his face.

'Your code. Nobody wakes up one morning and decides to be a serial killer with an elaborate code to outsmart the police. That happens over time. Also, I don't believe entry number one in your code is your first victim. I think there is another one, possibly two, victims out there we don't know about.'

'You're good,' he smiled.

'I'm right. Aren't I?'

He leaned forward. 'As it's just the two of us here, and as there is no evidence whatsoever, I'll throw you a bone. Yes, you're right.'

'How many more are we talking?'

'That would be telling.'

Olivia looked at him, looked deep into his eyes, studied what was going on in there. He was difficult to read, but not impossible.

'The first kill was an accident, wasn't it? You didn't mean to kill them, but something happened to you that convinced you to do it again.'

He swallowed hard, his Adam's apple bobbing up and down, and his cheeks reddened slightly.

'Let me ask you a question,' Olivia said, shifting in her seat. 'Can you point out the transverse cervical nerve?'

Isaac didn't answer.

'How about the sural nerve? The common peroneal nerve? No? What about the iliotibial tract?' She waited for a reply. None came. 'I didn't think so. They're just words to you, aren't they? I could be saying anything. Do you love Eleanor?' Olivia asked.

Isaac seemed to be perplexed by the sudden change in subject. He opened his mouth a few times to reply, but never said anything. He was weighing up which words to use.

'I've already said I do.'

'Then why are you doing this to her? Why are you letting her suffer like this? You're her father, her last surviving parent, and she doesn't know you at all. Don't you think that hurts?'

Isaac leaned forward again. There was that glint in his eye again. 'Tell me, how do you feel about knowing everything about your father?'

She needed to give the correct answer here or he'd gain the upper hand. 'I'll be honest with you, Isaac, I feel sick to the stomach. But I'm glad I know.'

'Why?'

'Imagine not knowing when others do? That's going to really mess with your mind when you eventually do find out. I'd be where Eleanor is now.'

'You think it's my fault she's like she is?'

'Who else's fault could it be?'

'I love my daughter.' Again it was said with purpose.

'You've already said that, and I believe you. But why did you have to destroy all of that? What did you gain by killing all these people? Why did you do it?'

'No comment.'

'Are we really going back to that?'

'I can't give you the answers you want.'

'I think you can. But if you gave me the answers, it would reveal who your partner is.'

'Is that so?'

'Yes, it is. Has he contacted you since your arrest? Has he visited you in prison?' She waited for a reply that didn't come. 'No, he hasn't. He's left you alone in here. Why is that? Are you collateral damage to him? What's it like to be separated, to have that strong bond you had broken? You'll never see him again. It's over.'

'I'm ready,' he called out to the guards behind the Plexiglas, signalling he wanted to return to his cell.

'I've hit a nerve,' she said.

A key turned in the lock and the door opened.

'I'm right, aren't I?' she asked as the guards entered and began releasing the cuffs from the table. 'There was a second killer. He's still out there, isn't he? Will he continue killing without you?'

Isaac stood up and made his way to the door.

Olivia jumped up from her chair. 'Isaac,' she barked.

He stood in the doorway and turned back. He looked at her over his shoulder and winked.

'Same time on Monday?'

She nodded.

Chapter Thirty-Eight

Olivia headed back for the police station. Linus had told her he was working on Saturday. She pushed open the door and found only Ryan Sweetland sitting at the large table, head down over his tablet as usual. He looked up.

'How did it go?' Ryan asked, his face expectant.

'As I expected it to,' she said, pulling out a chair and sitting down. 'Is it me, or is it cold in here?'

'I've only just got back from popping over to see Lesley Quinn. The heating has only just come on.'

'Did she say anything useful?'

'She wasn't in.'

'Oh.'

'Did Isaac give you any more insights?'

'I've managed to get him to admit he's killed more than these twelve.'

'How many more?'

'He wouldn't say. He also wouldn't confirm if he had a partner in crime or not. Reading between the lines, I'm even more certain he wasn't killing on his own.'

'Where do you go from here?'

'Today's interview was more of a meeting. He was trying me out and I was trying him out. Next time, it will be more open.

Isaac will reveal more when I see him next week. I know he will. Is Linus around?'

'Erm… no,' he said, looking back to his tablet.

'Oh. Busy with something else?'

'No. Not… no.'

'Ryan, never, ever, play poker. What's going on?'

Ryan sighed. 'DCI Wise has more or less forced DI Sutton to take the weekend off.'

'Forced him? Why?'

Ryan cleared his throat and shifted in his chair. 'I'm not really supposed to say.'

'But you're going to?'

'It's personal.'

'Is he ill?'

'No.'

'Ryan, we're dealing with a killer who I've just found out could have added to his tally of twelve. We need to be one hundred per cent focused on this. If there's something troubling DI Sutton, I need to know about it.'

'Tomorrow is the first anniversary of his wife's death,' Ryan said, softly.

Olivia's mouth fell open. 'I didn't even know he was married. What happened?'

'She was killed by a hit-and-run driver near the Arena.'

'Oh God.'

'She was on the phone to DI Sutton at the time she was hit. He heard everything.'

'Jesus Christ!'

'He took a few days off work but came back the day after the funeral. He's thrown himself into his work. He refuses to talk about her, he's taken off his wedding ring, and I've heard he refuses to scatter her ashes.'

'He's in denial,' Olivia said. 'Where can I find him?'

'At home.'

'Can you give me his address?'

It took a while for Olivia to find where Linus Sutton lived. He had a loft apartment on the Newcastle Quayside overlooking the Tyne. She pressed the buzzer and waited. It was another cold day and gentle flakes of snow were falling. It was only a light shower as the sky was relatively clear. A biting wind from the river dropped the temperature a notch.

'Hello?'

'Linus. It's Olivia. Any chance I can come up?'

Linus released a heavy sigh through the intercom. 'It's not really a good time at the moment, Olivia. Can I see you at the office on Monday?'

'I've not come to talk about the case. I... I know you've been advised to take this weekend off. I thought you might like someone to talk to.'

'I'm not really in a talking mood.'

'I can understand that Linus, I really can, but I'm a complete stranger. I'm not going to judge you. I'm not going to gossip about you around the station. I'll be gone soon.'

It was a long minute before she received a response.

'Top floor.'

The lock was released, and Olivia was more than happy to get in out of the cold.

She took the lift to the top and as the doors slowly yawned open, she found Linus standing in the doorway of his apartment waiting for her. He was wearing tracksuit bottoms and a black and white Newcastle United football shirt. He was unshaven, his unruly hair stuck up in random directions and his eyelids were heavy.

'I didn't have you down as a football fan.'

'I wasn't until I met Clara. She was football mad.' He turned on his heels and headed into the flat. Olivia followed.

'Clara was your wife?'

'Huh-uh.'

Olivia closed the door behind her and marvelled at the space. It was a stunning open-plan affair with floor-to-ceiling windows giving a wonderful picture view of the city melting into the countryside. The whole place was stylishly decorated, with bare brick walls and warm muted colours. Cleanliness, however, was obviously no longer a priority. Cushions hadn't been plumped in a while, kitchen surfaces were dull, and the floor was in urgent need of a vac.

'Can I get you a coffee or something?'

'Coffee's fine.'

He went into the kitchen and placed a pod in the Nespresso machine. Olivia went over to a leather sofa by the window and began removing her coat.

'Gorgeous view of the river,' she said. 'I love the steel bridge. From what I can see.'

'That's the Tyne Bridge. Almost one hundred years old. It's finally getting a makeover,' he said, handing her a coffee. He slumped into the matching armchair.

Olivia turned to look at him. He radiated sadness. 'Why didn't you tell me about your wife?'

He shrugged.

'I'm so sorry.'

'One of those things.'

'It's not, though, is it? You can't just dismiss it as a random act. It had huge consequences.'

Linus swallowed hard. He sucked in his lips to hide showing them quivering to Olivia.

'Ryan told me you were on the phone to her at the time. That must have been devastating.'

He nodded. 'She was going for a taxi. She wouldn't let me pick her up. She'd been to see a singer she liked with a friend from work. She was talking to me through her earphones on the phone. I heard the car hit her. How they didn't fall out of her ear, I don't know. I heard her... I heard her take her last breath,' he said, tears rolling silently down his face. 'She tried to talk, but she couldn't. I knew... I knew I was losing her.'

Olivia went over to the armchair, sat beside him and pulled him towards her. He needed to feel comfort right now.

'I ran,' he continued. 'I ran down the stairs. I ran out into the street. It was only when I was in the ambulance with her that I realised I wasn't wearing any shoes. Just socks. Huh. It's strange the things you think about, isn't it? There we were in the back of the ambulance. Clara was unconscious, tubes sticking out of her mouth and wires everywhere, and I'm looking at my feet.

'She was already dead by the time we got to the hospital. They rushed her into the emergency department, but you could see they were just going through the motions. There was no bringing her back. We'd only been married four years.'

Olivia squeezed him tighter.

'That's cruel,' she whispered. 'How did you meet?'

She felt his body begin to relax in her arms.

'We met in a bar in town. She was on a night out with a friend, and I was out with a few of the guys from work. As soon as I saw her smile, I knew she was something special. Have you ever just seen someone and known you had to be with them?'

Olivia couldn't answer that. Her mind immediately went to Ethan. She wished it hadn't.

'We arranged to go out on a date, and she took me to St James's Park. I've never been a big football fan, but seeing her enthusiasm just made me enjoy it more. We never missed a home match.' He smiled at the memory, but the smile quickly faded. 'Every time I think of her, I… for a brief moment I feel like she's still here, then I remember, and the pain…'

Olivia kept her arms wrapped around him. He held onto her. Tight.

'The pain won't go.'

'Because you're not allowing it to,' Olivia said. 'You're grieving, and that's fine. It's perfectly normal, but in order to stop the hurt, you need to let her go.'

'I can't do that.'

'Why not?'

'Because if I let her go it's like I'm saying goodbye.'

'But you are. You need to say goodbye to her in person. She's still with you in your heart and in your head. You can think about the good times, the memories, her smile, whenever you want, and they will be happy memories and not tainted by how she died. But in order to do that, you have to let her go. You can't hold onto something that is no longer here.'

Olivia closed her eyes. She constantly thought of her mother and sister. Twenty-five years after their deaths and she still missed them terribly. She often wondered what Claire would be doing now. She'd be thirty-one. What job would she be doing? Would she be married, have children? And her mum, her beautiful mum.

As Olivia's own tears began to run, she held onto Linus still tighter. The grief never left, no matter how much you tried to say it had, especially when those who had left had been so cruelly snatched away.

Linus wiped his eyes with the backs of his hands. 'I have to scatter her ashes, don't I?'

'Only you can decide that. No one is forcing you to do anything.'

'I've been putting it off. I've tried scattering them a few times, but always brought them back. I talk to them every night. I even have some in here,' he said, pulling out a chain around his neck that had a plain silver cylinder attached. 'She's always with me.'

Olivia couldn't think of anything to say.

'She'd hate me for being like this,' he said. 'It's been a year. A year tomorrow. If she could, she'd slap me across the face and tell me to pull myself together.' He laughed and wiped his nose with the back of his hand. 'Will you come with me? I don't want to do it on my own.'

'Are you sure?'

'I am. I don't have anyone else.'

'I'd be happy to.'

'Thank you, Olivia. You're a good woman.'

'I try to be,' she said.

Extract from a notebook allegedly written by Isaac McFadden

I like the night time. I love the darkness, especially in the winter when it's dark by four o'clock in the evening and sometimes, during the day, it hardly becomes light at all if the weather is bad. It keeps people off the streets. The only ones who are out are those who have to go to work and the hardy joggers and dog walkers.

Others who are out in the cold and dark are the ones who have no choice. Those without a home. Those with no family or friends to look out for them. Those who are lost.

It's much easier to choose a victim in the winter than in the summer. It's much easier to get away with things in the winter when everyone is home, and the curtains are drawn early. Driving around the streets at eight o'clock in mid-December you can be forgiven for thinking it's the wee small hours of the morning. So much more time to get things done.

The power of the night, of the silence, of knowing you've brought someone's life to an abrupt end, and you've been able to get away with it. It's electrifying. I can't explain it. I feel like a god.

Chapter Thirty-Nine

By the time Olivia left Linus's apartment, it was pitch-dark. She wasn't in the mood to spend any time on her own and, as she made her way back, she decided to sample some of the nightlife Newcastle had to offer. It was late evening and despite the temperature hovering around freezing, people were out in force. Young women linked arms as they hurried from pub to pub wearing impossibly high heels and skimpy clothing. They looked perished but were laughing and seemed to be having a good time. Young men in skinny jeans and tight polo shirts strutted with confidence. Their evening of drunken rowdiness was just beginning, and they were prepared for the long haul. Olivia had missed out on the recklessness of youth. She was never part of a group in her teens who bar-hopped and drunkenly staggered home smelling of some random fit bloke's aftershave. She feared letting her guard down from a young age. Any act of wild abandon was of her making and under her control. A lot of men found that a turn off.

She turned a corner and stopped in her tracks as she came face to face with a poster on a bus shelter, advertising the drama about her father starting on Monday. The man who was to play Richard was glaring at her. He had a sinister smile. The producers were turning her tragic childhood into a cheap thriller, and that sickened her more than anything. Sebastian had written a sensitive and mature account of what Richard had done, and the programme makers were doing everything in their power to sensationalise it simply for ratings. She pulled up her collar, put her head down and hurried on.

Olivia found a quiet pub, the Slug and Lettuce on Grainger Street. She felt the warmth envelop her as she entered, ordered a large glass of chardonnay and went over to a table by the window. She needed a distraction from the day of interviewing Isaac, discovering he had killed more than the twelve on his code, and Linus's personal tragedy. She sat back, looked out of the window and people-watched. It was one of her favourite hobbies and it was while doing it that she had first met Ethan Miller. They used the same swimming pool and she had been more than impressed with his physique, his designer stubble, his smiling eyes. She had invented a backstory for him, which, when she eventually got to know him, had turned out to be completely different to the truth. She missed him. She hated the fact she was missing him as she knew she couldn't sustain a relationship with him, but while they were together, all the horror and the pain inside her ceased to exist. She ordered another glass of chardonnay.

She dug her mobile out of her coat pocket and fired off a text message to him asking how everything was going in the Amazon. She had no idea if he had a signal or whether the internet connection was good or not, but she wanted him to know she was thinking of him often, even though she was planning on ending whatever it was they had when he returned.

A knock on the glass made her jump. She looked up and saw Eleanor McFadden staring at her from the street. She did a convoluted mime, asking if she could come in and join her. It was the last thing Olivia wanted but she felt she couldn't refuse.

'You looked a million miles away,' Eleanor said, as she breezed in, removed her beanie hat and shook it free it of a few flakes of snow.

'Just thinking,' Olivia replied.

'Mind if I join you?'

'Of course not.'

She pulled out a chair and sat down. 'I was going to call you on Monday. I want to ask your advice.'

'What for?'

'I can't decide whether I want to go and visit my dad in jail or not. I was wondering if you could help me make up my mind.'

'I think that's something you need to work out for yourself. Nobody can tell you what to do.'

'Have you been to see him yet?'

'Yes. I went today.'

'How is he?'

Olivia wasn't sure whether to tell Eleanor the truth or lie. She looked at her. Was she ready to take on more horrors about her father? 'He's… he's doing okay.'

'He's not… I mean, you read stories about prisoners beating each other up or getting knifed with a blade welded onto a toothbrush.'

'He's fine, Eleanor. He's adjusting.'

'Oh. Good. I know he's done some…' She stopped herself. 'I just don't want him being hurt.'

'That's understandable. He's still your dad at the end of the day.'

Eleanor nodded. 'Did you go and visit your dad?'

'No,' she answered sharply.

'Not once?'

'Not until last year when he had a heart attack.'

'Why didn't you go when you were younger?'

'I didn't want to. He'd killed my mum and sister.'

'Did your grandparents ask if you wanted to go?'

'No,' she answered. 'My grandparents were very good. They looked after me. They protected me. Whatever I chose to do, they backed me up.'

'That's nice.'

'Yes.'

'Are they still alive?'

'Unfortunately not, no.'

'When you went to see your dad in hospital last year, how did you feel?'

Olivia frowned. 'Why are you asking me all this?'

'I'm just… I'm trying to understand how I'm going to feel when… if I decide to see him.'

'You'll feel completely different to how I felt, Eleanor. Nobody knows how they're going to react. You have to trust your own instincts and hope they're right.'

'Will you go to see your dad again?'

'No. I have no intention of seeing him ever again.'

'Do you hate him?'

Olivia didn't answer that. She couldn't. She didn't know who her father was. It was difficult to hate someone she didn't know.

'You're still affected by him, aren't you? Even after all this time,' Eleanor said.

'I think I'm going to go,' Olivia said, standing up.

'No. Sorry. I shouldn't have said anything like that. It's none of my business. I'm sorry,' Eleanor said, flustered. 'You stay and finish your drink. I'll go. I appreciate you talking to me, though, Olivia, you've helped. I… thank you.'

Olivia watched her leave. She waved at her through the window before heading back to the bar for a third glass of wine.

Drinking alone, and on an empty stomach, it wasn't long before Olivia found herself light-headed. She needed to return to the hotel while she could still remember where it was. She hoped the restaurant was still serving food. She had a long day ahead of her tomorrow helping Linus to scatter his wife's ashes. She needed something rich and heavy to soak up this alcohol so she could have a good night's sleep.

As Olivia made her way down Grainger Street, she turned and headed for the Quayside. She passed the bus stop with the poster of the actor playing her father and glanced at him over her shoulder. She stopped and her eyes widened when she saw the poster had been vandalised. The glass had been smashed and the poster torn.

'The best thing that could happen to it,' she said to herself as she turned and continued on her journey.

Chapter Forty

'I'm sorry to call so late. Do you mind if I come in?' Lesley Quinn asked Eleanor when she opened the door.

'No. Of course not,' she said, stepping to one side to allow her to enter.

'Thank you. I was going to call but I thought it might be better said face to face. Then I wondered if I should wait until the morning, but I knew I wouldn't sleep if I didn't say something,' she said, her words tripping over each other.

Eleanor had been about to go to bed. She'd arrived home from seeing Olivia in the pub, had a shower and changed into her favourite pyjamas and comfortable dressing gown. She wasn't going to answer the door. It was never good news at this time of night, but she'd looked through the spyhole and seen a worried-looking Lesley Quinn on her doorstep.

They went into the living room. The central heating was on and the room cosy and warm. The large-screen TV on the wall was showing the menu for Netflix. Eleanor had been looking at their selection of horror movies. The entire back catalogue of *Halloween* films was at her fingertips.

'I won't stay long,' Lesley said. She kept her coat on and sat on the sofa. 'I've had a forensic psychologist sniffing around.'

'Olivia Winter? She's been to see me, too.'

'I looked her up. Do you know who her father is?'

'Yes.'

'And there's a drama about her on TV next week,' she added, incredulously. 'She might have letters after her name, but have you seen what she's been through? She's been stabbed more times than a pin cushion. It comes to something when the police are relying on someone like her for answers, doesn't it?'

'She seems to know what she's talking about,' Eleanor said, slumping into the armchair.

'Hmm, we'll see. I sometimes think these experts do more harm than good. Anyway, that wasn't why I came to see you. I've been out most of the day. I got back a couple of hours ago and Julie across the road came over. Hal Garfield was spotted going round the back of your dad's house.'

'What? Why?'

'I don't know. It's not the first time he's been seen either. I saw him a few days ago lingering at the bottom of the drive. He keeps asking me what you plan on doing with it. He says he'd like to buy it for himself, but I don't know. There's something fishy going on if you ask me.'

'In what way?'

'Why is he so interested in your dad's house all of a sudden? He's never shown an interest in it before. I think he's looking for something.'

'Like what?'

'I've no idea. Have you ever been in Hal's house?'

'No.'

'I have. A couple of times. He's very interested in true crime. He's got books and DVDs on it and textbooks based on criminal profiling. He works in computers, for crying out loud – why does he need to know about profiling?'

'Maybe it's a hobby.'

'A strange hobby if you ask me. I just... I'm worried he's looking for access to your dad's house because there's something in there he wants.'

'Such as?'

'I don't know. Maybe something… incriminating. For him.'

'I don't understand. Surely you don't think Hal and my father…?' She left the question hanging. 'He wouldn't break in though, would he?'

'I don't think so. He might not need to. Maybe he's got a spare key.'

'You think?'

'He and your dad were quite pally at one point. They were on the same pub quiz team at The Rose and Crown.'

'Yes, they were, weren't they?' Eleanor said, a heavy frown appearing on her face as she thought. 'I wonder… no.'

'What?'

'I was going to say, I wonder if the police have been to see him.'

'We've all been interviewed in the street, and I saw that Olivia Winter go over after she'd been to see me. Hal actually called her over to his place. I bet he couldn't wait to give her chapter and verse.'

'Lesley, the police were asking whether Dad had anyone close in his life. I told them he didn't. Anyway, I've been thinking about it and if he did kill twelve people, that's a lot for one person, choosing victims, hiding the bodies… Can one person do all that on their own?'

'You think your dad had a partner?'

'I don't know. I… I'm finding out all this new information about my dad and I don't know what to make of it. Is it possible Dad and someone else have been going around the north of England on a crime spree?'

Lesley took a deep breath. 'I liked your dad, Eleanor, I really did. He was a good man. But, if he has killed all these people, we have to ask ourselves if we really did know him in the first place. And if he did have a partner in crime, is he still out there?'

'Hal Garfield?'

'Can you think of anyone else?'

Eleanor thought for a moment. 'No.'

'Me neither,' Lesley replied.

They sat in silence and allowed the heavy atmosphere to envelop them.

Chapter Forty-One

Sunday 2nd February 2025

By the time Olivia fell into bed on Saturday night, she was exhausted. As she closed her eyes, images of her mother and Claire came to her mind. She remembered a Guy Fawkes night when they all went to a local fireworks display. They were wrapped up against the elements and gazed in awe at the colourful display as explosions lit up the night sky. Olivia couldn't remember how old she was, but it was Claire's first time seeing the fireworks. At first, she was scared of the loud bangs, but the beautiful colours made up for it. By the end of the evening, she was high on the excitement. It had been the perfect evening. Their dad had had to carry Claire home in his arms as she was too tired to walk. Trailing behind, Olivia held her mum's hand tightly. They'd been a happy family that night. Olivia wondered how many women her father had already killed by then. Another memory tainted.

The next morning, she woke early, and was cold. The duvet had been pushed onto the floor, one pillow was at the bottom of the bed and the fitted sheet had come away from two corners – evidence of a night thrashing and turning in the throes of a nightmare. Her brow was wet with sweat, and she could smell stale body odour. She was pleased she never remembered her dreams. She wouldn't be able to handle that.

She stumbled into the shower, stripping off her bed clothes as she went, and remained under the hot needles of water until she couldn't stand it any longer.

Olivia needed to disengage her mind. Today was all about Linus. He needed to say goodbye to his wife, a woman he clearly adored. The last thing he wanted was Olivia's terrors intruding.

They were going out into the countryside, to the Northumbria National Park, so she dressed in layers. Jeans, thick socks, walking shoes, T-shirt, a heavy jumper and padded coat. She wrapped a scarf around her neck, pulled down her beanie hat over her ears and put on thick woollen gloves.

Linus was waiting for Olivia when she arrived at his apartment. He was dressed in walking trousers and boots and had a thick coat on. In his hands, he held a cloth bag which Olivia guessed contained the urn with his wife's ashes. Judging by the expression on his face, that bag weighed a tonne.

'Good morning. Are you sure you want to do this?' she asked.

He nodded but didn't make a move.

'We don't have to.'

'No. I'm sure. What you said yesterday made perfect sense. This past year has been agony. I need to let go.'

'I know my opinion doesn't count for anything, but I think you're doing the right thing.'

'I saw Eleanor last night on the way back to the hotel,' Olivia said once they'd left Newcastle city centre behind them and were heading for open countryside in Linus's Audi.

'Really? At the hotel?'

'No. I called into a pub on the way back. I fancied a drink. She's in two minds whether to go and see Isaac in prison. She asked my advice.'

'What did you tell her?'

'I told her it was entirely up to her. Nobody can tell her what to do, and she shouldn't be listening to people if they start sticking their noses in, giving their twopenny-worth.'

'Good advice.'

'I love these sprawling views,' Olivia said. They were driving on the A696, leaving Ponteland behind them, and were surrounded by farmland. 'No matter what window I look out of in London, all I see are buildings.'

'Would you consider moving?'

'No. London is home. The countryside is a lovely place to visit when you want to clear your head and recharge your batteries, but I'm definitely a city girl.'

They both fell quiet for a few miles as Linus kept his eyes on the road and Olivia continued to marvel at the views.

'Where are we actually going?' Olivia asked as they turned off the A68 and onto a narrow lane towards a battered road sign pointing to a place called Sills.

'I was hoping to take an earlier turn-off, but it was closed. We're heading to The Drake Stone. It's a beautiful area and you can see for miles from there on a clear day. I have a photo of Clara leaning against the stone. The sun is shining in the background and her hair is all windswept. She was looking into the distance, and I just took this snap of her. She looks… It's my favourite photograph of her. We came back to this spot often. I thought she'd like to be scattered here.'

'That's lovely,' Olivia said.

'I remember…' Linus stopped as a beeping sound rang out from the dashboard.

'What's that?'

'I've no idea. I've never seen that light come on before.'

'Please don't tell me we're breaking down.'

'I wouldn't have thought so. It was only serviced at Christmas.'

Olivia looked around her with a worried expression. She couldn't see another building and hadn't seen one for miles.

'Have you noticed we've slowed down?' she said.

'Yes. I had picked up on that.'

Linus put the car into a higher gear and pressed his foot down on the accelerator. The engine made a sound like it was struggling to breathe.

'Shit,' he said, moving quickly down into a lower gear.

Olivia watched on in bewilderment as Linus wrestled with the car.

It wasn't long before they were merely crawling along the single track.

'I think you should pull over,' Olivia said. 'Maybe the engine has overheated or something and needs a few minutes to cool down,' she guessed.

Linus took her advice and pulled in to the side of the road. He turned off the ignition and the car fell silent.

As far as the eye could see, there was nothing but flat land, countryside, trees in the distance and the odd sheep here and there. No sign of life. No farmhouse they could walk to for rescue. Olivia couldn't remember the last time she'd seen another vehicle that wasn't a tractor.

'I hate to be a doom-monger,' Olivia began. 'But we're not going anywhere, are we?'

'I'm not sure, yet.'

Olivia shivered. 'Are you a member of the AA?'

'Yes, I am.'

'Please tell me you also know where you are when you call for help.'

Linus looked out of the windows around him before turning to Olivia. 'Not a clue.'

'I thought you knew this area. What did you call it, The Devil's Stone?'

'The Drake Stone. We're miles away from that.'

'Oh. Great,' she said, folding her arms tight against her chest.

'Shall I try the engine?'

'Go on then,' she said, giving Linus a nervous look.

He turned the key in the ignition. The engine ticked over. It was struggling to start, but it didn't. He tried again. The same result. He tried a third time, and nothing happened at all.

Olivia took out her phone and opened Google Maps. She zoomed in on where the blue dot signalled where she was, but there were no road names, no place names, no areas of interest listed, nothing.

'We appear to be nowhere,' she said, showing him her screen.

'That's fine. Don't worry. I'll use what3words.'

'What's that?'

'You don't know what3words?'

'Obviously not.'

'It's a geocode system that can identify any location on earth with a resolution of three metres giving each square three random words.'

'What?'

'Look.' He showed the app, which zoomed in on their location, seemingly in the middle of nowhere. 'We're here, and the three words for this point are feasting, prom, copy. All I need to do is tell the AA those three words and they'll find us easily.'

Olivia's expression was one of confusion and amazement. 'And this covers the entire planet?'

'Yes. Well, I've no idea if it includes the oceans, too. I don't really want to try it by getting lost in the Atlantic,' he said with a smile.

'So, where we were going, The Drake Stone, that will have its own three words?'

He typed 'The Drake Stone' into the search bar and it came up with 'clutches, gear, strictly'.

Linus laughed while he scrolled through his contacts to find the AA. 'It's funny – you know what the front door of 10 Downing Street is? It's "slurs this shark".'

Olivia tuned him out as a spark of an idea came into her head. She reached down to her bag in the footwell and brought it up onto her lap. She opened it and took out her tablet. Turning it on and looking for the file of Isaac's code, she looked at columns three and four with the four seemingly random words, one of which was in brackets. Could the other three words be locations where the bodies were buried?

'They're sending a breakdown vehicle. But we could have an hour's wait,' Linus said, ending the call.

Olivia held up the tablet. 'I think we might have cracked the final two columns.'

'Oh my God,' Linus said. 'It's been staring me in the face all this time.'

'But what does the single word in brackets mean?' Olivia asked.

'I don't know. Maybe it's something to do with what's at each location.'

12	M6	DATE EATEN EDGE (POPPY)	HELPFUL INDEED CRESCENT (HEAT)	BROWN BLUE BLUE BLACK 12/5/10/20	£

'Right, we'll use Sean Bridger's entry in the code,' Olivia said. 'Type in the three words in column three and see what comes up. Date, eaten, edge.'

'It's very close to Whitley Bay Cemetery. There are a few holiday parks and resorts around there.'

'That's close to Newcastle, isn't it?'

'Yes.'

'Did Sean have any connection with that area?'

'I've no idea. He travelled all over. Some of his homeless

friends we spoke to said he often went off for a few days and came back with a pocket full of cash.'

'I suppose it's possible he could have gone to these holiday resorts for either casual work or maybe he was… I don't know, selling himself to holidaymakers.'

'You think that's where Isaac picked him up?'

'I don't know. Try the words from the fourth column: helpful, indeed, crescent. What does that give you?'

'It's a narrow road near Eshott Airfield.'

'Was that close to where Isaac was stopped by police when he had Sean Bridger in the back of his car?' Olivia asked.

'Yes.'

'That's where he was going to bury him.'

'Jesus Christ!' Linus exclaimed.

'Column three is where he picked his victims up and column four is where he buried them. We've found them, Linus. We've fucking found them!'

Chapter Forty-Two

Monday 3rd February 2025

Olivia hadn't had much sleep on Sunday night. She was looking out of her hotel room window a little before seven o'clock and saw lights on in the offices of Forth Banks Police Station. She was starting to feel claustrophobic in her room so quickly showered and walked over.

She wasn't totally surprised to find Linus sitting in the office, laptop open, mug of coffee going cold on the table in front of him. Olivia guessed, like her, he'd been kept awake all night with finally cracking Isaac's code.

'Good morning, Linus.'

He looked up and smiled.

'You're in early.'

'Couldn't sleep.'

'Me neither.'

'Look, Linus, about yesterday,' Olivia said. She kept her coat on as she sat down. The room wasn't quite warm enough for her yet. 'Events sort of took over once the AA arrived, didn't they? We didn't get around to scattering Clara's ashes.'

'No,' he said, and bowed his head. 'I felt bad as I didn't give it any thought until I pulled into my parking space outside my flat and saw the urn on the back seat.' He shook his head. 'I'm putting work before everything else.'

'This is an unusual case. It's understandable. We can go out again if you like. This evening. Or tomorrow, maybe.'

'I think I want to hold onto them, just for a little while longer. I called Clara's sister last night. I told her I was ready to scatter the ashes and she's asked if I'll hang on until she comes back from Canada. We're going to make a special event of it.'

'That's good. That's healthy. I think you're doing the right thing,' she said, reaching over to him and placing a hand on top of his.

'Thank you. For everything you said yesterday.'

'You're welcome.'

'Now, on to this code,' Linus began. 'I've put the three words into what3words, and I've written down the locations and coordinates. If we're correct, several of Isaac's victims have been dumped around mines. I've looked online and they're all abandoned.'

The door opened and Ryan came in carrying a takeaway Costa cup. He was wrapped up in a knee-length reefer coat, scarf, bobble hat and chunky boots.

'Have you two been here all night?' he asked.

'I've just arrived,' Olivia said.

'I've been here about an hour,' Linus added.

'You should have called me; I'd have come in,' Ryan said, taking his satchel off over his head and removing his bobble hat. 'I haven't had a full night's sleep since my early teens. I'm always up early. I was researching those areas you emailed over,' he said to Linus.

'I gave Ryan the locations of the areas we believe Isaac picked up his victims and I worked on where he buried them,' Linus explained to Olivia. 'I thought it would be easier.'

'I did both,' Olivia said. 'I thought it might be better if we worked on the entry before Sean Bridger as it's the most recent where we have a potential burial site. Now, based on the fact we believe the Polish passport belongs to this one, we're clearly looking for Piotr Czajkowski. I've worked out the pick-up location as being in Morecambe and his burial point as being Robin Hood's Bay.'

Both Linus and Ryan nodded in agreement.

'More accurately, Morecambe train station,' Ryan said.

'Now, J9 in the code works out at being January 2024. I'm guessing too much time has elapsed to get CCTV footage from around that time, but would the local police be able to do a door-to-door enquiry with Piotr's passport photo and see if anyone remembers him?'

'I'll give someone a call at Lancashire police and see what they can do,' Linus said, making a note.

'Will your DCI now open an official investigation?' Olivia asked Linus.

'Not without firm evidence.'

'I thought not. In that case, I suggest we three go out to Robin Hood's Bay and see if we can find Piotr's body ourselves. If so, you can call out a full forensic team and go from there.'

'I was thinking the same,' he admitted. 'Aren't you going to see Isaac again today, though?'

'I'm going to put it off until tomorrow. It was Isaac who asked me to go back today. Never let a killer think he's in charge. Tomorrow, I'll go back to Frankland Prison and hopefully we'll be able to tell him we know where he buried the bodies, and I can show off and say his code was a piece of cake to crack.'

'Even though it wasn't,' Ryan said.

'He doesn't need to know that.'

'I suggest we wait until it gets light,' Linus said. 'How about we get something to eat, then go out to Robin Hood's Bay and go from there?'

'Good idea,' Olivia said. 'Where's good to go for breakfast? My treat.'

They didn't get as far as having breakfast. In fact, they didn't even make it out of the police station before a DS passed Sutton on the stairs, handed him a tabloid newspaper and told him to open it at the centre pages. Olivia and Ryan looked over Linus's shoulder to see what was so interesting and all three froze in horror, open-mouthed, as they took in the photograph of Eleanor McFadden beneath the headline 'MY FATHER THE SERIAL KILLER'.

'I think she may have misinterpreted my advice,' Olivia said.

They were back in the small office. Olivia had read the article and was fuming over her name being mentioned several times, and the fact that she was now in Newcastle helping police with their investigations.

'Why would she do this? She's just drawing attention to herself,' Linus said. He was pacing the room, hands on hips, steam coming out of both ears.

'I think she's taking ownership of what's happened rather than waiting for the media to start banging her door down.'

'On the plus side,' Ryan said as he read the feature, 'she's not giving much away. She's talking about her childhood and her father a lot, but she's not mentioned how many he's killed or about the code.'

'Maybe she's saving that until she gets her own slot on breakfast TV,' Linus said.

'Do you want me to have a word with her?' Olivia asked.

Linus was about to speak when there was a knock on the door. He yanked it open.

'DCI Wise wants a word,' a young uniformed officer said.

'I bet she does.'

'She's told me to tell you that the press office is being bombarded with calls.'

'Well, it'll give them something to do, I suppose.'

'Oh, and this arrived for Dr Winter,' he said, handing Linus a small padded envelope before leaving.

Ryan read from the newspaper. '*I was struggling to take in everything my father has done. The man who raised me by hand, the man* who I looked up to and cherished no longer existed. I went into a dark place and considered whether life was worth living. Then I met Dr Olivia Winter. She has been through a similar horror. If she can still get up in the morning and function, then so can I. I'm taking control of my life. Be more Olivia. Wow. She's really fangirling you.'

'Maybe I should start an Olivia Winter Appreciation Society,' Olivia said, flippantly.

'Here, this has arrived for you,' Linus said, handing her the envelope. 'I wonder what Isaac's going to make of this.'

'I'm more worried about what the second killer is going to make of it,' Olivia said as she opened the envelope. 'He'll scrutinise this word for word to see if there is anything that could point the police in his direction.'

The envelope was proving tricky to open. As she tugged the flap off with force, an item fell out and landed on the table with a heavy thud. They all looked at it. It was a watch.

Ryan reached out and picked it up. 'Wow, this is nice. Hugo Boss, too. That's not going to be cheap. Is it your birthday?'

'No,' Olivia said. She looked inside the envelope, took out the single sheet of paper and unfolded it. She could feel her legs give way beneath her and quickly found her chair behind her before she fell.

'Olivia, what is it?' Linus asked.

She handed the paper to him. 'It's a thirteenth entry for the code book.'

13	F4	(NIGHT) FREE COLLAR CHANGE	SLOW (CROW) DRINK GRAIN	BROWN GREY BLACK BLACK 10/5/11/18	&

'Jesus Christ,' Ryan said, almost dropping the watch when he realised he was holding something belonging to a dead man. 'I'll get an evidence bag,' he said, jumping up out of his seat and leaving the room.

'Different handwriting. We wanted proof of a second killer. This is it,' Linus said. He placed the paper on the table and slid it back over to Olivia.

'F4. February 2025. Brown hair, grey top, black trousers, black shoes. He was cut up into ten pieces, five feet eleven inches tall and eighteen years old. He was ranked seven out of ten. Bloody hell!' she exclaimed, running her finger through her hair.

'We need to find him,' Linus said. He grabbed his laptop and went to the what3words website. He typed in the three words from the fourth column of the code and hit enter. 'According to this he's in woodland close to Colt Crag Reservoir.'

'Where's that?'

'It's in Hexham. About thirty miles from here.'

Olivia stood up and grabbed her coat.

'Where are you going?'

'We need proof that these are drop-off points for the victims. You said so yourself. We need to go and see if this young lad is really there. It's a recent kill. There may be forensic evidence leading us to a second killer. We need to get to him before the local wildlife do.'

'I'm not having you walking into a fresh crime scene. Besides, he's cut up into ten pieces. Do you really want to see that?'

'In early 2020 I was in France helping the Police Nationale search for a man who had killed four women. Against my better judgement, the detective leading the case asked me to go on national television and tell the viewing public what kind of man they were looking for. I did. The next day, the killer called the police and told them where they could find victim number five. He'd mutilated a young woman, only nineteen years old. I won't go into the gory details, but he'd done things to her nobody should have to endure. Afterwards, he'd washed her body clean and propped her up in her bed. Carved into her chest with a very deep knife were the words "for Olivia".'

'Fucking hell! How do you sleep at night with all that shit in your head?'

'I have shares in Stolichnaya,' she said with her usual stoic smile, which hid a world of pain.

Chapter Forty-Three

According to the satnav in Linus's car, it would take thirty-seven minutes to get to Colt Crag Reservoir. When they set off from the police station car park, he called DCI Wise and told her of the latest developments. Olivia hadn't heard her reply, but Linus told her a forensic team was on standby should they have interpreted the code correctly and found a body waiting for them. In the back of the car, Ryan was scrolling through his tablet, having actioned various tasks following the watch and note being sent for testing.

'It's a nice watch, and looked new, but it's quite high-end. There are several places in Newcastle you can buy them from. I've asked DC Lowel to contact local sellers and get a list of buyers. If we get no joy from there, we'll cast our net wider.'

Olivia turned around in her seat. 'I didn't think to ask – where was this one picked up from?'

'The what3words gives the location of St Joseph's Church in Benwell.'

'Is Benwell in Newcastle?' she asked.

Ryan nodded.

'Who the fuck is this second killer?' Linus asked, slamming his hands onto the steering wheel. 'We've questioned his daughter, his neighbours, his colleagues. Not one of them stands out as being Isaac's partner in crime.'

'That's why I want to talk to Eleanor,' Olivia said. 'If we can find out what was going on in Isaac's life when he first started killing in April 2021, we can work out who he was close to around that time. Who came into his life then? Or who left his life at that time and has remained in the shadows ever since?'

'But you said there were previous victims before the code?'

'Yes, but something happened to make him start writing the code in the first place.'

'Ryan, get on to uniform,' Linus said over his shoulder. 'Tell them to go round to Eleanor's and bring her into the station.'

'Is that kind of tactic necessary?' Olivia asked.

'We can't wait any longer. Thirteen victims, Olivia. Thirteen. I will not have any more murders because of that man.'

'I just don't think sending a team of uniformed officers around to Eleanor is a good idea. She's a victim, too.'

'I don't care. The time for kid gloves is long gone. We need answers. I'm worried that now Isaac is in prison, this second killer might think we're going to be closing in on them and will want to go out in a blaze of glory. I don't want a massacre on my hands.'

'You won't. Isaac was arrested in March last year and he's waited eleven months to kill again. You don't need to worry about an elaborate endgame.'

'He wrote to you, Olivia. He sent the watch to you,' Linus said firmly. 'Don't you think that's a mind game of some kind?'

'He could have got Olivia's name from the newspaper,' Ryan said.

'No, he couldn't,' Olivia said as the realisation dawned. She felt an icy chill run up her spine, despite the heated seats. 'The article only went in the paper today, which is the third of February. This new victim will have been killed on the first. He knew I was here before the press did.'

'What does that mean?' Linus asked.

'The killer knows I've been here from the beginning, and I've probably already spoken to them.'

The car fell deathly silent.

Chapter Forty-Four

Eleanor read the feature on her iPad. She was still in her dressing gown, sitting at the kitchen table with a mug of tea in front of her and a slice of granary toast rapidly going cold. She wasn't happy.

She had arranged with the journalist over the phone to spread the information she had given him over several features, to be printed over five days for maximum impact. A new serial killer on the streets of England was exciting for the media. Damien Littlejohn had listened with rapt attention as she'd told him about her killer father, his code book, his trophies. He'd asked questions but his tone was flat. The moment Eleanor mentioned Olivia Winter he'd become more animated and started asking questions about her. In the first feature about her, Olivia's name was mentioned in the third paragraph and then constantly throughout. There was mention of the sodding drama going out on ITV1 tonight and an oversized photo of Olivia at the top of the page. This was supposed to be about her, not fucking Olivia Winter.

Eleanor's mobile rang. She fished for it in her dressing-gown pocket and looked at the display. Damien Littlejohn was calling. She swiped to answer.

'Sorry to call so early, Eleanor. I want to go over a few facts for the second feature.'

'Right,' she said, an iciness to her tone.

'You mentioned one of the trophies your father kept was a Polish passport. Did you get a look at the name of who it belonged to?'

'Oh. Erm, no, I'm afraid not.'

'That's a shame. Now, I've been in touch with a photographer I know in your neck of the woods. Is there a chance you can let him have access to your father's house? We'd love a photo of the garage.'

'Right. Yes, that shouldn't be a problem.'

'Excellent. I'll drop him an email. This code you said your father wrote, have the police been able to crack it?'

'I don't know. They haven't said.'

'Has Olivia Winter said anything about it?'

Eleanor visibly flinched at the mention of Olivia's name.

'Not to me she hasn't.'

'Did she tell you the psychological meaning behind creating a code?'

'No.'

'Will you be seeing her again?'

'I... Maybe, I—'

Damien interrupted. 'I think it would be useful to get her angle on things, especially if she's working with the police. She'll be able to offer an insight nobody else can.'

'I see,' Eleanor said, merely for something to say.

Damien cleared his throat. 'It's the premiere of the first episode of the drama about her father tonight. Will Olivia be watching? How does she feel about the drama being made?'

Eleanor squeezed her eyes tightly shut and sucked in her thin lips.

'Eleanor, are you still there?' Damien asked when she didn't say anything.

Eleanor disconnected the call.

Hal Garfield carefully cut out the feature from the newspaper. He'd kept a scrapbook of the investigation into Isaac McFadden's crime and subsequent trial. Now, the story was gaining traction once again. He wondered why Eleanor had decided to go to the newspapers to put her side of the story across. He didn't know her too well, but thought she wasn't the type of person to sell her soul to the press. He wasn't surprised about the lack of detail and information in the feature as Eleanor didn't visit her father often. They weren't the closest father and daughter in the world, something Isaac regretted, but she had her own life. Maybe Eleanor was the wrong person to go to the newspapers and tell them what Isaac was really like. Maybe the story needed to be told by someone closer, someone who lived bang opposite the murder house, someone who could see right into the living room from his bedroom.

Hal carefully placed the feature in his scrapbook, grabbed his tablet and turned it on. He was the administrator on a message board on the dark web – *Analysing the Killers Anonymous* – where members talked about recent murderers in the press around the world and tried to understand what made them kill and why, and how the victims had, inadvertently, put themselves in the path of their killers. He logged in and opened up a new conversation.

<<ISAAC MCFADDEN>>
Posted: Mon 3 Feb, 2025. 10:27.

ADMIN: You may have seen in the news this morning that ISAAC MCFADDEN, killer of Sean Bridger, currently serving a life sentence in Frankland Prison, has possibly murdered more people. His daughter, Eleanor, has given an interview with The Sun newspaper in which she states Northumbria Police are looking into her father's past based on new evidence and that renowned forensic psychologist, Dr Olivia Winter, is helping them. What do we think? Do we have a serial killer who has managed to outfox the police and is doing time for merely one victim? Hats off to Mr McFadden if so. However, what none of you will know is that I was a good friend of Isaac's. I live on the same road as him. The photo attached to this post is a picture of Isaac's house, the house where his murders seem to have been committed. Do I think he's capable of being a serial killer? Ask me your questions and I'll answer them.

FavaBeans: How many victims are we talking here? If you know him as much as you say you do then did you see him with one of his victims? Are you going to go to the police and tell them what you know?

>**ADMIN:** I've spoken to the police on numerous occasions. I've told them everything I know about Isaac.

AxeMan: I read that feature. It doesn't go into much detail. Reading between the lines, I don't think Eleanor was as close to her father as she was making out. She's riding on his coattails. She's probably hoping to be on the next Celeb Big Brother.

BabyFace: Olivia Winter is hot. I'd do her serious damage.

BlackDahlia: Surely Northumbria Police know if there's a serial killer on their patch. More info needed, Admin.

>**ADMIN:** The police are looking into unsolved murders. Isaac was a sales rep. He travelled all over the northeast. Who knows where he hid the bodies. This could be huge.

JeffreyDahmersHusband: No offence, Admin, but anyone could have taken that photo. How do we even know it's his house?

>**ADMIN:** It's his house. He'd lived there since the late 90s.

KeyserSoze: That does look like a serial killer's house. Bodies in the cellar I'm guessing.

JackTheStripper: Have you been in the house Admin? What's it like? How close did you come to being a victim?

> **ADMIN:** Isaac was a good friend. I was in his house often. I doubt I was ever close to being a victim. I never felt like I had anything to worry about.
> **JackTheStripper:** Think we need more proof that's his house.

No1Fan: I agree with JackTheStripper. Need more proof. If you were close to him, did you have a spare key? Surely there's something you can take that the police won't miss.

JackTheStripper: We need a selfie of you looking for victims under his patio. Haha.

> **ADMIN:** Leave it with me.

Chapter Forty-Five

COLT CRAG RESERVOIR, HEXHAM, NORTHUMBERLAND

Linus turned the bend on the A68 passing Barrasford Quarry.
'It's coming up on your right,' Ryan said, quietly, from the back.

'I'm aware,' Linus returned.

The atmosphere in the car had been heavy since Olivia had suggested the second killer had known from the beginning that she was here and helping the police. She had been racking her brain making a mental list of the people she had spoken to. Eleanor was the obvious one. After that there were Isaac's neighbours, Lesley Quinn and Hal Garfield. Linus, Ryan and other police officers in the station she'd said good morning to. Staff and customers of the hotel she was staying in, restaurants she'd eaten in and bars she'd drunk at. Was it possible she was being followed this whole time without realising it? If the second killer knew she'd been brought in to help, how close to the investigation could they be? Had Linus been followed down to London?

Linus slowed down. 'How far away are we from the drop-off site?'

'We're really close now. The square box on the what3words site is off the road in amongst these trees. I think you should probably pull up on your left, here, and we hop over the wall.'

'Right,' Linus said, indicating and pulling up on the grass verge.

Olivia struggled to get out of the car as it was parked close to a dry-stone wall so as not to obstruct passing traffic. The ground was squelchy underfoot and she was pleased to have worn sensible shoes rather than heels.

She buttoned up her coat and raised her collar.

Linus jumped over the wall and held his hand out to help Olivia over it. At only five foot two, she didn't have the length of leg to simply hop over. Ryan followed, his tablet under his arm.

The trees were bare, apart from a few evergreens, and the sky was dull. Another fall of snow was threatened. As they entered the woodland, the light faded, and the breeze rattling the naked branches together created an unsettling and eerie atmosphere.

Ryan looked down at his tablet. They were frighteningly close to where the code said the drop-off point was. He edged forward, leading the way with Linus and Olivia close behind.

'Are there traffic cameras on this road?' Olivia asked.

'Not on this stretch, no,' Linus replied.

'Surely whoever dumped the body here will have had to park close to where you did. They will have been obstructing traffic. Maybe someone will remember that.'

'We can only hope.'

Ryan had stopped ahead. Linus and Olivia edged around him so they were all level and could see exactly what he was seeing. There it was. Up ahead, sheltered by two trees close together, was a hint of red they all immediately recognised as the same red plastic clinical waste bag that was found in the back of Isaac's car when he was pulled over and Sean Bridger was discovered in his boot.

'You two wait here,' Linus said. He took his phone from his inside pocket, turned on the torch and headed around the other side of the trees.

Ryan looked away. 'It's one thing looking at pictures, it's a different thing entirely being this close to a dismembered body.'

'Are you all right?' Olivia asked.

He nodded, though it was clearly a lie.

Olivia went back to watching Linus. He was walking slowly and carefully, looking at the ground in case he stepped on something that might be forensically important. He passed the trees, looked back and pointed his phone towards the bag. Olivia couldn't quite make out his facial expression from where she was standing but seeing his shoulders droop and his head shake, she knew he was looking down at their thirteenth victim.

The road was closed off, which would be a massive disruption to motorists. Olivia waited in the front passenger seat while uniformed police officers set up a cordon and scene of crime officers donned their white paper suits and began a fingertip search of the area. A white tent was erected around the trees to hide the bags from public view and to protect the body from the elements. It had started sleeting and Olivia had been glad to return to the warmth of the car. Linus had told her there were three clinical waste sacks, dumped next to each other. As he led her back to the car by the elbow, she looked up at him, took in his ashen expression and knew this was grim. She wanted to question him more about what he had seen but knew he wouldn't tell her. Not yet.

While alone in the car, Olivia took out her laptop and began making notes. There was clearly a shared madness between Isaac McFadden and the second killer. But had the second killer, the dominant one of the two, replaced Isaac with an alternative subordinate, or was he out there on his own continuing the reign of terror they'd started together? How strong did a person have to be, especially physically, to dismember a body and transport the pieces to the middle of nowhere?

Forensic and postmortem examinations would be able to inform detectives if a person had been killed by one person or two. It was possible, from the range and extent of the injuries inflicted on a victim, to estimate the force of each blow or stab and work out the ferocity and strength of each killer. This fresh body could give more information than the previous twelve put together, since it had not been subject to decomposition before being located.

But what about when it came to dismembering a corpse? According to Linus, there were three bags hiding amongst those trees. Going back to the code, this latest victim was five feet eleven and eighteen years old. She had no idea if he was of slight build or muscular. Either way, he was going to be heavy. There was no way someone like Olivia, slight and only five foot two, would be able to carry three bags of body parts all the way out here on her own. She would struggle carrying them one by one. It would take time, and someone was bound to see her. Was this the work of one man? One incredibly strong man? Or was this the work of two?

It would be worth checking Isaac's garage again to find out if the second killer still had a key and was using their old murder ground to continue his work. If so, had Lesley Quinn or Hal Garfield seen anything recently? Had someone other than Eleanor been calling at the house over the past few months? Is that how the killer knew Olivia was working on the investigation, because they had been watching the house and had seen her arriving with Linus and then popping next door to talk to Lesley? Was the killer worried Lesley might have seen something and said something to Olivia? Could Lesley be on the killer's hit list as the endgame approached?

Linus rapped on the side window with his gloved hand, making her jump. She looked at him, took in his ruddy face, red from the biting wind, and lowered the window.

'Sorry, I didn't mean to startle you.'

'It's fine. I've just been making some notes. I think you should send someone over to Isaac's house and see if his garage was used to cut up this victim, too.'

'Good idea. We've got an ID on this one, by the way.'

'Really? So soon?'

'A wallet was found in the victim's jeans pocket. Inside there was a single ten-pound note and a provisional driver's licence.'

Olivia frowned. 'There wasn't anything left with Sean Bridger, was there?'

'No.'

'Why start leaving something now?'

'Well, we haven't found the other victims yet. We don't know if anything was left with them or not.'

'True. It just doesn't make any sense, letting you know who the body belongs to. In fact, it doesn't make any sense for the killer to send me the code and trophy. Why is he showing off all of a sudden, after Isaac has kept it a perfect secret for four years?'

'I feel like these are the questions I should be asking you.'

'I wonder if Isaac has been able to get a message to his partner from prison,' she said, more to herself. 'He knew I was going to visit him. He could have contacted them somehow and they've changed their MO in order to increase the danger value.'

'I thought the MO never changed,' Linus said.

'No. The MO can change. It's the signature that doesn't. Here, the signature is chopping the body up. Who is this young lad?' she asked, turning to him.

From behind his back, Linus brought out the evidence bag containing the wallet and provisional driver's licence. 'Thomas Landy. The address is for a house in Byker. We've got uniform going round there now.'

'Was there anything else in his wallet apart from the tenner and the licence?'

'No.'

'What happened to his bank card or credit card? If he was at university he'd have student ID. If he was working, he might have a key card to get into a building. Store loyalty cards, membership cards. Where are all of those?'

'You think it was emptied but the licence left so we could identify him quicker?'

'Possibly. And why leave the ten pound note?'

'I'll send them off to the lab for testing. Maybe there'll be prints or something on them. I'm going to have someone run you back to the police station.'

'Okay. Did you get in touch with Eleanor? Is she coming to the station? I'd really like to talk to her.'

'I don't know. It completely went out of my mind. I'll give someone a call.'

'Don't forget about Isaac's house. If his garage was used for cutting up this Thomas Landy, then you'll need to question his neighbours again, too. They might have seen someone coming and going.'

'Right,' he nodded.

'Linus, are you all right?' she asked, placing a gloved hand on top of his as he rested it on the lowered window.

'I'm fine.'

'No offence, but I'm the queen at saying I'm fine when I'm not. I know the signs of someone who isn't fine.'

He snorted a hollow laugh. 'I don't like killers playing games. Thomas Landy was eighteen years old. He was young, had everything to live for, and some sick bastard has decided to use him in his twisted fucking game. Life is precious, for crying out loud.'

There were tears in his eyes and Olivia knew he was thinking of Clara.

'Linus, a word of advice,' she said. 'I know things aren't great for you right now, personally, so don't let this, or Isaac, set up home in your mind. You have a team around you. Use them.'

Linus seemed to be thinking about this before he replied with a firm nod.

She watched him walk away. Olivia had travelled the world interviewing killers and she often felt she needed to talk to the detectives who had worked the original investigation. Many had been affected by seeing what a killer had done to a victim, by the mind games, the lengthy interviews, witnessing post mortems, late nights and grieving relatives. This was not a job for the faint-hearted, or for someone with a fragile personality such as Linus had at present. She didn't want to see him destroyed by this, and there was only one way she knew to stop that from happening. Olivia herself needed to step up her game.

Chapter Forty-Six

DC Ryan Sweetland dropped Olivia back at Forth Banks then, as per Linus's instructions, headed straight for Isaac's home in Blyth.

Olivia was pointed to a family room where Eleanor McFadden had been taken upon her arrival. As she wasn't a suspect, nor was she answering questions under caution, it was thought a cold, impersonal interview room would be inappropriate. When Olivia opened the door, she found Eleanor sitting on an uncomfortable-looking two-seat sofa nursing a mug of tea. She hadn't heard Olivia enter and continued to stare into her mug, a million miles away from where she was.

Olivia cleared her throat. Eleanor looked up at her and proffered a weak smile.

'How are you doing, Eleanor?' Olivia asked as she went to sit down.

'I don't know. I felt like I was a suspect, the way uniformed officers escorted me here. God knows what the neighbours are saying about me now.'

'Eleanor, why did you go to the press with your story?'

'I remembered what the press was like while Dad was on trial. They camped outside my front door. They followed me to the court and bombarded me with questions. I can't face that again. I thought, if I give an exclusive interview, it will stop that from happening again.'

'I don't think it will. Once the police give a formal statement regarding your father's crimes, they're going to be all over this. It's going to be front page news and as the closest person to your father, it's you they'll come for.'

Eleanor stood up and went over to the window. She looked out at the rear car park of the police station. 'How can you say I'm the closest person to my dad? He killed so many people and I didn't know about it.'

'Eleanor, we've been working on the code your father wrote. We think he killed his first victim in April 2021. Can you think of anything around that time that happened to your dad? Did anyone new come onto the scene? Did he mention a new name you hadn't heard before, or a new friend?'

'April 2021?' Eleanor asked herself as she seemed to be searching her memory. 'No. I... I don't think so. Weren't we still in a lockdown nightmare then with Covid?'

'We were coming out of a national lockdown around that time. People were being urged to stay local but non-essential retailers were still closed.'

'It seems like a different world talking about it now, doesn't it? I didn't see my dad much during the lockdowns. I have asthma so I isolated a lot and I worked from home a great deal, too. I saw Dad via Zoom. He occasionally brought me some shopping and left it on my doorstep. We'd chat through the living room window with him standing out in the street,' she said, a wistful smile at a happy memory in a bizarre time.

'So, you wouldn't have known if anything specific happened to your father around that time?'

'No. Thinking about it now, I think it was the summer of 2021 before I actually saw him in person again. We'd all changed, though, hadn't we? I doubt I'd have noticed anything different about him.'

'Right,' Olivia said. She sat back in the armchair and chewed her bottom lip as she contemplated. 'Eleanor, we've been informed of a thirteenth body.'

Eleanor turned back from the window. 'What?'

'An item – a trophy – was sent to me this morning along with an entry in the code book. DI Sutton and I went out to where the code said the body was hidden and we found it.'

'What... I don't understand. What does all this mean?'

'We believe there is a second killer. We believe your dad had a partner.'

Eleanor's mouth fell open in shock. It was a while before the news sunk in. 'A partner? I'm sorry, I can't take any of this in. You're talking about my dad like he's one of the killers in a *Scream* film. How would he have found a partner? He... I... No!'

'Eleanor, I know this is difficult for you to take in, but this is where the evidence is taking us. What we need from you is to help us identify the second killer.'

She shook her head. 'I don't know of anyone. Dad... we didn't spend a lot of time together. Sometimes, months could go by without me seeing him. We texted, obviously. He sent me funny dog videos and I sent him dad-joke type memes. I'm guessing he might have had friends I didn't know about.'

'Who would know about them?'

'I don't know. I'm guessing the police have been through his phone and computer. Surely, any other contacts will be on there.'

Olivia nodded. She was sure Linus would have told her if there were any unusual text messages or emails they'd uncovered, unless Isaac was using a separate device they hadn't found yet.

'Could your dad—'

'Can I go?' Eleanor interrupted. 'I'm not enjoying being here in this police station and every time I talk to you or DI Sutton, I find out something new about my father that scares me to death. I really can't cope with this right now.'

'Of course you can go.'

'Thank you.' Eleanor stood up, grabbed her coat and made for the door. She stopped and turned back. 'The drama about your dad starts tonight.'

Olivia swallowed. 'Yes,' she said. She looked at Eleanor, expecting her to say more. She didn't. She opened the door and went out into the corridor, closing the door firmly behind her.

Olivia remained in the impersonal family room. She frowned as she thought about the conversation she'd just had. Why did Eleanor bring up the drama? Why didn't she ask anything about the thirteenth victim?

'It could be just possible that Eleanor knows who the second killer is and she's protecting him,' Olivia said to herself. 'But why would anyone do that?'

Olivia had interviewed many killers whose wives had known what their husbands were doing yet had remained silent. Even when they were caught, they sometimes stayed by their side and visited them every week in prison. Why? Why would anyone support a person convicted of murder, especially serial murder? Joseph Lansbury, the Seattle Slasher, whom Olivia had written a book about, had a wife who didn't give up her husband when police named him as a suspect. Olivia had interviewed her for the book and asked her why she stayed by him. She answered straightaway. It was a simple answer: 'He's my husband. I love him.' As far as Olivia was concerned, love was not an excuse for murder.

Olivia's phone vibrated in her pocket. She took it out and saw it was Linus calling her. She swiped to answer.

'Are you on your own?' he asked.

'Yes. Eleanor's just left.'

'Isaac's garage is covered in blood.'

Chapter Forty-Seven

Olivia had stepped out of a long shower, and now, wrapped in her dressing gown, towel around her head, she relaxed on the bed with a bottle of vodka she'd bought from a supermarket on her way back to the hotel. She had poured a healthy measure before she went into the shower and was now on her second. Her hopes for a night of drifting into drunken oblivion were ruined by her phone ringing and Linus Sutton telling her he was downstairs in reception if she could spare the time. Of course she could spare the time. What else was she going to do this evening apart from drown herself in a bottle of vodka?

She quickly dressed, gargled with mouthwash, then ate a couple of macadamia nut cookies to mask the smell of the mouthwash. At this time of day, the distinct smell of cool mint triple-action Colgate could only mean one thing – she was covering something up.

Linus was sitting on one of the sofas in reception. His shoulders were slumped, and his head was down. His hand was fiddling with the pendant around his neck where he kept a sample of his wife's ashes.

'Linus,' she said, softly, as she approached.

He looked up. He attempted a smile, but it didn't work.

'Sorry to call on you without asking first. I didn't think. Do you have plans?'

She almost laughed. Plans in the evening meant a social life. Olivia didn't know the meaning of the concept. 'No. Just me and a tub of Ben and Jerry's,' she lied.

'Can we talk somewhere private?'

'Sure.' She looked over to the restaurant. It was full of evening diners, laughing, joking, enjoying themselves. They didn't need to be put off their monkfish and rare steaks by looking at two gloomy people talking about disturbing crime scenes and bodies cut into pieces. 'We'll go up to my room. Are you hungry? We can call for room service.'

'I can't remember the last time I had anything.'

'Me neither. They do a really nice pan-fried salmon here.'

Olivia had no idea why, but as he lifted himself up from the sofa, she linked arms with him and led him to the lifts. Linus, this evening, seemed as if he needed human contact.

Once in the hotel room, food ordered, Linus sat on the chair at the desk while Olivia sat on the edge of her bed. He told her about the latest victim, Thomas Landy.

'Thomas lived with his mother in Byker in a council house. Last year, his mother was diagnosed with breast cancer. It was aggressive and spread quickly. She died in January this year, a day or so after Thomas's eighteenth birthday. Because they lived in a council house, and because it was in his mother's name, Thomas wasn't eligible to stay in a three-bedroom property on his own.'

'They threw him out?'

'They offered him alternative accommodation. Unfortunately for Thomas the only accommodation available was the Egremont Bed and Breakfast.'

'Judging by the look on your face, it isn't a twee coastal B&B run by a kindly old lady.'

'I wouldn't wish the Egremont on anyone. The council use it as a dumping ground for immigrants and people who've come out of prison. The only other people who use it are prostitutes paying by the hour.'

'Jesus. And they sent a grieving eighteen-year-old there?'

'I'm afraid so.'

'Didn't he have a father or other relatives?'

'His father died not long after he was born. There was no one else. Anyway, last week, Billy Driver, a notorious drug dealer, walked into the Egremont and shot Patience Winstead three times in the head. The place was a crime scene and had to be locked down. According to Raymond, the manager, Thomas was really down on his luck and had nowhere to go for the night. Raymond told him to wander around the local hospital waiting rooms, catching some sleep where he could, pretending he was a relative. He slipped him a tenner and told him he'd look after his things for him until he could come back the next day. Only…'

'He never came back,' Olivia said.

'No.'

'Where did the code say Thomas was picked up from again?'

'A church not far from the B&B in Benwell.'

'Is there any CCTV around there?'

'Some. We're going through it. It's following a similar pattern, isn't it? The second killer is going around and finding people who are at their lowest, or, like you said, have fallen off the radar.'

'It would appear so. The question is, has the second killer replaced Isaac with a third, or is he working on his own?'

'How do we find that out?'

Olivia shook her head. 'Has the post mortem been done?'

'Boyd Hailstones made it a priority. He believes Thomas was strangled and the body was taken apart in a similar way to Sean Bridger.'

'There's no way Isaac could have taken a body apart like that. When I reeled off a list of names of muscles, he looked at me like I was speaking a different language. The second, more technical, killer is doing all this.'

The knock on the door made them both jump. It was a waiter with their food.

While they were eating, the conversation strayed from work matters to more pleasant territory. Olivia told Linus all about the miniature dachshund she'd inherited, Stanley, and how he was a mischievous character, and about his best friends, two huge German Shepherds who were incredibly gentle with him. She showed him a photograph on her phone of the sleeping sausage dog snuggled in between two hairy Alsatians. She had to zoom in for Stanley to be visible.

'I used to go swimming a lot,' she said. 'Not so much anymore. But Stanley means I have to go out every day and take him for a walk. It helps to clear my head,' she smiled.

'Dogs are great for that,' he said. 'It's not practical me having one at the moment in the flat. Plus…' He paused. 'Clara was allergic.'

'What happened to her was horrific.'

'I miss her so much,' he said. His words sounded painful. 'Every single day, I miss her. I know I need to move on. What you said was absolutely right. But it's difficult, isn't it, when you're with someone you love so much you physically ache for them, and they're no longer there.'

Olivia thought of Ethan. She knew that if they settled, they would turn into every other couple. The sex would become pedestrian before becoming non-existent. They would spend their weekends planning how to decorate the spare bedroom or walking around garden centres and trying to decide how to celebrate Christmas from mid-October. She couldn't do that. She couldn't do domesticity. It was obvious that was what Ethan wanted. He'd have to find it with someone else.

'Are you all right?' Linus asked.

'Yes.'

'You seemed to zone out a bit there.'

'Did I? Sorry. I was thinking about something.'

'About the case?'

'N—yes,' she corrected herself. She was on safer ground if she only spoke about things work-related. 'Tell me, what do you think about Eleanor?'

'It's difficult to know what to think about a person when they're struggling against everything. Why?'

'I made a call to a detective I know to give one of his journalist contacts a ring. This interview Eleanor gave to the newspapers, it's not a one-off. It's the first of a series. They're going to be running one a day for the next week.'

'Really?' He frowned. 'How much information has she given them?'

'That's what I wondered.'

'Why would she do that?'

Olivia shook her head. 'She could be doing it as a form of therapy. It's cathartic to reveal everything that's on your mind. She said she had trouble trusting an actual therapist, but a journalist isn't going to sit in judgement, is he? He's just going to listen and write what she says.'

'In theory. We both know what journalists are like. They turn anything into sensationalism to sell more papers. Who's to say that by mid-week, if the articles aren't having the desired effect, there won't be a swift rewrite and Eleanor's story will be pure fiction?'

'I'm worried about her,' Olivia said. 'She was struggling with what her father has done but, there's something else eating away at me.'

'What?'

'I don't know. When I told her about a thirteenth victim, she was shocked, yes, but she didn't ask anything about him. I can't help but think she knows more about what's going on than she's telling us.'

'Is it possible Eleanor is the second killer?'

'Of course it's possible. Isaac has lied to everyone in his life. He has mastered the art of misdirection. It's fair to assume the second killer would have done so, too.'

'How *likely* is it for Eleanor to be the second killer?'

'I've asked myself that question a few times and I can't answer it. Then again...'

'Go on,' Linus prompted.

'According to my detective friend, Eleanor has been paid an undisclosed five-figure sum for her story by the papers. Maybe she does know more about what's going on than we realise. Maybe she's trying to make as much money as she can out of being the daughter of a serial killer before the attention starts to wane.'

'Do you think we'd get anything out of her if we questioned her under caution?'

'You don't have proof of any involvement to issue a caution.'

Linus frowned. 'A father and daughter killing couple. Is that a thing?'

'There is a history of families killing together. I know of sisters and brothers killing together, but never a cross-generational coupling.'

'Why does the answer to every question I have lead to more questions?' Linus asked.

Olivia sniggered. 'Welcome to my world. All I do is ask people questions and rarely do I get an answer I can trust.'

'So, when you do get an answer, what do you do with it?'

She took a deep breath and slowly blew it out. 'I hope I can find the evidence to back it up.'

Linus reached across for the wine bottle and half-filled his glass. 'I honestly do not know how you do your job. When I catch a criminal and they're in prison it's on to the next case. It's not like that for you at all, is it? You must have so many killers in your head screaming for attention.'

She tried to smile as if it wasn't a problem, but she felt her lips quiver.

'Sorry,' Linus said. 'Have I said the wrong thing?'

She shook her head. 'When you go to a football match and you're in the stands and everyone's cheering, it's a wall of noise, isn't it? Imagine standing there among thousands of people and trying to listen to each and every voice.'

'It's not possible.'

'Precisely. That's what it's like in my head. And the loudest one is my father.'

'Jesus Christ, Olivia. That's not natural. Surely you have something other than work to offer a distraction? And don't say all you have is your sausage dog.'

Olivia swallowed her tears. 'I'm afraid he is all I have.'

'What? But, as a psychologist, you must know that's not a normal way to live.'

She shrugged as if to say, 'That's life.'

'You need an outlet, Olivia. You're going to end up getting sectioned if you're not careful.'

She drained her wine glass. She placed the empty glass on the desk and looked up at Linus. He was blurred. She thought it was the drink until he told her she was crying. She hadn't realised. Olivia was so numb to her own emotions that she no longer knew when they were on display.

'Oh, God, Olivia, I'm so sorry,' Linus said. He went over to her and wrapped his arms around her, pulling her to his chest in a comforting, manly hug. 'I didn't mean to upset you.'

She sniffled. 'I know it's not normal. I just… I can't let go.'

'There must be something you can do to unwind, to switch off. It can't all be mass murderers and sausage dogs.'

She laughed through the tears and pushed herself out of his embrace. She looked up at him. His brown eyes were wet, filled with tears waiting to fall, looking bigger, sadder. He needed comfort as much as she did. She reached up on tiptoe and kissed him softly on the lips. They made eye contact. There was a small hint of lightness behind his eyes. They kissed again, more urgently this time.

They should stop. Linus knew it was wrong. His wife had been dead a year. Just one short year. In those twelve months he hadn't even looked at another woman. He hadn't missed sex or even thought about it, but right now, he needed to do this. But a small part of his mind was telling him to stop, to put Olivia down, pick up his jacket and leave. Now. Go now, before it's too late.

It was too late. He lifted Olivia up off her feet. She wrapped her legs around his waist, and they kissed hard. Her hands reached up and pulled at his hair. He pushed her down on the bed, climbed on top of her and began unbuttoning his shirt. He was taking too long. Olivia reached up and tore it open, sending buttons flying. She pulled him back down onto her and kissed him hard, biting his lip and his tongue. She ran her fingers up his back, under his shirt, and dug her nails into his skin, dragging them down. The pain ran up his spine. He hated it and loved it in equal measure. He sat back up again and undid his belt. While he unzipped his trousers, Olivia reached for the bedside lamp and turned it off before undoing her own shirt.

'Do you have any protection?' he asked.

'Just fuck me, Linus,' she hissed.

Chapter Forty-Eight

Lesley Quinn sat down on the sofa, legs tucked up beneath her, and turned the television on to ITV1. It was nine o'clock and *The Riverside Killer* was about to start. She'd seen the drama advertised on TV for weeks but hadn't been interested in it until she met Olivia. The subject of the drama had been in her house, had sat on her sofa, and now her life story was being told on television. It was exciting.

The programme opened with a young girl crossing a street to an unassuming house. It was dusk and flakes of snow were falling from the sky. The caption in the bottom corner of the screen read 'December 21, 1999'. Lesley guessed this was the young Olivia Winter, or Button, as she was then known, arriving home after seeing a friend. The drama was about to begin.

Across the street, Hal Garfield was also sitting on his sofa in front of the television. Whereas Lesley was watching for entertainment purposes, Hal was hoping to learn something. On the coffee table in front of him he had a notebook and pen, ready to make any notes that might come in handy later.

The lights were off, the living room lit only by the muted

colours from the television screen in the corner. Hal hadn't had a good day. The comments on the message board hadn't been what he'd expected. He thought people would have been impressed by the fact he lived opposite a serial killer. Instead, they wanted proof. How was he going to do that?

Then it came to him. He had a spare key Isaac had given him years ago when he had his chest freezer delivered. When the drama was over, once the street was quiet, and lights extinguished, he was going to pop over there and prove to his online friends that he knew Isaac McFadden far more than anyone else.

Eleanor had been tormenting herself all afternoon. Once she'd arrived home from the police station, she'd sat down, opened her laptop and Googled Olivia and this sodding drama about her father. Features had been written in all the national newspapers. The drama was on the cover of the *Radio Times*. The whole country seemed to be fascinated by Richard Button and his murders and the mystery surrounding his surviving daughter. Eleanor assumed Olivia thought that if she ignored the press and refused to give interviews they'd leave her alone. The opposite had happened. Olivia's silence had made the reporters eager to discover more about her – and if they couldn't get direct answers from her, they'd use other sources, including Eleanor herself.

Damien Littlejohn had been salivating whenever Eleanor mentioned Olivia's name. He'd call her tomorrow after the second feature was printed, she knew he would. He'd ask about Olivia again, and this time, she'd tell him.

Eleanor smiled to herself as the drama on television began. Poor little Olivia was being chased through the house by her father, dripping with the blood of his wife and youngest daughter. It was a shame he hadn't caught her and killed the little bitch.

Ryan Sweetland hadn't said he was going to watch *The Riverside Killer*, but then he hadn't said he *wasn't* going to watch it either. Linus had categorically stated he wouldn't be viewing. He didn't like true crime adaptations, but Ryan was fascinated. He knew not to expect a psychological profiling of a serial murder. He knew this was an entertainment programme, but it would be interesting to see what Olivia went through and how she was able to survive and cope with the aftermath.

Sitting in his small flat on the outskirts of the village of Wideopen, Ryan watched the drama begin in the style of a slasher horror film as Olivia discovered the bodies of her mother and younger sister before being attacked by her father. As the final knife came down on the nine-year-old Olivia, the camera angle was from her point of view and the dripping red blade swiped in slow motion across the screen before cutting to the main opening titles. This was gratuitous entertainment. Ryan got himself comfortable and settled in for the evening.

Hal waited until gone midnight before risking going over to Isaac's house. After the drama, which, in his opinion, was way over the top, he'd watched the news and had a cup of tea and a few biscuits while reading one of Olivia Winter's books. Every now and then, he got up and went over to the living-room window, peeling back the curtains and risking a glance outside to see if there was anyone around. He saw the odd dog walker taking their pet for a final pee of the night, but most of the houses were in darkness. He waited a little while longer and read another chapter of *The Secrets of a Serial Killer*, Olivia's first book on serial killers, and one Hal had read a few times already.

Eventually, he tore himself away from his book and left the house by the back door, taking the long route round to Isaac's house.

The police had been there for most of the day. Various CSI vans had pulled up, and white-suited forensic officers had gone inside and come out again. From the discreet distance of his living room, Hal had risked taking a few snaps on his mobile and uploaded them to the message board. The final van had driven away around teatime. Hal had watched as a man had locked the front door and pocketed the keys. He'd noticed a marked police car drive by slowly over the past couple of hours. They were obviously keeping an eye on the house. What did they know? And, more importantly, why didn't Hal know about it?

It was a cold night. Temperatures were a few degrees below zero and Hal's breath appeared in great clouds as he exhaled. Dressed in black from head to toe, he tried to be inconspicuous and stealthy, while also looking as if he was simply on a late-night stroll, should anyone notice him. He walked in silence, and once he was in Isaac's back garden, he was pretty sure nobody had seen him. He certainly hadn't seen anyone else.

He slowly inserted the key into the lock and turned it. He wasn't sure if it was his overactive imagination or the silence of the night, but he was sure the sound of the lock mechanism was echoing around the quiet neighbourhood.

He opened the door. The alarm started beeping straightaway. He ran on tiptoe into the house and tapped into the code on the alarm panel. 1170. The beeping stopped. Hal remained still for a while and allowed the silence and the darkness to wrap their fingers around him. The magnitude of the occasion was not lost on him. He was alone in the house of a serial killer. He couldn't keep the smile off his face.

'Where to begin?' he asked himself quietly.

The garage was the obvious choice. Hal often wondered why Isaac had gone to the expense of having a garage built when he never parked his car in it. What was he hiding in there? Or to be more accurate, what was he hiding *under* there?

He went into the kitchen and over to the door leading into the garage, pushed down the handle and opened the door. What he saw was not what he was expecting. Not in his wildest dreams would he have guessed that.

'Oh' was all he managed to say.

Extract from a notebook allegedly written by Isaac McFadden

I met a murderer once.
I didn't know it at the time, but when he was arrested and appeared on the news, I recognised him. He was a barman at a pub I used to drink in when I worked for Carter, Weddle and Thropp. He was a nice bloke. He was approachable, personable. You need to be in that job.
Often, I'd go in on a weeknight after work and prop up the bar with a pint or three before going home and we'd chat about this and that. He was a few years older than me, slim, good looking, always smiling. A few of the regular lasses fancied him. They'd do that coy smile thing at him yet pretending they're not looking at him. He played up to it.
Next thing I know he's on the front page of every newspaper in the country. Scott Knight had killed his girlfriend, and her mother and father in a frenzied attack, stabbing all three of them a total of more than one hundred times.
I've no idea of his motive. I followed the case in the news, but it soon disappeared. I did think about going to see him, but, well, everyone who does this kind of thing are different, aren't they?

That was probably when my fascination for murder began, though I didn't do anything about it until much later.

Looking back, I didn't really have much choice in the matter. It was circumstance that led me to murder. It was an alignment. It wasn't manufactured. How could it have been? I didn't start it.

Chapter Forty-Nine

Tuesday 4th February 2025

Olivia had forgotten what it was like waking up next to someone she hardly knew. For the last year, the only man who had stayed over in her house was Ethan Miller. In the past, if she met up with a stranger, they usually left after the deed was done. She would hear them leaving the house, the front door closing behind them while she was curled, foetal, in her bed, holding back the tears and internally screaming. As she looked over at a sleeping Linus Sutton, she realised it had been a long time since she'd had sex with a stranger. When Ethan hadn't been available, she'd settled for an early night and a good book, with Stanley curled up at the bottom of her bed. As time went on, she was realising dogs were more reliable for company than men. Dogs gave you their love unconditionally. One look into the big, deep, dark eyes of a dachshund and the love was more than reciprocated. Maybe Olivia should have brought Stanley to Newcastle with her.

Linus began to stir. As he woke up, Olivia tried to put herself in his position. How would he be feeling this morning when he opened his eyes and the realisation dawned that he'd slept with someone who wasn't his wife for the first time since she died? She hoped he wouldn't be full of regret, anger, grief, and torment. There wasn't enough room in the bed for two people to be suffering such emotions.

'Morning,' he said in a tired voice, a smile warming his face.

'Good morning,' she returned. 'Sleep well?'

'Yes. Fine. You?'

'Not bad.' She didn't add that she'd spent the best part of four hours wide awake trying to make sense of the noises in her head. 'Are you... okay?'

'I'm fine,' he beamed. 'Thank you, for last night,' he said.

He placed a warm palm on her bare shoulder. She tensed and tried not to flinch. She didn't like being touched. Well, she did, but only on her terms.

'You're welcome,' she said. 'It was fun.'

'Yes. I enjoyed it. It's just... you know... I mean...'

'It was just sex, Linus,' Olivia quickly jumped in.

'Oh. Good. That's what I was trying to say. I'm nowhere near ready to...'

'No. We were just having fun.'

'Absolutely.'

She swung her legs out of bed and wrapped her dressing gown around her. 'Well, I was thinking that we still need to go out to Robin Hood's Bay?'

'Yes,' he said, sitting up and rubbing his eyes.

'I know the entry sent to me in the code matched where Thomas Landy's body was found but I still think we should take a look for ourselves.'

'Yes. I want to make sure we're one hundred per cent certain before I tell DCI Wise.'

'That's very wise,' she said with a grin.

'It's too early for bad puns. Mind if I jump in the shower?'

'Sure. I'm going to order some breakfast. Do you want anything?'

'I can't stomach anything first thing. The strongest coffee they can do is fine with me.'

Olivia opened her mouth to say something then stopped

herself. She was about to say he was a man after her own heart. She was glad she had caught herself in time.

As Linus made his way to the en suite, Olivia looked up and saw the lines of scratches on his back. She looked back to the bed and saw a clump of black hair she must have torn out of him during their violent sex. She smiled to herself. It had been a very good night.

Olivia went over to the desk, a mess of paperbacks and notebooks. She moved some of them around and the photo of her with Ethan came into view. She picked it up and looked down at it. Before he left for the Amazon, he printed off two copies and handed one to her. He said they could both take it out and look at it whenever they wanted, knowing the other was also looking at it at some point that day. It was a sweet thing to say, if slightly sickly, but it had made Olivia smile, and despite not liking how she looked in photographs, she had to admit she genuinely loved this one.

'Who's that?'

Olivia must have drifted. She turned to see Linus standing over her, his hair dripping from the shower, towel wrapped around his waist.

'This is Ethan,' she said, handing him the photo.

Linus smiled. 'You look completely different in this picture.'

'Really? It was only taken a few months ago.'

'You look so… happy.'

Olivia didn't know how to respond to that.

'You like him, don't you?'

She struggled to find the right words. 'Yes. I do.'

'What are you scared of?'

'I'm scared of hurting him,' she admitted. 'I can't be a normal girlfriend to someone. I can't share things. I can't open up to him. That's what partners do. I'd ruin him.'

'Are you sure you're not scared of falling in love, of being happy? It's not a crime to enjoy life, Olivia. I'm no forensic psychologist, but don't you think you're punishing yourself for surviving when you mother and sister didn't?'

Olivia was struggling to hold back the tears.

'I'm not trying to hurt you, Olivia,' Linus continued. 'But don't give up on this man.' He handed back the photo. 'It's obvious you like him. It's obvious he likes you. Give it a try. Nobody knows what's around the corner. I never thought I'd be a widower, but here I am. If you find even a modicum of happiness, grab it with both hands.'

Linus leaned forward and hugged her. She placed her head against his wet chest, smelled the familiar shower gel. She felt safe in his arms.

According to Linus's satnav, it would take one and a half hours to get to Robin Hood's Bay by car, traffic depending. They decided to skip the coffee and pick up a takeaway Costa on the way and hopefully beat the rush-hour traffic. They set off a little before seven o'clock. It was still dark, and Olivia watched as early morning commuters made their way to the train station wrapped up in layers against the cold, faces hidden behind scarfs pulled up over their mouths, hats pulled down low.

'Winter seems to be lingering,' she said as she noticed a few flakes of snow hit the windscreen.

'It tends to linger longer in the north. There's the rest of February, March and April for more bad weather. We generally wait until late May before we can say winter is definitely over.'

'Bloody hell, I'd go mad.'

'You like the sun?'

'I'm not overly fond of hot weather, but it's nice to look up and see a blue sky from time to time.'

'Are you having a holiday this year?'

'I've been invited to guest lecture in Germany in June and San Francisco in September. I'll add a couple of days to my visits there.'

'Don't you ever take time off?'

She didn't answer that question.

'What's the plan for Ryan today then?'

'He's back out at Isaac's house with the forensic team. They're doing a full sweep of the whole house in case the killer used more than the garage. I've asked him to talk to the neighbours too; see if they've noticed anything in the past few days. Let me put the radio on and see if there are any traffic updates,' he said, as he played with the buttons on his steering wheel.

The news was just beginning. The hurried presenter gave the headlines. She had a soft Geordie accent which Olivia found quite soothing.

'... And in a second interview with *The Sun* newspaper, Newcastle woman Eleanor McFadden reveals more information about her father Isaac McFadden, sentenced to life in prison last year for the murder of homeless man Sean Bridger. In today's interview, Ms McFadden states she believes her father could have killed as many as twelve men. Northumbria Police are currently investigating and are being helped by forensic psychologist Dr Olivia Winter. Dr Winter is the daughter of serial killer Richard Button. Last night, the first episode of a four-part drama telling the story of his crimes and capture aired on ITV1. It has been met by—'

Olivia reached out and turned the radio off.

'I completely forgot about the drama last night,' Linus said.

'So did I.'

'How are you feeling?'

Olivia was looking out of the window, watching the dark world go by at high speed. 'How are you feeling?' should be such a simple question to answer. For Olivia, it had the potential to open more darkness than Pandora's box.

'I'm fine,' she said, turning to him with a fake smile. 'I just hope they've made me a six-foot leggy blonde,' she said. It was her usual remark when she was asked how she felt about the drama. It was starting to wear thin. Even she no longer believed herself.

The Devil's Code

They approached Robin Hood's Bay via the B1447. As they turned right off Raw Pasture Bank, Olivia told Linus to slow down as, according to what3words, they were almost at their destination. It was a similar location to where they found Thomas Landy. A single-track road, no place to pull over, with woodland on either side.

'We're going to have to get out and walk,' Olivia said.

Linus indicated and pulled over.

Olivia took off her seat belt, opened the door and stepped out of the car. She was hit in the face with the smell coming in from the nearby North Sea. She could hear the waves crashing on the shore. She couldn't remember the last time she heard the ocean. It brought back memories of her grandparents taking her on holiday abroad, of running in and out of the warm water, the sun on her bare skin, not caring if anyone saw her scars. As a child, she was immune to the stares of others and basked in the innocence of youth. But the holidays were always tinged with sadness. Her younger sister Claire would have loved those trips. She loved the beach so much.

'I haven't heard the sea for so long,' she said, the ghost of a smile on her face. 'I think I might have to treat myself to a holiday at some point.'

'Clacton?'

'Nowhere so exotic. Maybe Grimsby,' she said. This time her smile was real.

Linus smiled back. 'Which way are we heading?'

Olivia looked down at her tablet. 'Over the wall and into the woods again.'

'We're going to get a reputation if we keep doing this,' he said as a car slowed down to pass them, the driver giving them a strange look.

'We don't have Ryan with us this time. It looks even stranger when two guys and a woman enter the woods,' she winked.

Linus helped Olivia over the wall and they entered the thicket of woodland, making their way over uneven ground, passing gnarled trees and ducking beneath low branches.

'Do you think Eleanor will tell the press about us looking for a second possible killer?' Linus asked.

'I'm not sure. I've no idea what she's thinking at the moment. It might be worth saying something to your DCI Wise about releasing a statement.'

'I'll have a word when we get back. If we're going to start finding bodies, she'll definitely need to inform the press.'

They continued walking on in silence for a few minutes.

Further into the woods, Linus climbed over a felled tree. He turned and held out a hand for Olivia to hold so he could help her over. As he turned back again, something caught his eye in the hollow trunk. He reached into his pocket, took out his mobile phone and turned on the torch.

'Have you found something?' Olivia asked.

'Hold this.' He passed her the phone while he took a pair of latex gloves from his coat pocket and struggled to put them on over cold hands. He reached inside the tree, grabbed something and began to pull it out. Whatever it was seemed to be either wedged in tight or snagged, as it took several tugs for Linus to bring it out into daylight.

Olivia knew they'd found what they were looking for. She could see the edge of a red clinical waste sack, dulled and decayed over the past year. Linus gave one final tug, the plastic tore and out fell a bundle of decomposed limbs.

Olivia staggered backwards as a half-decomposed skull, muscle and sinew still attached in places, rolled towards her and stopped at her feet.

Chapter Fifty

Olivia was left waiting in Linus's car, alone, for a long time when officers from nearby North Yorkshire Police arrived. Linus took them into the woods, showed them what he found and explained why he was looking for it.

A forensic van pulled up in front of the car just as Linus opened the driver's door and climbed in. Olivia couldn't take her eyes from the team in front of her putting on their paper oversuits. Some people questioned how Olivia could sit down and chat to serial killers while they admitted and revelled in their disturbing crimes. She would much rather do that than have to painstakingly pick through a dismembered body and work out which part went where.

'As far as we can tell, there is no ID on this one like there was on Thomas Landy,' Linus said as he closed the door behind him, keeping the cold outside. 'There are three bags in total. Two contain body parts, the third is clothing from the victim. I really hope we're able to positively identify him.'

'I know you said Piotr had little family but surely there's someone you can get DNA from to make a positive match,' she said, still not taking her eyes from the forensic team. She pulled a face and placed a gloved hand over her nose and mouth. Linus had brought into the car the stench of death.

She looked down at her tablet and Isaac's code she had open on it. 'He was only twenty-one, six feet, and cut into eight pieces. Then he was put into plastic bags and dumped like rubbish at a tip.' There was sadness in her voice. Before, it was clinical. She had been looking at a code on her laptop, trying to understand how Isaac's mind worked. Now, she was facing the reality of everything he'd done and putting a rotting human face to it.

'Olivia, I will do everything in my power to make sure this is Piotr and find someone who can give him a proper burial.'

She turned to him and saw the sincerity on his face.

'I hope so. I hope he doesn't end up being cremated by the local council with nobody to say goodbye to him.'

Linus reached over and placed a cold hand on hers. 'I'll say goodbye to him.'

She looked into his eyes and saw that he meant it. 'You can't say goodbye to them all.'

'I can. And I will.'

'Thank you. So, what happens now? Do we need to give a statement or something?'

'No. The DI is going to contact me later. We'll liaise on this one. I know him; he's a good bloke. Do you want to head back to Newcastle?'

'I suppose we should. We're obviously right about the code. You need to get DCI Wise to open an investigation and send a team out to all the other sites and find the rest of the bodies.'

Linus nodded. 'Do you need to rush back?'

Olivia looked at the time. It wasn't even half-past nine yet. She felt like she'd been up for hours. 'No.'

'We could take a detour. Nidderdale is only a couple of miles west of here. That's where victim number ten is. What3words points to an abandoned mine.'

Olivia looked down at the code again. Whoever's resting place was Nidderdale was only nineteen years old and had been cut up into nine pieces. She couldn't leave them there a moment longer. They needed bringing back up to the surface.

'Let's go,' she said.

Chapter Fifty-One

HM PRISON BELMARSH, THAMESMEAD, LONDON

From the outside, Belmarsh Prison, opened in 1991, looked like a characterless building with its well-maintained grounds and brickwork. Behind those tall security doors lived some of the most dangerous men in Britain. Former inmates included Wayne Couzens, police officer and murderer of Sarah Everard, Islamist terrorist Michael Adebowale, and John Worboys, known as the Black Cab Rapist, who was convicted in 2009 for attacks on twelve women. Current inmates included Ali Harbi Ali, who murdered MP David Amess, David Carrick, serial rapist and former Metropolitan police officer, and Stephen Port, known as the Grindr Killer.

Dr Sebastian Lister had been in this prison on numerous occasions. Like Olivia, entering a prison no longer fazed him. Neither did the inmates. The majority liked to frighten people for shock value. Sebastian could no longer be shocked. He entered the prison with his head high and a strolling gait as if he was entering his local Tesco. The staff knew him, and he chatted animatedly as he signed in, emptied his pockets and walked through the scanner that checked he wasn't hiding anything he shouldn't be. He was then led through the labyrinthine corridors to a special room where his meeting with Olivia's father, Richard Button, was to take place.

While Sebastian was researching his book on Richard, he had visited him in Belmarsh many times. Their interviews were always conducted one-on-one and away from other inmates.

Last year, when Richard suffered a heart attack, Sebastian visited him in hospital. Before that visit, it had been a number of years since they'd last met and Sebastian was surprised by the change in his appearance. He seemed much older and fragile, but once he built his strength back up, the disturbed and twisted psychopath inside came back to the surface. Richard was not a man to be trusted.

Sebastian was shown into a room where Richard was waiting. He was now back to full health and seemed to radiate a warm glow as he looked up and smiled at his visitor. Richard always enjoyed keeping himself fit. He used the prison gym on a regular basis and was a fan of running on the treadmill and lifting weights. His physique was trim, his hair buzzcut-short, and he was clean-shaven. Even his eyes sparkled when he smiled. He seemed to be revelling in life behind bars.

'Sebastian, long time no see. Are you well?' Richard asked. He stood up and held out his hand for Sebastian to shake.

'I'm doing very well, thank you. Yourself?' Sebastian asked, taking his hand in his and squeezing hard.

You could tell a lot about a person by the firmness of their shake. A manipulative killer was an expert in mind games and, even though they had met many times in the past, Richard would consider it one–nil to him if Sebastian's palm had been clammy or the shake weak in any way. Sebastian made sure his grip was firmer.

'Can't complain. Did you see the drama last night?'

'No,' Sebastian said. He'd watched the first half and couldn't cope with the hatchet job the writers had done on his book.

'It was good. I enjoyed it. Though I didn't like the tart they cast as my Geraldine,' he said, referring to the wife he stabbed to death. 'They got some woman who used to be in *EastEnders*; gave my Geraldine a Cockney accent. She never spoke like that. Still,' he clapped his hands together and grinned, 'it's given me some cachet in here, a little bit of celebrity. Good for the ego.'

'I didn't think your ego needed boosting.'

'Being confined to this place for the rest of your life tends to put a dent in your confidence, Sebastian. I'm only human.'

As much as Sebastian wanted to react to that, he decided against it.

'I'm guessing there's been a revival of interest in your book,' Richard continued. 'You must be making a fortune out of my story. And Olivia's too. How's she doing?'

'Olivia is the reason why I'm here today.'

'Did she watch the drama?' he asked, eyes wide and smiling.

'I very much doubt it. She's away with work at the moment. I'm looking after her house. You've been sending her a lot of mail lately.'

'I hope you haven't been opening post that isn't addressed to you, Dr Lister.'

'Olivia gave me permission,' he said and almost hated himself for justifying his actions to him. 'Why are you bombarding her with requests to visit?'

'I want to see her.'

'You know that's not going to happen.'

'You need to make it happen,' Richard said, his expression suddenly serious.

'Why?'

Richard shifted in his chair. He leaned forward. Sebastian glanced over Richard's shoulder to make sure the guards were still keeping an eye on the room.

'Me and Livvy, we have a connection, a bond. We've got a lot in common.'

Sebastian raised an eyebrow. 'You think so?'

'Oh yes. I sent her a letter last year, just after she killed Jamie Farr.'

'The man you sent after her.'

'I knew she could hold her own against him. She did me

proud,' he beamed. 'The thing is, Seb, I'm in here and, well, it can get a bit boring, a bit lonely, and you know, as a killer, you're going to get caught one day and spend the rest of your life banged up. So, you need to keep things exciting, and you do that by withholding certain things and revealing them when the time is right.'

Sebastian swallowed hard. He thought he knew everything there was to know about Richard Button and the crimes he'd committed. What else was there to divulge?

'Olivia won't want to hear you try to justify what you did.'

'That's not what I want to do. I have something I want to get off my chest, something… well, let's just say I need to put things right.'

Sebastian frowned. He couldn't read Richard at all. What was he playing at?

'Richard, you know Olivia won't come to see you. If you really want her to visit, if you have something to say, she's going to need to hear it beforehand.'

Richard seemed to think long and hard before he spoke again. 'Before I met Geraldine, I had a little ground-floor flat in Peckham. Not the nicest place in the world, but a lovely bit of garden. Did I ever tell you about it?'

'No.'

'That's what I want to talk to Livvy about. My life before I met her mother. Remind her that people don't just wake up one morning and decide to kill. Remind her that murder is an evolutionary process.'

'She will not come here on the basis of a few cryptic clues, you know that. You need to tell me—'

Richard interrupted. 'No. It doesn't work like that. You come here and have Livvy sitting next to you, and I'll give you chapter and verse.'

'Olivia won't agree to that,' Sebastian stated.

Richard mimed zipping his lips closed.

Chapter Fifty-Two

BLYTH, NEWCASTLE

DC Ryan Sweetland wasn't enjoying his visit to Isaac McFadden's house. Standing in the hallway at the entrance to the garage, looking at all the blood, turned his stomach. He had only attended two truly gruesome crime scenes in his short career and had been ill at both of them. The concrete floor was a river of red. Sprays and splatter adorned the walls. The smell of metal was in the air. He could taste it. It was scratching at his throat.

A hand slapped hard on his shoulder, making him jump. He turned around and looked into the pinhole eyes of DC Edgar Lowel.

Lowel was in his mid-forties. He had high blood pressure and was overweight. He lived on a regime of late nights, cholesterol and caffeine. When he smiled, he revealed a graveyard of crooked teeth, and his long thinning hair resembled a comb-over. When out of earshot, he was called Homer, for obvious reasons.

Lowel didn't make waves. He didn't volunteer for overtime, he didn't stick his neck above the parapet, and he didn't go above and beyond the call of duty. He performed his job by the rule book, and he collected his wages at the end of the month. He also expected everyone else to do the same. One thing he didn't like was university graduates entering the police force straight into plain clothes with no experience under their belt, especially when said detectives had an impressively high IQ. His favourite person at Forth Banks was certainly not DC Ryan Sweetland.

'I love the smell of dried blood in the morning,' he said to Ryan.

Ryan recoiled. Lowel was a stranger to toothpaste and mouthwash. His breath was pure Greggs Steak Bake.

'What's the matter, Sheldon?' Lowel asked. 'Is the smell bringing up your granola and Greek yoghurt?'

'No,' Ryan said. A lie. 'You'd need to have a heart of stone not to be affected by a sight like that, surely. A person has died. It's sad.'

'People die every day, Ryan. Suck it up. I'm going next door to interview Lesley Quinn. You coming?'

'Me?'

'You can impress the DI with your meticulous notes and shorthand,' he said, heading for the door.

'I don't do shorthand,' Ryan said, following.

'Hello, Mrs Quinn. I'm not sure if you remember me. I'm DC Lowel from Northumbria CID. I interviewed you last year when Mr McFadden—'

'Yes. I remember,' Lesley interrupted.

He gave her his best placatory smile, keeping his mouth closed to avoid frightening her with his stained teeth. 'This is DC Sweetland. I was wondering if we could come in and have a word.'

'What about?' she asked. She had barely opened the door and only poked her head through the gap. She looked worried, scared, and kept glancing beyond the detectives and out into the street at the drama of police cars and forensic vans blocking the road. 'Has something happened next door? Has there been a break-in?'

'If we could just come in, Mrs Quinn. It would be better than chatting on the doorstep.'

The Devil's Code

'Of course,' she said, though she seemed reluctant to allow them entry.

'Thank you,' Lowel said, wiping his feet exaggeratedly on the coconut matting. 'It's parky out there,' he said.

'Come on through to the living room. I've got the fire on.'

As the detectives entered the house she went to close the door but looked around outside first to see if anyone was watching. Luckily, there was nobody about. Julie's blinds were half closed and it was all quiet at Hal Garfield's.

Lesley pointed the detectives to the sofa, and she sat on the armchair opposite.

'I saw the police vehicles yesterday afternoon,' she said. 'My office overlooks the front. I thought someone might have broken in, but, well, I've seen my fair share of police dramas to know you don't send that many vehicles out for a break-in.'

'No. We don't,' Lowel said. 'Mrs Quinn, have you seen anyone hanging around next door recently?'

'No,' she answered quickly.

'Has anyone knocked, asking about next door?'

'No. I had a few journalists knock during the trial, but that's all finished with now.'

'Do you have CCTV?'

'No. I have a burglar alarm. Look, what's happened next door? Has someone broken in? Does Eleanor know?'

'Mrs Quinn. Lesley. I'm sorry, but I have some distressing news for you,' Lowel said with a tinge of sadness in his voice. 'We have a forensic team next door looking through the entire house. A body was found yesterday near Colt Crag Reservoir, and we have reason to believe the victim was killed in Mr McFadden's house. The garage is covered in blood.'

Lesley looked at Lowel in disbelief. She opened and closed her mouth a few times as if unsure of what to say. She blinked hard several times. 'I'm sorry. I have no idea what you've just said. Someone killed someone in Isaac's garage?'

'Yes.'

'What? How? I mean, how did they get in? Who?'

'We're asking ourselves those questions at the moment. What we want to know is if you've seen anyone hanging around next door in the past forty-eight to seventy-two hours?'

'No. I haven't seen anyone. I haven't been looking, to be honest. When Isaac was first arrested there were a few broken windows. I called Eleanor and she sorted it out. Wait a minute, is this like… what do you call it when someone commits a crime similar to one that's been done? Copycat. Is this a copycat killing?' Lesley asked. She wiped a tear from her cheek.

'We don't know.'

'Will there be more? Am I in danger? Should I move out?'

'Lesley, please, calm down,' Lowel said. 'We have no evidence that you, or anyone else in this street, are in danger. However, we will be increasing patrols in the area and keeping an eye on the house next door.'

'It's some sick fantasist, isn't it? The internet loves things like serial killers and all that weird true crime stuff. There should be a ban on all these podcasts that are doing the rounds. It's feeding people's imagination. Him opposite, Hal Garfield, he loves all that kind of stuff. It's not normal, is it?'

'I couldn't agree with you more,' Lowel said, standing up. He fished inside his jacket pocket and pulled out a creased business card. 'These are my contact details, Lesley. If you think of anything, give me a call. Or, if you see anyone hanging around next door, let me know.'

'Thank you,' she said, taking it from him and studying it. 'Will you… will you keep me informed about what's happening next door?'

'Of course,' he said, leaving the living room and heading for the door.

'Thank you for your time,' Ryan said, offering her a sweet smile as he left the house.

'You're welcome,' Lesley said. She closed the door on them and double-locked it.

Lesley remained in the hallway, a perplexed expression on her face. She looked back at the business card DC Lowel had given her. There was a grease stain on it. She placed it in the pocket of her trousers, turned and headed upstairs to her office.

In the box room overlooking the front of the house, she peered around the curtains at the events taking place next door, then went to her desk and pulled out the chair.

Waking up her computer, she went on to the BBC News website. There was no mention of Isaac McFadden being a serial killer, or of another body being found in his house. She tried Sky News, and there was nothing there, either. She typed 'Isaac McFadden' into Google, then clicked on the news tab. She was presented with images of Eleanor and various headlines all saying the same thing: 'KILLER'S DAUGHTER SPEAKS OUT', 'MY FATHER THE SERIAL KILLER', 'GROWING UP WITH KILLER DAD'.

Lesley clicked on the link for *The Sun* newspaper and read the feature focusing on Eleanor's childhood.

'Jesus Christ, Eleanor, what have you done?' she asked herself.

Chapter Fifty-Three

NIDDERDALE, NORTH YORKSHIRE

Nidderdale was listed as an Area of Outstanding Natural Beauty in 1994. From where Olivia Winter was standing, there was nothing outstanding or naturally beautiful about an abandoned mine that had been allowed to rot. As Olivia looked around at the exposed buildings, missing doors and windows and crumbling brickwork, she found it difficult to picture this as once a prosperous business with hundreds of workers.

'Welcome to Black Watch Drift Mine,' Linus said. He was sitting on the edge of the boot of his car as he replaced his shoes with wellington boots.

Olivia looked down at her feet. She was wearing boots but they were not practical for trudging around an old mine. She was going to get soaked, she knew it.

'Do you know what a drift mine is as opposed to a shaft mine?' he asked.

'Well, I know that a shaft mine goes straight down below ground,' she replied.

'A drift mine is on a gradient rather than straight down. If you look over there –' he pointed over his shoulder '– you'll see exposed track lines. Coal was brought out in tubs on those tracks.'

'You sound very knowledgeable.'

'I come from a mining family. My grandfather and great-grandfather worked the mines. I spent a lot of time with my grandad growing up. He told me plenty of stories,' he said with a smile. 'He told me a lot of swear words, too.' He slammed the car boot closed. 'How far off are we from the what3words site?'

Olivia glanced at her tablet. 'Not far.' She pointed up ahead.

They made their way over the unstable ground. The recent snow falls and rain had caused the ground to be muddy and slippery underfoot. Olivia was careful where she stepped. Linus walked confidently, trusting the grip of his boots.

Olivia spotted the tracks and followed them into an archway cut into a stone wall. She dreaded to think how far down the mine went and shivered at the thought of being enclosed in the darkness for several hours each day.

'Is this place maintained at all?' she asked, slipping and having to hold onto a skip to keep her balance.

'See those things over there?' Linus pointed to a row of three stainless steel tanks. 'It's a pumping site. The mine is flooded, and those tanks are bringing it out and cleaning the water. It's full of metals – iron, lead, zinc, cadmium. And all of it is flowing into our rivers.'

'Who's responsible?'

'The Coal Authority Board, I suppose.'

'How long has this place been closed down?'

'Decades. I'd say late eighties.'

'And it's been like this ever since? Can't they, I don't know, fill the mine in or something?'

'I'm sure there's a reason why it's not that simple.'

'Oh God,' Olivia said. 'It's in there.' She pointed to the archway where the tracks went into the blackness.

Linus came back for her. The land grew steeper the closer they came to the entrance to the mine, and she was struggling up the slippery incline. He took her hand and pulled her up. The entrance archway was barely five feet high, and even Olivia would have to duck down to enter.

'This looks like the kind of place Pennywise would live,' Linus said, referring to the clown from Stephen King's horror novel.

'Something tells me we shouldn't be going in there.'

Linus looked at her with a face of concern. 'No. But we've come all this way.'

'Surely we can call someone from the Coal Authority Board. They'll come out on a regular basis to inspect the site, won't they? They'll have all the safety equipment to go in there.'

'If this place was regularly inspected, the body would have been found by now. Besides, look around you. Do you honestly think this place is visited often?'

'I suppose not.'

'Look, you stay here. I'll go in. I won't go far.'

'Shouldn't I go in instead of you? I'm smaller.'

'Do you want to go in?'

'There're going to be rats in there, aren't there?'

'I hadn't thought of that,' he said, shuddering in horror.

He took his phone from his back pocket, turned on the torch and pointed it inside the drift mine. The ground underfoot was unstable, with track lines, loose stone and bricks that had fallen from the roof. He bent almost double as he entered and looked up to the roof.

'Jesus,' he muttered to himself. 'It's all bowed in here. The weight of the land above it is pressing it down.'

'You really shouldn't be going in there, Linus. Come back out. We'll get someone who's into potholing or something, or someone who owns a hard hat, at least.'

'How close are we to where the code said the body was?'

She looked down at her tablet. 'Well, if each square is three metres, you're about twelve metres away.'

'I can't not go further, can I?' he asked, looking back to her from inside the mine.

Olivia chewed her bottom lip. She could feel her face frowning in worry.

'Your face isn't inspiring confidence,' Linus said.

'What do you want me to do, wave you off with a mariachi band?'

Painfully slowly, Linus eased his way further into the mine, disappearing into the blackness. It wasn't long before Olivia couldn't see him at all, or even the weak beam of his torchlight. She stepped closer to the entrance, turned on the torch on her own phone and pointed it inside. She looked at the brickwork of the walls and roof.

'There's no cement at all between these bricks. It's all worn away. What the hell is holding it up?'

'Thanks for that,' Linus's voice echoed.

'How far down does that thing go?'

'I've no idea. Maybe one hundred and fifty to two hundred metres.'

Olivia blew out her cheeks. The thought of going all that way underground filled her with dread.

'Can you see anything?'

'Actually, I think I can,' he said.

Olivia could see him squatting. She heard him straining as he moved a heavy stone.

'I could do with an extra pair of hands,' he called out over his shoulder.

'You can piss off,' she called back.

'I need you to hold the torch while I pick this thing up.'

'Oh. I see. Shit. Do you seriously want me to come in there?'

'If you wouldn't mind.'

'Can I play the pathetic-weak-female card?'

'You can but I'll play the feminist-we're-all-equal card.'

Carefully, and reluctantly, Olivia stepped into the mine.

'It's at times like this I wish the suffragettes had stayed at home and made a Victoria sponge for their loving husbands.'

Linus laughed.

'Have you seen any rats yet?' Olivia asked.

'I've seen a dead one.'

'Fuck, fuck, fuck, fuck,' she said with each short step.

'The quicker we do this, the quicker we can be back out in daylight.'

'This mine could collapse at any minute,' Olivia said. 'I don't want to risk slipping and falling and disturbing any bricks. How the fuck did Isaac McFadden get in here in the first place? He's taller than you.'

Linus turned to see Olivia over his shoulder. She shone the torch in his face. In this dim light, he almost looked sinister.

'Maybe he didn't.'

'Whenever I think of a second killer, my mind immediately jumps to Eleanor, yet I can't find a single shred of evidence.'

'She'd certainly fit in here. She's not much taller than you.'

Olivia reached Linus. He handed her his phone.

'Shine both torches down here. I need both hands to lift this.'

Olivia did as she was told and concentrated on her breathing. The further into the mine she had gone, the more claustrophobic it had become. She wanted to get out. She needed fresh air and a wide-open space. She needed to breathe.

'Okay, hang on,' Linus said, straining to move whatever it was on the floor. 'Can you point the phone over here now?'

'I can't get round you,' she said.

'Pass me the phone.' He wiped his hands on his trousers and took his phone from Olivia, pointing it where he needed it. 'Jesus Christ!' he hissed.

'What is it?'

'It's what we expected. There's only one bag this time, though.'

Olivia remembered the code. 'He's six feet tall, nineteen years old and has been cut up into nine pieces. All that wouldn't fit into one bag, surely.'

'Maybe it's not all here. Maybe some of it has drifted further down the mine. Look, slowly back your way out and we'll see what we've got in daylight.'

Just outside the entrance to the mine, Olivia released a deep sigh of relief as Linus, filthy, placed the clinical waste sack down on a pile of leaves. It was difficult to tell what was inside given how dirty the bag was.

'There's a hole in it,' Olivia pointed out.

'I'm guessing that's where rats might have opened it up and feasted on what's inside.'

'Will there be anything left of him in there?'

'I don't know. Look, I've got some hand sanitiser in the car. I'm going to wash my hands then I'll call North Yorkshire Police.'

Linus returned to the car, leaving Olivia standing sentry over the bag. She squatted down and tried to peer inside. A disturbing, sickening smell emanated from the tear. She pointed her phone towards the hole, turned on the torch and sneaked a look. She could make out the edges of a bone, and an item of clothing, but nothing else. She felt a tear roll down her cheek.

'I'm so sorry,' she said.

By the time Linus returned, he was putting his phone in his back pocket.

'Police are on their way.'

'It's bad enough for someone to murder someone, but to then make it so their body is never found is beyond evil. I want to see Isaac in a courtroom charged with twelve murders. I want him on the never-never list. But I don't think that's going to happen, do you?' she said, clearly fuming.

'Look, go and wait in the car and try and calm down. Maybe you should cancel your visit to Frankland Prison this afternoon.'

'Oh, absolutely not. I'm going into that meeting and I'm telling Isaac McFadden exactly what I think of him,' she said, storming off to the car, not caring if she slipped and fell in the mud.

Chapter Fifty-Four

FRANKLAND PRISON, COUNTY DURHAM

The drive to County Durham from Nidderdale should have taken a little over one and a half hours. However, Olivia and Linus had stopped twice. The first time was at a nearby service station so they could freshen up and the second time was so they could have a sit-down somewhere warm and comfortable for something to eat and drink. By the time they pulled up outside Frankland Prison, Olivia had calmed down, slightly.

There was no way Linus would be allowed into the interview room and Olivia doubted Isaac would reveal anything with a detective inspector present, so he decided to wait in the car and possibly catch up on some sleep while Olivia headed for the main entrance, folder in hand.

She underwent the usual security checks and had her pockets emptied and folder searched, and then was led deep into the bowels of the prison where Isaac McFadden was already waiting for her. He was sitting up straight in his chair, a rueful smile on his cleanly shaven face.

'It's lovely to see you again, Olivia,' he said.

Olivia didn't say anything. As she walked into the room and saw his face, the rage came boiling back to the surface. She thought of Sean Bridger, of Thomas Landy, of Piotr Czajkowski and Shane Waterhouse. Four men so far, all of them young, with their whole lives ahead of them and the freedom to do what they wanted, and it had all been torn away because of one man's sick desires. If she could get away with it, she would jump across the table and punch him continuously in the face.

The problem with interviewing serial killers was that Olivia needed to leave her emotions outside the door. Multiple murderers are manipulative, and despite what they've done, they'll sit on the other side of the table with the calm contentment of an innocent child. It's almost as if they have done nothing wrong. It was that attitude that immediately raised the hackles and Olivia had to dig deep to find the strength to conduct the interview in a professional manner. She was searching for answers. She wanted the victims found and returned to their families. This was not about her. Whatever she felt for the loathsome creature across the table was academic.

'We're finding your victims, Isaac,' she began. 'Two so far, but police teams are out in force across the north of England locating your hiding places.'

'You've cracked my code,' he said, a twinkle of happiness in his eyes.

'We have. It'll all be making the news in the coming days. How will your partner react?'

He remained still and silent.

'Speaking of the news, Eleanor has been to the newspapers to give her side of the story.'

'I've seen.'

'She's not coping with this very well at all, Isaac. She's hurting. She's struggling to understand who you really are. She's so petrified of the media camping out on her doorstep when your crimes are revealed that she's selling her soul to the press while she still has some hold over events. You're destroying her life.'

Olivia watched Isaac and waited for a response. None came. He was clearly struggling with what was happening on the outside. He loved his daughter, there was no doubt about that. Olivia hoped that the more she expressed how difficult Eleanor was finding it to cope with her father's actions, the more likely

Isaac was to reveal the identity of the second killer. Olivia prayed to God it wasn't Eleanor.

She reached for the folder and took out the paperwork. 'Shall we talk about your victims? Number eleven,' she began. 'Piotr Czajkowski. You killed him in January 2024, picking him up from Morecambe before dumping him in woodland at Robin Hood's Bay. He was twenty-one years old, six feet tall, and you cut him up into eight pieces. He had blond hair, was wearing a white top, black jeans and black and white trainers. You ranked him nine out of ten. I can go through the rest of the code if you wish?'

Olivia spoke firmly and decisively. She needed to come across as the strong one in this exchange and not allow Isaac to gain the upper hand.

'You haven't worked out the whole code,' Isaac said, that knowing glint in his eye back to taunt her.

'Haven't I?'

'No. The words in brackets. What do they signify?'

A thought entered Olivia's head. Why hadn't she realised this before? She might be wrong, but it was worth a stab. She had never heard of the what3words website before. Linus had. Maybe if he'd seen three random words, he might have guessed the link sooner, but the addition of a fourth word ruled it out straightaway. The fact it was bracketed added mystery. But what if it was meaningless?

'The fourth word means nothing. You knew that one day this code would be found, and you decided to add an extra word so whoever found it wouldn't get the what3words link. The word in brackets is pointless.' She might have sounded confident, but Olivia was shaking inside. She hoped she was right.

'Congratulations, Dr Winter,' Isaac said.

She hoped she wasn't showing the smile on her face that she felt glowing inside her.

'Where do we go from here?' he asked.

'Tell me who the second killer is. Thomas Landy was killed on the first of February this year. He was picked up from Benwell in Newcastle and dumped near Colt Crag Reservoir. He was eighteen years old, five feet eleven inches tall, and cut into ten pieces. He had brown hair and was wearing a grey top, black jeans and black shoes. He was rated seven out of ten. His blood is all over your garage floor.'

'Oh,' Isaac said, surprised. 'A copycat killing.'

'No. A continuation. There is no way you killed all these people on your own. The second killer is still out there. You see, I've watched your recorded interviews with DI Sutton at Forth Banks police station. I've read the court transcripts. You're not a devious and psychopathic killer. On your own, you may have harboured thoughts of taking a life, but you would never have done it if you hadn't met a second person who was just that bit more disturbed than you and edged you into a life of murder. When two people commit murder together, one of them is the supplicant and the other the dominant. You are in no way a dominant personality. If you were, once arrested, you would have sat back and spoken about your crimes. DI Sutton would have had trouble shutting you up. Knowing the bodies would never be found, you would have given him chapter and verse. But you didn't. Why? Because you were told to keep your mouth shut if you were ever caught disposing of your victims. You had to protect your partner from capture, and that's why you gave "no comment" answers to every question put to you.'

'Is that so?'

'It is. Who is the second killer, Isaac?'

They maintained eye contact, neither wanting to be the first to look away.

As much as Olivia wanted to ask if it was Eleanor, she decided to keep her mouth shut. If she was wrong, and she hoped she was, Isaac would laugh in her face. He would love how completely off the mark she was.

'We will find out who it is eventually,' Olivia continued. 'You put the body parts in clinical waste sacks you sold through your job as a rep for MediSupplies UK. Their supplier reference number is on the barcode, for crying out loud. And do you honestly think you're not going to have left your DNA behind while stuffing the body parts into the bags? You could save the police time and effort by telling me, right now, who the second killer is.'

Isaac looked away, as if weighing up his options. He inhaled a deep breath. He nodded and leaned closer to Olivia across the table.

'I'm saying nothing.'

'You're killing your daughter,' Olivia shouted.

'I killed her when I killed my first victim. You of all people should know there was no coming back from that. I maintained the facade of a father, but I'd ruined everything. Just like your father did with you and your family.'

Olivia hated people knowing who her father was. They always threw it back at her. Her thick skin needed to be thicker to withstand a blast from a manipulative murderer.

'You have the chance here to do the right thing.'

'Why should I?'

'Eleanor is on a slippery slope to God knows where. You can stop all of that. It's not too late for her to be able to pick herself up and move on.'

'No. I can't,' he said, his voice back to being calm. 'Once the truth is out, the whole truth, she'll be back on that slope.'

'What do you mean?'

'You figure it out. You're supposed to be the great forensic psychologist.'

Olivia bit the bullet. She had no proof, but it was worth a stab in the dark. 'You killed your wife, didn't you?'

'A mercy killing.'

'Still murder.'

'She was suffering.'

'It had to be the first of the month, didn't it?'

'My special day,' he smiled.

'Who else is there? How many more victims are there that aren't on this code?'

He winked at Olivia.

She wanted to laugh. He was trying to come across as being

sadistically vague, but it wasn't working. The eyes revealed the truth. He was keeping quiet because he had been told to do so.

'Isaac, I'm asking, one last time, tell me who your partner was in all this. End this now.'

'Sorry. I'm saying nothing more.'

'More people will die. What if the next victim is Eleanor?'

'I don't care.'

'You don't care about your own daughter?'

He thought about this for a moment. 'No. I really don't.'

'If you're saying that to shock me then there really is no need. I'm not shocked, and I am not playing your games.'

He shrugged.

'There really is no point in me being here,' she said, gathering her paperwork. She stood up, went over to the door and knocked to alert the prison officers she was ready to leave. 'I won't be coming back, Isaac.'

He shrugged, unperturbed.

She paused, waiting, hoping he would say something to keep her in the room. She turned her back on him, walked out and listened to the door slam closed behind her. In the corridor, Olivia leaned back against the wall and sighed.

'I could have handled that much better,' she said to herself.

It didn't matter what else happened now, she couldn't go back on her word and return to interview him. He would see her as weak. She just hoped Linus and his team found the second killer before he had a chance to strike again.

Chapter Fifty-Five

Eleanor risked a look out of her bedroom window. She didn't want it to appear too obvious, so she remained in the shadows of the room and carefully peeled back the edge of the curtain and glanced down. The press was there. Newspaper reporters, both local and national, and there was someone she was sure she recognised from reporting on *BBC Breakfast*. The crowd had been steadily growing throughout the day. Her door had been knocked on several times and she'd ignored it. Her phone had rung more times than she could remember. All calls went unanswered. She had signed a contract with *The Sun* to give them an exclusive interview which would run over five consecutive days. Only after that would she be allowed to talk to other media outlets.

The problem Eleanor faced now, however, was that she needed to leave the house. She was running low on milk and cereal, and she was starting to feel like eating something more substantial. Taking control of events had brought back her appetite. She fancied chicken. Roast chicken with a few roast potatoes and maybe a Yorkshire pudding. Her dad had showed her his special way of making Yorkshire pudding so that it came out risen and crispy every time. She found herself almost salivating as she thought of such a meal. To make it, she would need to leave the house to buy the ingredients and she would be hit with a barrage of questions and photographed.

Eleanor sat at her dressing table and looked at her reflection. She had lost weight since her father's arrest and incarceration. Her cheekbones were now clearly defined. That wasn't a bad thing, she thought, as she turned her head and looked at herself from different angles. She applied blusher to give her pale skin some colour and highlight her cheeks. Black mascara extended her lashes and a touch of eyeliner made her eyes look deeper set. She didn't want to appear to be making herself up for the media so she applied a natural-looking lipstick, just to take away the dryness. She leaned back in her seat and looked at herself. She looked like a new woman.

She put on skinny black jeans and an oversized jumper, black boots and a cream bobble hat. Her roots desperately needed doing. She didn't want to be judged by her appearance, but she decided to leave her thick winter coat open despite the cold.

At the doorway, she checked she had everything she needed – wallet, keys, phone – and braced herself for the onslaught. She took a deep breath and pulled open the door. The blitz from the journalists started straightaway.

'Eleanor! Eleanor!' the calls came, followed by camera flashes. She kept her head down as she tried to fight her way through the scrummage.

'Eleanor, have you been to visit your father in prison yet?'

She didn't answer.

'Eleanor, you said you think your father has killed up to twelve more people. Are you helping the police with their enquiries? What are they doing about it?'

She had no idea what the police were doing. She didn't want to know.

'Did you ever feel in any danger as a child? Did your father frighten you, threaten you?'

She had been over her childhood many times. There were no signs. Her father was perfect to her.

'Dr Olivia Winter has been seen with the police. Have you spoken to her?'

Eleanor hesitated. She paused, briefly, before continuing in the direction of the shops.

'What can you tell us about Dr Winter?'

'Has she spoken about her own father?'

'Has she seen the drama on TV?'

Eleanor pushed a reporter out of the way. She was suddenly clear of them and was able to get to the other side of the street. She picked up the pace and headed for the shops. She swore to herself. Not everything was about Olivia fucking Winter.

It was growing dark by the time Olivia and Linus returned to the police station in Newcastle. Although they had progressed enormously in locating the bodies which would hopefully lead to them being positively identified, Olivia berated herself for how she had reacted to the interview with Isaac. She had wanted to remain cool and calm throughout, but her emotions were close to the surface, and she'd allowed Isaac to see how near she was to displaying them. She would not go back to see him again. She couldn't allow that.

On the journey back to Forth Banks, Linus had been able to see Olivia was upset and had kept the topics of conversation away from the McFadden family and Isaac's victims.

He cleared his throat. 'I spoke to Clara's sister, Jill, in Canada last night. She's booked to come over next month. We're going to make a bit of an event of scattering the ashes.'

Olivia looked over at him. She could only see him in profile, but he seemed brighter, his head held high, his shoulders relaxed.

'That's good. I'm so pleased, Linus. It's important to remember those we've lost, but it's equally important to remember that we're still alive and need to move on.'

He glanced at her. 'Do you ever take your own advice?'

She didn't want to answer that question, but Linus's silence

The Devil's Code

showed he wasn't going to let her get away without saying something.

'No, I'm afraid I don't,' she said.

'Why not?'

Olivia didn't reply. She knew what the answer was but was afraid of saying it out loud. The reason she hadn't moved on was because she felt guilty that her mother and sister were dead while she had survived.

Linus turned the corner and almost slammed his foot down on the brake pedal when he saw the swarm of people gathered outside the main entrance to the police station. They both knew straightaway they were journalists.

'Shit,' Olivia said to herself.

Linus turned again to find a parking space and pulled up.

'It's hardly surprising,' Linus said. 'Do you want to talk to them?'

'Definitely not. I'm not here for that.'

'It shouldn't take us a minute to get from the car to the foyer,' he said. 'Try to tune out their questions.'

'I always do,' she said with a false smile. She was never able to tune them out. Their questions were always blunt and hit home like an arrow direct to the heart. On the darkest of nights, she could still hear the calls from reporters when she was nine years old and attending the funeral of her mum and sister.

'Olivia! Olivia! We've got a message for you from your dad.'

'Ready?' Linus asked.

'Sure.' She tried for nonchalance, but she wasn't sure if she'd pulled it off. Linus's worried expression told her she hadn't.

They made their way to the front entrance and as soon as the reporters saw them, they lunged towards them, phones held aloft, ready to record anything they said.

'DI Sutton, is there a serial killer on the streets of Newcastle?'

'I can't answer any of your questions right now,' Linus said. 'We will be releasing a statement soon.'

'Olivia, you're the serial killer hunter, what does your presence here mean?'

Neither of them said anything.

'Did you watch the drama on Monday night, Olivia?'

'Have you been to see your dad in prison lately?'

'Do you have anything to say about the private prosecution Suzanne Farr is starting against you regarding the death of her son last year?'

Olivia stopped dead in her tracks. This was the first she had heard about any such prosecution.

'What?' she asked.

Linus put his arm around her shoulders and urged her towards the entrance of the police station. He whispered something in her ear, but she hadn't heard him. Her gaze was locked on the journalist. He was smirking at her.

'It's all over the papers, Olivia. She believes you caused the unnecessary death of her son.'

'I did—'

'Leave it, Olivia,' Linus interrupted, pushing her further towards the doors.

Once inside, Linus let her go. Olivia headed for the stairs and took them two at a time. She needed to get to a computer to find out what was going on. She rarely read the news and only searched its archive if it concerned a serial killer she was preparing to interview.

She threw open the door of the small room she, Linus and Ryan had been using for their investigations. Ryan was sitting at the paperwork-strewn desk, studying his tablet.

'I didn't think you'd be coming back today. We've had some huge developments,' Ryan began.

Olivia wasn't listening. She sat down, pulled her laptop out of her case and switched it on.

'Three more bodies, or rather body parts, have been found in locations around the north of England. And I've just got off the phone with DI Duggan in Carlisle. He's had a team out at Downdale Colliery in Armathwaite all day and they've found—'

'Ryan, not now,' Linus said as he followed Olivia into the room.

'What is it? Has something happened?'

'Jesus Christ, she is as well,' Olivia said, sitting back and looking at the screen.

'What?' Ryan asked.

'She's given an interview to the *Daily Mail* stating that she's taken legal advice and she's going to sue me for the unlawful death of her son. Jamie Farr was a bloody serial killer, for crying out loud!' Olivia fumed. 'He didn't just kill his victims, either – he tormented them. He attacked DI Foley. He stabbed me four times. What I did was in self-defence.'

'Ah,' Ryan said. 'I saw that earlier. I was going to call you but…' He trailed off.

'You'd think she'd want to forget about what her son turned into.'

'Olivia, I can't see this actually getting anywhere,' Linus said, soothingly. 'I'm sure this is just in the early stages. She'll have got a shyster lawyer who is hoping to get a decent payout. No judge will hear this case. If you hadn't killed him, he would have killed you.'

'And why did I have to hear it from a fucking journalist?'

'Well, that's good, isn't it?' Ryan asked. 'I mean, if she was taking a prosecution out against you, you would have heard about it by now. It's probably just rumour at the moment.'

'Ryan's right,' Linus said. He removed his coat and took his phone out of his trousers pocket. 'Shit. Ryan, we haven't got a charger for a Samsung lying around, have we?'

'Yours is still plugged in over there,' he pointed out.

'Oh. I wondered what I'd done with that,' he said, plugging his phone in. He looked at Olivia, whose face was steely as she continued to read from her laptop. 'Ryan, you were saying about Carlisle.'

'Oh. Right. Yes. Well, I called them up earlier and DI Duggan sent a team out to Downdale Colliery. It's an abandoned mine. It's been closed since the mid-1980s. According to what3words, the place the body was dumped was down a mine shaft. They managed to send a team down there and they've found remains.'

| 2 | O1 | BAIT ANGEL COG (KITE) | DREADING ORIGIN GANDER (GRINCH) | BROWN GREY BLACK BLACK O/?/? | & |

'Where did Isaac pick him up?' Linus asked.

'Somewhere around Whitby.'

'So, he picked him up in Whitby and drove him over a hundred miles to dump him in Carlisle intact? How has he managed to drop an entire body down a mine shaft? There's no way he could have done that on his own, surely.'

'The body is heavily decomposed. It's practically skeletonised. The post mortem is going to take place first thing tomorrow and DI Duggan will let me know the results. I mean, this victim could have been a child, or someone slight. Isaac could have done this alone.'

'No,' Olivia said. She closed the laptop. 'Isaac had a partner. I don't know why he chose not to cut this one up – there are many different scenarios, and I don't think we're going to get all the answers we're seeking, if any – but Isaac did not act alone in any of this.'

'When we catch the second killer,' Ryan began, 'would either of them talk then and reveal everything? I mean, you can understand Isaac keeping his mouth shut now as his partner is still out there, and if he's the submissive one, then he's going to want to make sure he doesn't say anything to drop him in it. Once the other killer's caught, there's nothing left for him to be quiet about, is there?'

'The dominant one won't talk,' Olivia stated. 'So long as we're in the dark about some of the victims, he'll have a hold over us. Revealing information isn't in his interest at all. It is possible that Isaac could talk, eventually, once the second killer is arrested and sentenced.' While she was speaking, she was frantically typing an email on her phone to Sebastian, asking him to find out more about the prosecution Suzanne Farr had allegedly taken out against her.

'But we're still no closer to finding who the second killer is,' Ryan said. 'Oh, bugger,' he said, finding a Post-it note stuck to his tablet cover. 'DCI Wise said she wanted to see you as soon as you came back. She wants to put out a statement about Isaac McFadden now that it's obvious he's a serial killer.'

'Yes, I emailed her in the car. I might be some time. Olivia, don't hang around, I'll give you a call when I'm finished.'

'Right,' she said. 'I think I might head back to the hotel anyway. I feel dirty after being in that mine.'

Linus grabbed his laptop and a folder before leaving the office and heading for DCI Wise's room.

'Olivia, can I ask you something?' Ryan asked.

'Of course.'

Ryan had a heavy frown on his face. There was obviously something troubling him. 'Isn't it odd that we've got Isaac, who we know to be a serial killer with an elaborate code he's created, but if he has a partner in crime, we have no idea who that other person is? Is it just possible Isaac did all of this on his own?'

'No. He didn't do this on his own. He couldn't have done.'

'I'm not doubting you. You're the expert on this. But without clear proof, how can you know that?'

She looked at Ryan and found herself smiling. She liked him. He was always questioning and asking for evidence. She wished her students were like this.

'You're right. There is no definitive proof right now, but the main proof is that whoever cut up these bodies needed medical training and Isaac doesn't have that.'

'So, who in his life does?'

'That's another head-scratcher for you to find out. Oh, did you get copies of Isaac's work diary and appointments going back to when the code started?'

'Yes,' he said, opening his tablet once again. 'It's quite simple early on, as for all of 2020, 2021 and the first part of 2022 his appointments were via Zoom because of the pandemic.'

'Okay. So, we know the dates when Isaac killed his victims because we've worked out the code to the second column. We have the month and the year and it's safe to say he killed on the first day of the month as we know that's a special date for him. If we look at his appointments schedule, we can see where he was in relation to the pickup place for his victims. Sean Bridger, for example, was picked up in Whitley Bay. Where was Isaac on the first of March 2024?'

Ryan looked down at his tablet, looked for the correct file, then began scrolling through. 'Let's see. The first of March 2024 was a Friday. He had a ten o'clock appointment at St Jude's Hospice in Monkseaton, Whitley Bay.'

'Look at the rest of the entries,' Olivia said. 'If there are any that you can't match, where Isaac might have been too far away from the pickup point, it's possible the second killer could have chosen that victim and brought him back to Isaac's house. The garage, as we found out with Thomas Landy, was the place where the victims were cut up. It's just possible that Isaac was the one who was in charge of hiding the bodies. After all, he was found alone on the night he was arrested.'

'But what about the body found in Carlisle today? He wasn't cut up.'

'Perhaps he was a hitchhiker. Maybe Isaac picked him up on his way to Carlisle and just killed him and dumped him there. It's a change to the signature, but sometimes the urge to kill is too strong to allow for planning.'

'That's a frightening thought.'

'It is. In 2017, I was in California at a correction facility. There was a man, Carl Lee Harris, who was jailed for killing four women. He said he heard voices telling him to kill them, that the world would be a better place without them in it. I interviewed him three times. On the fourth occasion, I went into the room and the atmosphere felt different. Carl was a polite young man and we got on well. This time, he seemed quiet, and he wasn't as forthcoming. I kept asking if he was feeling unwell and wanted to postpone the interview, but he said no. After about twenty minutes, he jumped up from the seat and ran to the door, begging the prison officer to unlock it. He was screaming and crying and scratching at the door to be let out. The guard opened it and asked what had happened. Carl told him that he had to go because he was going to kill me, and he didn't want to because he liked me. He was fighting against the voice telling him to kill. He hadn't ignored the voice for the other victims because he didn't know them.'

'Bloody hell. I bet you were scared to death, weren't you?'

'A little.'

'What happened to Carl? Is he still in prison?'

'No. He killed himself about a year later. He was receiving psychiatric treatment, and he couldn't cope with what he'd done.'

'That's sad.'

'It is. Right,' Olivia said, standing up. 'I'm in urgent need of a hot bath and something alcoholic. Is there a back way out of here to avoid the press?'

'Yes. I'll show you down.'

'Thanks. Ryan, do me a favour, don't spend too long agonising over all of this,' she said, pointing to the mass of paperwork and photographs. 'I know it's fascinating and you're full of questions, but don't let Isaac's crimes set up home inside your head.'

'I won't. I promise. I'll be going home myself, soon.'

After Ryan had shown Olivia out, he went back to the office, closed the door behind him and pulled the Venetian blinds shut. He spent the next hour comparing Isaac's appointments diary with the code. He looked at his watch. It was almost six o'clock. He should be heading home. He'd been at work since seven this morning and he needed to catch up on some sleep. The problem was that investigations like these came along so rarely. He was absolutely fascinated by it and wanted to live, breathe, eat and drink everything he could get his hands on. He decided to give it another hour and then he would force himself to go home.

One thing Ryan still couldn't get his head around was Isaac's garage. Why didn't he park his car there? Why leave it on the driveway? He could understand it if the garage was chock-full of crap, but it wasn't. It was neat and tidy. Yes, he used the garage for cutting up his victims, but he could have left his car out on the drive whenever he was doing that.

He pulled up the file on his tablet showing the photographs of the garage when the police first visited the house. It had the usual detritus of a normal garage – storage boxes, shelves, tins of paint, ladders leaning against a wall – but there was something wrong with the photographs. Something at the back of his mind was troubling him about the layout of the garage, and he couldn't shake it off. It was driving him mad.

He opened Google and typed in 'Citroen Picasso', Isaac's car, and looked up the dimensions of the make and model Isaac drove. He needed to measure the garage and see if the car fitted. If it did, then it was simply an ordinary garage with an extraordinary owner. If the car didn't fit, then the garage was built for nefarious purposes and maybe it *was* worth digging it up to see what might lie beneath.

Chapter Fifty-Six

Olivia walked out of the en suite bathroom with an oversized bath robe wrapped around her body and a towel around her head. She felt so much better for washing off the detritus of the day. Her skin was red from the heat of the shower. Olivia always had the water scalding hot. It was a cleansing ritual. The needles of water needed to almost pierce her skin. She stood beneath the shower for as long as she could take it before turning the temperature down to a more manageable level.

She sat on the edge of the bed and dried her hair. Her laptop was open but switched off. Her mind hadn't fully been on work today. Maybe that's why she had snapped at Isaac in prison and ruined any further chance of interviewing him. There was something nibbling away at her synapses, and it didn't matter how much she tried to focus, it was constantly nagging at her.

'Fuck it,' she said to herself.

She went to the desk, turned on the laptop and went to the ITVX homepage. The drama about her father was prominently placed. All episodes were available now to watch. She shouldn't be doing this. It would be incredibly bad for her, but she needed to know, she needed to see what the viewing public had seen.

Taking a deep breath, she started the first episode.

The opening shot was of an innocuous-looking house in a suburban road. It was dusk. There were no lights on inside. A caption came up on the screen: 'December 21, 1999'. A young girl came into view and headed for the house. The viewer could only see her from the back. Olivia knew this was supposed to be her as a nine-year-old.

She opened the front door, closed it behind her and walked into the living room. It looked nothing like Olivia's childhood home in Kingston-upon-Thames. The layout was all wrong. Her mother took pride in their home. She wouldn't have had the clutter on the coffee table or the cushions on the sofa squashed, and she certainly wouldn't have had a fake Christmas tree. She always had a real one.

'Mum! Claire! I'm home,' the fake Olivia called out.

She looked in the kitchen for her mother and sister. There was nobody there. She went back into the living room, then into the hallway, and stood at the bottom of the stairs. As she looked up, the camera panned upwards at an odd angle to show something dark and disturbing was waiting for her upstairs.

With every step, the intensity of the music grew. The camera kept switching from the young Olivia's face to her point of view. She already looked scared, which was anathema to Olivia watching on her laptop. Why should she be scared in her own house? She wasn't yet aware that anything had happened.

'Mum. Are you up here?'

The young Olivia opened a couple of doors and looked inside. She eventually turned to the main bedroom, the door of which was ajar. A shadow moved on the other side, indicating that someone was in there. The intrusive music increased in volume and suspense. Olivia reached out, placed the flat of her hand on the door and pushed it open. Tentatively, she stepped inside, and the viewer saw what she was seeing.

It was a bloodbath. It was a horror film. Blood spatter adorned the walls and ceiling. The carpet was saturated with it. It was dripping off the lightshades on the bedside table. There was a mound on the bed that Olivia guessed was supposed to represent her little sister Claire. That wasn't what it looked like. Her mother was cradling Claire. With her dying breaths, she was still holding onto her dead daughter.

The woman playing her mother, whose hair was all wrong, was leaning against the headboard. She was soaked in blood. She opened her eyes and told Olivia to run.

That part was true and Olivia, watching in the safety and comfort of her hotel room, slapped a hand to her mouth as the memory came flooding back.

'Olivia! Run!'

Her father came out of the en suite, blood-dripping knife held aloft.

Olivia turned and ran, and the music was kicked up a notch as she was chased into the main bathroom, where she slammed the door behind her and locked it.

The rest of the opening scene played out as Olivia remembered it. She struggled to climb out of the bathroom window, dropped down onto the roof of the extension at the back of the house, jumped onto the grass and ran to the fence at the back, which she fought to climb over. Her father called out to her. She stopped and looked round as a police officer came through the back fence. Her dad lunged out and stabbed him before turning his attention back to his daughter. A *Scream*-style chase through the woods, father pursuing daughter, was overly dramatic. He caught up with her, leaned over her and told her he loved her before stabbing her repeatedly. The screen went black, and the title of the drama, *The Riverside Killer*, faded in as if written in blood drops.

Olivia slammed the lid of her laptop closed. She ran into the bathroom and vomited.

Blyth was nowhere near where DC Ryan Sweetland lived. It was a good thirty-minute drive away, but the niggling suspicion in the back of his mind that there was something lurking beneath the floor of the garage, that it had been built purposely to kill in rather than house a Citroen Picasso, would give him a sleepless night if he didn't find out for sure.

He pulled up outside Isaac McFadden's home and turned off the engine. He looked up at the house. In the darkened street, it looked isolated and lonely. In every other home, a typical weekday evening was playing out. Isaac's, a house of horror, was already descending into decay.

He took a tape measure and a notebook from the glove box and climbed out of the car. A fine drizzle was falling. A few flakes of snow, too. It was going to be another bitterly cold night. He took the keys for the house from his coat pocket and made his way up the driveway to the front door.

The sound of her mobile ringing made Olivia come out of the bathroom. She had vomited everything she had eaten today, and more. By the end, she was just dry heaving. The display said Sebastian was calling and she swiped to answer. Right now, she needed to hear the voice of someone she loved and trusted.

'Olivia, I haven't heard from you for a few days. I thought I'd check in and see how you are.'

She sat down on the edge of the bed. 'Have you seen it?' she asked.

'What?'

'The drama. Did you watch it?'

'I... A little. I watched until the second ad break.'

'What did you think?'

'Does it matter?'

'Yes, it does.'

'It was a travesty. Gratuitous. I hate myself for selling the rights just so I could keep my head above water. I'm so sorry.'

'It might be dirty money, but you've put it to good use. That's the main thing.'

'I suppose. Olivia, please don't tell me you've watched it.'

'I saw the opening scene.'

'Jesus, Olivia, you said you wouldn't.'

'I know. I was... curious.'

'And?'

'It looked like a cheap slasher film.'

'Don't watch any more,' Sebastian said, sternly.

'I won't.'

'You said you wouldn't watch any of it. Olivia, if you watch more it's going to burrow itself into your head. You don't need that.'

She wiped away a tear.

'Are you still there?' he asked.

'Yes. The press has discovered I'm up here.'

'I've seen the stories in the papers by Eleanor McFadden. What was she thinking?'

'I don't know.'

'Daisy's been keeping an eye on social media. She's already being vilified. People are saying she's cashing in on the torment of the victims. Some are saying she must have known what her father was doing. There's very little sympathy for her.'

'It's my fault. I told her she needed to prepare for the press onslaught. She's actually gone out and struck first.'

'It is not your fault, Olivia. Eleanor is a grown woman. She can make her own decisions.'

'Do you think I should go and see her?'

'It might be worth just telling her to take the comments with a pinch of salt. The world is full of keyboard warriors. They say these things for shock value, so they're noticed. It's all about attention.'

'But when you're feeling vulnerable, you don't see it like that.'

'No.'

'Did you look into the Suzanne Farr thing?'

'Yes. I can't find any evidence of her launching a prosecution. I've forwarded your email to Amyas. He's looking into it for us.'

Olivia's phone pinged a second incoming call. She looked at the screen and saw that Ryan was calling. She ignored it and returned to Sebastian.

Ryan stood in the cold of the garage and looked around him. He'd taken the measurements, and a Citroen Picasso would fit, just about, but there was still something strange about this garage that didn't make sense.

There were two strip lights on the ceiling, of different wattage. The one close to the door was a brilliant, blinding white, the one at the back, if it worked, would have been dimmer. And those shelves on the side wall. They didn't belong there. They should be on the back wall. That was why a Citroen Picasso wouldn't fit perfectly in here because the shelves were in the wrong place. Why was that?

Ryan turned on the torch on his phone and walked to the shelves, his shoes echoing on the concrete floor. Close up, he saw what he'd missed the last time he was in here. The shelves were in a recess. It was only a narrow space, but there was definitely a recess in the wall. Putting the phone in his back pocket and struggling under the dull lighting in this corner of the garage, he grabbed one of the shelves and found it wasn't secured to its bracket. He took it down and propped it up against the wall. He removed all the other shelves and stood back, looking at an insert in the wall.

At some point, there had been a door here and it had been bricked up, though not professionally. He grabbed his phone and took a couple of photos. He then decided to give Olivia a ring and tell her what he had discovered. Maybe being a detective wasn't what he was supposed to do with his life, but unravelling the dark life of a serial killer definitely was.

Olivia didn't answer. He tried Linus, but it rang several times before the voicemail kicked in. He decided against leaving a message.

He was about to leave, head back to the warmth of his car, when a light was turned on somewhere and a sharp line appeared at the bottom of the recess. Slowly, it began to open.

Chapter Fifty-Seven

Olivia couldn't get Eleanor out of her mind. There were times when she thought she was the second killer, but more often than not, she saw her as another victim of her father. If Eleanor was a killer, would she have drawn attention to herself by selling her story to the press and allowing a tabloid to print features over five days? No, definitely not, especially not with a thirteenth victim being discovered. Nobody was *that* complacent, surely.

Eleanor was a victim, and she was struggling to come to terms with everything her father had done. Olivia, more than anyone, could understand what she was going through. At least, when Richard's crimes were discovered, Olivia had her grandparents to shield her from the media circus, but who did Eleanor have? She was completely alone in all this.

Olivia dressed in jeans and a jumper. She threw on her coat and boots and left the warmth of the hotel room. She needed Eleanor to know she wasn't alone, that there was someone she could talk to.

An Uber took Olivia to Eleanor's house in Heaton. She had expected to see a scrum of journalists camping outside her door, but was pleased to see nothing apart from a litter of cigarette ends and wrappers they'd discarded. She rang the doorbell and stood back, looking up at the dark house. It wasn't late, but maybe Eleanor had decided on an early night, to block out the horror of what she was going through and hope her dreams would make sense of it for her.

The door opened and Olivia was bathed in a warm glow from within. She smiled.

'Eleanor, I thought I'd come round to see how you are.'

'Oh, that's nice of you. Come in,' she said, stepping to one side.

Olivia entered the house and wiped her feet on the mat. 'The press was outside the police station when I arrived earlier. I wondered if they'd been bothering you.'

Eleanor closed the door. 'They were here most of the day. When it started to go dark, and I went around closing all the curtains, they seemed to take the hint. I'm assuming they'll be back tomorrow. Go on through to the living room.'

Olivia took off her coat as she made herself comfortable in the warm lounge. She sat down on the sofa. 'They can be very insensitive with their questioning. Their words can sometimes hurt.'

Eleanor sat on the armchair and looked at Olivia with icy disdain. Her smile looked almost painful. 'They can.'

A silence fell between them.

Olivia cleared her throat. 'I just wanted you to know that I know what you're going through. If there's anything I can do or if I can help in any way, or even if you just want to vent some frustration, I'm here for you.'

'Yes. I'm sure you are,' Eleanor said, an edge to her voice.

'I'm sorry? Is everything... has something happened?' Olivia asked, confused.

'They don't want me,' she said. 'Typical, isn't it? My father is in prison. He could be a serial killer. All those journalists out there are wetting themselves for an exclusive, but it's not me they want to hear about.'

Eleanor was knotting her fingers together. She was red with rage, seething as the anger within threatened to explode.

'Oh, they ask a few questions to begin with,' she continued.

'Did you know your father was killing people? Did you know any of the victims? But it's not long before they move on. You've met Olivia Winter. What's she really like? Has she mentioned her dad? What does she think about the drama? How well do you know her? Is she as fucked up as she seems? It's all Olivia, Olivia, fucking Olivia,' she ranted.

Olivia watched, wide-eyed, as Eleanor crumbled and fell apart in front of her.

'Eleanor, I'm so sorry. Some reporters, they don't—'

Eleanor interrupted. 'I've been talking to Damien Littlejohn from *The Sun*. He's been asking me questions for the features. It's blatantly obvious he's not interested in my dad, in me, and he'll find any opportunity to bring your name up. He's even emailed me a list of questions to ask you on his behalf. Can you believe that?'

'I think what you're best off doing—'

'No!' Eleanor shouted. 'I do not want any more of your advice, Olivia. All I wanted was just a little bit of attention, someone to sympathise with what I was going through, but no. While you're around, you're the only one they want. You're the elusive final girl. There can only be one.'

Olivia took a breath. Suddenly, coming here tonight didn't seem like a good idea after all. She stood up.

'I think it's probably best if I go,' Olivia said. 'I can see you're hurting. I don't want us to get into an argument and one of us say something we might regret.'

Eleanor jumped up from her seat and reached the door to the hallway before Olivia could. She slammed it closed, blocking her from leaving.

'You're not going anywhere. Like I said, there can only be one final girl. And it's going to be me.'

Chapter Fifty-Eight

Linus left DCI Wise's office and stretched his aching body. He had been in there for hours working on a statement and trying to include each police force that had helped in recovering victims. So far, five had been found, though no new ones had been identified, and Linus couldn't even begin to guess which of the trophies Isaac saved belonged to which body. Between them, DCI Wise and Linus hoped that a full national press conference, at which the victims were described as accurately as possible from information gleaned from the code, and the trophies would be shown, would get people coming forward to say they were friends or family of the missing. Then there was the question of a report to the Crown Prosecution Service in the hope of being able to charge Isaac McFadden with a dozen more murders.

However, it seemed that some victims might never be found. The code for victim four stated that he was buried, or dumped, at Rockman Colliery in Carlisle. Police had visited the mine this afternoon and the what3words location had taken them to the mine shaft. Upon removing the cover for the shaft, it was obvious they were not going to be able to send someone down to look. It was flooded, the water running fast below ground, its temperature in the twenties. If a bag had been dumped there, it could have been swept out to sea, or if it had become stuck, the heat of the water and the chemicals and minerals in it would have eroded the plastic and eaten away at the body. He had been down there since July 2022. There would be nothing left by now.

Linus left DCI Wise's office and headed back to his own. The station was quiet, running on a skeleton staff in the hours of darkness. He yawned. His stomach growled. He wanted nothing more than to go home, fall onto his bed, and sleep until at least midday tomorrow.

He unplugged his phone from the charger and saw he had three missed calls from Ryan. He called him back, but it went straight to voicemail. It obviously wasn't important. He'd try him again in the morning.

By the time Ryan had worked out what he was seeing, he'd been hit on the head by a blunt object and was unconscious before he dropped to the floor. When he came to and opened his eyes, he was tied to a chair, his hands behind his back, his legs at the ankles. His head throbbed, he was cold and shaking in fear, yet in front of him what he saw defied belief.

The concrete garage floor was awash with blood. Body parts were strewn about. He spotted an arm, a leg, a foot, a head. There were tendons, muscles, veins and bones sticking out of various chunks of body. The air was filled with the metallic stench of blood. He could almost taste it. His eyes went back to the head. He recognised it as belonging to Hal Garfield, but it didn't seem real. It was like a model, a plaster cast, a waxwork impression of a head.

In the centre of the nightmare, dressed in a clear plastic onesie, Lesley Quinn had a wide-eyed, determined look as she set about detaching a thigh bone from the torso. She wiped her brow with the back of her hand then went back to snipping away at veins and sinews. She was oblivious to Ryan having regained consciousness. Eventually, the leg came off, she sat back on her haunches and released a heavy sigh of relief. She looked up and spotted Ryan watching her for the first time.

'Oh good, you're awake,' she said. 'I was worried I'd hit you too hard. I don't know my own strength sometimes.' She looked back down at the mound of body parts. 'You know, I've never liked Hal. Right from the first time I saw him. Isn't it strange how you can just take against someone without even knowing them? He was a nosey bugger. Isaac wanted to kill him a while back, but that would have brought the police right to our doorstep. I couldn't have that.'

'You,' Ryan said. He was in shock. He was in the middle of a nightmare. There were so many questions in his head he wanted to ask but he couldn't seem to get them to come out of his mouth. 'You're… Why? Why are you doing all this?'

Lesley placed the blood-soaked scalpel on the floor. She flexed her fingers and cricked her neck. She was obviously in pain from being hunched over the body.

'It's a long story. Me and Isaac were sort of a couple. I fell for him as soon as he moved in next door. He had a wife then, as you know. I liked Louise. I would never have come between them. When she fell ill, I helped as much I could. I watched as the cancer took hold and slowly killed her. I couldn't stand seeing her fade away so slowly and in so much pain. Isaac said he wanted to end her suffering. I was with him when she died. I held his hand as he held hers.

'I stayed in the background from then. I played the long game. I'd be there for Isaac when he wanted me. But he went off the rails slightly and left me looking after Eleanor. I could see he was heading for destruction, so I had to give him an incentive to get back on track. Eleanor didn't have an accident at school. I made sure she took a tumble in the park. A slight concussion but she was soon right as rain. That's all it took for Isaac to see he had something to live for.

'Unfortunately, it went too far. He put all his energy into looking after Eleanor, working all hours to provide for her, so that he didn't see me. I was the invisible woman in the background looking after his daughter for him.

'I told him one night that I liked him, that I wanted to take our friendship further. He said he still loved Louise, that there couldn't be anyone else. I wanted him, though. I had to have him. Have you ever loved someone so much that you physically ache when you're apart from them?'

'No,' Ryan said.

'No, I don't suppose you have. You're only young. Anyway, I decided to make Isaac jealous. I went out with this bloke a few times, made sure Isaac saw me with him, happy, smiling, having fun. It worked, too. He came round one night, Isaac, and he told me the truth. He said he liked me but since Louise's illness, he'd suffered with… you know… not being able to maintain an erection. He said it wouldn't be fair on me to be with someone who couldn't perform.

'We tried everything. It didn't work. Even Viagra wouldn't touch him. It started to drive a wedge between us, and we decided to call it a day. To say I was disappointed was an understatement. Still…' She shrugged. She paused and took off the blood-streaked latex gloves she'd been wearing while cutting up Hal Garfield.

'I rejoined Tinder,' Lesley continued. 'I met a man on there who, well, he was no Isaac, but he'd do. I invited him back here, but I changed my mind. It was like if I couldn't have Isaac, I didn't want anyone else. Unfortunately, he was the type of man who wouldn't take no for an answer, and he tried… I don't need to go into details, do I? I hit him. I grabbed the nearest thing to hand, and I smacked him over the head. I didn't intend to kill him. That wasn't supposed to happen. I dragged him in here then called for Isaac to come round and help me. I didn't know what to do. I was frantic. I shouldn't have moved his body, I knew that, I didn't know what I was thinking, but it was too late. We decided we had to just get rid of him, dump him somewhere. We wrapped him up, carried him out to Isaac's car, drove out to Ripley Mill, an abandoned mine just off the A696, and dropped him down the shaft. I looked up at Isaac and I saw something different in his eyes. Something had clicked. We had sex right there and then at the mine. It was amazing,' she said with a grin on her face. 'I thought we'd turned a corner, but we hadn't. It turned out the only way he could have sex was when there was an element of danger.

'It was Isaac's suggestion to do the murders. He's always had a fascination with taking a life, he told me. He'd met a murderer once. He said he was surprised by how ordinary he was. You always expect people who do extraordinary things to be... different, somehow, don't you? I'd have done anything Isaac said if it meant I could be with him. Unfortunately, I had to be the stronger one. Isaac was terrible at luring in the victims.

'We killed two more men I found on Tinder before we realised people were missing them and we'd need to be a bit more creative. There are so many homeless, drifters and illegal immigrants that we were spoilt for choice.'

'How many have you killed?' Ryan asked. His voice was low. He'd sat and listened to her story in disbelief.

'I didn't keep a count. I didn't know about Isaac's code until he showed me when we were on the eighth one. Silly sod. He was more emotional about it than I was. I suppose that's why he saved trophies from them all, too. Idiot. I told him from the very beginning that nothing could connect us to them. Nothing.'

'We thought we were looking for someone with medical training,' Ryan said.

Lesley looked up at him. 'But I do have medical training. I was a nurse for years until I helped Isaac kill his wife. The hospital found out I'd stolen drugs to give to her. There'd been a scandal the year before about a surgeon scorching his initials on people's organs so I said I'd resign quietly to avoid a media storm.'

Ryan swallowed his tears. One escaped and ran down his cheek. 'Are you going to kill me?'

'I don't want to. You're a lovely young man. But you really shouldn't have come here on your own. You've left me very little choice.'

Chapter Fifty-Nine

'We're very alike, you and me,' Eleanor said. She had Olivia trapped. The door to the hallway was closed, Olivia was pressed up against it and Eleanor was leaning in close, her hand firmly against the door.

Eleanor had a few inches on Olivia. Even barefoot, she towered over her. Olivia felt the oppression of imminent danger closing in around her.

'We've both got fathers who are serial killers. We've both had a childhood that we thought was perfect but turned out to be a complete lie. We're both fucked up beyond belief. Now, the problem is, there can only be one of us. The press and the public prefer a sole survivor, someone they can champion and look to as a beacon of hope in these bonkers times we live in. Do you know what else the great British public love? They love to see someone fall from grace. And that person is going to be you.'

Eleanor was frightening Olivia. Gone was the painful expression of disbelief as she tried to understand the extent of her father's actions, being constantly on the verge of bursting into tears whenever she thought about her supposedly idyllic childhood and the uncertainty of the future. It had been replaced with a wide-eyed determination to make something happen, something she could be in control of.

'One of us is bound to snap one day, right?' Eleanor asked.

Olivia looked up at her. She wanted to plead with Eleanor that what she was doing was wrong, but in this state it wouldn't take much for her to flip completely and do something she would later regret.

'And it's more likely going to be you rather than me. You've got people writing all kinds of crap about you on social media. Your peers are questioning your work. The drama was the last straw. You saw me as someone who could usurp you, be the victim everyone wants you to be, and you couldn't stand the competition, so you came here, you tried to kill me, but I was just that little bit too strong for you. And I won. I promise, I'll make it quick.'

'Eleanor, is this really the route you want to go down?' Olivia asked. 'Nobody will believe I tried to kill you. Everyone who knows me will know that's not who I am.'

'You killed Jamie Farr last year. His mother is taking out a private prosecution against you. That's bound to be messing with your head.'

'That won't even reach a courtroom. What you're doing is ridiculous. You need help, Eleanor. Not this.'

'Help? I need help?' she asked, raising her voice. 'Have you seen yourself? If anyone needs help around here, it's you. I was watching you in that pub for ages before I came in to see you. You were necking the wine back like it was water. How much do you drink in a single day? What else do you do to numb the pain? Do you take drugs? Do you self-harm? You cannot lecture me when you're just as fucked up.'

Olivia looked away. She knew she was fucked up. She knew she wasn't coping with the hand life had dealt her, but it was up to her to tell herself she was fucked up, not somebody else.

Eleanor grabbed Olivia by the throat and turned her face so they made eye contact.

'I need to do this,' Eleanor said, forcefully. 'All my life I've been in the background. Mum was ill – she couldn't help that, obviously, but she took priority. Then she died and Dad was grieving, and I was left with Lesley looking after me. If we hadn't come up with our plan, then who knows where he would have ended up.'

'Your plan?'

'Dad needed something to focus on. He needed to realise life was still continuing without Mum. Lesley managed to convince me. She threw me down on the ground, cut my head and rushed me to hospital so that Dad would see how much he was neglecting me.'

Olivia frowned as she tried to remember the story Lesley gave her.

'Who came up with that plan?' Olivia asked.

'Lesley. I wasn't happy about it as I knew it would hurt. She said she knew how to do it so that it wouldn't cause much pain. I mean, she should know, she was a nurse, after all. Unfortunately, it did hurt. Someone else who lied. Just add them to the list. I've still got the scar to this day,' she said, lifting back her fringe and showing the soft white line on her hairline.

'Lesley said you fell over in the playground at school,' Olivia said.

'Well, she's not going to admit assaulting a five-year-old, is she?'

'She was a nurse?' Olivia asked. Confusion ran over her face. 'She told me she was an accountant.'

'An accountant? No. I mean, she does a lot of office-based stuff, but she's not trained. She was a nurse for years.'

'What happened? Why did she leave?'

'I... I don't know. Why all these questions about Lesley all of a sudden? Look, stop stalling. Stop trying to make me change my mind about all this.'

'Eleanor, wait. Why aren't your dad and Lesley a couple?'

'What?'

Olivia took her chance during Eleanor's lapse in concentration. She ducked down under her outstretched hand and moved over to the window, putting some distance between the two of them.

'Eleanor, just listen to me for a moment,' Olivia said. 'Why aren't your dad and Lesley a couple?' she repeated.

'Dad didn't want anyone else. He always said he was in love with Mum still.'

'How does Lesley feel about that?'

'I always thought she wanted something to develop with Dad. She's always dropped whatever she was doing to help him if he needed her. They work well together; I thought something would have happened.'

'What do you mean by "they work well together"?'

Eleanor looked confused, as if wondering where this was leading. 'They work together. Lesley gets Dad his appointments, does his paperwork and invoicing. All the sales reps at MediSupplies UK are on a freelance contract and have to get their own customers. That's why Dad was always their top salesman. While all the others were doing admin, Dad was out getting new deals because he had Lesley at home doing the office-based stuff.'

'So, Lesley works with your dad? For how long?'

'For… ever, I suppose.'

'Shit!' Olivia exclaimed. She put her hand in her jacket pocket and pulled out her mobile.

'What are you doing?' Eleanor lunged forward.

Olivia's lapsed Krav Maga training suddenly kicked in. She dropped her mobile and shoved a palm into Eleanor's left shoulder, pushing her back at an angle, tilting her torso. With her other hand, Olivia grabbed Eleanor's right shoulder and pulled it towards her, spinning her around. With a quick movement, Olivia put Eleanor in a chokehold. Eleanor still had the height advantage, so Olivia kicked her at the back of the knees, causing her to drop to the floor. With all her energy, Olivia squeezed tight around Eleanor's neck. She didn't want to cause her any harm, simply subdue her. When she felt Eleanor relax in her hold, she pushed her away, bent down and picked up her phone.

'You'll be fine,' Olivia said. 'We'll not say anything more about this, but you need to seek help, Eleanor, and I'll bloody make sure you do, too.' She scrolled through her phone, found Linus's number and called.

He answered almost straightaway. 'I was just this second about to phone you,' he said by way of a greeting.

'You need to get over to Isaac's house,' she said, urgency in her voice.

'What? Why?'

'I think Lesley is the second killer.'

'Lesley? As in Lesley Quinn?'

'Yes. She's been lying to us. She's closer to Isaac than she's been making out.'

'Where are you?'

'I'm at Eleanor's house.' She turned to Eleanor, who was still sprawled out on the floor, her face red. 'Do you have a car?' she asked her. Eleanor nodded. 'Get your keys.'

'I'll go over there now,' Linus said. 'Have you heard from Ryan? I've had several missed calls from him.'

Olivia had been halfway to the living-room door when she stopped in her tracks. 'Ryan,' she said. 'Oh my God! Linus, you need to hurry.'

'What? Why?'

'Ryan had a bee in his bonnet about Isaac's car not fitting in the garage. He said he wanted to measure the inside and see if Isaac's car would fit. He might have gone over there to test out his theory.'

'Shit! When did you last speak to him?'

'I don't know. An hour ago, maybe. I don't know.'

'I'm on my way.'

Olivia ended the call. She turned to Eleanor, whose face was pale with shock. It had obviously just dawned on her what she had been about to do to Olivia.

'I'm sorry,' she cried.

'We don't have time for that. Car keys. Right now.'

Chapter Sixty

'Ryan. Ryan. Come on young man, wake up.'
Ryan slowly opened his eyes. He felt dazed and didn't have a clue where he was. Someone was slapping his face. Someone was calling his name.

He tried to speak but his mouth was dry. His eyes focused and he saw Lesley leaning over him, a sickly smile on her lips.

'There we are. You're awake. I tried bringing Sean round, but he was weak. That's the problem with people who take drugs, you've no idea what they've taken over the years and what it's done to them. Their own fault, really. I've no sympathy.'

Ryan tried to move but found he couldn't.

'It's all right,' Lesley said. 'I'm going to look after you. I'm going to make sure you're comfortable. Would you like a drink?'

She lifted a bottle of water to his lips. He sipped, but most of it dribbled down his chin. She wiped it away with a soft towel.

'I've tied off the blood vessels and stemmed the bleeding. I've wrapped the wound up nice and tight so you can't see anything. But that's one piece of you gone,' she said, holding up a foot.

He looked down at his outstretched legs, saw the space where his foot should have been and then everything went black.

'I'm sorry. I'm so so sorry,' Eleanor said. She was standing in the doorway of her house, a look of horror and confusion on her face. 'I don't know what came over me. I really don't. I just... I... I don't know what to say.'

'Eleanor, we don't have time for this. Which one's your car?'

'What?'

'Eleanor! Your car!' Olivia shouted.

'Black Peugeot.'

Olivia looked around her and spotted the car. She turned back and saw Eleanor hadn't moved. She was stood, stock still, in the doorway. Olivia ran back to her and snatched the keys from her hand.

'Eleanor, you need to snap out of this. A young man's life is in danger. I'll drive but I need you to direct me from here.'

'I was going to kill you,' she said.

'Yes, well, you wouldn't be the first to try that,' she said, flippantly. 'The main thing is you came to your senses before you had a chance to do anything. That tells me you're much stronger than you think you are.'

'Really?' Eleanor looked at her pleadingly.

'Yes. You know, what you said in there about us being alike – it's very true. We are alike. Another way in which we're alike is that we are both incredibly strong-willed, determined women. Anything thrown at us, we can survive.'

'Can we?'

'Of course we can. But right now, we need to work together to stop Lesley from taking another life. We can stop this,' Olivia said.

Eleanor nodded. 'You're right.' She took her keys back from Olivia. 'It might be quicker if I drive.'

Linus struggled to get out of Newcastle city centre due to traffic. He had tried Ryan's phone a few more times, but it went straight to voicemail. It was either switched off or damaged. He had no idea what he was going to find when he arrived at Isaac's house, but he would never forgive himself if anything happened to Ryan. He was young, he was keen to learn and impress. He knew he was being taunted by some of the other plain-clothed detectives, most of whom resented Ryan for not climbing the ranks and paying his dues in uniform first. He should have protected him more.

He turned right, passing Exhibition Park, and joined the Great North Road, where he slammed his foot down on the accelerator. He reached across for his airwaves radio.

'Oscar Delta from 347. I need all available units to 17 Ridley Road. Potential hostage situation. Approach with caution. 347 en route.'

Linus hoped he wasn't too late.

'I'm going to take your leg apart at the knee, now,' Lesley said.

Ryan was flat on the floor of the garage. He was unconscious but his eyelids were flickering. Lesley hoped he could hear her.

'I'll be separating the femur and the tibia. I'll be cutting through the patella tendon, the anterior and posterior cruciate ligament and the hamstring muscle, which is at the rear of your knee. Now, that's a tough muscle to cut through, but I have plenty of scalpel blades. I don't want you to worry.'

She leaned down and with gentle pressure, she cut the skin, just above the patella.

Ryan didn't feel a thing.

Under normal circumstances, it would take just over half an hour to drive from Eleanor's house in Heaton to her father's house in Blyth. However, breaking every traffic rule in the Highway Code, Eleanor managed it in a record-breaking twenty minutes. She turned onto Ridley Road without slowing down and pulled up at the end of Isaac's drive.

As Olivia jumped out of the car, she looked around. The street was quiet. So much for increased police patrol. There were no lights on at Hal's house across the road, no ill-parked police cars or unmarked vehicles, though she recognised Ryan's red Fiat Punto. She must be the first to arrive. She hesitated for a moment. It wouldn't be the first time she would have to apprehend a killer single-handed. It just wasn't something she was relishing.

'Do you have anything we can use as a weapon?' Olivia asked Eleanor. Her voice was urgent and resounded around the quiet neighbourhood.

'No,' she said, incredulously, in a 'why would I?' voice.

'Shit.'

Olivia ran to the front door and found it unlocked. This did not bode well.

She pushed open the door and headed inside. It was freezing cold, and all the lights were off. Ryan had a fixation with the garage, so she headed straight for the kitchen. The door leading into the garage was ajar. She slowly went through, looking around her at the empty, dark space.

Ahead, where the shelves were, was a recess in the wall. A connecting door was open. She looked back over her shoulder to Eleanor.

'I had no idea,' Eleanor whispered loudly.

'What's through there?'

'I don't know. It backs onto Lesley's garage.'

'Fuck,' Olivia mouthed.

They both headed, silently, towards the doorway. There was a dull light within, and they could hear the soft voice of Lesley, but couldn't make out what she was saying. As they reached the door, Olivia placed a hand on the door frame and tried to make sense of what she was seeing.

The floor was awash with blood. There were four clinical waste sacks overflowing with body parts and blood-soaked clothes, and she was sure she could see hair. She had no idea who this latest victim was.

'Run! Olivia, run!'

Movement at the edge of the garage caught Olivia's eye. She looked over and saw Lesley, leaning over a prostrate Ryan, carefully taking apart his leg.

Eleanor gasped, slapped a hand over her mouth and looked away. Despite the darkness, Olivia could see she had turned pale.

'Lesley,' Olivia said softly.

Lesley paused and looked up. She looked confused, as if wondering who had called her. She looked around before her eyes landed on Olivia.

'Oh. It's you,' she said.

'Lesley, step away from Ryan. Leave him alone.'

'But I haven't finished.'

'Is he dead?'

'No,' she said, looking back at Ryan. 'I've tied off the blood vessels in his leg. He's not losing any blood. Not yet,' she said with a smile.

'I need to get him to a hospital.'

'No. I haven't finished,' she said, more forcefully.

Eleanor stepped past Olivia and into the garage.

'Lesley, why are you doing all this?' Eleanor asked. She tried to not look at the bloodbath in front of her, but it wasn't easy.

'Because I love your father. We've been in love for so long, since you were a child. I told the young man here everything. It was something for us to do together, something to…'

Olivia looked down at Ryan. He was pale. She looked at his chest. His breathing was slow. She stepped forward and Lesley jumped up and pointed the bloody scalpel at her.

'You can't save him.'

'I can,' Olivia said. 'And I will. I will not let you kill another one.'

'Who's that over there?' Eleanor asked, nodding towards the bloody sacks.

'There? That's Hal Garfield.'

'Oh my God,' Eleanor said, buckling slightly. She reached out to the door frame to keep herself upright.

Outside, the sound of a car screeching to a halt could be heard.

'That's the police, Lesley,' Olivia said. 'In a few minutes, they'll be barging in here. It's over. It's all over.'

'No. It really isn't.'

'You've lied. All this time,' Eleanor said, struggling to compose herself. 'You've killed and you've lied, and you and my father have been cutting up innocent people for… for what? For fun?'

'You wouldn't understand.'

'Try me,' Eleanor said, finding the courage from somewhere to raise her voice.

Olivia made to move closer to Ryan.

'You need to stay where you are!' Lesley screamed at Olivia, pointing the scalpel back at her.

'I'm helping him,' she said.

'No. One step closer and I'll cut you up, too.'

Linus ran into Isaac's garage and heard the commotion through the connecting door. When he had pulled up outside he had recognised Ryan's car, but saw no other vehicle belonging to the force. He thought others would have been here by now. He took his radio from his pocket and pressed the emergency red button on the top. That closed down all radio traffic except for his and the communications room back at HQ. It opened a frequency and everyone on the same channel would be able to hear what he said for ten seconds before it closed.

'Officer down. Urgent assistance required at 17 Ridley Road. Potential hostage situation,' he whispered.

In the control room, Linus's location would be known because of the GPS tracking in the radio.

'I'm saving Ryan's life,' Olivia called out. 'It's over, Lesley. The police are outside.'

'Don't go an inch closer. I'm warning you. I'm fucking warning you!' Lesley screamed.

'Olivia,' Eleanor called.

Olivia turned to look at her. She saw the hint of resignation and sadness in her eyes.

'Help him,' Eleanor said.

Olivia didn't have time to stop her. Eleanor lunged forward and grabbed Lesley, tackling her to the ground.

Olivia ran over to Ryan. Blood was pouring from an open wound on his knee. She grabbed bandages and wadding that Lesley had ready and placed it over the top of the knee to stem the blood flow. She lifted Ryan up, but he was a dead weight.

Linus entered the garage. He stood in silence, looking down at Olivia cradling the bloodied DC.

'Don't even think about coming closer,' Lesley said.

She had scrambled to her feet, Eleanor in front of her, arm wrapped around her throat, scalpel held to her neck.

Sirens outside began to sound louder as the emergency services got closer to the house.

'It's over, Lesley,' Linus said. 'Your house is surrounded.'

'This could still end up as a bloodbath. I could take all three of you.'

'That's not going to happen.'

'Really? Watch this.'

With a swift movement, she sliced through Eleanor's neck with the scalpel, severing the external jugular vein. Eleanor's hand went up to her neck to try to stop the gush of blood. Lesley pushed her out of the way and ran towards Linus, scalpel aloft, screaming at the top of her voice.

Linus reached out with his right hand, grabbed her right wrist firmly and pulled her down to the floor. He stood on her arm with all his weight so she would let go of the scalpel. He kicked it away and then pressed his foot on her lower back so she couldn't get up.

As uniformed officers filled the garage, he gave the instruction to cuff her and arrest her, only releasing his foot once she was secured.

He turned back to look at the scene of horror in front of him. All he saw was red.

Chapter Sixty-One

Wednesday 5th February 2025

Olivia knocked on the door of the private hospital room. She didn't wait for a reply. She pushed open the door and went inside. Ryan was sitting up in bed. His eyes were half closed, and his face wore the dazed expression often seen in people who had recently undergone a general anaesthetic.

'Olivia,' he said slowly with a soppy smile.

'How are you feeling?'

'Great. I'm feeling great.'

She couldn't help but smile. 'That'll be the drugs.'

'I'm so hungry. You know what I fancy? Fish and chips, but I want to eat them on the beach. There's a shop in Whitley Bay. They're so nice.' He was practically salivating.

The door opened and Linus entered.

'How is he?'

'Smacked off his face,' she replied.

'Probably for the best for now. Can I have a word?' he asked Olivia, nodding for her to step out of the room.

'Sure. I'll come back and see you in a while, Ryan.'

'Have you seen my tablet?' Ryan asked. 'I need to update my tablet.'

'I'll see what I can do.'

She went into the corridor and closed the door behind her. 'I wouldn't mind some of those drugs myself. I didn't sleep a wink last night.'

'Me neither.'

They sat down on a row of three seats.

'They had to amputate Ryan's leg below the knee,' Linus said. 'He'll be fitted with a prosthetic when the wound's healed. Which it should do.'

'Poor lad. A desk job for him from now on.'

'You're welcome to poach him for the Behavioural Science Administration,' Linus said. 'I believe he'd be happy there.'

'If he wants to be poached, he'd be very welcome.'

Linus looked down at the floor. It was clear he had more to say. He took a breath. 'Eleanor didn't make it. She died about an hour ago.'

Olivia deflated in her seat. She shook her head. 'I didn't think she'd survive. She lost so much blood in the garage. Is Lesley talking?'

'Yes and no. She's only telling us what she wants, which is very little. She's refusing to tell us about any of the other victims. Whenever we ask a question, she sits there with a smug smile on her lips that I want to slap right off her. Oh, she did tell us that she posed as one of Isaac's customers. She was Melanie Knox, who Ryan interviewed on the phone. She slipped into a perfect Irish accent with ease.'

'Why did she pose as one of his customers?'

'So they could order bandages, scalpel blades, clinical waste sacks, ties, everything they needed.'

'Wow,' Olivia said, impressed by their ingenuity.

'Lesley also said it was killing and dismembering that gave Isaac a charge, made him physically able to perform.'

'Erotophonophilia,' Olivia said. 'I've never come across that before. People being aroused by killing someone. It's a power trip. The surge of adrenaline. I'm guessing Isaac was impotent, which is why he didn't engage in a relationship with Lesley, but then something happened, they both found themselves standing over a dead body, and suddenly Isaac feels something stirring.'

'And Lesley manipulated that, do you think?'

'Yes. I think she genuinely loved Isaac in the beginning, but he was married and then grieving for Louise. She made sure he fell in love with her eventually and that it was all down to her that he was cured of his impotence. Like a sap, he believed it. She was a domineering woman, just like his mother. Maybe she reminded Isaac of his mother, who knows?

'She lured the victims in with her kind-lady act. She purposely chose the homeless, the addicts, those who needed someone to hold out a hand, and she took advantage of that. She also had medical training so knew how to cut the bodies up. Isaac was muscle. He hid them.'

'But Shane Waterhouse wasn't homeless. He was picked up outside a nightclub at New Year's.'

'Which I'm guessing was one of Isaac's victims. Any anomaly would be when the one who didn't usually perform that task had a go. I imagine when Isaac returned home with Shane Waterhouse in his car, Lesley was not happy. She would have gone through with their ritual, but she would have made sure Isaac knew not to do it again.'

'So, Lesley was the dominant one and Isaac the supplicant?'

'It was obvious from the start Isaac was covering up for someone.'

'I always thought it would be another man.'

'So did I. Never underestimate the power of women,' she said, a glint of a smile in her eyes.

'Why did she kill Thomas Landy? Why continue killing after Isaac was caught?'

'To prove she was able to do it all on her own. To show us that she was the brains and Isaac was merely the muscle.'

'Will she tell us everything now she's been caught?'

'No. She'll maintain an air of mystery. She's drip-feeding you, and she'll continue to do so for years to come.'

'She truly is a psychopath, isn't she?'

'Absolutely. She's mastered the art of manipulation and has been doing so for so long that she won't be able to stop herself.'

'Bloody hell. I never asked, why were you at Eleanor's last night?'

'It doesn't matter now,' she said. Nobody needed to know what Eleanor had in mind.

'Will you go and see Isaac again?' Linus asked.

'Oh yes. I'm looking forward to this visit,' she said with an evil smile on her lips.

Olivia walked into the room where she had interviewed Isaac McFadden before. As she saw him, she took in the look of gloating on his face, as if he'd known she would be back. She was about to bring him down to earth with a massive thud.

'Couldn't stay away, could you? I knew you wouldn't be able to resist,' he said, sitting back in his seat, arms stretched out in front of him, cuffed at the wrists.

Olivia didn't sit down. She had no intention of staying.

'Lesley Quinn has been arrested.'

Isaac's smile dropped, but one suddenly appeared on Olivia's face. The ball was now firmly in her court.

'The police know everything,' she continued. 'Lesley has told them how you were impotent until you had a dead body in front of you. You're pathetic. When I first saw that code you'd written I actually thought I'd found someone who had the mettle to be a prolific and intelligent serial killer. I should have known that you wouldn't be an original. You're like all the others. An inadequate. You're not clever, you're not smart, you're not special. You're a pathetic little man who needed a woman to take control of you in order to perform. A weak man with a mother fixation. You couldn't be more of a cliché if you tried. You're not even worth writing about.'

Olivia walked over to the door and reached for the handle, then stopped and turned back.

'Oh, one more thing. Lesley killed Eleanor. She sliced her throat open with a scalpel. You've nobody left. You've nobody to come and see you. You're going to remain in here for the rest of your life and slowly fade away. And I can't think of a better punishment.'

She left the room, closing the door behind her with a loud slam.

Isaac remained seated, his face void of expression or emotion. A hand eventually slapped down on his shoulder. It belonged to one of the guards who would take him back to his cell. He stood up, turned and walked out of the interview room with his head down, dragging his feet, all life drained from him.

Chapter Sixty-Two

Friday 7 February 2025

Olivia was almost packed and ready to leave Newcastle. She was sorry she hadn't been able to explore the city as she had wanted to. It seemed like a friendly and welcoming place and the countryside looked stunning. She would like to return here one day, sample the restaurants and the nightlife, maybe go walking on the hills or along the beaches. She could bring Stanley. It would be a while before she would be able to think of Newcastle as an ordinary city in the north of England, though. At the moment, it was a place of murder and destruction.

She took the framed photograph of her mother and sister from the bedside table and placed it in her bag with the photo of Ethan Miller. She had received an email from him this morning saying he was returning to London early - next Monday. He was looking forward to seeing her. She heard Linus's words echoing around her mind. She planned to lay everything on the table for Ethan. She couldn't do a relationship and domesticity. She had no intention of giving him a spare key, attending dinner parties together and walking around DIY shops at the weekend choosing wallpaper to decorate the box room with, but if he wanted to be in her life as… as… whatever… then she would try her hardest to make it work between them.

There was a knock on her door. She opened it to find Linus standing on the threshold. He looked dapper in his freshly ironed shirt and skin-tight trousers.

'I've come to drive you to the station,' he said.

'It's less than a ten-minute walk.'

'I know, but I've still come to drive you.'

'Come on in. I'm just checking I've got everything. How's Ryan?'

'He's doing very well. Healing nicely. I think he'll be sending you an email once he's discharged and used to walking on his prosthetic leg. He's keen to work alongside you again.'

'Tell him there is no rush. He needs to concentrate on himself for now.'

'I've said that. We've identified two more victims,' he said, sitting down on the beautifully made bed. 'Jack Penhaligan, aged twenty-one, originally from Devon. He's been missing since October 2021. He had a breakdown after his best friend at university killed himself. Nobody seems to know how or why he came up north, but he somehow managed to cross Lesley Quinn's path. We've found some of him at Downdale Colliery in Carlisle, but not all of him. The other victim is Paul Devlin. He was a young homeless man from Whitehaven. Twenty-one years old. His parents died when he was a child. He'd been living with his sister. They had a big argument and he just walked out one day in June 2022. His sister identified his medical alert bracelet from the trophies Isaac kept. It's a long process, but we're slowly getting there.'

Olivia nudged him to get up off the bed she'd recently made and smoothed where he'd been sitting.

'Hopefully you'll be able to identify them all eventually.'

'We're not even going to find them all, especially the ones down the mines. Lesley is denying all knowledge of where they were hidden. She said she left that to Isaac. I called the prison yesterday to arrange to see him and according to the staff, Isaac is going on hunger strike.'

'For what reason?'

'He wants to die.'

'Coward,' she spat.

Linus parked in a space reserved for taxis and helped Olivia to the platform with her cases. She looked up at the board. Her train was due in seven minutes.

'It's been an absolute pleasure and delight to meet you, Dr Winter,' he said above the din of the station.

'And you. It's a shame we didn't meet under more salubrious circumstances.'

'Some of the nicest people I've met have been over dead bodies.'

'You need a hobby,' she said.

He laughed. 'Tell me about it. I'll keep you informed of any further development with the code and the victims.'

'Thank you.'

'No. I should be thanking you. You've been a massive help to us, to me in particular. I know I haven't scattered Clara's ashes yet, but I've a plan in place and I feel… I don't know, lighter, somehow.'

'There's no doubt in my mind you'll never forget her. Just… don't dwell on her.'

'I won't. Now, promise me you'll not dismiss Ethan out of hand.'

'I promise.'

'Good.'

The train pulled into the platform. Linus stepped forward and pulled Olivia into a tight embrace.

'Thank you again. For everything,' he whispered into her ear.

'You're welcome,' she said.

They pulled out of the hug and Olivia stretched up and kissed him on the cheek. 'If you're ever in London, don't be a stranger.'

'The same applies for you if you're ever in Newcastle.'

The door to the first-class carriage opened and Olivia struggled on with her bags. Once she found her place, she sat down, looked through the window and saw Linus standing on the platform, watching her. He seemed brighter, healthier, than when she first saw him in her office all those weeks ago.

She waved and he waved back. As the train pulled away slowly from the platform, she glanced through the window and saw he'd already left.

She faced forward and let out a deep breath. She took her phone out of her inside pocket and sent a text to Sebastian, telling him she'd left Newcastle on time and would see him in roughly four hours, depending on delays.

He sent back a selfie of him, Daisy and Stanley smiling at the camera.

Olivia couldn't wait to get back home and see them.

Chapter Sixty-Three

BELMARSH PRISON

Tuesday 18th February 2025

Against her better judgement, Olivia had relented and gone with Sebastian to see her father in prison. There was obviously something he wanted to talk to her about. However, she told Sebastian that at the first sign of him gloating or any snide comments and remarks, especially about that sodding TV drama, she would walk out, and she would never go back.

They sat in the small room, waiting for Richard to arrive, in silence. It was a cold room. The radiator was making a few gurgling noises, but it wasn't giving off any heat.

Olivia had dressed in understated clothing. She didn't want to give her father anything he could use against her, and that included criticising her dress sense or anything that might show off her scars.

The television drama had gone down well with viewers, though critics hadn't been as kind, calling it sensationalist. Based on the little she saw, Olivia agreed with them. Sales of Sebastian's book had shot through the roof, though now the drama was finished, the displays had vanished from shops and the book was back on the regular shelves in the true crime section. The billboards had been replaced and even the journalists had stopped calling. For now. As Olivia had expected, the fanfare had died down as quickly as it had started.

The door on the opposite side of the room opened and her father, dressed in blue jeans and a blue jumper, came through, handcuffed at the wrists, a guard on either side. He was sat down and the guards left, closing the door behind them.

Olivia looked at her father, took in his craggy face with his grey stubble and smiling eyes. Below the table, her hands were squeezed into fists. She could feel her fingernails digging deeply into her palms. It hurt, but it kept her strong emotions in check.

'You wanted to see me,' she said. Her voice was icy and professional.

'I did. How are you?'

'What did you want to see me about?' she asked, ignoring his question.

'Livvy, I want to know how you are?'

She felt herself balk at him calling her Livvy.

'Why?'

'Because I'm your father.'

'So. I'm your daughter, but I've no interest in knowing how you are.'

He smiled. 'Feisty.'

'I am very busy. If you have something to tell me, then tell me. If not, I'm going.'

'Fair enough,' he said, relenting. 'Does the name Janet Brown mean anything to you?'

Olivia frowned. She looked to Sebastian then back to her father. 'No.'

'I didn't think it would. I met her long before I met your mother. We got engaged. Briefly.'

'Okay,' Olivia said, wondering where this was going.

'I'd like to tell you where she is.'

'Why?'

'Because… I've been doing a lot of soul-searching recently. The heart attack last year has made me realise things need putting in order before it's too late.'

Again, Olivia looked to Sebastian. He looked as confused as she did.

'So, why do you want me to know where this Janet Brown is? What is she to me?'

'She's nothing to you. But she deserves to be found. So she can have a proper burial.'

Olivia felt her stomach plummet. Beneath the table, Sebastian reached across and held her hand.

'She's...' Olivia began.

'She's victim number one, Livvy,' Richard said with a smile.

Acknowledgments

I would like to thank the incredible team at One More Chapter and HarperCollins who have worked tirelessly to put this book into your hands. My editor, Jennie Rothwell, really is a superstar, there is no other word to describe her. Tony Russell, Hana Rowlands, Kara Daniel, Arsalan Isa, Toby James, Simon Fox, Lucy Bennett, Chloe Cummings and Emma Petfield who all had a hand in shaping this book into its final form; thank you so much for everything you've done.

I wouldn't have written this book at all if it wasn't for my agent championing me and my work. A big, massive thank you to Jamie Cowen and everyone at the Ampersand Agency.

It's strange but there are times when I love researching more than I love the writing. To discover all about mines, I called upon Chris Schofield who took me on a tour of abandoned mines in the north of England and went into all the places to take photographs that I was too scared to enter. It was a cold and miserable day, and I got soaked, but we had a laugh, and I loved every minute of it, even the accidental chicken sandwich.

Philip Lumb is an eminent pathologist who is incredibly busy, but he always finds time to answer my questions. I am appreciative of his detailed emails regarding the dismemberment of bodies. I must remember not to read an email from him while eating lunch.

Simon Browes for his unwavering support and detailed knowledge of all things medical and for giving me the names of arteries to cut and how to tie off veins. Fascinating and gruesome in equal measure.

Andrew Barrett who always goes above and beyond when I

ask him questions about crime scenes. He knows what I want, and he supplies the information perfectly. We really are a pair of sickos, aren't we, Andy?

"Mr Tidd" for all the police procedural information. Despite writing crime thrillers for the past decade, I still get it wrong, and he always puts me right. Thank you.

Scott Burden pointed out the areas of Newcastle I could use, Tom Wood told me all about Krav Maga and my Mum supplied me with home baking to keep my spirits up. Thank you all.

Finally, without the readers, the bloggers, and book sellers, you wouldn't be reading this book. Thank you for your continued support. I hope you enjoy the second Olivia Winter novel, and I'd love to hear from you all. You can reach out to me via social media, but please only say pleasant things.

Now, onto book three we go… let's spill some more blood.

The author and One More Chapter would like to thank everyone who contributed to the publication of this story...

Analytics
James Brackin
Abigail Fryer

Audio
Fionnuala Barrett
Ciara Briggs

Contracts
Laura Amos
Laura Evans

Design
Lucy Bennett
Fiona Greenway
Liane Payne
Dean Russell

Digital Sales
Lydia Grainge
Hannah Lismore
Emily Scorer

Editorial
Kara Daniel
Simon Fox
Charlotte Ledger
Ajebowale Roberts
Jennie Rothwell
Tony Russell
Helen Williams

Harper360
Emily Gerbner
Jean Marie Kelly
emma sullivan
Sophia Wilhelm

International Sales
Peter Borcsok
Ruth Burrow
Colleen Simpson

Inventory
Sarah Callaghan
Kirsty Norman

Marketing & Publicity
Chloe Cummings
Grace Edwards
Emma Petfield

Operations
Melissa Okusanya
Hannah Stamp

Production
Denis Manson
Simon Moore
Francesca Tuzzeo

Rights
Helena Font Brillas
Ashton Mucha
Zoe Shine
Aisling Smythe

Trade Marketing
Ben Hurd
Eleanor Slater

The HarperCollins Distribution Team

The HarperCollins Finance & Royalties Team

The HarperCollins Legal Team

The HarperCollins Technology Team

UK Sales
Isabel Coburn
Jay Cochrane
Sabina Lewis
Holly Martin
Harriet Williams
Leah Woods

eCommerce
Laura Carpenter
Madeline ODonovan
Charlotte Stevens
Christina Storey
Jo Surman
Rachel Ward

And every other essential link in the chain from delivery drivers to booksellers to librarians and beyond!

Read on for an extract from *The Mind of a Murderer*, the previous book in the Dr Olivia Winter series.

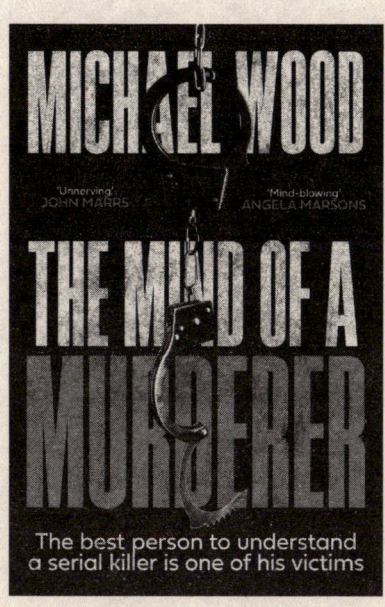

Extract: The Mind of a Murderer

Chapter One

Dollis Hill, London
Thursday 15th February 2024

After a double shift at the Royal Free Hospital, Phoebe Harper was hoping to get home, order a takeaway, have a long soak in the bath until the delivery arrived and spend the evening in front of the television gorging herself on spring rolls and crispy duck. As soon as she turned the corner and entered the road where she lived, she knew her quiet evening was ruined before it had even begun.

Her next-door neighbour, Donna Fletcher, was forty today and was having the party to end all parties. Phoebe had known about it for months – she'd even been invited – but had turned it down because she knew she'd be tired after work.

The road was packed with randomly parked cars. Donna's driveway was cluttered, and it wasn't difficult to spot the party house; a light was on in every room. The front door was wide open, and people were spilling out onto the street, bottles in hand. Thumping music sounded from within.

Donna, dressed in an unflattering little black dress, trotted unsteadily down the street towards Phoebe. She was wearing a plastic tiara on her head, a pink feather boa around her neck, and had an open bottle of prosecco in her left hand.

'Pheebs,' she slurred. 'You're home. Please tell me you're going to join us.'

Phoebe could smell the alcohol on her breath before she even opened her mouth. 'I'd love to, Donna, but I'm dead on my feet. I've been at the hospital for eighteen hours.'

'Pleeeeease?' Donna begged, managing to stretch the word for longer than was necessary. 'For me? Just one little drinky?'

'I can't. I've got to be back at work by eight tomorrow morning. I've got this weekend off. I'll take you out for lunch on Saturday if you're free.'

'I never say no to a free lunch,' Donna said with a smile. 'Thanks for your present. They're gorgeous.'

Donna put her arm around Phoebe and led her up the street to their homes. 'It's a shame you can't come. Roger's here. I've told you about Roger, haven't I? He's gorgeous. Six foot something, amazing body on him, and my James has seen him in the showers at the gym. I don't know any measurements but even James was impressed, and I've told you how big he is.'

'Yes, Donna, you have. Many times.'

'According to James, Roger is a sucker for a nurse's uniform too. He'd be on you in seconds.'

'As fun as that sounds, I'm really not in the mood tonight.'

'Never mind. I'll introduce you to him another time.' Donna took a swig from the bottle of prosecco and proffered it to Phoebe who waved it away. 'Listen, any chance we can park a couple of cars on your driveway? The net curtains are twitching. I don't think it'll be long before them across the way call for the police.'

'Yes, sure. No problem. Why don't you invite them over? They can't complain if they're invited.'

'I did. I went round on Saturday. He gave me a right earful about council regulations regarding loud music and occupancy levels. Boring old bastard.'

'Donna!' The call came from the doorway of the party HQ. They both turned to see James stood on the doorstep. 'Alice's been sick. Where's the mop?'

'She's such a lightweight,' Donna said to Phoebe. 'She only has to hear a cork popping and she's heaving.' She kissed her on the cheek. 'We'll try to keep it down,' she said, stifling a laugh and heading back to her house through the maze of cars.

'Don't worry about it,' Phoebe called.

She unlocked the door, stepped into the house and closed it

behind her. From inside, all she could hear was the dull thud of music and muffled laughter. Once she had the television on, she was sure she wouldn't have her evening interrupted.

She locked the door, put the security chain on and picked up the post. She flicked through the brown envelopes as she headed into the kitchen, slapping them down on the worktop. She switched the light on with her elbow. The whole room lit up in a brilliant white light. She went to the fridge, pulled out a bottle of wine and poured herself a glass. Unconsciously, she let out a heavy sigh.

There was a loud bang on the patio door at the back of the room that made her jump. She turned and saw James standing outside. He waved to her.

Phoebe took the key from the hook on the dresser, unlocked the door and pulled it open. A blast of cool air hit her in the face.

'Jesus, James, you scared the life out of me.'

'Sorry, I thought you'd seen me. Look, I know it's an imposition, but can we borrow your patio chairs?'

'What?'

'I know it's February, but we're having a barbeque and we haven't got enough chairs. Can we nab yours?'

'Course you can,' she smiled.

'I'll bring them back round tomorrow, once I've sobered up.'

'I doubt they'll be getting used until the summer. Keep them as long as you like. They might be a bit damp though. Do you want the cushions?' she asked as he began grabbing the wooden seats.

'Please. I'll have them cleaned if anything gets spilled on them.'

'Hang on.' Phoebe went back to the dresser. She opened a drawer and took out a key. 'Here you go. They're in the shed. Just pop them back in when you're done with them.'

'You sure?'

'Yes.'

'Thanks. Are you sure you can't pop round for a quick drink?'

'I'd better not. Once I get started, I don't know when to stop.'

'Donna's the same. I hope this is the only time she plans on turning forty. She was thirty about five times. See you later.'

Phoebe smiled and closed the door. She watched as James took the four chairs and squeezed through the gap in the fence between the two houses.

Phoebe refilled her glass of wine and took it upstairs.

The house was warm, the heating having come on as timed at six o'clock. She started running the bath, poured in a large amount of bubble bath, then went into her bedroom to change. Before stripping off her nurse's uniform, she looked out of the window into the garden next door. The party was in full swing. She could see the silhouettes of people dancing inside cast onto the lawn. She would love to be with them but didn't dare risk being late for work tomorrow. The hospital was struggling to cope as it was, being understaffed and with extra patients following the harsh winter.

She closed the curtains and tried to block out all sounds of the party. If she couldn't hear it or see it, she wouldn't feel so bad about missing it.

Phoebe wrapped a pink towelling dressing gown around her. She went back to the bathroom and removed her make-up in the mirror above the sink. She couldn't believe Donna was forty. She certainly didn't look it. As she wiped away the foundation and eye shadow, the lines and wrinkles were revealed. It would be another three years before Phoebe hit the big four-oh, and she wasn't looking forward to it. Donna was married and had two children, a good job, holidays twice a year and a new car every eighteen months. Phoebe was single, childless, had a demanding job and no money for a holiday or a car. Things would have to change this year. She'd been thinking about entering private practice, but that would mean turning her back on helping real people at the heart of the NHS, something she loved doing.

She sighed and turned away from her tired reflection. She pulled out the hair tie and allowed her dull hair to fall down her shoulders. The bath was full, the room had filled with steam and a relaxing aroma rose from the bubble bath. She turned off the tap and threw the dressing gown to the floor. She was just about to step into it when the doorbell rang.

Phoebe sighed. She put her dressing gown back on and headed for the stairs. She opened the door, expecting it to be Donna or James or maybe even the hunk from the gym.

'Sorry to interrupt,' a man of average height with neat dark hair and staring blue eyes said. 'I've come from next door. I've been sent round to ask if you can spare any wine glasses. There seems to be more people here than expected.'

Phoebe looked out at the madness of the party. The other neighbours wouldn't be as accommodating as her. She doubted it would be long before the police turned up.

'Sure, come on in,' she smiled, opening the door wider.

'Sorry, I haven't woken you up or anything, have I?' the man asked, noticing her dressing gown.

'No. I've just got home from work. I was about to take a bath. How many glasses do you want?'

'I'm not sure. How many can you spare?' he asked from the hallway.

She opened the doors to the dresser and began to reach up for a glass. As she did, her shoulders were grabbed, and she was pulled backwards from behind. She felt a kick to the back of her knees, and she buckled to the floor. Shocked, she looked up and saw the man standing over her, a sweet smile on his face and a twinkle dancing in his eyes. From behind his back, he pulled out a large carving knife.

He held the knife aloft. He was about to bring it down when Phoebe swiftly kicked him hard between the legs. He let out a shout and doubled up in pain. She pushed him to one side and ran out of the kitchen and into the hallway. She pulled at the front door, but it was locked, and the chain had been replaced. In her panic, she grabbed at the security chain, but her shaking fingers couldn't get any purchase on it.

'You fucking bitch.'

She turned to where the voice was coming from and ducked just in time as the large knife slammed into the wooden door. She scrambled to her feet and headed for the stairs, quickly crawling up them on her hands and feet. She could hear the intruder following behind her.

She ran into the bedroom and slammed the door closed behind her, but she was too slow. The man had managed to get to it before it closed and was forcing it open. He pushed as she struggled to keep him at bay.

As loudly as she could, Phoebe screamed, hoping someone, *anyone*, would hear and come to save her. The noise from Donna's party was getting louder. There was no way anyone would hear her cries.

The bedroom door was forced open and Phoebe fell backwards onto the carpet. The man entered and stood over her, knife aloft in his right hand.

Phoebe was crying. Her breathing was erratic as he came towards her.

'Please. Please don't kill me,' she pleaded.

He brought the knife down quickly, but Phoebe's reactions were quicker. She kicked him hard in the shins. His knees buckled and he fell, but not before the knife had pierced the skin on her exposed leg. She screamed out in pain, and looked down at the blood seeping out of the wound.

She tried to stand up. She pushed her attacker out of the way. He fell backwards again and hit his head hard against the fitted wardrobe door. She pulled herself to her feet and stumbled out of the bedroom, limping towards the top of the stairs, half running, half falling down them.

Out of breath, panicking, frightened and bleeding, Phoebe struggled with the front door. Her fingers were shaking so violently she couldn't find any grip on the Yale lock. She pulled the door open, but the security chain was still on.

'Fuck!' she cried.

She closed the door, ripped off the chain and opened it once again.

It was pitch-black outside. All she could hear was thumping music and raucous laughter coming from next door. Ahead, three people made their way up the cul-de-sac, heading for Donna's house. Two had a bottle in hand and the third was carrying a large present with a red bow on it.

She stepped out into the cold air.

Phoebe opened her mouth and let out a piercing scream as her intruder grabbed her by the collar of her dressing gown and pulled her back inside, slamming the front door closed.

She fell to the ground, but was able to look up and watch as the attacker leaned down towards her.

'I knew you'd be a fighter the moment I first saw you,' he said calmly into her ear. 'I love a woman who likes to play.'

Available in paperback, ebook and audio!

DCI Matilda Darke Series

Have you discovered the DCI Matilda Darke Thrillers?

DCI Matilda Darke Series

DCI Matilda Darke Series

DCI Matilda Darke Series

DCI Matilda Darke Series

DCI Matilda Darke Series

DCI Matilda Darke Series

DCI Matilda Darke Series

One More Chapter is an award-winning global division of HarperCollins.

Subscribe to our newsletter to get our latest eBook deals and stay up to date with all our new releases!

signup.harpercollins.co.uk/join/signup-omc

Meet the team at
www.onemorechapter.com

Follow us!
- @OneMoreChapter_
- @OneMoreChapter
- @onemorechapterhc
- @onemorechapterhc

Do you write unputdownable fiction?
We love to hear from new voices.
Find out how to submit your novel at
www.onemorechapter.com/submissions